THE FRANCISCAN CONSPIRACY

john sack

RiverWood Books
Ashland, Oregon

Inquiries should be addressed to:
RiverWood Books, PO Box 3400, Ashland, Oregon 97520.
Website: www.riverwoodbooks.com

First printing: 2005

Cover art © Francisco de Zurbarán (Spanish, 1598-1664), *Saint Francis
of Assisi in Tomb*, 1630-34, Oil on canvas, 80 3/8 x 44 5/8 in.,
Milwaukee Art Museum, Purchase, M1958.70
Interior images © Gary Kliewer. Illustrations from the
Wittenburg Bible, 1584, Private collection
Cover design by David Ruppe, Impact Publications
Interior design by Christy Collins

Library of Congress Cataloging-in-Publication Data

Sack, John R.
The Franciscan conspiracy / by John Sack.
p. cm.
ISBN 1-883991-91-9
1. Francis, of Assisi, Saint, 1182-1226--Death and burial--Fiction. 2. Francis, of Assisi, Saint, 1182-1226--Cult--Fiction. 3. Italy--History--1268-1492--Fiction. 4. Assisi (Italy)--Fiction. 5. Franciscans--Fiction. I. Title.
PS3619.A29F73 2004
813'.6--dc22

2004012871

ACKNOWLEDGEMENTS

To the Northwest Writing Institute of Lewis and Clark College for the Walden Residency and valuable gift of time,

To the Blue Mountain writers and White Cloud readers for invaluable advice and encouragement,

And above all to Francis, who insisted this story be told, *Grazie molte*.

Saint Francis' Blessing of Brother Leo.

If Satan existed, the future of the order founded by Saint Francis would afford him the most exquisite gratification. ... The net result of Saint Francis' life was to create yet one more wealthy and corrupt order, to strengthen the hierarchy and to facilitate the persecution of all who excelled in moral earnestness or freedom of thought. In view of his own aims and character, it is impossible to imagine any more bitterly ironical outcome. — Bertrand Russell

Do not tell me that Francis failed. The Spirit of Compromise captured his dream and pared it down; it captured his brothers ... and changed them, as it had tried to change him from the first, into good but commonplace monks. It captured his body and buried it in one of the greatest churches of Italy. It captured his dangerous life-story and put it into censored and adapted biographies. But it could not catch Francis. ... Francis succeeded; it was the others who failed. — Ernest Raymond

Facsimile of the letter written by Saint Francis about 1220 to Brother Leo.

CAST OF CHARACTERS

THE FRIARS MINOR (FRANCISCANS)
  Ministers General (1212-1279)
  1212-1226 San Francesco d'Assisi
        Vicars: Pietro Caetani, 1212-1221
        Elias di Bonbarone, 1221-1227
  Secretary: Leo d'Assisi
  1227-1232 Giovanni Parenti
  1232-1239 Elias di Bonbarone

  Secretary: Illuminato da Chieti
  1239-1240 Alberto da Pisa
  1240-1244 Haymo of Faversham
  1244-1247 Crescentius da Iesi
  1247-1257 Giovanni da Parma
  1257-1274 Bonaventura da Bagnoregio

  Secretary: Bernardo da Bessa
  1274-1279 Girolamo d'Ascoli

THE BROTHERS
  Conrad da Offida, a hermit of the Spiritual faction
  Federico, a visitor to Assisi
  Lodovico, librarian at the Sacro Convento
  Salimbene, a scribe and chronicler
  Tomas da Celano, first biographer of San Francesco
  Ubertino da Casale, a novice
  Zefferino, companion to Fra Illuminato

FROM ASSISI COMMUNE
  Angelo di Pietro Bernardone, a wool merchant
  Dante, eldest son to Angelo
  Piccardo, son to Angelo
  Orfeo, a mariner, youngest son to Angelo
  Francesco di Pietro Bernardone (San Francesco d'Assisi),
    brother to Angelo
  Giacoma dei Settisoli, a widowed noblewoman, formerly of Rome
  Roberto, steward to Donna Giacoma
  Neno, a carter
  Primo, a farmer
  Simone della Rocca Paida, signore of the major fortress of Assisi
  Calisto di Simone, his son
  Bruno, hireling of Calisto
  Matteus Anglicus, an English physician

FROM FOSSATO DI VICO
Giancarlo di Margherita, a retired knight, former mayor of Assisi

FROM GENOA COMMUNE
Enrico, a farm boy from Vercelli

FROM ANCONA
Rosanna, friend to Fra Conrad da Offida

FROM TODI COMMUNE
At the Coldimezzo
Capitanio di Coldimezzo, donor of the land for the Basilica di San Francesco
Buonconte di Capitanio, son to Capitanio
Cristiana, his wife
Amata, his daughter
Fabiano, his son
Guido di Capitanio, brother to Buonconte
Vanna, his daughter
Teresa (Teresina), his granddaughter
From Todi City
Jacopo dei Benedetti (Jacopone), a public penitent
Cardinal Benedetto Gaetani
Roffredo Gaetani, brother to Benedetto
Bonifazio, Bishop of Todi, brother to Capitanio di Coldimezzo

FROM VENICE
Lorenzo Tiepolo, Doge of Venice
Maffeo Polo, a jewel merchant
Nicolo Polo, brother to Maffeo
Marco Polo, son to Nicolo

THE POPES (1198-1276)
1198-1216	Innocent III, approved Order of Friars Minor
1217-1227	Honorius III
1227-1241	Gregory IX (Ugolino da Segni, former Cardinal Protector of Friars Minor, 1220-1227)
1241	Celestine IV
1241-1243	Twenty-month vacancy
1243-1254	Innocent IV
1254-1261	Alexander IV
1261-1264	Urban IV
1265-1268	Clement IV
1268-1272	Four-year vacancy
1272-1276	Gregory X (Tebaldo Visconti di Piacenza, former papal legate to Acre in the Holy Land)

PROLOGUE

ASSISI

25 MARCH, 1230

S IMONE DELLA ROCCA PAIDA scanned the alley where the friars would emerge. *Come on; come to me now, you verminous church mice. Let's be done with this sorry business.* The knight straightened in his saddle and loosened his sword in its scabbard. His tongue had gone dry as wool.

The crowd made him edgy. All morning spectators had streamed into the piazza, ignoring the ankle-deep muck and the hint of another downpour to come. The chief administrator of the city, Mayor Giancarlo, had declared a holiday and no mere spring shower, nor even the barrier erected overnight, could spoil their festive mood. Giancarlo's civil guards had dragged timbers and marble blocks from the new basilica's half-completed upper church to create a low wall across the square. Now, the guards shunted the townspeople behind it like fish into a holding pond, where they squirmed and wriggled for a prime view. The din increased with the congestion. Those who strained to hear the chanting of the friars above the noise wasted their effort. They could only fix their eyes in the same direction as Simone.

At last the knight saw the incense boiling from the alleyway. A tall crucifix bobbed above the smoke and the skullcaps of the boys who swung the censers as the procession entered the square. *Too late now for misgivings.*

Simone had mounted his horsemen to face the clearing from the porch of the upper church. He nodded to the other riders and placed his helmet over his head, brushing the tuft for luck. His hand twitched over the hilt of his sword while he squeezed his knees against his horse's ribs. He swallowed hard against the dryness in his throat and nudged the animal slowly forward, into the space between the people and the procession.

The hooves sucking at the mud with each step, the deceptively gentle pinging of the knights' armor, hardly ruffled the chant as a double file of cardinals in red cassocks and copes inched like a brilliant centipede along the boards laid across the piazza. Neither they, nor the ermine-cloaked bishops who followed, showed the slightest alarm as the horses plodded nearer. Nor did the people crossing themselves and genuflecting behind the barricade.

And why should they? These were the warriors of the Rocca Paida, the hilltop fortress that protected the city from danger. Everyone had heard the rumor that the Perugians planned to kidnap the saint's remains. Or so Simone hoped. Surprise would be his best ally.

Behind the bishops marched the friars and, at the heart of their column, the coffin bearers. They crossed the piazza along the ledge of the embankment that marked its southern boundary. The crucifix, cardinals and bishops had already disappeared down the dirt path leading to the lower church and waited in formation in the courtyard outside.

Simone's moment had come. When the coffin tipped down the path also, he yelled, "*Adesso!* Now!" and dug his spurs into his mount. The animal bolted into the line, smashing out with its front hooves as he'd trained it to do in battle. Bone snapped and a friar disappeared under the charge with a cry of pain; another dove over the embankment to avoid the huge horse. Simone grinned beneath his helmet and slashed wildly with his blade. As he swung his mount in a slow circle, he saw the civil guards skirmishing with a cluster of men trying to scale the spectator barricade.

"Seal the top of the path," he called to the rider beside him. Two of his horsemen had already started down after the coffin, herding the pallbearers toward the lower courtyard. At first the friars cooperated, rushing for the sanctuary of the church and the protection of the mayor who waited at the base of the path with the rest of his civil guard. But instead, Giancarlo's men used their pikes to scatter the prelates from the courtyard in a flurry of miters and cloaks and gathered skirts, fighting their way upward toward the coffin. Too late the friars realized they were caught in the pincers of a trap.

Simone plunged his horse down the hillside alongside the path. Just below him, a friar seized a guard by the arm, screaming shrilly. The man sent him hurtling off the path with a blow from his metal gauntlet and

Simone's horse had to leap the tumbling figure as it skidded headfirst down the hillside.

The knight looked back only when he reached the bottom of the hill. The friar's cowl had flown off, freeing a long black braid. The Roman widow! Damn her! She had no business marching with the friars. Blood spurted from her cheek as she finally managed to right herself, but she seemed neither to notice nor care. She shook her fist and her green eyes blazed at him. "How dare you, Simone?" she shrieked. "How dare you steal our saint?"

The knight inhaled sharply, hearing himself accused by name. He wished again that the mayor had hired warriors from another city to do this dirty work.

He wheeled and galloped for the church door. The guards had the coffin now, peeling off one last friar, small as a boy, who clung to the lid with all his strength. That would be Leo the dwarf, Simone guessed from his size. With the plank box surrounded, Giancarlo's men wedged in behind Simone while the churchmen pelted them with curses. The knight jumped from his horse and flipped the reins to one of the guards.

"You'll burn in hell for this, Simone!" someone bellowed close to his ear. He turned and raised his sword, but the Bishop of Assisi held up the cross that hung around his neck to ward him off. Simone bit his bottom lip and ducked into the church. The mayor joined him immediately. Just inside the doorway, the wool merchant waited alongside the castellan from Todi commune.

"Set down the coffin," Giancarlo shouted to his men. Then he shoved them back outside to defend the courtyard. With the guards gone, he and the knight lifted a heavy beam across the door. The mayor leaned against the carved panel, breathing hard, while Simone raised his helmet and wiped his forehead on the sleeve of his quilted gambeson. Only when the knight sheathed his sword did he notice the drying streaks of crimson on the blade. *Worse and worse*, he thought blackly.

The dark entrance and the muffling of the confusion outside the church settled his nerves. He glanced around at the blanched face of the castellan, the disdain curling on the merchant's lips, the mayor's rigid jaw, wondering why each had involved himself in this sacrilegious business. He suspected the merchant would happily sell off the relics, bone-by-hallowed-bone, albeit they were the remains of his only brother.

A voice rang from the far end of the nave: "Hurry. Bring the coffin here." Two friars, the master builder Fra Elias and his lackey, waited on either side of the main altar. A circle of torches flamed from the stanchions behind them, recalling to Simone the bishop's threat of hellfire. The torchlight cast Fra Elias' shadow out into the church, where it projected far larger than the light-boned conspirator who had plotted the theft. Simone's face flushed with heat, despite the chill draft in the church. He wondered whether Elias could shrive him before they left the church, even though he'd been an equal partner in this sin. He dreaded the prospect of facing that mob outside with his soul in mortal peril.

When the four men reached the front of the nave, they found the main altar moved off its base and a deep excavation scooped from the rock beneath. The men settled the box onto ropes laid out parallel to the hole and, with the help of the friars, lowered it into the sarcophagus. They tossed the ropes in behind the coffin. Then Elias twisted one of the ornate, miniature pillars on the back of the altar until it clicked. The massive block ground in a heavy rotation over the hole. Finally the friar scuffed at the dirt around the marble base, smoothing it with his sandal.

"The workmen began tiling the apse yesterday," he said. "They'll cover this area tomorrow. There'll be no trace. No one will know where he rests."

He dropped to one knee beside the altar, inclining his head in the general direction of the sarcophagus. "No trace, Padre Francesco," he repeated in a satisfied whisper. "Your secret remains your own."

Simone thought back to the meeting at Giancarlo's palace when this friar Elias had argued that the body must be hidden, even from the faithful, to protect it from relic hunters. He doubted the man's motivation from the first. The way the knight read the situation, Elias still seethed from the election he'd lost after San Francesco's death. The brotherhood had named another friar to succeed the saint as minister general of their Order an aged, spiritual man, but one who possessed less administrative skill than filled Elias' little finger. Elias had turned defeat to advantage, however, when the pope asked him personally to build this basilica. Now he had deflected his consolation prize against his detractors and hidden the Order's most-prized relics where they would never be found. Next time, the brothers would think twice about voting against him.

After he'd smoothed the area around the altar, Elias signaled to his lackey: "Fra Illuminato, fetch the coffer."

The young man disappeared into the shadows of the transept. When he returned a moment later, he carried a small, golden reliquary. Elias raised the lid and took out a ring set with an etched, pale blue stone. He slid it onto his finger while his assistant handed identical rings to the others.

"This day is formed the *Compari della Tomba*, the Brotherhood of the Tomb," Elias said. "Let us swear under pain of death never to reveal where these bones lie."

"And death equally to any man who discovers this place by chance," Giancarlo added grimly. "As God is our witness."

"As God is our witness," the others repeated. They raised their ringed fists high into the torchlight and brought their hands together. Each opened his fingers to grasp the wrist of his neighbor.

"Amen! So be it!" they shouted in unison.

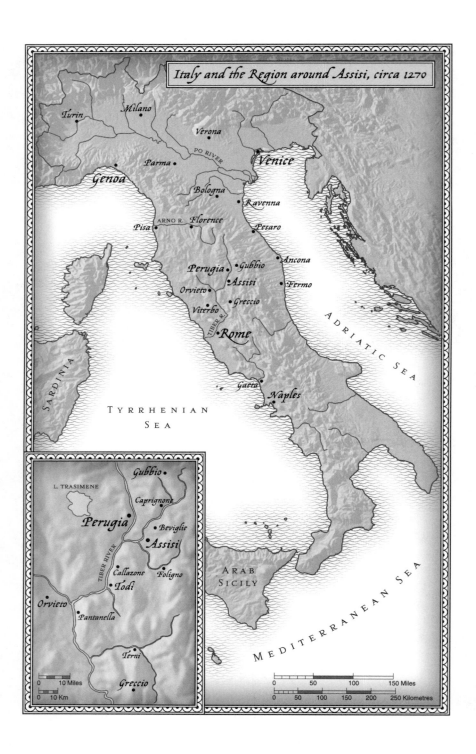

Italy and the Region around Assisi, circa 1270

Turin
Milano
Verona
PO RIVER
Parma
Venice
Genoa
Bologna
Ravenna
Pisa
ARNO R.
Florence
Pesaro
Perugia
Gubbio
Ancona
Assisi
Orvieto
Fermo
Greccio
Viterbo
TIBER R.
Rome
ADRIATIC SEA
SARDINIA
Gaeta
Naples
TYRRHENIAN
SEA
ARAB
SICILY
MEDITERRANEAN SEA

L. TRASIMENE
Gubbio
Caprignone
Perugia
Beviglie
TIBER RIVER
Assisi
Callazone
Foligno
Todi
Orvieto
Pantanella
Terni
Greccio

0   10 Miles
0   10 Km

0   50   100   150 Miles
0   50   100 150 200   250 Kilometres

PART ONE

THE GRYPHON

I

Festa di San Remigio

1 October, 1271

F RA CONRAD FROWNED as he reached the top of the trail that zig-
zagged up to his hut. The squirrel lashing its tail and scolding from the
window ledge warned him that a visitor waited inside, someone other
than Rosanna's man.

"Shush, Brother Grey!" he chided as he tumbled a bundle of sticks from
his shoulder. "Welcome the stranger as you would me. He might be one of
God's angels."

The hermit scooped up the squirrel in his hands and tossed it lightly onto
the black bole of a nearby pine. It clambered to a higher branch as Conrad
stepped through the doorway.

Oblivious to the chatter, the visiting friar slept with his head cradled on
the hermit's table, his face hidden beneath his cowl. Conrad grunted his
approval. If he must be sociable and converse, at least the subject matter
would be spiritual. His guest's leather sandals and soft, new mouse-grey robe
pleased him less. Most likely a Conventual, one of those pampered friars who
lived more like a cloistered black monk than a rootless son of San Francesco.
He hoped the talk wouldn't degenerate into the old quarrel about the nature
of true poverty. He was both weary and wary of that argument; it had caused
him nothing but pain.

He fetched the deadwood he'd gathered earlier, carrying the bundle by its withe binding. The sun plunged early into the Apennines these autumn afternoons and the mountain air already grew cold at night. He carried in several handfuls of dead leaves, pine cones and dry needles and heaped the tinder into the circle of flat stones in the center of the room. While he kindled the fire with his flint, a sleepy murmur drifted from the corner.

"Fra Conrad da Offida?" The surprisingly high-pitched voice was that of a choirboy's before it reaches the crackling and wavering of puberty. His visitor was a novice, he guessed, and probably under-aged at that. Theoretically, the Order took no candidates younger than fourteen, but the authorities often ignored the prohibition.

"Yes, I'm Fra Conrad," he said. "God's peace be with you, young brother." He remained kneeling beside the fire ring.

"And with you. I'm called Fabiano." The child rubbed his nose with the back of his hand, muffling his words.

"Fabiano. Good! And welcome. Once the fire's going, I'll cook up soup. I have fava beans soaking in the kettle."

"We brought food too," the boy said. He jerked his thumb toward a net bag hanging from the rafter. "Cheese and bread and grapes."

"We?"

"Monna Rosanna's manservant led me here. His mistress sent along the extra food—in case you didn't have enough for yourself and a guest."

Conrad smiled. "That would be the lady's courteous way."

The fire snapped loudly now, filling the room with the scent of smoldering Aleppo pine. Smoke meandered up into the soot-blackened thatch and out the small hole in the ceiling. The firelight sparkled in the visitor's eyes, which shone dark as ripened olives from inside his hood. Conrad set the kettle into the flames and took down the bag of food. Rosanna, bless her generous heart, had sent an onion too. He cut off two slices to eat raw with the cheese and quartered the rest into the soup.

"Who sent you to Monna Rosanna?" Conrad asked.

"My superiors in Assisi. They said to seek her out in Ancona, and outside Ancona I met two friars who told me where to find the signora's house. She seemed so *very* curious when I told her I needed to find you ..." The comment hung unfinished, more like a question.

"We grew up together," he said, "almost as brother and sister. She—that is, she and her husband—still look after me when they can." A flotsam of memory drifted through his mind, two children sharing biscuits on a dockside while the sun shimmered off the water beneath their feet. The image fragmented at once, just as their reflections had scattered in the ripples that long ago afternoon, for the visitor immediately resumed his chatter.

"Are you an orphan? Is that why you lived with her family?"

Conrad puffed out his cheeks in a slow exhalation. "This creature's past is unimportant," he said. This was not the spiritual conversation he had hoped for.

He'd have dropped the subject there, but Fabiano looked so disappointed that he added: "Yes. My father was a fisherman in Ancona. God took him in a storm while I was but a small boy. Monna Rosanna's parents took me in. They felt I should be educated, and delivered me to the friars when I turned fifteen. Now, fourteen years later, I'm here, and that is my whole story." As he stirred the soup, his eyes watered ever so slightly. He wiped at them with the cuff of his sleeve, about to comment on the strength of the onion, when the boy interrupted again.

"Where was your mother?"

"In heaven no doubt. My papa said she died calling on the Blessed Virgin as she gave me life."

The aroma of the cooking favas filled the hut. The child inhaled deeply and scratched his head. "I love to hear about people's lives. I wish I could spend my life wandering over the world collecting histories, like Fra Salimbene. Do you know Fra Salimbene?"

Conrad scowled. "He's not a friar *you* should emulate," he said. "Why don't you tell me why you needed to find me?" He stared again into the dark eyes, which suddenly brimmed with compassion almost to the point of tears, and at once he understood.

"Fra Leo?" he said, answering his own question.

"Yes."

"Did he die in peace?"

"He did, in the same hut where San Francesco passed away."

"That must have pleased him."

The hermit sagged back onto his heels. The loss of his friend and mentor was hardly unexpected. Leo had seen more than eight decades after all. But this death was still a blow.

Who could fathom the divine plan? Leo had begged to be taken with his master San Francesco, yet God had bound him to life for another half century, working and writing. The little priest had been the founder's personal infirmarian, changing the dressings and rubbing ointments on the lesions that erupted on his hands and feet and side after the terrible vision on Monte LaVerna. Leo had also been the saint's confessor and secretary—potentially the most powerful positions in the Order had he been interested in power. But Francesco had chosen his companion precisely for his marvelous simplicity. With his love of nicknames, he had rechristened Leo the lion—"*Fra Pecorello di Dio*," Brother Little Lamb of God.

Even the younger friars like Conrad knew the famous tale of Leo's skirmish with Elias after Francesco's death, how he shattered the great vase where the minister general collected donations for the new basilica. Elias had him beaten and banished from Assisi for that act of rebellion. Leo retreated into obscurity and began writing his tracts denouncing laxity and abuses within the Order. He became the conscience of the friars, citing both the rule and spirit of San Francesco as his inspiration, and the Conventual faction hated him for it.

Conrad wondered whether Fra Bonaventura, the latest in the line of Elias's successors, had risen above the old quarrel. "Did the minister general bury Fra Leo with dignity?" he asked.

"Oh yes. In the basilica, beside his companions. They say it's the highest honor."

"And such did he deserve," Conrad said.

The boy pulled back his hood as Conrad stirred the soup. Black, close-cropped hair hung straight to the tips of his ears. His almond-shaped eyes had a startled, doe-like expression accentuated by his long lashes. The milky skin about the cheeks and temples shone so translucent, even in the poor light, that Conrad could trace his veins. His grin was wide, his nose long and straight with flared nostrils. A noble nose, Conrad thought. This child is altogether too *pretty* to be living with older friars, especially friars who wished to emulate the black monks. God alone knew which of the plenitude of monastic vices they imitated by now.

When Conrad took a break from the stirring, the boy reached inside the pouch he'd left under the table and took out a rolled-up parchment. "My novice master told me to give you this letter. Fra Leo said it was absolutely urgent you get it after he died."

The hermit uncurled the lambskin vellum beside the fire. He glanced through it several times.

"What does it say?" Fabiano asked.

"It's not sealed. I'm surprised you didn't read it. Hasn't your novice master taught you your letters yet?"

"Some. I could only make out a few of the words. I asked the friars I met on the road to read it to me, but they only called it—*uninteresting*."

Conrad rolled his eyes heavenward. The boy was shameless. And maybe dangerous in his naivete. "Did those friars tell you their names?" he asked.

"No. But one was older than time, and the other had blond hair, if that helps."

Conrad pursed his lips. "It doesn't." They might in fact be troublesome. Hopefully the boy's lack of judgment would prove harmless.

He scanned the vellum again. "Maybe *you* can tell *me* whether the letter's interesting or not," he said. "It counsels me to goodness, as Leo certainly would, but the message doesn't sound like the priest I knew." Holding the parchment closer to the firelight he read aloud.

"*To Conrad, my brother in Christ, Fra Leo, his undeserving companion, offers dutiful reverence in the Lord God.*

"That's Leo, so far. But listen to this:

"*Remember how we counseled you to study and learn. Read with your eyes, discern with your mind, feel in your heart the truth of the legends. Servite pauperes Christi.*"

Conrad held out the parchment toward Fabiano. "Serve Christ's poor ones?" He paused to let the words sink in, as though the boy should grasp their significance, then finished with a wave of his hand.

"*Written at Assisi in the fourteenth year of the administration of Bonaventura di Bagnoregio, Minister General, Order of Friars Minor.*"

The hermit scratched the back of his neck. "Leo would *never* ask me to study, not even the accounts of San Francesco's life—if those are the 'legends' he means. Francesco preached that scholars wasted time better spent in prayer. As for serving the poor, it was Leo who sent me into these mountains. Now he wants me to devote myself to service? It seems odd to me."

He flicked at the vellum with his fingernail. "This isn't even Leo's writing. Much too large and clumsy. Leo was an elegant scriptor."

The hermit held the letter to the firelight one final time. An oval border framed the letter, but in the poor light he couldn't see any consistency in its pattern. Leo wasn't one to call an *uninteresting* letter *urgent*, but from what he'd read, Conrad had to agree with the two traveling friars.

He tossed the parchment onto the table where it coiled again into a cylinder. It might be no more than the babbling of an old man's dotage. But Leo's mind held so many secrets. Given the unfamiliar writing, the message could even be a trick by Bonaventura, but to what point? Still, the lad was from the Sacro Convento, the motherhouse of the Order, and that alone roused Conrad's fears.

"Let's get you fed and back to sleep," he said at last. "You've had a tiring journey." He could mull this message while they rested, and hope for some inspiration by first light.

He filled two wooden bowls from the kettle. Fabiano meanwhile ran his fingers slowly and thoughtfully through his fuzzy hair until it stood up straight as a hedgehog's. "Were you sad to leave her?" he asked finally.

But Conrad was not about to reopen that childhood wound. He touched his finger to his lips. "We should observe silence while we eat, little brother. Our founder wished his friars to be eager for silence from evening until dawn. We've talked enough for one day."

LEO, THE CANNY BASTARD, had known all along. All these forty-five years he'd nurtured his cache like a protective broody hen, too stubborn even now to quit the nest and take his secrets to the grave like a reasonable man.

Instead, he'd passed his stillborn hatchlings to one of the hermit rebels.

Fra Illuminato slapped at a mosquito sucking on his wrist, wishing he might squash the hermit as easily. He reined in his donkey and mopped his sleeve across his forehead. Even in October, a day in the sun could sap a traveler's strength, especially one of his advanced years. With Leo gone, he was the last of the first-generation of brothers who had actually lived with San Francesco.

"I need to rest, Fra Zefferino," he said to his companion. "These fragile bones can ride no further today."

"As you wish, padre." The younger friar swung his leg over his donkey's neck and slid to the ground. Then he helped the priest dismount.

Illuminato pressed his hands against his hips and arched his back, stretching like a stiff old cat. He shook his shoulders, then limped the few paces to the top of the rise. "Magnificent," he said finally, sweeping his arm across the valley carved by the River Tescio. Rows of Lombardy poplars ranged like sentinels alongside the road below, brilliant in their autumn golds. Other daubs of yellow marked the holm oaks scattered among the evergreens of the surrounding forests. At the bottom of the hill a number of wooden buildings huddled around the brick campanile of a church, and somewhere in that cluster the road forked: northwest toward Gubbio, south and west to Assisi.

Illuminato's companion held both sets of reins in one hand, while with the other he waved at a fly that buzzed around his straw-colored tonsure. "Do we sleep in Fossato di Vico tonight?" he asked. "I have a friend among the cathedral canons there."

"Sleep? No, Zefferino," the priest replied. "You'll have no sleep before tomorrow."

Illuminato stared into the man's puzzled blue eyes. "We can't lose any time," he said. "I want you to go ahead of me into the village. On the hill opposite the cathedral you'll see a palazzo. Ask there for Signore Giancarlo and tell him 'Amanuensis' would stay with him this evening."

"*Amanuensis?*"

"He'll know what it means. Beg him also, for love of that same name, to exchange your donkey for a fresh mount, a fast horse if possible." The old priest pointed to the forks below. "Ride the north road as hard as you can to the friars' house in Gubbio. Tell the brother prior that if the hermit Conrad comes through the mountains and stops to rest there, he must hold him—by force if necessary. I'll continue on to Assisi and warn the minister general."

"And how will the prior know the hermit?"

Illuminato crinkled his hairy nose and his eyes glistened. "Pah! He's a zealot, one of those stinking '*zelanti*,' proud as the Evil One that he never bathes. They'll smell him long before they see him. He also wears the black beard of an ungodly Saracen, and a shaggy mane where once was a priest's tonsure."

He spat into the dusty roadbed to underscore his disgust and added, "The boy could be with him too, but he should be no problem. Have the prior hold him too."

Illuminato took back his reins from the other friar. "Go now, brother, and Godspeed. There'll be a reward in this work for each of us."

He watched Zefferino whip his donkey down the hillside, until man and beast disappeared around a turn in the road. Then he followed at a more comfortable pace, leading his own animal. His slack hamstrings and scrawny haunches could endure but so much punishment and had suffered bruising enough for one afternoon.

Hadn't he warned Elias, those many decades ago, not to flog that pesky gnome Leo? *Let him rant*! he advised. But that was 1232, and Elias, flushed with his new power—Minister General of the Order at last—harried Leo from Assisi, and with the same blows opened the fissure that now gaped like the infernal abyss, ready to swallow both factions of the Order.

The priest ground his snaggly teeth, irritated at Elias all over again, and suddenly at himself as well. He should have snatched Leo's letter from the boy. His wit worked so slowly anymore. At the palazzo he would ask the aged *signore* for parchment. He had to record as much of the message as he could recall. Old Giancarlo wore the ring of the confraternity; he'd spare no pains to quell this latest threat to their oath.

II

CONRAD AND FABIANO lay curled up inside their cloaks on opposite sides of the fire. The boy's breathing eased into a regular rhythm, while the hermit watched the ceiling shade from vermilion to grey. Mice scuttled through the hut in search of bread crumbs and scraps. Larger night hunters foraged in the brush outside and from a distant pool a chorus of frogs kept up a steady chant. A cool gust through the window caused him to shiver. Most nights, deep in contented sleep, he wouldn't have noticed either the breeze or the night creatures.

Over and over he reread Leo's letter in his mind. Everything about the message felt wrong—the handwriting, the words, even the creamy vellum on which it was written. Leo worshiped Madonna Poverty as passionately as San Francesco himself. Had he any money, he'd not have spent it on expensive lambskin. No, he'd have given it to some poor person.

Conrad wondered too what to make of the courier. He couldn't believe Leo would have delivered an important message to this imp from the Sacro Convento. His mentor trusted no one at the mother house. These last decades he'd scrupulously hidden his tracts from the other friars for fear they'd be confiscated. He'd even entrusted only one of his scrolls to Conrad, whom he regarded as his spiritual son. The rest Leo left with the Poor Ladies of San Damiano. In their convent, where no man but their father confessor had permission to enter, his manuscripts lay safely hidden, beyond reach of Bonaventura's ferrets.

On the other hand, this Fabiano *had* survived a perilous trek through the Apennines and managed to track Conrad to his hermitage. The boy had to be resourceful. He even spoke familiarly of Fra Salimbene, though Conrad couldn't imagine what this tadpole might have in common with *that* old toad. He remembered the obese chronicler's visit to the Sacro Convento during one of his endless wanderings. Salimbene kept a cluster of brothers sniggering at his bawdy tales for the better part of an afternoon. The image of the friar's bloated features and sagging jowls—testimonies to a life of feasting at the courts of the nobility—his bald pink head trickling with sweat in the hot sunshine, caused Conrad to cringe now as it had then.

As he stared across the fire ring, the hermit saw that the sleeping Fabiano shivered too. The child would be unused to the chill mountain air. Twisting onto his side, he blew on the remnant of embers until he stirred up a shower of orange sparks. He added more wood and prodded the coals until he felt the fire could keep itself going for a while.

"Stop it!" Fabiano cried out suddenly.

Conrad froze. What had he done to alarm the boy? "Stop what?" he asked softly.

Fabiano didn't answer, and Conrad realized the novice had never been awake. The shout sprang from some nightmare. The boy's feet twitched beneath his cloak, trying to outrun something or someone.

Conrad watched until Fabiano calmed again. Then the hermit finally closed his eyes. The knot of frustration in his stomach loosened, his heartbeat slowed, and his wrestling mind quieted.

He wasn't conscious of how much time had passed, of being either asleep *or* awake, when a pale, bluish light seemed to expand behind his eyelids. Two ragged friars, their outlines blurred in the sapphire glow, hovered over him. The younger brother rested a lacerated hand on the shoulder of the elder.

"Conrad," called the one with the white tonsure through lips that didn't move. The gentleness and affection of the voice tingled the hermit's limbs. He recognized his mentor and from the wounds in the younger friar's hand, he knew who Leo's companion must be. "Fra Leo! Padre Francesco!" He wanted to speak, but no sound escaped his throat.

"Discover the truth of the legends." Leo repeated the gist of the message. His words reverberated through Conrad's mind, although Leo seemed only to think, rather than speak, them.

"Then the message *is* from you? It seemed so unlike . . ."

"Treat the messenger with courtesy. She has finished a hard task here. Discount her lack of years. You will need her help in the work ahead."

Conrad's eyes snapped open. Again he found himself staring at the shadowy thatch of the ceiling.

She? Her help?

He sat bolt upright and peered across the flames at Fabiano, whose narrow back lay toward the fire. Was there a curve about the hip line he hadn't noticed before?

A vision of God's saints must be taken seriously. Voices heard in deep prayer or deep sleep always spoke truth. For now they said he could not remain in the hut with this Fabiano. Hadn't San Chrysostomo warned: "It is through women that the devil penetrates men's hearts?"

Conrad put the last of the dead branches on the fire. He swung off his cloak and spread it over the sleeping figure, then tiptoed through the straw to the door. Mice scurried away toward the corners of the hut until he'd passed.

The cold air assaulted the hermit's ears and cheeks. He curled against the wall nearest the doorway, his arms hugging his knees, and raised his eyes to the clear, frigid sky.

Leo, what have you done to me? You know I have no experience of females. He'd been only a teenager when he'd parted from Rosanna's family and had had almost no contact with women since. During their last summer together even she, with a suggestive smile or a deliberate flash of her dark eyes, could start his pulse pounding and a tempest whirling in his heart. Over the years he'd come to accept the exquisite ache he'd suffered when they separated as a saving blessing from God. He hadn't even had a chance for a real farewell. Rosanna's mother said the girl was too ill to join the family for breakfast the day her father whisked him so abruptly to the friar's house in Offida.

The eye shine of a yearling doe browsing a few feet from the hut caught his attention. "Chiara" he'd named the animal as a fawn, for the pure lightness of her high-striding movement. Conrad grinned for the first time since he'd read Leo's message, happy that *something* in his world remained constant.

He held out his hand and the animal came to him. He scratched the stiff hair on her neck for a moment, the neck he checked every week for ticks, then gently pushed her away. Here was a fitting female companion for a hermit friar. *God spare me the company of women*, he begged as he tried to doze again.

CONRAD NORMALLY WELCOMED the dawn, a time when he sucked in the pure, cold air and added his morning prayer to the lilt of wakening sparrows and the hooing of turtledoves. As the first light filtered through the treetops today, however, his brain still teemed with thoughts of women.

If Fabiano is a girl, he reasoned, that would explain her frivolous questions. But how could Leo possibly say he'd need the help of this gossipy creature?

He remembered how Leo had loved and praised Santa Clara. The foundress of the Poor Ladies had shown indomitable strength, clinging to poverty after Francesco's death more steadfastly than any of the friars. Bedridden and broken by fasting and austerity, she held on to life for another thirty years, until the Holy Father finally approved her strict rule for the Poor Ladies. Leo had knelt by her pallet at San Damiano two days after the papal sanction, watching in sorrow as she kissed the decree and finally released her soul. But this will-o'-the-wisp Fabiano—this smidgen—and the blessed Clara shared nothing in common but their female gender.

Leo had spoken well of another woman also, the wealthy widow who had comforted Francesco on his deathbed. Over the decades, she'd also helped Leo, giving the Order money for a robe after his disintegrated in tatters, housing him during his years of exile. Donna Giacoma dei. . . someplace or other, some district in her native Rome.

Conrad rubbed his numb cheeks as he pondered a new possibility. Donna Giacoma—Leo's benefactress—certainly could, and would gladly, have supplied him with fine writing materials if she were still alive. She had to be of an age with Leo, though, already widowed when San Francesco first met her. But if she *had* provided the vellum for the letter, that would add some sense to this garbled business.

Conrad heard the novice, if such he was, or *she* was, rustling in the straw. He ducked his head and pretended to sleep as Fabiano stumbled through the doorway and into the trees. He was tempted to follow with his eyes to see whether his visitor stood or squatted, but modesty prevented him.

The thought did offer another potential clue, though not one Conrad was eager to follow. Like most seminarians, he'd read Pope Innocent's *De Contemptu Mundi*. He still remembered the passage that detailed the great pontiff's abhorrence of menstrual blood. *By contact with it grain does not ripen, bushes dry up, grasses die, trees lose their fruit; and if dogs eat it, they become mad.* If Fabiano were a girl, and if she'd reached puberty, and if by a stroke of luck her monthly flow were in progress, he need only check the spot later.

Just recalling the text raised sour bile in the hermit's throat, however, and his stomach turned suddenly queasy—the same reaction he'd had when he first learned of the female curse from Rosanna, and later when he'd crossed paths with the witches of the South who were said to stir catamenial blood into their love potions. He'd just turned eleven when Rosanna, a year older than himself, explained why she wouldn't be racing up the foothills with him that afternoon. She seemed to have aged into womanhood and grown beyond him overnight, and he could only look at her with awe thereafter.

Conrad finally made up his mind. He couldn't deal with this raw, primal femininity. He clambered to his feet and headed away from the hermitage in the opposite direction from Fabiano. He'd have to take another tack to uncover the novice's identity.

Fabiano appeared sullen as they returned to the hut and nodded to one another at the doorway. Conrad motioned toward the table as he took down the food net from the rafters. He poured water from a clay jug into two cups, sliced a loaf of bread lengthwise with his eating knife and loaded the bread with cheese slices and grapes. He spoke casually as he handed the trencher to Fabiano.

"Is Fra Hilarion still master of novices at the Sacro Convento?" he asked.

"Oh, are we breaking silence now?" Fabiano seemed more annoyed than surprised by the friar's question. "Fra Conrad, if you want to know something, just ask me. It's clear you've figured out that I'm a woman. You don't have to play stupid tricks."

"What do you mean?" he asked. He felt suddenly very clumsy.

"I wake up with an extra cloak over me and you're sleeping outside. What am I supposed to think? A courteous man has discovered he's sharing his hut with a woman and gives her his cape. For this I thank him. On the other hand, a brainless man decides he'd rather freeze than risk catching female depravity like a pox, so he flees to protect his most pure soul. *For this I thank him not!*"

She tore off a chunk of bread with her teeth as though she wished it were his flesh. "Do I read you right?" she said. The pale skin on her face and neck took on a rosy sheen and menace gleamed in her black eyes.

Conrad's face warmed too. Her bold speech embarrassed and dumbfounded him. She had undermined his transparent attempt at cleverness—fair enough—but in doing so, showed a total lack of deference to his priesthood. He really should be furious with her, for the sake of his office, if not on his own account.

"My real name is Amata," she continued before he could protest. "Fabiano is—or *was*—my brother's name."

She fiddled with Leo's parchment as she ate, chewing and talking at the same time. "I should say *Suor* Amata. I'm a servant sister at San Damiano. The steward of a grand lady brought this message to our house and Mother Prioress entrusted it to me. I run many of her errands."

She glared into his eyes. "Do you know, brother, how dangerous it is even for a *man*, even a *friar*, to cross these mountains alone? If a gang of *banditi* found out they'd caught a woman ... and not just a purse of silver or a pair of new sandals, I'd be better off with my throat gaping like a castle gate. Life would be worse than death, even eternal death in hell."

"Take heed, child! You blaspheme!" Conrad said. "Nothing could be worse than eternal separation from the Beatific Vision."

Amata shot him a sidelong, sardonic glance. "I know what I'm talking about, brother, though I'm not sure you do. It's called the real world, a place you haven't seen in some years, I suspect. And another thing, don't call me 'child!' I'm almost seventeen. Were I not bound to a convent, I'd be running my own household with babes hanging onto my skirts by now." She smiled, but the smile wasn't pleasant. "Was your Rosanna not married by my age?"

Conrad glowered in turn. Rosanna was none of her business. He'd shared too much already.

In fact his friend had married *late,* at just sixteen. He'd been but two months with the friars when her letter arrived. Her parents had betrothed her to the merchant Quinto, she wrote, and she asked for his prayers and blessing. He fasted for several days to atone for his thoughts on reading *that* news. The prayers didn't flow until much later.

With her elbow Amata spread Leo's message flat on the table while she popped grapes into her mouth with her free hand. A quizzical expression rose in her eyes. Her anger slackened as quickly as a fussing baby handed a new trinket.

"Are these words?" she asked, tracing her finger along the border framing Leo's message. "I see an *M* here and what looks like an *A.*"

"Where? Let me see."

Conrad snatched the parchment from her hand and rushed to the doorway. The border was indeed a series of small letters, a minuscule script that Conrad recognized as Leo's own. He searched for a starting point from which to find series that formed words and sentences, but what he found was a number of disconnected fragments. The border began with the same command that ended the main message, *Servite pauperes Christi.* He murmured aloud as he read.

"*Serve Christ's poor ones. Fra Jacoba knows much of perfect submission. Who mutilated the Companion? Whence the Seraph? The first of Tomas marks the start of blindness; the Testament sheds the first shards of light. The dead leper's nails are crusted with truth. Servite pauperes Christi.*"

He'd come full circle around the border, but its meaning was as dark as when he began. "Why does he write in riddles?" Amata asked.

"I suppose if I can't understand it, then Bonaventura wouldn't either, had this fallen into his hands." He rolled up the letter and tucked it into his tunic. "This much I do understand. I need to see the legends and the testament Leo mentions here and the library at the Sacro Convento has what I need."

Just saying the words made Conrad go rigid. Friars like him, who practiced total poverty, weren't welcome visitors at the mother house. Living there as a young priest, he'd landed himself in serious trouble by pointing out the brothers' misuse of "property."

The brothers shall acquire nothing as their own, neither a house, nor a place, nor anything at all, he had quoted from San Francesco's Rule. "Look at us with our soft clothing, shiny faces and fine food. We own books. We own this opulent friary. The only thing we lack here are wives."

That had happened seven years before, in 1264, soon after he returned from Paris and after Fra Bonaventura had replaced Giovanni da Parma as minister general. Bonaventura had little tolerance for contentious friars like

Conrad who kicked against the goad. He introduced the new priest at once to one of the clammy dungeons excavated deep beneath the Sacro Convento. Had Conrad not promised, at Leo's urging, to live in isolation and forswear preaching, he'd be languishing there still—like Giovanni himself.

"Giovanni da Parma is a living martyr," he said. He'd become so accustomed to talking to himself or to his squirrel friend Brother Grey that he forgot Amata still sat at the table. When he looked up, he saw her head cocked in the querulous pose the animal often adopted.

"All will unfold as God wills," he said, as though that explained his other comment. "I have to leave for Assisi, sister. This very morning."

"Can I come with you? I'd feel safer if we traveled together."

Conrad hesitated. Another conundrum. San Francesco told his first followers never to journey with women—nor even to eat from the same plate in the courtly fashion of the nobility for that matter. He may already have pushed the limits of that rule when he shared his breakfast table.

"I promise to behave with utmost modesty," Amata added. She thrust out her lower lip, but Conrad also saw the sparkle in her eyes. The girl mocks me, he thought. But she's right about safety in numbers.

Then the hermit remembered that the second version of Francesco's Rule said only that brothers were not to associate with women in ways that might *arouse suspicion*. Who'd suspect a friar traveling with a novice named Fabiano? In fact, San Francesco ordered his friars to travel in pairs; a friar traveling without a companion *would* arouse suspicion, as Amata no doubt had when the two friars met her on the road. And he wouldn't even be violating the *spirit* of the Rule, for he felt no affection for this outspoken, disrespectful elf. Temptation of the flesh would not be an issue.

"See you keep your promise," he said. He glanced around the room, planning what they'd need to bring, what needed to be settled before they left. Again he hesitated. "Did you notice whether the friars who read Leo's message also read the border?"

"They may have. The old one turned it from side to side. Did I do wrong to let them see it?"

"I fear you did! Whether or not the message might lead us into danger, I can't say, since I don't know what it means. My Conventual brothers suspect that anything Leo wrote smacks of sedition—and they might be right."

He stooped into the shadows behind the table and hoisted an urn onto the bench. "You should know about Leo's scroll—in case I don't make it back here." He removed the lid from the urn and took out a tubular packet. The pungent odor of decayed fish escaped into the room, a comforting smell to Conrad who always associated it with his father and the docks of Ancona. Gingerly peeling away the greenish-yellow oilskin sheath and several layers of discolored linen, the hermit finally uncovered a thick manuscript and spread it the length of the table. Amata rubbed the material between her fingers.

"It's called a paper scroll," Conrad explained. "Fra Leo said it's a new material imported from Spain—by the same lady who delivered his letter to San Damiano, I suspect. He loved it. No parchment to scrape and smooth, and his pages never got out of order.

"He sent for me last spring, knowing his time was short. He asked me to make copies of this chronicle for the Spiritual brothers hiding in Romagna and the Marches. The handful of us are the only ones who can keep the truth alive."

"What truth?"

"The true history of the friars minor since San Francesco's death. Sadly, our Order has become a monstrous gryphon. Half eagle, it soars on wings of holiness and devotion. I could name you dozens of friars who rise on such wings. But it is also half lion, and hides the claws of cruelty and injustice. Leo witnessed the ordeals of those brothers who remained faithful to the Rule. After Elias became minister general, he jailed and tortured many of them and even murdered Fra Caesar of Spires; later, when Crescentius succeeded Elias, he scattered their party. Some he sent to martyrdom in Lesser Armenia. Bonaventura..."

"But Fra Elias built the basilica," Amata interrupted. "All the world flocks to Assisi to see *that*!"

Conrad let his breath out slowly, and reminded himself to be patient. This Amata obviously knew little of the division in the Order. She had much to learn before she could be the help Leo promised. He assumed the indulgent tone of a schoolmaster.

"Although Elias was as close to San Francesco as any friar save Fra Leo, he missed the whole point of our founder's life. Francesco, in his humility, asked to be buried outside the city walls, on the Colle d'Inferno, where Assisi's refuse was dumped and the common criminals buried. But what did Fra Elias do? He arranged to have the entire hillside donated to the Order, an Order which owned nothing while his master lived, and built there the most magnificent basilica in Christendom—such a gigantic mausoleum for *Il Poverello*, as the people called him, God's little poor man. *That's* how meagerly Elias understood him."

Amata's face brightened. "I *do* know about the Colle D'Inferno," she said. "My grandfather Capitanio was the one who gave it to Fra Elias."

Conrad stared in disbelief at the novelty across the table. First she claimed to know a worldly friar like Fra Salimbene, and now this bondwoman had the temerity to tell him her family donated the land for the grand basilica?

Amata spread the scroll with both hands. "Shouldn't we take this with us? We could hide it with Mother Prioress."

"No. We'd be fuel for the Inquisitors if they caught us, and the chronicle would be the kindling. I'll bury it in its urn. Only you and I know it exists. If I don't make it back here..."

"Oh no!" Amata waved her hands like an alewife shooing gnats from her brew. "I can't help you with that. I'm not free to wander where I will. This is the only time I've ever crossed these mountains."

"God alone knows why you're involved in this matter, sister, but if He wants you to be His instrument, He will give you the means."

To reposition the manuscript in the urn, Conrad first had to remove a linen bundle tied with twine. It slipped from his hands and clattered to the straw, scattering quills, an inkhorn, pumice stone, ruler, stylus and chalk. He blushed at his own clumsiness as he bent to gather up his paraphernalia.

"You see, I have everything to make the copies but parchment. I meant to ask Monna Rosanna to start including a few sheets each time she sent me food."

Amata laughed loudly, but not, as he imagined, at his awkwardness. "And *you* called *scholars* time wasters? I knew you didn't believe that."

"Did you? And how were you so clever as to decide that?"

"Look at your robe. The seat and elbows are *far* shinier than the knees. You're as comfortable on your butt as any scribe at his desk."

Conrad couldn't decide whether to laugh or take offense. He decided on the first. "I confess," he said. "I studied and debated with the great ones in Paris. Held my own, too. We students thought we grasped the keys to the universe, somewhere there in our quibbling syllogisms and hair-splitting disputations. My head aches, just to think of those years."

He grinned as he walked to his garden to fetch a digging tool. *And I still don't know how many disembodied souls it would take to fill a soup bowl,* he recalled.

"Wait outside a while," Amata called out to the hermit through the window. "I have to take care of ... a female matter."

Conrad immediately turned his back to the hut. Female matters again! He'd already ruined his appetite enough today reflecting on that subject.

He seized the moment to stare off into the trees that still glistened with dew like a million tiny bonfires. In that instant he sensed just how deeply he'd miss his forest. Although Amata seemed to be taking forever, all his urgency to be on the road suddenly drained away. He realized he might be leaving forever this spot he'd come to love as a foretaste of heaven. The hermit wanted to drink in its stillness, the serenity he'd felt here, one final time. He decided he would leave the door of his hut open, in case his forest friends needed shelter. He wondered if they would miss him, or was he being heretical to ascribe human feeling to soulless animals?

"I'm ready," Amata called at last. "I repacked the urn for you too."

The hermit dug a hole in the corner where the table stood. Amata watched closely while he fitted the urn into the hollow and covered it with straw. She even held the lid tightly in place while he tamped dirt around it. As Conrad wiped his wooden spade, he imagined he saw a firmer set to her chin, a resolve he'd not seen earlier. Could it be that this fatuous sister, for all her impertinence, possessed some measure of a man's courage and resolution? *She'll need both*, he thought, *if she's to weather the storm ahead*. And the storm—inevitable as approaching winter—would surely come.

In that instant the image of his drowned father, struggling in the black froth of the squall that devoured him, thrashed through his mind. *God pity us all*, he prayed.

III

ORFEO BERNARDONE MOPPED his face with the flowing sleeve of his Arab robe. He raked his fingernails through the hair clotted against his neck and readjusted the red levantine cap that hung like a purse over one ear. The sun beat without pity on the port of Acre this rare morning, rare because no breeze blew off the sea and the Holy Land felt more like a scorched wilderness than the Land of Promise. The mariner squinted against the glare from the white Moorish houses and the distant domes of mosques and palaces. Tall palms clustered their few, clicking leaves at the tops of slender trunks, as though begrudging their shade to the humans below.

"You're a marvel, Marco," he said to his companion. "Your coif's as dry as the moment you tied it on." He tugged at the blond curls protruding from the headdress of the young master Polo. "And now only one hair's out of place."

The teenager pushed his hand away. "A rising merchant has to keep a cool appearance," he said. "Should another trader see you sweat, he'll know he's outbargained you."

They entered among the shaded stalls and intersecting alleys of the bazaar. Orfeo inhaled deeply of the blended scents of cloves, mace and nutmeg, sacks of cinnamon and ginger from the Indies, and musk from Tebeth. Princes of the court and Church paid small fortunes for these spices in Rome, but here he could enjoy the same sensual delights with a simple morning stroll. What a wonder was this Orient!

Ragged children chased through the market place and shy, veiled women balanced jugs on their heads, reminding him of the housewives who fetched water in the hilltop villages of his native Umbria. Umbria was cold as a virgin's vows compared to Acre, however. In the streets of the port, crusaders rubbed elbows with Saracens, black Moors and Jews bargained with Armenians and Nestorian Christians—all linked as wheel spokes to the hub of money. Like the sailors beached on the island of the lotus eaters, the converging races soon seemed to forget their holy crusades and jihads, even their homelands, and wanted only to remain throughout eternity on this pleasurable coast.

The tolerance of the city amazed Orfeo even more than its inhabitants. In Umbria, a man might burn because his tattered clothes offended a wealthy bishop or because he compared heaven to a round of cheese to make some theological point. But in Acre, every culture and philosophy found a home. The minarets from which the muezzins called faithful Muslims to prayer shared its skyline with the bastions of the European nobility: the towers of the Countess of Blois and King Henry II, of the Hospitalers, Templars, and Teutonic Knights and—down where the city walls met the harbor—the castles of the Patriarch of Acre and of the Papal Legate, Tebaldo Visconti da Piacenza. In the labyrinth of squares and alleys Orfeo met Greeks, Normans, Aragonese, Kurds, Turks and, of course, merchants from Pisa and Genoa. It was mainly because of these fellow countrymen that the two young men wore swords belted over their robes.

Their destination this morning lay beyond the bazaar, in one of the narrow corridors twisting away from the trading center. Up that alley, musicians sang provocative, intertwined melodies to the strumming of zithers in a house where a pair of twin dark-skinned courtesans waited to receive them. "Once more before we sail to Laiaissa," the Italians had promised the day before. The prospect of budding adventure had them as roused as the thought of this last pleasure call on the hot-blooded sisters.

"Marco, why do you withhold your father's answer?" Orfeo asked as they threaded their way among the stalls. "Tell me if I'm to be a rising merchant too."

Marco's face was a noncommittal mask. "He deals with realities, *amico*. He's a man of logic." A scowl darkened the mask as he imitated the expression of the elder Polo. "Orfeo's an oarsman. Beyond boarding raids on Genovese merchantmen, what training has he in weaponry? Why should we take him with us as a man-at-arms? Can he even sit a horse, let alone a camel? Will not the Tartars laugh at us when they see what we call a horseman?"

The darkness spread from Marco's face to Orfeo's spirit. So it was to be as he feared. Ever since he'd hired on to crew the Polo's sleek Venetian galley, he'd dreamed of going the next step with the jewel merchants, traveling as part of their caravan across Lesser and Greater Armenia, Turkey and Cathay to the court of Kublai Khan himself. *Jesu*, what an experience of a lifetime that would be! He was but a few years older than Marco, and wouldn't he return rich also, rich enough to live the same excitement Marco had been born to? But as he listened second-hand to Nicolo Polo's somber assessment, he felt more doomed than ever to the lot of the seaman. His savings would never be enough to set him up as a trader, and he'd long since severed all ties with his merchant father and brothers. His head drooped and he studied his sandals as they scooped through the dust of the street.

"Oh, and one final thing he said," Marco added. "His peroration was, '*but, after all, he is your friend, my son. As you love him, we'll find a place for him.*'"

"What! Is it true?"

Marco grinned.

"All the holy confessors be praised! I'm going to Cathay!" Orfeo shouted. He grabbed the teenager and kissed his cheek, then lifted him off his feet and hugged him so hard he grunted in pain.

"You're supposed to protect me, not crack my ribs," Marco gasped.

Orfeo laughed, then suddenly became deadly serious. "Beginning now, maybe," he said. Over Marco's shoulder he'd spotted three men approaching. They wore the colors of Genoa.

He sized them up rapidly. They weren't large, probably not worth a hundred drachmas the lot in the slave market. Orfeo on the other hand had a wrestler's physique, and often bragged he could pull an ox to a standstill. Years at the oar had transformed his pudgy boyhood frame. Still, they were three and likely to rely on their swords rather than brute strength.

Whether overly excited by Marco's good news or simply inspired by his new role as his master's bodyguard, he felt an impulse to brawl. He spoke loudly as the men approached.

"Is it not true, Marco, that Genoa is peopled by geldings who lack all faith and women who lack all shame?"

He glared at the men as he spoke. They returned his stare and one retorted, "Nay, but it *is* true that all Venetians are ass-licking liars."

Marco spun around so that he and Orfeo stood shoulder-to-shoulder facing the Genovese. All five reached for their swords simultaneously.

"Sior Polo. Sior Polo," a breathless high-pitched voice cried out behind them. "Come quickly. Your father says you must return to camp at once."

"Oh, Sior Polo," one of the Genovese mimicked in the same mincing voice. "You'd better run to your papa before you get scratched."

"Please. All of you. Put away your swords," the eunuch squealed. "This is *important.*"

"What is it?" Marco snapped without taking his eyes off the three men and the menacing blades. "What's so damned important?"

"We have a pope, Sior Polo. After thirty-one months, we finally have a pope."

IN THE GREAT HALL of his castle Tebaldo Visconti da Piacenza waited to receive the Polo entourage, dabbing at his moist temples with a scented, embroidered handkerchief. Bright sunlight flooded through the arched windows that lined the western wall of the room.

Had it already been two years since Nicolo and his brother Maffeo arrived in Acre as emissaries from the Great Khan? The more he aged, the faster the months passed. He remembered his first impression of the two Venetian merchants: well-instructed, discreet men. To Tebaldo, as Papal Legate of Acre, they'd delivered the Emperor's requests.

"Kublai Khan, supreme chief of all the Tartars, asks the Sovereign Pontiff of Rome for one hundred men of learning, thoroughly acquainted with the Christian religion as well as the seven arts, qualified to prove by just and fair argument that the gods of the Tartars and the idols worshiped in their houses are but evil spirits, and that the faith professed by Christians is founded upon more evident truth than any other. The Great Khan further wishes a vial of holy oil from the lamp that burns at the sepulcher of the Lord Jesus Christ, whom he professes to hold in veneration and to consider as the true God."

But that was the Year of Our Lord 1269, and Pope Clement IV had died the year before. "His seat is still vacant," Tebaldo told the Polos. "Return to Venice. Visit your homes and families and await the election of the new pope."

This they did and Nicolo had discovered that the wife he'd left pregnant fifteen years before had borne him a son. She named him Marco after the city's patron saint. Nicolo also learned that she herself had died bringing the boy into the world. But finally, two years after their first meeting with Tebaldo, the brothers had returned to Acre with Marco in tow. They could wait no longer, they said. Kublai Khan would take their continued absence as an affront, with grave consequences for Christians everywhere.

Now, just as they prepared to resume their journey, the conclave of cardinals had defied the clamors for a French pope from the Angevin faction in their ranks and announced their choice. They'd elected the Papal Legate of Acre to be their next pope.

Tebaldo rose from his throne of Lebanon cedar as voices and footsteps echoed in the stone corridor leading to the hall. Maffeo Polo entered at the head of the family entourage. He genuflected and kissed Tebaldo's ring.

"Your Holiness," he said. "What a wonderful surprise. By what name shall we know you in future?"

"I've decided on Gregory—Gregory, the tenth pope of that name."

He sat again while the visitors remained standing before his throne. They'd always been respectful of his Legate's role, but the extreme deference he saw in their faces now embarrassed him. In his most ambitious dreams he had never imagined himself as the pope. And now that he had been named leader of the whole Christian church on earth, he preferred to focus on one of the papacy's humbler titles: *Servus servorum Dei*, the servant of the servants of God.

"The news could not have been more timely," he said. "Another day and you would have sailed for Lesser Armenia." He motioned to a cleric who waited by a half-open side door. The cleric beckoned in turn and two portly Dominican friars came into the hall.

"*Signori*, I give you Fra Guielmo da Tripoli and Fra Nicolo da Vicenza. By the grace of God they were here in Acre when word of my election arrived from Rome. They're not the hundred scholars the Great Khan wants, but they are men of letters and science." This really was the best he could do on such brief notice, and he prayed the paucity of missionaries would not be the deciding factor in converting the pagan Tartars to Christianity. Studying the two soft preachers, he wondered if they'd even survive the rigorous trip to Cathay.

The cleric approached the throne and handed Tebaldo a vellum parchment secured with his personal seal. "Besides my greetings to Kublai Khan, this papal letter authorizes these friars to ordain priests, to consecrate bishops, and to grant absolution as fully as I could do in my own person.

"My blessing goes with you all, for your health and safety. I know you will be impeded by ice, sand, floods, wars, barbarian raiders and numerous other dangers." He spoke the last words for the benefit of the two Dominicans, and watched as they exchanged nervous glances. He feared his selections would prove unlucky, but they truly were the only trained scholars available in Acre that day. He might as well have given the Polos his cleric.

Having disposed of the formalities of the merchants' mission, Tebaldo allowed himself to sink against the throne's carved backrest. He took a deep breath while he dabbed again at his temples. "To tell you the truth, my friends, I shan't be sorry to leave Acre. Your fellow merchants and even our brave crusaders have made my life here one of endless frustration."

The entourage fidgeted at his words, unsure whether to look guilty or contrite, or how they were expected to respond. Tebaldo smiled wearily at their bewilderment. "Surely you understand?" he said. "We've transported the finest warriors in Christendom here to regain the Land of Promise. Yet Baibars Bandukdari and his Mameluks continue their predations. Just this year they took the Templar castle at Safed and beheaded the knights there. They razed Antioch and massacred all its 80,000 souls save for those few whom Baibars' soldiers were too arm-weary to kill, and those few are now enslaved. Within the decade I expect him at the walls of Acre itself. And do you know what? He will take it, for we Christians bicker so among ourselves that we never oppose him with a united front. Your brother

Venetians sell arms to Baibars. The Genovese feed his slave trade. The Templars and Hospitalers feud among themselves and both thwart our efforts to negotiate with the Saracens, refusing to exchange their Muslim prisoners. 'We need their artisan skills,' they tell me. Everyone thinks of his own profit instead of God's will, or even our mutual good."

He leaned his head against the backrest and sighed aloud. "Forgive me, *signori*. You are but jewel merchants and have served our cause well. It is not of you that I complain. My time here has taken its toll. I'm just tired and eager to be back on familiar soil."

He sat upright again and looked over the gathering. "Ah, there's your Marco. But I don't think I know the young man with him. Is this another of your sons, Sior Polo?"

"No, Your Holiness. Permit me to introduce Orfeo di Angelo Bernardone, a friend of my son and a man-at-arms in our expedition."

"Another of your Venetian countrymen, then."

"An Assisan, Excellency." Then, as if to salvage an uncomfortable situation, the merchant added, "He is a nephew of the most blessed San Francesco of that city."

"Indeed?"

Tebaldo scrutinized the sturdy youth. He considered himself a keen judge of character. The young man carried himself well, and Tebaldo liked the energy and curiosity in those brown eyes. They spoke of liveliness and a quick wit. *Too bad this one has no theological training*, he thought, and then another idea crossed his mind.

"Sior Bernardone," he said, "with the leave of the Polos, I would have you sail with me to Venice. With you on board, we can be sure to gain the protection of your holy uncle. I do not doubt that he stands nearer to the throne of God than any saint, save Our Lord's own blessed mother."

The brothers Polo quickly bowed their agreement, but Tebaldo saw a shadow of disappointment and confusion darken the Assisan's face. He seemed less than honored to have been singled out by the papal request. Marco scowled at his friend and whispered something in his ear. The young man nodded and walked stiffly forward. He knelt before the throne, bowed until his forehead touched Tebaldo's white silk slipper, and kissed the hem of the legate's robe.

"I am your servant and God's, Your Holiness. All that I am, and all that I have, is at your disposal."

IV

AMONG THE JUMBLED boulders of an ancient scree, Conrad set down their food pouch and waited for Amata. The sun hadn't yet reached its highest point, but the rocks were already warm and likely to grow hotter—one of those odd October days that clung stubbornly to summer. They'd left all shade behind when they cleared the tree line more than an hour before and the slight breeze that stirred the hillside scrabble offered scant relief from the heat.

The hermit seldom ranged from his forest, either to descend to the coastal villages or to climb up here into the starved barrens. When he did venture to some peak, it was usually to celebrate a special holy day in contemplation. The crags afforded a pure panorama, range after range of blue and purple mountains, mantled in snow or cleft by stunning waterfalls, a breathtaking display of God's generative power through which Conrad crawled as small and grey as the spiders that scaled the wall of his hut. City dwellers, clustered in dense webs of their own construction, might feel superior to their surroundings, but God's Appenines dwarfed all human pride.

He withdrew his gaze from the horizon and looked back at the trail he'd just climbed. "Are you sure you're part mountain goat?" he called as Amata straggled up.

The girl plopped down on a nearby boulder and sucked in the hot air, one hand rising and falling on her heaving chest. When she'd caught her breath, she said, "I may have exaggerated a bit. I'm not used to climbing such high mountains."

"But you spoke truly when you said you have no fear of heights?"

"Just lead on. I'll be right behind you. If your shortcut saves us a week of travel, I'll be grateful to you for taking it."

"We'll come soon to a footpath carved by goats across the face of the mountain," Conrad explained. "The narrowest section lasts but two hundred yards, but a single misstep will plunge you *six* hundred yards to the valley floor." He scraped absent-mindedly with a small stone on one of the boulders, deliberately avoiding looking at her as he added: "I should think that only an innocent soul who has no fear of God's judgment would dare attempt it." This was a matter between the girl and her conscience, and he didn't wish to see the state of her soul reflected in her eyes.

"If you're not afraid, I'm not," Amata said. "The climb would be a lot easier, though, without these long robes. My hem keeps catching on rocks and tripping me. I heard a rumor that the Order plans to return to short tunics like the first friars wore. I wish they'd already done it."

"The first friars worked for their food like ordinary laborers," Conrad said. "As you so quaintly pointed out this morning, we brothers-come-lately spend most of our time on our backsides. The friars of the Sacro Convento now earn commissions for copying manuscripts, just like the black monks. Besides, even if the Order does restore the tunic for its friars, you and your cloistered sisters will still be wearing full-length robes in the name of decency."

"A shame, don't you think?" Amata said behind him.

Conrad swung around on his perch. She stood grinning at him with her robe pulled up well above her knees. The hermit jerked his hand up to shield his eyes and turned his face away from her.

"Sister! For love of the most pure Virgin, cover yourself!"

"What's the matter?" Her voice had taken on a playful tone. "If you were a ploughman and I your loving mate, I'd dress like this every day as I worked beside you—and give you much pleasure in doing so."

"But I am *not* a ploughman and *you* are *certainly* not my mate. I'm a friar and priest consecrated to God's service. Should I draw but an *instant's* pleasure from the sight of your long legs, that instant could be the first link in the chain that drags me into the abyss. Keep to the promise of modesty you made at the hut."

He hadn't meant to say *"long"* legs. He hadn't actually meant to look at her legs either, but his brief glance startled him. Not that he should have been surprised. Her baggy habit might have hidden any form possible to women. He just hadn't thought of her until now in terms of limbs or torso—or the length of her legs.

If Amata noticed the slip, she was kind enough to let it pass—which made him think she hadn't caught it. He already realized she wasn't one to pass up a chance to needle him. To his relief, she changed the subject as they set out again.

"You're a *queer* sort of priest, aren't you? You haven't touched your breviary once, and here it's almost midday."

Conrad smiled. Did nothing escape the child? Had she not been born female, she might have made a decent student of canon or civil law.

"The roads to heaven are many, sister," he replied. Again he assumed the pedagogic tone he had used when he explained about Elias and the basilica. "Some, for example, choose the physical path, using their bodies to gain salvation. The crusader finds God in the decapitated Saracen or in his own martyrdom. *Flagellanti* whip themselves with leather disciplines while they recite the penitential psalms."

Amata grimaced. "Ugh! I saw a band of flagellants once, when I was a little girl. They passed through our commune on their way to Todi. Their bloody flesh spattered everyone and everything in range. I hid my eyes, they were so disgusting."

"They've been everywhere these last eleven years. Many people thought 1260 would be the year of the apocalypse." Conrad thought again of Giovanni da Parma, secluded in his cell. And for what? For nothing more than continuing to believe the prophecies of the clairvoyant Abbot Joachim di Flora after they'd fallen from fashion among the Church hierarchy. After a pause to reorganize his thoughts, he resumed his lecture.

"Cloistered religious like the black monks of San Benedetto, on the other hand, pass their lives on the devotional path, chanting and praying by the book." He pulled a breviary from inside his robe and flipped its pages. "Seven times a day and in the middle of the night, as the Psalmist instructed.

"I myself first tried the way of the intellect, beginning with the *trivium* and the *quadrivium*."

"The *who* and the *what?*"

"The seven arts prerequisite to the study of theology: the *trivium*—grammar, rhetoric, and dialectic—and the *quadrivium*—music, arithmetic, geometry, and astronomy."

He slowed his pace to catch his breath, for the path still climbed before them. "Then, after I tutored in theology in Paris," he resumed, "I returned to the mother house in Assisi and began to practice the devotional formalities of conventual life. Oddly enough, after several years of study and routine prayer I found myself growing estranged not only from Our Lord, but from my brothers as well. The conventual life lacked something for me. It was then that I started to wonder about the hermit friars, and whether they lived closer to God than the rest of us."

He warmed to his theme. He could teach Amata so much. "It is only in these mountains, sister, that I've finally begun to see God—still 'through a glass darkly' as San Paolo said, but perhaps as clearly as one can hope to on this earth. And how do I do that, you may ask? I *sit*. Nothing more, I just sit. I lean against the wall of my hermitage and let God come to me. If I sit with my eyes closed, He appears within me. If I open my eyes, I see Him in every creature that walks or crawls past my door. He's in every tree and bush, in every..."

Amata cut him off with a wave of her hand. She stopped in her tracks and placed her hands on her hips, appraising him like a noblewoman deciding whether or not to buy a slave. "Like I said, you're a queer sort of priest—and turning into a considerable talker. I'm not sure hermiting is your vocation either. Maybe you should have joined the preaching friars of San Domenico instead of the minorites."

Conrad's mouth hung open, arrested as he had been in mid-speech. *Why did he cast his pearls before this shoat? Most scholars wouldn't bother instructing any female—let alone a bondwoman.*

They had come to a precipice where the path gave way to a sheer drop. Far below them a thin, glittering ribbon twisted through a mottled greensward. Despite Amata's perversity, Conrad couldn't resist the lesson presented by the scene. "Here is an example of the hermit's life at fullest advantage. The mighty Hercules couldn't throw a stone across that river down there. The trees on its banks that seem but mere clumps of greenery from here are taller than ten men. From this height one sees the world through God's own eyes, in all its insignificance, a view worth volumes of philosophy. Drink it in while you have the opportunity, sister."

Whether she actually drank he couldn't tell, but at least she didn't dispute his point. He led her along the rim of the cliff until they came to a narrow ledge that crossed the scarp to the West. "That's our path. You may want to tie your sandals around your waist so you can grip with your toes." He added: "We'll only lose one day's journey if we turn back here and set out from the hut again tomorrow."

Amata squinted at the goat trail, taking its measure. Her lips moved, and Conrad wondered whether she prayed or just firmed up her courage. He thought of asking if she'd feel safer holding onto his cincture, but that would only be inviting physical contact and he let it pass.

"Are you ready?" he asked finally.

The girl swallowed, took a deep breath, and nodded as she slipped her feet out of her sandals.

"Don't look down," he cautioned while she tied the sandals to her waist. He knotted their food pouch at the back of his own cincture. "Face the wall and slide along sideways feeling for hand holds. Don't concern yourself with how long we take. Just focus on your next step."

He studied her face. Her skin color had faded even whiter than its normal shade. Although she chewed at her lip, her eyes showed the same determination he'd seen just before they left the hermitage.

"All right, then. May God protect us," Conrad prayed. They crossed themselves and side-by-side stepped out onto the edge of the world.

ALTHOUGH HE MIGHT have welcomed a cooling wind earlier, Conrad thanked God for the calm air now. Sweat crawled like vermin down his neck and back and he had to blink the gnats away from his eyes. Still he knew that one powerful updraft from the valley could billow their robes like sails, lifting them off the face of the cliff as easily as seeds blown from a dandelion.

He kicked away loose rocks as he sidled inch-by-inch, smoothing the footpath for Amata. She followed closely, more silent than the plummeting stones. He knew she itched as much as he. If anything, her new robe would be heavier than his threadbare one. He wondered what might be going through her mind, but didn't want to disturb her concentration. When he did speak, it was only a supportive murmur to keep her focused: "One step ... one step."

They came to the bend that marked the halfway point in the trail. Around the corner, he knew, was a widening of the path protected by an overhang—a cavity where they could rest for a moment and relax the tension from their arms and shoulders. He turned to tell Amata about the ledge just as the rock she was gripping cracked off in her hand. She gave a sharp cry and began to teeter. Conrad reached back and snatched her sleeve to steady her. He heard a clattering above their heads and a trickle of pebbles pelted down on them.

"Hurry! We have to make it to the corner," he said.

Amata froze against the wall. The falling fragments were larger now and the trickle had become a stream. A rock the size of her head struck her left shoulder. She screamed as Conrad shifted his grip around her waist, a knot of robe wadded in his fist, and half-led, half-dragged her toward him.

"Stay with me!" he cried. "Don't quit now!"

Amata's legs began to shuffle stiffly. Using his free arm for hand holds, Conrad inched her across the scarp and around to the wide spot in the path. He eased her into a seated position with her back to the cliff. Then he slid down beside her, keeping his arm curled around her shoulder as a violent trembling began to shake her entire body. She tried to speak, but the chattering of her teeth prevented her, and she could only sob.

He'd seen such quaking fear before, in a fox that darted into his hut to escape a pack of baying hounds. It had a sizable lead on the pack and Conrad closed the open doorway before the dogs could follow the animal into the hermitage. He held the door shut with the fox quivering against the back of his calves until a group of hard-breathing horsemen pounded up the path in the dog's wake.

"Sanctuary," he called out to the hunters. "Brother Fox has claimed the sanctuary of this hermitage." Through a knothole in the door he kept an eye on the clan of nobles, a brutish bunch in general, and hoped his local reputation as an eccentric holy man would give them pause. Why should they risk his curse and jeopardize their souls over a mere fox? The looks directed at his hut ranged from resentment to wroth. They glowered and grumbled as they conferred, but finally wheeled their horses. They called the dogs after them as they threaded their way back down his mountain.

"The shaking will pass, sister," he said. "It's the dance of San Vito. The fiercest warriors have such tremors after the battle's won." He began to rock her gently like a father calming a frightened child, and to his own surprise began to hum a lullaby. He felt he embraced a piece of his own youth, for when he blinked his eyes he imagined he held Rosanna—Rosanna as he remembered her at sixteen, not the plump thirty-year-old survivor of eight pregnancies and three live births who sent food to his hermitage once a week. Amata even gave off a light fishy scent reminiscent of the children of Ancona, probably from handling the wrapper on Leo's scroll.

They had a different view now that they had rounded the bend in the path. Conrad pointed across the valley. Here and there on rocky outcroppings umber-colored blocks clustered atop one another. "There's the village of Sassoferrato and way off to the right you can make out Fossato di Vico. We'd have been four days getting there by the southern route."

A feeling like tenderness filled his heart, an emotion he might reasonably expect during a meditation on the Holy Infant. But he wasn't prepared for feelings of fondness toward a flesh and bone female. Conrad grew suddenly fearful that God might hurl him from their perch if he gave way even slightly to impulse. He tried to dredge up some of the antagonism he'd felt just before they stepped out onto the ledge, but her vulnerability had flushed that particular silt from his soul. For all her brashness and bravado, she needed his protection.

Finally the trembling subsided and he withdrew his arm from around her shoulders. "I think you'll be all right now." He answered her deliberately, clipping out the words he knew he *should* say. He had to change the mood, and quickly.

"How is your shoulder? Can you lift your arm?" he asked.

Too eager to help, he grasped her forearm to help raise it. Instead of muscle, he felt something solid through her sleeve, like a splint, and thicker than bone. Amata yanked the arm away, wincing as she did so.

"It's not broken," she said, "but I don't think I'll be much help with the grape harvest when I get back to San Damiano." She shifted her legs, struggling to get up. "We should start moving."

By touching whatever Amata concealed in her sleeve, he'd spurred her to action. He wanted to ask, but decided this wasn't the time to press her.

"You're sure you don't need to rest a while longer? Most people wouldn't shrug off a brush with death so easily. Especially someone as sheltered as you've been."

He'd meant to be reassuring. Her face reddened and her eyes narrowed to slits.

"Sheltered? What do you know of my life?" she said. She turned away from him towards the remaining section of trail. "You are a complete fool sometimes, brother, but you did just remind me I have another reason to get back to Assisi in one piece." She tried to push herself up with the uninjured arm.

"Stay another moment, sister" he said. "Tell me what you're talking about." It was a clumsy sort of apology. He'd meant to say, *If I knew more about you, I wouldn't make stupid remarks.*

"If we come off the trail in one piece, I might," Amata said.

The sky had begun to cloud and thunderheads rose to the Southeast. The distant, disordered ridges took on the look of hostile, wind-whipped waves as the gloom deepened and spread across them. Those clouds might be harbingers of rain. Or worse, the cooling air might create the updrafts Conrad had feared earlier. They really should be going.

He supported Amata's elbow, steadying her as she stood. Once she had her balance, he untied the loops in his rope cincture and held it out to her. "Loop it through your cincture before I tie it around my waist again," he said.

"Aren't you afraid I'll drag you with me if I slip?"

"Whatever happens befalls us both, sister. God has linked us in this undertaking. I believe He means us to continue, or end, together."

"That's a pretty speech for a friar," Amata smiled. "Coming from a suitor it would've been absolutely romantic." Then she added seriously, "Thank you for your concern. I've been rough on you. I've little love for the religious habit we share and for some men I've come up against in the past. You're a good person and you've treated me well. I want to say I'm sorry before we risk the path again."

"And I too, for any harsh feelings I've held towards you."

Again she smiled, but her eyes grew sad. "My brother Fabiano used to say: 'A kiss goodbye, in case I die.'" Conrad could see she was close to tears. He leaned toward her and allowed his lips to brush her forehead.

"In case we die, little sister," he said.

Amata reddened and lowered her eyes. She crimped his cincture in her fingers for a moment, then intertwined it with her own.

V

WHERE THE GOAT TRAIL faded onto a bare broad plateau they finally collapsed. Amata lay on her back in the dirt waving her arm and laughing wildly. Still linked to the girl by their cinctures, Conrad stretched beside her, his heart pounding against his breastbone as the anxiety gradually relaxed from his limbs.

"Oh God, we made it," Amata said.

"*Praise* God, we did," the hermit gasped in turn.

A bright patch in the clouds showed where the sun dipped toward the tallest peaks. "We should find a place soon to make our camp," he added. "We've worked hard enough for one day."

The view now spread north and east from the plateau, as well as to the south. More villages and an occasional enclosed croft could be seen on the spurs of the mountains. They were still far from a real settlement, but within a day they could expect to come across other people.

"We're headed just over that farthest range," Conrad said. "If there's an opening in the clouds this evening, watch where the sun sets. It marks our course for Gubbio. From Gubbio we follow the banks of the Chiagio to Assisi. We'll be there in two days, three at most."

Amata sat up and peered into the distance toward the ridges to the North. "Will we catch sight of the castle of the Malatesti? I'd love to see it, even from a distance."

Conrad laughed. "Not a chance," he said. "It's many leagues from here, almost on the coast."

She shuddered. "I hate lords. Especially old, deformed, evil lords like Gianciotto Malatesta."

Conrad knew the tale, gossip so choice that even Rosanna's man couldn't resist sharing it when he brought Conrad's food. The Malatesta clan of Rimini and the Polenta lords of Ravenna wished to form an alliance and arranged a marriage between Gianciotto and Francesca Polenta. The bride would have been about Amata's age, Conrad guessed. Aware that Francesca would probably reject Gianciotto because of his advanced years and ugliness, the Malatesti sent his younger brother Paolo, *Il Bello*, to stand proxy at the wedding. Some time after the ceremony, so the story went, Paolo and Francesca were reading a romance of Lancelot in the castle garden. Moved by the handsome knight's yearning for the married Guinevere, they began to embrace and kiss. They read no more that day. Apparently their passion also overwhelmed their caution, for one of Gianciotto's servants saw what happened and reported to his master. The end proved tragic, the very kind of romantic tripe a young female like Amata would find irresistible.

"Gianciotto will surely burn in hell for murdering his wife and brother," Conrad said. "But the lovers no doubt suffer for their sin also."

"Their sin? Is it a sin to love, then? Did not Jesus tell us to love one another?"

"Even as He loved us, sister. He was not speaking of carnal lust when he said that. Besides, Francesca was married to Paolo's brother."

"As though she had a voice in the marriage. These spoiled lords marry whom they will, and never for love. For land or money or to seal a treaty. Never for love. They take what they want and kill those who counter their wishes. I hate them with my very soul!"

"There *are* evil lords, to be sure, but good lords also, just as you'll find good and evil villeins. They are all part of God's plan."

"I know about the good men too." Amata's voice became dreamy. "My father was an honorable man. But men like Gianciotto Malatesta..." Her jaw muscles clenched and her face contorted, first in sorrow, then in rage. She would talk now, Conrad sensed.

In silence the hermit observed the copse of twisted oaks spread across the slope below. Shadowy birds flitted among the branches, their singing muted and sporadic.

He sniffed the air. He could smell the impending storm and apparently the birds sensed it too. He could always count on the first rain of the season to be a real downpour. At least he and Amata would have plenty of wood to ward off the dampness. Broken, windfall branches littered the ground beneath the trees; oak firewood burned better than any other.

He chewed on the seeming contradiction of a noble-spirited peasant, which he assumed best described Amata's father—an easy enough guess, since nine men in ten tilled the soil. In his experience, most villeins and tenant farmers were too busy working to brood on higher ideals. Their religion amounted to little more than charms and spells to ward off sickness and make their harvests abundant. Given a holy day's respite from their chores, they usually reverted to drinking, brawling, and all sorts of licentious mischief. Yet, as a confessor, Conrad had known occasional exceptions, laborers who far outstripped their masters in virtue.

"Was your father abused by his lord?" he asked finally.

Amata huffed. "Abused by his lord? My father was praying to his Lord, unarmed, gathered with his wife and children in his family chapel, when the devil in human form burst through the doors and hacked him to death. Mamma threw herself across his body while a son of the same Satan ran his broadsword through both of them. My brother tried to escape by leaping through the chapel window."

She paused. "He screamed my name as he fell. Then he made no noise at all." She hid her face in her hands. Her shoulders and back shook in a dumbshow of grief, for her sobs remained silent. "I don't even know whether they had a fitting burial."

Conrad looked away at the shadows deepening under the trees. He almost feared to ask the next question, but having heard so much of the slaughter of her family, he had to know the rest.

"How did you escape alive?"

"I tried to run, but I slipped in my parents' blood. It ran everywhere on the tiles of the chapel floor. I remember thinking that the tiles and the blood were almost the same color. It seemed like a bad dream in which the tiles were really just melting, and that when I woke soon, none of this would be happening. I rolled over and saw an ax raised above my head. I thought I would be the next to die.

"But I wasn't to be freed so easily. Their leader yelled to the knight to stay his arm. I was just eleven and he wanted me as a maidservant for his daughter. The raiders took me with them."

"She was the woman who entered San Damiano?"

"Yes. She hates the lot as fiercely as I do." Amata stiffened her back. She spoke calmly now. "The lady made me part of her dowry to the convent. I was thrilled, though in truth I care not a whit for the life. But I would have killed myself rather than be left behind with her father and brothers."

"And damned your soul by your suicide," Conrad reminded her. "Were your families at war, Amata? Was there some feud or bad blood between you?"

"No. Purely a case of silver and gold. Three lives lost, at least, and I don't know how many of our servants, all to save the price of a toll. Our estate lay where the communal borders of Perugia, Assisi and Todi meet. We called it Coldimezzo, 'the hill in the middle.' Naturally, we charged a fee to the merchants who carted their wares across our property. The Assisan wool merchants would scream and threaten us, but my papa and his brother Guido just laughed and threatened them right back. My mistress told me later that it was one of the wool merchants who hired her father to kill us."

She appeared to stare at the shade creeping up the hillside toward them, but Conrad guessed she actually saw again the bloody chapel of the Coldimezzo. After a prolonged silence, she turned to him and shrugged. "There's my sheltered life," she said. All the fear and ferocity had leached from her voice.

And *there* also was the reason she was determined to get back to Assisi, Conrad thought, and a reason for him to stay away. War seemed to rage wherever people crowded together. Cities and countries clashed over trade routes and territory. Within the city walls, middle-class Guelphs and aristocratic Ghibellines fought out their allegiance to the Pope or Holy Roman Emperor. Families battled to settle some antique grudge, and children killed their parents and each other to speed their inheritance. Death by murder was the common end for noblemen, and for the ordinary citizens the ensuing duels, funerals and lawsuits formed the theater of life. Widows, widowers, and orphans proliferated, all of them spurred to revenge. The spark of the vendetta kept many a ruined life aflame.

"You didn't mention the others of your family," he said at last, "your Uncle Guido and his household. Weren't they caught up in the attack too?"

"No. The cowards even knew *that*. My cousin Vanna was to marry a notary from Todi that month. Her mamma and papa had gone to the city with her to prepare the feast. We were supposed to join them in a matter of days."

She lay back in the dirt and closed her eyes. Gradually, she started to hum, a popular dirge of the country people. She had retreated to a private place within her mind, and Conrad understood that he would hear no more.

She must have mourned often during these five years, even as her hatred grew and she plotted her revenge. Perhaps she wondered why her uncle hadn't come for her. Maybe he didn't even know where she'd been taken or who had committed the murders. He'd have ridden back from Todi to a scene of carnage. The servants might have fled or, if they remained, been unable to name the assailants.

He wondered, too, what sort of knight would hire out as a paid killer. And why had Amata remained at San Damiano? Why had she delivered Leo's letter at great hazard, when she could have run away and made the relatively easy journey by good roads to the Coldimezzo? Maybe she feared that nothing remained to run home to. The more he learned of the girl, the more she puzzled and intrigued him.

He felt a powerful urge to soothe her hair as he had the fur of the shivering fox. As he stretched out his hand, however, he also felt an aching sensation in his groin that warned him to stay his touch. "I'm truly sorry, Amata," he said.

"Piss on your wasted pity," she snapped. "It won't bring my family back to life." She kept her eyes clamped shut, but he could see tears gathering in the corners.

He took advantage of her closed eyes to search her face, hoping to find there some clue to help him understand this enigmatic woman-child. Her jaw knotted in taut fibers and the tears flowed softly down her temples and into the earth. She'd exposed herself where she hurt most, and he had eavesdropped on her powerlessness. But her crude reply had gotten him off the hook in a way. It dropped him back into reality. He stared in awe at his hand, the one he'd almost used to caress her hair. *That* close he'd come to unraveling all he'd gained spiritually during his years in the wilderness.

As a boy he often dove for sponges in the harbor of Ancona. Once, during a meditation, he'd found himself comparing the creatures to human souls. Left to dry in sunlight the sponge became light and airy, like the soul exposed to the blinding rays of God's grace. His own soul had nearly attained that weightless state he used to hope, before Amata arrived with the letter. But in the two days since, it seemed his spirit had grown heavy and bloated as it absorbed first Leo's, then the girl's, concerns—as it soaked in one long-forgotten emotion after another. He needed suddenly and desperately to be alone.

"I'm going to look for a shelter," he said. "We're in for heavy rain tonight. I'll be back soon."

Amata resumed her keening. He untwined their cinctures, then rose and brushed the dirt from his robe. As he walked off the plateau down toward the trees, he turned for one last look at the solitary figure stretched out on the hilltop, then ducked his head and plunged into the tenebrous woods.

REGRET STILL WEIGHED on Orfeo as he watched the tide carry his friend toward the mouth of the harbor. The oarsmen launched the galley smoothly through the sheltered stretch of water.

Goodbye, Marco, he waved. *Go enjoy your journey of a lifetime. I will think of you as I walk the piazzas of Venice, and every other courtesan I will dedicate to your memory.*

Were it possible, he'd have purged from his mind the elder Polo's stories of the ladies of Kinsai, the most beautiful in the world, who swayed in decorated litters with ivory combs in their jet black hair and jade ear rings bobbing against their smooth cheeks. Or the tales of the palace ladies who, tired of coursing game with the royal dogs, flung off their gowns and dove naked and giggling into the lakes where they sported like shoals of silver fish.

Addio, compare, he waved one final time as the galley cleared the breakwater. *Addio, Cathay.*

He shuffled toward the end of the quay, ignoring the tang of the salt air and the wheeling and shrieking gulls overhead, until he came to an English man-of-war being provisioned for the trip to Venice. The Anglican prince, Edward, the new commander of the crusader forces, had volunteered a convoy of his warships to the pope as soon as he'd learned of Tebaldo's election.

The mariner in Orfeo could not but marvel at the ship. The deck beams projected through the sides of the vessel, secured with pegs in the southern fashion, but the width-to-length ratio of the beams themselves was perhaps three-to-five, unlike the one-to-five of the sleek Venetian galleys. The man-of-war clearly had been built to withstand heavy northern seas and open ocean, while a galley like Niccolo Polo's sliced smoothly through calm Mediterranean waters. Both the forecastle and aftercastle of the warship rose several levels in the manner of Saracen caraks, and a top castle towered above its single mast. Archers and slingers aboard the man-of-war held a decided height advantage over lower-slung fighting galleys. The ship's builders had grouped the oar openings with but two handbreadths between thole pins and could easily engage two hundred rowers in a bireme or trireme array. With a strong trailing wind, the craft might reach a speed of twelve knots. No pirate would dare attack a flotilla of such ships.

Orfeo grunted in self-pity. Pirates might at least liven up the voyage. He turned back toward the city with downcast heart and eyes. He saw Acre's towering bastions mirrored in the harbor, drifting and scattering in the waves like a mirage. If the pope-elect already spoke with the infallibility of papal vision, these monuments to power would be dashed to rubble in a few years. All Orfeo knew now, though, was that—through a whim of this same pontiff—the barely raised storehouse of his own hopes and fantasies had crumbled beyond recovery.

He lifted his chin as if to stare down the towers of the port. They stood tall and cold and stiff as the father and big brothers who'd dominated his boyhood. As a child, he would run to his grandmother when the older men tried to quash his small spirit. Through all the years since, women had continued to comfort him while the men of his family, his comrades, his shipmates, only left him in pain.

And so it must be tonight. Having turned his back on the man-of-war, he directed his steps toward the alley where he and Marco had been heading in such high humor just that morning.

VI

FUCKING MUD! FUCKING puny-assed ox!" Primo slammed his huge fist
against the plank seat of his tumbrel. He kicked off his clogs and tossed
them onto the load of firewood, then climbed down shin deep into the
mushy cart path. He glowered first at the animal, then at the solid wooden
wheels bogged down in the ooze. The storm that swept through the mountains the night before had turned the path into a quagmire. "You'll spare your
worthless hide a beating if I don't have to unload this cart again."

He waded off the narrow roadway and ripped furiously at branches from
the nearest pines. He strewed them for traction in front of both wheels and
slogged around behind the tumbrel.

"Haw. Gee up there, Jupiter," he yelled, grunting and shoving on the back
end of the load. The axle creaked and the wheels rolled slightly forward.
"Move your bony rump!" He spun around so that his back rested squarely
against the load and drove his heels into the mud. His feet slipped and he sat
down hard. With a low moan, the cart settled back into its rut.

"*Porco Dio! Putana Madonna!*" He grabbed a fistful of the clay-red slop and
flung it down the road in the general direction of two approaching friars.
They followed the tracks left by his wheels. The heavier one had a bag slung
over his shoulder and seemed not to notice the wet footing. He plowed
straight ahead, while the small one lifted his robe daintily and danced off to
the side of the road.

*Merda! Here's all I need. Priests passing me on the road. And begging friars at
that.* Primo had crossed paths with a padre the day before his mamma's fatal
sickness set in. He knew through the primal lore in the marrow of his bones
that the unlucky meeting with the priest had caused her death. Like his fellow

villagers, he had a morbid dread of clergymen, but unlike them, he met his dread head on. As the friars slogged into hailing range, Primo glared at them with heart-felt animosity.

"I got no money, no extra food, and I don't want saving," he yelled out. The short one laughed, a high-pitched, almost girlish giggle. The farmer shook his head in disgust. *Not two priests. Just one sodomite priest and his novice whore.* He was as hot as the next man and never missed his mark in a dark corner at a festival—but he never did it with little boys like a pagan Greek.

Primo grabbed a cart rail and pulled himself onto his feet. He scooped the slime from his tunic, leaving ruddy streaks that gave the unbleached wool a pied effect. The clay even caked the thick hair on his naked legs.

The two pulled up a few paces from his cart. The small one piped up first. "*Servite pauperes Christi*, padre. Just like Leo said."

"What's that he said?" Primo asked. "If he's making fun of me I'll split his skull, novice's habit or no."

"He said we should give you a hand," the older friar answered.

Primo pulled off his round cap and used it to wipe his face. "What? And dirty those anointed fingertips of yours? I thought you was only allowed to touch holy things and money."

"Do you want help or not?" the friar asked. He spoke in a flat tone and obviously had no sense of humor.

"Sorry, sorry padre. Course I do. Never piss off a gift horse, as they say."

He tossed the ox goad to the novice. "Here, *fratellino*. See if you can prod some life into that lame excuse of an ox. We'll push from the back if the padre's willing."

The friar studied the beast. "He's not very big."

"Aye. That would be my problem. He's only twice a yearling, but he's all I got left. The pastor took his dam for the burial fee when my mamma died. Being one of the thieving breed yourself, you know how that goes."

"Your pastor was entitled to his *heriot*. Taking the survivor's choicest animal is an ancient custom." The friar's colorless eyes stared directly into Primo's. "For a man in need of help, you don't mind your mouth well."

Primo straightened to his full height and was about to tell the man to suck himself when the boy interrupted: "I'm ready whenever you two want to start shoving." The friar continued to stare hard at him with those creepy grey eyes that could curse a man just by looking on him. The farmer dropped his gaze. He couldn't afford to make an enemy of the friar just now and motioned to the back of the cart. "After you, padre."

The men set their shoulders to the large wheels. With a shout the boy began to pull at the front of the cart while he goaded the ox with his free hand. The pine branches crackled underneath the wheels, releasing a scent that momentarily overshadowed the musky odor of the animal, and ever so slowly the cart groaned forward. The bell around the ox's neck clanked rhythmically.

"Keep pushing," Primo shouted. "Get me to the top of this grade and it's rides for all. We can coast the next couple of leagues."

All three bent to their work and even the animal seemed revitalized by their forward motion. "Good ox. Good Jupiter. There's my good boy. Keep those wheels turning."

The friars cheered as they crested the rise and Primo thumped the older one between the shoulder blades. The blow startled the man, but he responded with a broad grin. "Well done all around," he said.

Primo clambered back onto his seat. He was in top spirits now. "Anybody tired? There's room for one of you at a time up here."

"No, we're used to walking," the friar said. "But we thank you all the same."

"I could use a ride," the novice interrupted. He held out his right arm. "I've hurt my other shoulder. Can you help me up?"

Primo grabbed the outstretched forearm. "Give him a goose, padre."

The boy laughed heartily. "You heard him, Fra Conrad. Give me a goose."

"Fabiano! Be mindful to whom you're speaking."

Primo guffawed. He gave a yank and the boy landed hard against him. The friar scowled furiously, especially when the novice poked his tongue out at him.

"I hope I'm not too heavy against you. This plank's pretty narrow," the boy said.

"I'd a cow once'd make twenty of you," Primo said. "I daren't milk her near a wall. She'd have leaned me right through it." He peered around the boy. "I thinks your priest is a touch jealous, though." He winked at his own wit and began singing nonchalantly:

"Through the leafy forest, Bovo went a-riding,
While his Rosabella trotted on beside him."

"Fabiano!" the friar barked suddenly. "There's naught wrong with your feet."

"Let the green-eyed monster sleep, padre," Primo said. He chuckled and added: "I've no craving for your novice."

The friar swung his head around angrily, but the boy spoke first. "Are you married, *signore?*"

"Nay, though I'm ripe to, since mamma died. Papa and I could use a woman around the place."

"I had that hope once," the novice said, "just to marry and make babies."

"Well, you may make babies yet if they don't geld you and let you keep wandering from your friary," Primo said. "There be more than one little bastard in our village has the pastor's blue eyes." He thumped his passenger's thin leg so hard the boy winced.

The friar had seen and heard enough. He yanked his cowl up over his head, picked up speed and strode out ahead of them. His feet kept slipping in the mud, but through dogged perseverance he managed to create a slight distance between himself and the other two.

"Hey. Hold up, padre," Primo called after him. "I wants to ask you a question. Something serious."

The friar stopped and waited for the cart to catch up, but he refused to lower his cowl. As Jupiter pulled alongside, Primo said, "Did you hear the one about the churchyard dancers?"

The farmer couldn't see the man's face, but a guttural growl satisfied him that the friar listened. "It was a feast day of the Virgin, the whole village drunk as guild masters, skipping around the tombstones and singing. All night long the same chorus, 'Sweetheart, take pity.' And some did take pity in the shadows, you know. But meanwhile, what with all the racket outside his chamber window, the old pastor don't sleep a wink.

"Well, you can decide for yourself how he looks at mass next morning, all bleary-eyed and grabbing onto the altar just to keep to his feet. Then he raises his eyes to heaven to begin the prayers, but instead of 'Lord have mercy,' out comes 'Sweetheart take pity.'" Primo roared and pounded his fist on the boy's thigh again. "What a scandal. It brings tears to my eyes even today."

The boy grabbed his leg in pain, but managed a laugh anyway. To Primo's disappointment, however, the friar still refused to play. Instead he stepped up his pace again.

"Nothing personal, padre," the farmer shouted after him. "It's just whenever I sits up here on the seat of my cart staring at Jupiter's asshole, it reminds of the priest who took his dam. It's nothing to do with you." He doubled over in his seat and roared until he started choking.

As the friar moved a good hundred paces ahead, the boy started to fidget. He began to pick at his neck and a worried look crept into his dark eyes. "You went too far," he said. "You made him really angry."

"Nay. He'll live. He's got a thick enough hide, and I needed a good laugh after that night of rain."

"Still, you didn't have to make fun of him like that. I'll go talk to him. We're better off to stay together."

The boy jumped down from the cart and splashed after his companion. When the novice finally caught up to the older friar, Primo found himself on a front row bench for the entertainment. *Aiee. The tad's getting a head scrubbing now*, he thought. *And giving it back too.* In their muddy long robes, they looked like the puppet Puncinello and his wife, scolding each other and flinging their arms around like grain flails. He waited expectantly for the girlish one to get a clout alongside his head, the way his papa used to knock his mamma when she nagged him. But maybe friars weren't allowed to box their darlings' ears.

In the end the friar shortened his stride and once more waited for the ox cart to draw alongside. "What's your destination, *signore?*" he grumbled.

Primo removed his cap and tried to look sufficiently sheepish. "The abbey of Sant'Ubaldo outside Gubbio, your reverence. I'm taking this wood rent to the monks there. I got to bring a load to the abbey before I can cut firewood for myself from their forest. We'll be at the front gate by afternoon if we get no more rain and Jupiter's back don't give out."

"Then you serve the black monks of San Benedetto?" the friar asked.

"It's worse even than that; in spite of the sermon's warning, I serve two masters. I can't say I loves one and hates the other, though, for I'd just as soon be quit of both. My first master, that'd be the County Alessandro, killed one of his cottagers for moving off the road too slow. Spurred his horse right over the man. He was shriven, rightly enough, the cottager being his own serf and all, but for his penance he gives the monks some pasture, half his woods, and half of myself. What you're looking at is half a man. Half of me's at the beck of the monks' steward and half belongs to the County's reeve, though I can't tell you which half's worked the hardest—and all the while my own piece sits untended."

The friar drew back his hood. He brooded beside the cart, while the novice dropped a few steps behind. For a time the only sounds were the ox's bell, the grating of the tumbrel, and the squishing of hooves in the mud.

"San Francesco spoke aright," the friar said at last. "It's a sad day when men of God decide they need property; even sadder when they sell absolution to gain it."

"Your saint said a lot that was right, albeit he was a disgusting sort of beggar in his own way. You know what I mean, padre?" He glanced into the friar's face.

"No, I can see you don't," Primo continued. "It was in the year twelve and twenty-five, when my ancient papa, being then the age of your novice here, saw the holy man in the flesh. The brothers led him on a donkey, blind as a bat in daylight, his hands and feet all wrapped to cover the Christ wounds, you know."

"There's nothing disgusting about either his blindness or his wounds," the friar interrupted. "He contracted an eye disease in Egypt, trying to convert the Sultan to Christianity. As for the stigmata of the crucified Christ, that was the greatest gift ever bestowed on any son of mortal man."

"Oh you're right, you're right of course, but you didn't hear me out. My papa's watching him, like I said, when out from the bushes hobbles this leper, shaking his clapper and holding out his alms bowl. 'Bring my brother to me,' says the saint and starts groping for the bugger's head. As soon as he finds the face and lips, he kisses him like he's the fairest of the fair and the sweetest of the sweet. Now you might want to speak for yourself, but I calls that disgusting."

"You'd not be alone in thinking so," the friar admitted. "I would not have such strength. Holy zeal is a gift of God too."

While Conrad talked, the tumbrel rounded a curve in the soggy road. Everywhere among the blue mountains, the morning mist lifted in feathery wisps. The farmer could just make out, several leagues off, the great, grey monolithic towers of the abbey carved into the slope of Mont'Ingino. Below the abbey, at the base of the mountain, nestled the village of Gubbio.

"See there, brothers," he said. "That's the end of my day. You'd do well to put up there tonight yourself. Dom Vittorio sets a grand table."

WITH THE MIST finally burned off, the sun soon dried the road to a crusty marl. The ox cart rolled more easily toward its destination. Sometime between None and Vespers, the three travelers reached the monastery gatehouse.

Conrad paused to bend his knees, enjoying the stretch in his calf muscles, happy to be near the end of another day of walking—and happy to be parting ways with the noisome farmer, although he still had to contend with Amata. With the man egging her on, she had amused herself at Conrad's expense for most of the day. *What a trial she must be for her Mother Prioress and her sisters at San Damiano!* The sooner he had her back behind the convent walls, and the sooner he could be on his own again, the better.

He inhaled deeply, filling his lungs with the fragrant air, still sweet with rain. A cool breeze swirled up in a fitful gust, rattling the yellow leaves of the forest, then subsided as abruptly as it had begun.

Ahead of them, an elderly monk squinted from the doorway of the gatehouse. Beyond the tiny shack a timber bridge spanned the headwaters of the Chiagio and led to the massive iron-banded gate of the monastery proper. Its walls seemed fit for a military fortress with its peepholes and slots for protruding weapons. Conrad suspected the main gate even hid a portcullis behind it.

On the opposite bank of the river, a solitary turtledove bobbed through the brown weeds, pecking from time to time at the seed knocked to the ground by the storm. *That will be myself in a few more days,* the hermit mused—sifting through dead parchments, hoping to find a single grain to give meaning to this journey.

For the last hour of their walk, with the farmer and Amata finally worn out by their games and the long sunny road, Conrad's thoughts had returned to Leo's message. His heart sank to realize he'd soon be in Assisi with no more idea what he searched for than the first time he read the letter. Discover the truth of the legends, Leo had said—a clue barely larger than the seed stalked by the dove.

"Ho, Primo," the porter called. "You've been away too long. Take your load around to the north gate and claim a mug from the cellarer."

The two exchanged pleasantries as the cart rolled past. Then the old monk turned to the friars.

"God's peace be with you, brother," Conrad said.

"And also with you," the monk replied. "Do you stay the night with us?"

That, of course, would be impossible. To bring a female within the monastery's walls would be a serious breach, despite Amata's disguise. Nor was Conrad sure she could keep up her pose. Even if they spent most of their time in the monks' guest quarters, they would have to interact with the community at some point.

"God bless your kindness," the hermit said, "but we want to go on to Gubbio while there's daylight left."

WHILE CONRAD WAS REFUSING the porter's offer of hospitality, a rumble began to shake the road beneath their feet. The elderly monk showed no alarm and pointed down the hillside where a half dozen heavily-armed monks raced up toward them from the valley. Their galloping mounts were no dainty palfreys, but huge warhorses, as tall at the withers as a man's jaw, with chests broad as water casks. A pack of dogs ran with them, loping on the fringes to avoid the pounding hooves and flying mud. The horses lunged on a straight course toward the travelers, mouths spraying foam and ears laid flat. Paralyzed, Conrad could only cross his arms in front of his face. At the last instant, the leader yanked up his horse's head, straining his feet against the stirrups while his powerful hands hauled on the reins. He looked to be a man of much physical strength, and the jeweled cross bouncing on his wide chest identified him as Dom Vittorio, the abbot of Sant'Ubaldo.

"Well met, friars!" he hollered down at Conrad and Amata. He stood in his stirrups and appeared to address them from the very treetops that framed his balding head. "God's providence surely sent you to me so this day wouldn't be a total loss."

Conrad's eyes widened at the display of pikes and halberds, the full quivers poking over their shoulders, and the maces and crossbows swung from their saddles. They'd been hunting fiercer game than deer.

The abbot followed his stare. "Those cursed Perugians," he explained. "God melt their souls in hellfire. They've hired a gang of highwaymen to plague our passes, but we found no sign of the bastards today."

Conrad recalled that the abbey of Sant'Ubaldo owned most of the farmland and forests surrounding Gubbio, and would naturally act as manorial lords, periodically protecting their fiefdom from raiders and predators. *Another curse of property*, he thought. Another reason to be grateful for his Order's love of Madonna Poverty—or at least its hypothetical love for the lady.

Dom Vittorio waved the other monks toward the monastery. The huge gate swung open from inside to the scraping of chains and crossbars. When the last horse had clattered over the bridge, he turned his attention again to Conrad and Amata. The hermit had already taken several strides down the road toward Gubbio while Amata trailed behind.

"Wait, brothers. I want you as my guests tonight."

"*Grazie molte*, Reverend Father," Conrad said, "but there's a house of our own Order in Gubbio. We plan to sleep there." He knew that the town also had a convent of Poor Ladies where Amata could stay, although he'd prefer spending the night in the trees to either possibility. He wanted to avoid complications this close to Assisi.

"Nonsense. I *insist* you stay." The emphatic way the abbot said "insist" made it clear the man always got his way. "I want you to lead the services tomorrow. After all, it's the feast day of your founder."

October fourth already? Conrad couldn't believe he'd forgotten the Feast of San Francesco, the most important day in the Order's calendar. That's what came of breaking faith with his breviary. Sudden compunction squeezed his chest. He could only reply weakly, "We're not familiar with your rituals."

"Ah, but you can at least read the Vigil lessons. I'll take your willingness as a personal favor." The abbot's measured tone implied he'd also take any refusal as a personal rebuff.

Checkmate! How could he deny the monk without admitting he'd been traveling with a female the last two days? He peered at Amata. With his eyes he pleaded for support. He hoped her quick wit might find a way out of the dilemma, that she might finally be the help Leo had promised.

With her back to the abbot, she shot Conrad a mischievous grin. "Let's do stay, padre," she said. "I've never spent a night in an abbey of these monks." Her eyes widened in a callous mockery of innocence. For a flickering instant, Conrad pictured himself thrashing her thoroughly with the thickest pole he could get his two hands around.

From his tall horse, Dom Vittorio bowed gallantly to Amata. "Thank you, young friar," he said. "You shall be treated as cordially as a visiting cardinal or papal envoy. If your churlish companion insists on going his way, he can do so without you."

Conrad lowered his head to hide the exasperation tightening the corners of his mouth. They had him beaten. He could do nothing but shuffle in their wake as the abbot prodded his stallion over the bridge and Amata trotted dutifully behind. He had to join them, if only to keep an eye on *her.* God only knew what trouble she might stir up should he abandon her to her whimsy.

VII

CONRAD COUNTED SOME hundred and twenty men and boys as he watched the monks file into the refectory after Vespers—a huge monastery. They took their seats along two rows of trestle tables that ran the entire length of the long hall. Dom Vittorio led Conrad, Amata and his prior along the short wall at the far end of the refectory to a smaller table on a raised platform. The *hebdomedary*, the reader of the week, climbed the steps to his lectern, completing the procession.

Conrad's stomach welcomed the prospect of food after their day on the road, even though it might not be a full meal. In a strict monastery, the monks would have eaten their large meal at midday. On the other hand, Dom Vittorio hardly struck him as strict. Conrad viewed the abbot more as a country castellan, one of those hospitable, tower-dwelling remnants of a dying feudal era—much as Amata's father must have been. The savory odor of hot viands drifting from the kitchen confirmed his impression.

The evening air had cooled quickly, but the brother kitchener had seen to it that the fireplace already blazed comfortably. Conrad noted that the refectory also served as the monastery's armory. All around him the orange firelight reflected off the polished crossbows, metal shields, breastplates and iron weapons hanging on the wall. Judging from the trappings, he could be dining in the great hall of the Duke of Spoleto.

At a signal from Dom Vittorio, the lector began reading the biography of a Benedictine saint from the Order's necrology. Immediately, the level of whispering at the tables increased. Heads began to turn in their direction. Conrad noticed that the attention fixed more and more on Amata; worse yet, she returned the monks' stares with that wide, compelling smile of hers.

Didn't she realize that, even disguised as a boy, she was in no less danger among undisciplined monks than she was as a girl? He felt like Lot sheltering his angel visitors from the townsmen of Sodom and Gomorrah. Not that Amata could be considered an angel by *any* stretch of the imagination. Still, he felt responsible for her. He leaned toward the girl and whispered, "Modesty, *brother,* modesty."

Fortunately for Conrad's nerves, the food arrived at that moment. Instead of the weak broth and a horse bread of coarse grains and dried peas he might have expected for the monks' light collation, the cook and his small army of kitchen helpers carried in platters of roast pork and cheese slices. One young helper sliced trenchers of delectable white bread before them. Another filled their goblets with aromatic wine, and all the while Dom Vittorio beamed at his guests with affable sociability. "Eat up, brothers. Tomorrow you take to the road again. Build up your strength."

The earlier murmuring grew to a crescendo of frenzied eating, totally drowning out the reader. As Conrad looked down the length of the hall, he saw that the hunting hounds had invaded the room and paced in the cleared space between the trestle tables. Occasionally one of the monks flipped a scrap of meat or bread into the air, setting the dogs growling and snapping at one another. Down among the novices at the lower end of the hall, the game seemed to be to land the scrap on the edge of the opposite table, forcing some brother novice to salvage his meal from a vaulting hound.

Although his conscience berated him for eating as voraciously as the monks, the hermit's stomach overruled its objections. He finished every morsel of the extra-thick slab of pork offered him as a guest. Amata too ate with gusto, and when the meal ended she cheered with the monks as the tables were tipped on their trestles. Empty tin goblets clattered to the flagstones along with the food scraps, while the hounds capped the uproar with their furious yapping and baying as they leapt upon the leftovers. Through all the bedlam, Conrad saw the lector's lips continue to move, until finally the monk closed his book and blessed himself with the sign of the cross.

Supper was done.

The kitchen crew lined up against the wall, waiting for the dogs to finish. The monks formed ranks and filed back toward the abbey's basilica for Compline, the final service of the day. As they entered the nave and took their assigned positions in the choir stalls, Conrad and Amata broke off from the line. The two grey friars stood apart in the north transept while the black monks prayed for a peaceful sleep and protection from the Devil whom their psalms warned would make his rounds *sicut leo rugiens,* like a roaring lion, in the coming night, seeking whom he might devour. Conrad bowed his head, and wished Amata knew enough Latin to take the advice to heart.

The hermit had lived outside any religious community for so long he'd forgotten what a mighty reverberation so many young and old male voices singing in unison could produce. For all their slack behavior, he thought, these monks could chant. The bassos, in particular, made his chest rumble. As the basilica grew dark and the worshipers were hidden from one another in the deepening gloom, he allowed joyful tears to overflow his heart and glide down his cheeks. He didn't know, nor did he care, whether Amata noticed. For the moment, he stood as alone in the packed basilica as she had been, keening on the plateau, the evening before.

A period of silent meditation followed the final hymn and then Dom Vittorio sought out the friars and motioned to them to follow him. He led them to a bedchamber adjoining his office.

"This is normally where I sleep," he said, "but our guest house is unfortunately under repair. I yield my bed to my honored visitors."

A single candle lit the room, but it disclosed more comfort than Conrad would have thought possible in a monastery. A stuffed reading chair sat in front of the leaded glass window and a high padded stool stood beside the abbot's writing desk. Two large tapestries insulated the stone walls, one a scene of a boar cornered by hunters, the other a falconer in the act of removing the hood from his bird. What astonished him most, however, was the abbot's bed. A monk should sleep on a simple mattress, usually a large cloth sack filled with straw. This bed had a wooden frame that raised the mattress well off the cold floor. The canopy of curtains tied to the bedposts parted wide enough to reveal a down comforter and a bank of pillows as large as wheat sacks. When closed, the curtains would keep out winter drafts or summer mosquitoes. Very likely the mattress had been stuffed with goose feathers also. Conrad wondered whether any pope had ever slept on such a bed.

The abbot stepped close to Conrad and said in a low voice: "The bed's big enough for you both. Or I can have a separate mat brought in for your novice." He watched Conrad's face closely as he spoke. The hermit knew Dom Vittorio's remark was a test as much as a suggestion.

"Oh, no. No!" Conrad stammered. He backed toward the door. "The same room? That wouldn't..."

The abbot nodded and held up his hands. "Say no more. You're quite right to avoid even the suspicion of impropriety. There are those in my house, I'm ashamed to admit, whose minds are too much preoccupied with impurity of the flesh. They might misinterpret your sharing a bedchamber. The boy shall sleep in the novices' dormitory." He turned to Amata. "Come with me, son."

Amata shrugged at Conrad. *What can I do? I have no choice*, her manner said. She smiled and started after Dom Vittorio.

"Wait," Conrad blurted out. Without thinking, he grabbed the girl's injured shoulder, causing her to yelp in pain. Her high-pitched squeal startled all three of them. The flustered Conrad spoke again quickly, trying to cover for her and divert the monk's attention.

"I failed to mention, Reverend Father, that Fabiano hurt his arm in an accident yesterday." His voice trembled, just enough that he feared he'd give everything away, but their only hope seemed for him to keep talking. "He should have the comfortable bed. A pallet in the priests' dormitory will more than suffice for me. I normally sleep on the ground."

Dom Vittorio stared curiously at Amata as he followed the hermit toward the door. "As you wish, Fra Conrad." He looked back once more as they were leaving the room. "Ignore the Vigil bell, young friar, and take your full rest. If the injury still pains you in the morning, I'll have the infirmarian look at it by daylight."

Amata bowed—a little too eagerly, Conrad felt. The poor girl seemed too terrified to speak again for fear her voice should betray her.

Conrad could see already that there would be no relaxation for him until they escaped this place. His stomach muscles convulsed as he and the abbot stepped into the cloister; the rich, fatty pork gurgled in his intestines. The slap of Dom Vittorio's sandals on the tiled walkway, and even the whisper of Conrad's bare feet, bounced back from the cloister walls, eerily loud in the dark silence of the unfamiliar setting. The friar glanced around the dim square anxiously, almost able to sense the shadowy, cowled figures lurking impatiently behind every moonlit column. *Please be wise through this night, Amata*, he implored, but of course she couldn't hear his plea as she snuggled down for the night in her commodious bed.

ACCUSTOMED TO SOUNDS no louder than the occasional scraping of pine boughs against his cottage wall, Conrad tossed on his mat. The dormitory had been divided so each sleeper had his own small cell, but the head-high wooden partitions afforded no barrier against the hoarse cacophony of dozens of snoring monks.

Even had the room been calm as a graveyard, though, his apprehension for Amata would have kept him awake. Every rustle of a mattress, every creak of a floorboard, brought him fully alert. Hour after hour his imagination pictured monks leaving and returning to their beds. Finally, in the middle of the night, sheer weariness overwhelmed him and he slid into an uneasy sleep. The rest proved short-lived. Sooner than seemed humanly decent, the monk on night watch clanged his hand bell announcing it was time to rise for Vigils.

In his somnolent condition, Conrad repeated the Psalmist's words he'd quoted to Amata the previous day: "Seven times in the day will I praise

Thee, and in the night I will call upon Thy name." *Curse King David and his insomnia,* he muttered to himself, but immediately reproached both his blasphemous mind and slothful body. He'd obviously treated his temple too leniently in his forest retreat. Even these riotous black monks put him to shame. The friar rubbed his eyes, stretched, and stumbled after the silent brothers toward the basilica. He chafed his hands and arms as he walked; night air chilled the cloister and the sun wouldn't rise for another five hours. Inside the church, the black monks formed into four rows, two down each side of the nave, with the priests ranked along the raised aisles closest to the wall and the novices on the ground level below them. Having no seniority in the group, Conrad took the lowest position at the end of one row of priests. He didn't see Amata. Apparently she had taken Dom Vittorio's advice and slept in.

The hermit snatched another moment's sleep while his choir neighbor arranged the silk markers in the large Psalter and Antiphonary balanced on the bookstands they shared. When he forced his eyes open again, he felt mildly justified to see others as weary as himself. Even Dom Vittorio appeared to have slept badly. His eyes were puffy, his cheeks blotched, and his voice creaked like the rusty chains of a drawbridge when he intoned the blessing to open the service: *Jube, Domine, benedicere.*

One by one the hymns and psalms and antiphons limped off Conrad's tongue, until the time arrived for the first reading. At Dom Vittorio's signal, he bowed a small reverence and mounted the pulpit that rose behind the abbot's stall. One of the monks had already opened the book to the passages he was to narrate.

Conrad's priestly training took over as he intoned the first four lessons from the Common for Confessors. The further he read, the more he began to enjoy his role in the black monks' service, proud that San Francesco was so honored by the members of another, sometimes even a rival, Order. As he turned the page to begin the fifth reading, however, he fell suddenly mute. Three times he scanned the heading: *Lectio de Legenda Major Ministri Bonaventurae.*

He wondered: *Is this why God put me through this night of torment?* The remaining text came from the "Major Legend," Bonaventura's biography of San Francesco. Here at last could be a clue to understanding Leo's message. Again, a fragment from his mentor's letter coursed through his mind as he stood dumbly, gripping the sides of the lectern: *Read with your eyes, discern with your mind, feel in your heart the truth of the legends.*

A round of coughing in the choir just below him brought him back to the task at hand. Rows of pale annoyed faces stared up from the torch-lit aisles and once again Dom Vittorio conspicuously cleared his throat. Conrad bowed his apology and resumed the recitation.

Franciscus, Assisii in Umbria natus, he intoned, *Francesco, born in Assisi in Umbria* ... and soon flowed into the narrative again. About halfway through the seventh lesson, however, Conrad stalled once more. The passage described how, two years before Francesco's death, a seraph with six fiery and shining wings appeared before the saint and impressed on the saint's hands and feet and side the wounds of the crucified Christ.

Conrad would likely have paused at this section anyway. That moment when the angel imprinted the holy stigmata on San Francesco's body was the most dramatic and touching in the chronicles of the Order. Any friar would have been moved. But even as his heart stirred at the image, one of Leo's questions nagged at his brain. *Whence the Seraph?* Was this the seraph Leo meant? Most likely not, since the angel obviously came from heaven. So what could Leo have meant by "whence came?"

He wished he might pause to untangle the connections rushing pell-mell through his head—but he had to keep chanting. When he finally finished the passage, he tried again to collect his thoughts while the monks sang the *responsorium* and *versicle* that followed. However, a movement at the front of the basilica distracted him further. One of the black monk novices had just arrived and prostrated before the main altar to atone for his tardiness. As he took his place in the choir, he whispered behind his hand to another novice and both began to giggle. Conrad followed their eyes down the dark nave and saw that Amata had just arrived also. She went to the stall at the end of the row of novices facing the laggard and (was it possible?) seemed to smile furtively at the young man. Conrad squinted, trying to sharpen his vision in the poor light of the basilica. Had he really seen that smile, or did his eyes trick him? In the dim, unsteady flicker of the tapers, and from the distance of the pulpit where he stood, he couldn't be certain.

Again the choir called him back to duty. Almost as if it were part of the service, the monks began coughing in unison, somewhat more loudly and irritably than the first time, Conrad realized. He launched into the final lesson. Still only half-awake, and burdened with the baggage of so many new questions, his brain felt as slow and dense as Primo's ox.

Why should he care what Amata did? An unexpected anger welled inside him as he sang the concluding passage. San Francesco's death scene could not compete with the swarm of thoughts quarreling in his brain.

Isn't my anger righteous? I'm responsible for her, after all.

But not really. God gave her free will, just like any other human being. And besides, she wouldn't have slept here last night except for her own trickery.

But woman is the weaker vessel. She needed my strength. I should have figured out a way to guard her room.

He managed somehow to finish the service and started down the steps from the pulpit. It was then that the contentious voice suggested, *Fra Conrad, are you jealous?*

That's preposterous! He shot Amata a furious look as he passed down the nave in front of her on his way back to his seat. He saw the girl flinch, but he turned his face away from her.

Once he had rejoined his choir neighbor, he sank against the back of his choir stall and stared down at the close-cropped, drooping head in the row below. A deep crimson flush colored the back of her slender neck and her small shoulders trembled ever so noticeably. The hermit's chest deflated in a mournful sigh while the Gregorian chant swelled all around him. He turned his eyes mournfully toward the golden tabernacle mounted on the main altar.

God forgive me my suspicious heart, he begged. *I've wronged her, wronged her terribly.*

VIII

ONRAD, TAKE THIS FOOD! It's killing my shoulder." Amata and the hermit had barely crossed the wooden bridge outside the monastery and were still within sight of the old gatekeeper.

"*Mi scusi*, sister. Be patient. We have to show Dom Vittorio your injury's better. Otherwise, he'd want to send you to the infirmarian."

"That he would not," the girl answered matter-of-factly.

"How can you say that? You heard his words last night."

"And I still say he wouldn't have sent me to the infirmary this morning. Anyway we're outside the abbey now." She winced as she swung the sack off her shoulder and held it out to the hermit. The cellarer had generously restocked their provisions.

Where the path dropped toward the city below, Amata stopped and pointed back toward Sant'Ubaldo, a black bulwark against the roseate sky. Above the abbey, the clouds that hung grey as muddy fleeces had begun to brighten to fiery pink. "Don't you find it strange," the girl said, "that the sun always rises in the East?"

"What? What has that to do..."

"Haven't you ever thought about it? The sun falls off the western edge of the world every evening, but by daybreak it's right back where it started. How did it get there during the night? Doesn't it make you wonder?"

"No, it doesn't. I know all things are possible with God, and that is understanding enough for me."

"And all that time we were chanting in the dark, the sun was already warming our new pope. Dom Vittorio said he should be at sea by now, sailing from the Land of Promise to Venice. Did you pray for his safety and the safety of all the young seamen this morning?"

"I hadn't even heard of the election until we broke silence after Prime. Of course I wish the Holy Father Godspeed. Yes—and those who sail with him too."

Amata smiled, as demure and contented a smile as Conrad had seen their entire trip. Since Vigils he'd been gracious, trying to atone for his earlier presumption. She didn't question his change in behavior, but responded with ebullience. She persisted, though, in dancing around his questions about her night in Dom Vittorio's chamber. Conrad suspected she teased him deliberately, which of course he deserved for imagining the worst of her. He knew that questioning her about the tardy novice would be a fruitless exercise on his part too.

The morning *Angelus* pealed up the twisting trail, signaling the city's night watchmen to open the gates. Gubbio spread like a dusky foot on the valley floor, its large toe thrust into the gorge created by Monte Calvo to the west and Mont'Ingino, where they now stood. Beyond its walls Conrad could see the ruins of the ancient Roman theater. Apparently *Iguvium*, as the city was known when the Caesars still ruled, once extended well into the plain of the River Chiagio—before centuries of warring with rival city-states had forced it behind its present barriers.

The tortured screech of the city gates swinging open to admit the new day rasped against the drowsy quietude of the dawn. The hermit recalled his last trip through Gubbio, the spring he received the scroll from Fra Leo. "Are you familiar with the *Corsa dei Ceri*, sister?" he asked.

Amata shook her head.

He paused and set down his burden. "I saw it once. Each fifteenth of May, on the eve of their patron, the Gubbians race up Mont'Ingino from this gate below us to the abbey. Three teams of ten men carry three enormous wooden candles up this path. The candles are tall as any six of them and ponderous as iron, and each is crowned with the wax figure of a saint—Sant'Ubaldo, of course, and San Giorgio and Sant'Antonio Abate. It's a wonderful festival, teams grunting away as they climb, saints careening on their poles, and the whole city chasing hard after them."

"Which saint won the year you were here?"

Conrad shrugged. "The race doesn't really matter. Sant'Ubaldo, as the city's patron saint, must always win. San Giorgio always finishes second and Sant'Antonio is always last."

Amata laughed. "Then why do they race at all?"

The hermit started down the path again. "You must understand, sister, the rite exists only to increase the devotion of the peasants. Being illiterate, they can't draw inspiration from the scriptures as lettered bishops and clergymen can. The faithful need an image or a spectacle to gather around and, through this *corsa,* they refresh their dormant faith each spring. The annual race does for their souls what the return of warm weather does for their fields."

At the bottom of the trail, they saluted the gatekeeper and crossed into the city. A small boy, his skinny legs streaked with scratch marks, ran by them driving a herd of goats. The miniature bells of the kids jounced noisily as they leaped past the milk-laden nannies or butted their tiny heads in carefree combat. Conrad looked askance at the animals. For all his kinship with the creatures that roamed the woods around his hermitage, including wild goats, he shared the popular view of the domestic version. They weren't actually demons, although something satanic lurked behind those preternatural yellow eyes. Their secret power seemed more akin to the ancient satyrs, with their cadaverous rib cages, curling horns, pendulous teats or testicles, wild wispy beards—and their blood so hot that the bestiaries claimed it could melt diamonds. He shuddered and crossed himself as they passed.

On this high end of the city, many of the houses were built of stone. All around Conrad and Amata doors and shutters opened as the serving women began their morning chores. The trail had already dropped two thousand feet from the monastery to the city walls. The equally narrow and steep, unpaved city streets were still slippery from the rain two nights before, so that they had to pick their way carefully to avoid sliding or stepping in the offal tossed from the doorways and windows.

Conrad knew the streets of Gubbio well. He planned to cross the Piazza Grande, follow the Via Paoli down through the Piazza del Mercato, cut through the marketplace, and exit the city quickly by the Porta Marmorea. He wanted to leave Gubbio behind as quickly as possible. The close-packed houses leaning against one another at their upper stories and the wakening households made him claustrophobic. Amata had never seen Gubbio, however. She asked about every building of any size, from the oddly-constructed cathedral of Santi Mariano e Jacopo Martire, with its rear wall embedded in a hillside, to the Palazzo Praetorio. Windowless fortress towers of noble families stabbed the skyline, the wooden hovels of the lower classes crowded the alleys, and all of them fascinated the girl. By the time they finally reached the Piazza del Mercato, many merchants had already opened their stalls and begun hawking merchandise, destroying with strident finality the last vestiges of morning calm.

"*Buon giorno,* brothers," sang a woman balancing a jug on her head as she passed. A tiny, shy girl carrying a loaf as long as she was tall lagged behind the woman. The child wore the habit and wimple of a nun, no doubt to fulfill some vow her parents had made. Her bare feet glowed pink from the cold and Conrad wondered why the mother hadn't provided her daughter with boots like her own. Perhaps the child was only a servant.

The village baker traditionally laid out his wares before the other merchants, and the aroma of fresh-baked bread made Conrad's mouth water. Amata turned pleading eyes in his direction and joined her palms prayerfully, but Conrad only shrugged.

"You know we haven't a denarius between us, sister. And we don't need to beg with all the food we've been given." Her face contorted in a playful pout, which he did his best to ignore. She was so frivolous this morning!

The hermit skirted the edge of the piazza, headed in the general direction of the Convento di San Francesco on the opposite side. Earlier in his career, he might have prolonged his trip to visit his brother friars from Gubbio, but he felt too much the stranger after his years alone. A chill shivered his spine as they passed under the friary wall, an odd sense of anxiety. Ahead he sighted the open Porta Marmorea and the empty road that led toward Assisi. He quickened his pace, urged on by the clamor swelling all around them.

They had nearly made it across the marketplace when three shrill trumpet blasts from the far corner of the square throttled the babble of the merchants. "Repent! Repent!" a man's voice boomed out. "*Penitentiam agite*! The kingdom of heaven is approaching, sooner than you expect."

Early shoppers milling and haggling before the stalls abruptly broke off and moved in the general direction of the commotion. "It's Jacopone!" voices called out to the people poking their heads from doorways and windows.

A group of small boys, frustrated by unsuccessful attempts to stone a cat off the roof where it had retreated, happily restocked their fists with rocks and slipped in among their elders. Pelting a madman would more than compensate for the cat. He presented a larger target too, standing fully head and shoulders taller than the people gathering around him.

"Let's get on the road while they're distracted," Conrad said over his shoulder. When Amata didn't reply, he turned to discover she'd run off behind the urchins.

He spotted her in the crowd, and struggled through after her. Somehow she'd wormed her way into the very front circle. The man called Jacopone stood atop the base of the marble fountain at the center of the piazza and glared down at the multitude. The windows around the piazza were all open now, and a few pale *nobildonnas* even strayed out onto their balconies—a rare public appearance, Conrad realized. Such grand females only came down into the streets for Sunday mass, for fear of soiling their splendid trains in the mud. As a rule, only female servants and common women walked out in public.

Jacopone raised his hands toward the heavens and turned in a slow circle, seizing the onlookers with his bloodshot hazel eyes burning from deep-set sockets. His cheekbones protruded sharply from his wasted skull, scarcely concealed by his scraggly beard. He wore only a loincloth and a black sheepskin cloak with a huge red cross smeared down the back from collar to hem and shoulder-to-shoulder.

"I've just come from Rome," he began. "I went to see the papal court."

A few of the townspeople tittered, but their laughter came uneasily and their neighbors hushed them quickly. No more than two or three of the listeners could have made the same claim. Jacopone took no notice of the murmuring.

"Let me tell you about the workday of the cardinals of Rome, the *cardinales carpinales*. Each morning, after the papal consistory where they debate the cases of kings and lawsuits and other such worldly business, these—*grabinales*—eat and drink like pampered swine. Then they waddle off to their couches for their midday naps. All afternoon they laze about their apartments, exhausted with idleness, or they amuse themselves with their pet dogs and horses, their jewels and their noble nephews and nieces."

He had spoken calmly to that point. He paused for a moment, then pointed accusingly at the church of San Giovanni Battista across the piazza and thundered, "Should we be surprised that the Franks have unearthed a horrible letter, a letter penned in blood from the deepest pit of hell by Lucifer himself, and addressed affectionately to his dear friends, the prelates of the Church? 'We give you abundant thanks,' it reads, 'for all the souls committed to your care are transmitted to us.'"

Conrad hadn't heard of this letter before. A sudden terror rooted him where he stood, as if some evil spirit from the underworld had slipped through his body leaving a dread *rigor mortis* in its wake. An almost palpable tension spread through the crowd.

Again Jacopone roared his condemnation. "Is it only an accident that the words *Praelatus* and *Pilatus* are so similar, when the wealthy and noble prelates by their actions crucify the impoverished Christ as surely as the evil Pilate did twelve centuries ago?"

Again he paused to let his words sink in, but this time a noblewoman in a crimson gown yelled down to the square in a shaking voice, "You lie. You've never been to Rome or you would not speak irreverently of these holy men." She spread her hand on her outraged bosom, fingering the filigreed brooch pinned there. A servant appeared on the balcony behind her and curled a winter *mantello* trimmed with black fur around her bare shoulders.

"Go on, Jacopone," bellowed a woman from the crowd. "Her uncle is one of those fat cardinals."

Jacopone pulled his own cloak closer around his bony rib cage. He glanced for an instant at the balcony and closed his eyes. "Let me tell you about women, about the *vanitas feminorum*." He sang the words, his eyelids still shut, as though he called a chanson or poem to memory.

"Woman, you have the power to strike mortal wounds. The basilisk's gaze is fatal, your glance no less so. But unless man steps on the basilisk by chance, it hurts no one, while you move about openly, freely, poisoning with a glance.

"You paint your face for your husband, you say, who takes delight in you. But you lie. He takes no joy in your vanity, knowing you adorn yourself for someone else.

"But you're clever, devilishly clever. With high pattens you transfigure your tiny self into a stately lady. Your pale complexion becomes rosy-hued and your dark hair turns fair with a hairpiece of vile-smelling fibers. To smooth your face you apply a cream better fit for old, scuffed boots. And when you give birth to a baby girl, if her nose is misshapen, you'll pinch and tug 'til you utterly reshape it. You lack strength to fight, but the weakness of your arm is more than made up by the vigor of your tongue."

Serenity spread across Jacopone's features as he sang, and his eyes remained closed even when the noblewoman screamed, "He's a madman! Chase him outside the walls!"

A boy standing beside Conrad took the woman's cry as his cue. *"Pazzo! Pazzo!* A madman!" he screamed. He raised his arm to hurl a rock at the preacher, but Conrad caught him by the wrist and the stone clattered harmlessly against the fountain.

"He's no madman. He's a holy *bizzocone,"* Conrad said, using the term for wandering public penitents. "There's wisdom in his words, even for imbecilic little boys."

Jacopone opened his eyes and seemed to see Conrad and Amata for the first time. Slowly a wave of sorrow washed over his large features. He bowed his head and started to sing again, but this time his voice emitted the deep, rich despondency of a funeral dirge.

"Brother Rinaldo, where have you gone? Are you in glory, or hotter where you are? Now you're gone where the Truth is clear, your cards on the table, good and evil face up. Too late to form sophisms, prose or rhyme. Only the truth will out. In Paris you earned your Doctorate. Great was the honor and great the expense, but now that you're dead, the final examination begins. For you there's only one question: did you truly feel the greatest honor was being a poor and despised friar?"

The song stunned Conrad. Decrying the vanity of women was one thing; disparaging a deceased friar quite another. "You injure the memory of a good man, Sior Jacopone," he interrupted, loud enough that the whole crowd could hear. "Fra Rinaldo and I shared the same classes at Paris. He never sought honors for their own sake. God gifted him with natural brilliance."

Jacopone did not reply. He merely lowered his eyes again and folded his hands in a prayerful pose. To Conrad's astonishment, a close imitation of his own voice rose meekly from the penitent's throat.

"I am a friar. I've studied the Scriptures. I've prayed, endured illness with patience. I've helped the poor, kept vows of obedience, poverty too, and even chastity..."

Jacopone opened one eye, winking at Amata, "...as well as I could, calmly accepted hunger and cold, rose early to pray, Vigils and Lauds."

Suddenly the penitent's tone grew gruff and his face red with anger. "But let any speak words that sound harsh to me and I quickly spit out fire. See now how much good this friar's robe has done. I hear but a word upsetting to me, I can scarcely forgive and forget."

Jacopone stared mildly at Conrad while the people hooted. Someone shoved at Conrad's back, pushing him stumbling into the cleared center of the circle and almost against the preacher.

"I've composed another laud, in praise of humility," Jacopone whispered close to his ear. "Do you wish to hear it?"

Conrad trembled with fury, and his throat constricted in such a knot he couldn't even manage a reply. A hand reached under his arm and tried to drag him back into the crowd. "He's right, you know, padre," Amata said. "You have a very short temper." The girl grinned, trying to cajole him. He let his arm go limp, finally, and surrendered to her tugging.

He hardly heard the rest of the sermon. Jacopone's and Amata's words filled him with remorse. Around him the people had begun to sob and beat their breasts, begging forgiveness of God and one another, while Conrad silently begged pardon for his pride. The crescendo of their wailing increased, then abruptly came to an end.

Jacopone sat down exhausted on the edge of the fountain. "Away, children," he waved. "I'm tired now. Go in peace and serve God." He scooped up a handful of water and lapped it with his tongue. The townspeople drifted back to the vendor's stalls more slowly and thoughtfully than they'd come, for the preacher had given them much to ponder.

After the center of the piazza had cleared, Conrad approached the penitent. "Forgive me, Sior Jacopone. I don't know what came over me. I haven't lost my temper like that in years. I still have so much work to do."

A light chuckle disrupted his apology. Arms akimbo, Amata squared off in front of him. "Fra Conrad," she scolded, "you haven't had anyone to lose your temper *at* for years." She turned to Jacopone and rolled her eyes in exasperation. "I just dragged him out of the mountains."

"You're a hermit?" Jacopone asked.

Conrad nodded.

"And you choose to return to the city?"

"For now. I have a mission, in Assisi. I don't know how long I'll be there."

"I would prefer to be a hermit too, but seem bound to this public life. You must bear in mind, Fra Conrad, that if a man does well, God is really in him and with him *everywhere,* on the streets and among people just as much as in a church, in a desert place—or in an anchorite's cell. He has only God and thinks only God and everything and everyone are nothing but God to him. Neither can any person disturb him, for he looks for nothing but God. The man who must seek Him by special means or in special places, such a man has not yet attained God."

Conrad bowed his head and blushed like a small boy being lectured by his tutor. "And such a one am I," he confessed.

"And such a one is everyone I've met, and myself as well," the penitent said.

"Where do *you* go from here," Conrad asked.

Jacopone shrugged. "Anywhere. Nowhere."

"Then come with us. I've been starved for spiritual discourse."

"As you wish. It seems God's plan for this day is still unfolding." He rose stiffly and joggled the folds out of his heavy cloak.

A yellow-haired teenager had been eyeing the men while they talked. Now, as they prepared to leave, he stepped forward bashfully. When he didn't speak, Conrad said, "Peace be with you, son. What is it you wish?"

"My name is Enrico," he said. He hesitated, already having managed to say more than he expected, swallowed, then forced himself to speak again. "Did you say you're going to Assisi?"

"We are."

"May I travel with you? I'm headed there too—to join the friars at the Sacro Convento."

IX

ENRICO DREW A SHEET of parchment from his belt. "I have a letter from the Bishop of Genoa. He asks the minister general of the friars to accept me as a novice."

"I knew you came from somewhere up north," Amata said.

The boy grinned and relaxed a bit as he tugged at his hair. "Yes, from the parish of Vercelli. You don't see many towheads in Umbria, I think."

She returned his grin. "About as often as we get a new pope. Though I did meet a friar with blond hair and blue eyes just four days ago."

She liked the look of him. His felt boots, short wool tunic, and hooded shoulder-cape marked him as the son of a peasant. He'd certainly known hard work; his chapped hands and sturdy legs showed that. Like many Northerners, he also had a large frame. When he filled out, he might be as big a man as Dom Vittorio. She also found his smile pleasant, if too quick. Those light azure eyes intrigued her most, however—clear and beautiful. But they lacked something too, some spark of intensity. Without that spark, they betrayed his timidity, the soft will of a born follower.

The weak blue eyes of a mamma's boy, she thought. He'll always need a woman to tell him what to do with his life. And if he ever leaves the Order, he'll be a most unreliable husband.

Amata smiled to herself. *Here the boy's only two days away from joining the friars, and I already have him deceiving his wife.*

Conrad handed back Enrico's letter. "I don't need to see it. You're welcome to join us, of course. We can talk about the Order as we walk. You should know, Assisi isn't necessarily the best place to follow the Rule of San Francesco."

Amata yawned. Good old Conrad. Ever true to his obsession—about to mount his pulpit and pound away once again at the split between the Conventual and Spiritual friars. Jacopone kept pace and seemed interested too, but she wasn't. She let the men move ahead of her as they left the city. She preferred to watch the morning unfold, the cottagers going about their work in the vineyards near the city. The children in the smallholdings were slow to feed the long-horned oxen today, judging from the animals' urgent lowing. In the fields, sweet-smelling, new-mown hay lay heaped in conical piles around center poles, weighted down by splayed branches. Gourds ripened on the cottage roofs, and grain hung on the trees to dry. From a distance, the rap of wooden clappers and a shout of angry voices sliced through the crisp air as farmers chased deer from the fields. Winter would settle in soon. How had her father described it? The season that divides the satisfaction of harvest from the itch of spring.

When she tired of the scenery, she used her rear vantage to imagine the bodies of the three males moving beneath their clothing. Jacopone was a cadaver, thin as a beggar's tunic, inside his full-length cloak. So much she already knew, for his loincloth left nothing to fancy—except to wonder whether his hidden part was in proportion to the overall length of him. Now *that* would be worth seeing! Conrad, on the other hand, had a slight build, no more than a thumb's breadth taller than Enrico and probably no heavier. He had to be a virgin, too, in spite of his friendship with Monna Rosanna. His tight walk lacked all flow, any swing or looseness in the arms and shoulders. But then, he probably wasn't aware anymore that he still lived in a body. Ah, but Enrico. She admired again the boy's nicely-muscled calves and with her mind's eye surveyed the remaining length of his legs to his slim hips and taut buttocks—a pleasurable fantasy.

Another day and she would be back in San Damiano, *Suor Amata* again. The thought depressed her. For all his quirks and gravity, she'd enjoyed these four days with Conrad. She enjoyed being in the company of all three of these men, even though she traipsed behind and took no interest in their conversation. Men seemed impervious, or maybe just oblivious, to the petty wounds that sent her sisters crying and complaining to Mother Prioress all day long. But for their gift of speech, these three could pass for the slow, good-natured farm brutes they'd just passed.

God, she wanted out of the convent! Not that Mother Prioress treated her badly. She led a pampered life compared to the austerities the voluntary nuns practiced. And she really had nowhere else to go with no family, no money, and no way to protect or support herself.

Still, sainthood and divine love had never appealed to her. Human love, the love her mother had known with her father and prepared her for—this was what she yearned to experience. Real love, not her great-uncle

Bonifazio's deceit or the brutish lust of Simone della Rocca and his sons. She folded her long sleeves across her lower abdomen and rubbed herself as she fantasized. An involuntary moan caused Conrad to stop and look back at her. She blushed and raised her hands quickly, but he'd seen her.

"Does your stomach ache, Fra Fabiano?" he asked with genuine concern.

What an innocent! "Yes, padre," she whimpered. "I have a definite aching in my stomach." She grimaced to validate her pain. "Don't slow down for me, though. I can keep up with you."

Jacopone resumed the conversation as they began walking again. "No, Enrico," he said, "a poem doesn't simply express feeling; it speaks of *experience*. To create a single line, a poet must visit many towns, many people. He must root and squeal with animals and soar with birds and stretch with the smallest movement of a wakening bud. He must journey back through time to foreign roads and unexpected meetings, to childhood sicknesses and—pardon me padre—even to nights of love, each different from any other, and the pale skin of women ... of women ... asleep between their sheets."

His voice caught as he spoke of love. He turned his head away from Conrad, and Amata saw the anguish in his sunken eyes. The arrogance and self-righteousness of the piazza had crumpled, and his complexion faded, wan as a grave marker.

Mother of God, Amata thought. *The woman on the balcony was right. He is mad—mad from grief for some lady love.* She doubted that Conrad and Enrico had even noticed.

The travelers walked in silence for a furlong before Jacopone cleared his throat. When he spoke again, it was still with difficulty and much emotion. "The poet must sit beside the dying, by the open window, hear the wailing outside and the fitful breathing in the room. And last of all, he must allow these memories of his to fade, then wait with great patience for them to return again."

"And from these memories the verses come?" Enrico asked.

"Not yet, son. Not yet. Not until they become his blood and flesh, thoughts with no name and indistinguishable from himself. Then, in that most pure, most rare of moments, can the poet distill from them the opening word of a verse."

"Taste and see that the Lord is good," Conrad quoted.

Amata recalled the friar's mental vaults at the hut. The blank look on Enrico's face amused her now. Jacopone saw it too.

"Fra Conrad is saying that the Psalmist, whom he quotes, being a poet and a mystic, understood that experience is at the heart of both roles. To read about the Lord from the Scriptures or hear about Him from preachers is not enough. You must *taste* Him, experience Him yourself. A farmer can brag to you about the special flavor of his olives, but his words mean nothing until you bite into one. Experience is the essence of everything."

A fine time to tell him that, when he's about to shut himself away in a friary for God knows how many years, Amata thought. *If he's smart, they'll make a scholastic of him, like they tried to do with Conrad. What will he experience then? Long, unpronounceable words! He'll be better off if he proves a dullard. That way, at least, he'll never realize what he's missing.*

They climbed the high road linking Gubbio to Perugia, following the ridge of the Gualdo Mountains. At a break in the thorny hedge that walled in a series of crofts, Amata could see Assisi far to the south. All in all, Gubbio had struck her as a somber, brown, muddy city. But Assisi, balanced on its rocky outcropping, suspended between Monte Subasio and the valleys of the Tescio and Chiagio rivers, resembled a translucent pendant on a backdrop of green felt. The pink- and coral-marbled churches, walls and towers radiated with morning sunlight. Its warmth marked a sharp contrast to dreary Gubbio, just as the balmy air wafting up from Assisi's valleys clashed with the cold winds swirling around Gubbio's mountain strongholds.

The philosophers of poetry, busily talking of the merits of experience, had missed the view. She wanted to draw their attention to it, but Conrad had returned to his favorite theme. "By all means, Enrico, go to the Sacro Convento. Discover all you can about our traditions, learn to read and write, study in Paris if they're willing to send you. But never forget that one day you'll have to choose: do I want to be a *true* son of San Francesco and live by his Rule and Testament, or will I settle for the easier path of the Conventual friar? But know also, that should you decide to join the Spiritual brothers, to choose the path of total poverty, you also choose the path of persecution. Friars have died for this choice already."

Amata groaned. *Fra Solemn, they should call him*! She wanted to tiptoe up behind the hermit, grab him around the waist, lift him off the road and not let his feet touch dirt again until he promised to laugh at least twelve times a day. The crowd had laughed *at* him, and he'd even laughed at himself when he told her of his university years, but this division in the Order had totally snuffed the light in his spirit. Worse yet, the gloom seemed to shroud him more thickly the closer they came to Assisi.

Maybe he's just frightened. Maybe, in talking so to Enrico, he's reminding himself that he's already made his choice—preparing himself for whatever is to come of it.

Men could be so odd. What they deemed vital, the things they'd willingly suffer—even die—for, seemed to her so remote. How could they even talk of experience, when they spent all their time in their heads? Dumb brutes indeed! Well, not all of them, she mused. *Jacopone is a thinker, but he's obviously lived too, and his passion's nearly done him in. Enrico should know a few things, too, if he's kept his eyes open around his father's barnyard.*

A wicked, most delicious, notion came to her as she watched the sway of the boy's tunic. Maybe in the cover of this night's darkness and the privacy of some sheltered grove...

She suddenly realized the other three had stopped again, waiting for her to catch up. "This is where we leave the high road," Conrad said. "The path takes us to the Roman bridge at the bottom of the gorge."

Like most mountain trails, it sloped steep and narrow. Amata silently cheered, for they'd be walking single file and that would put an end to Conrad's sermonizing for a while. They'd also be back among the trees; the hot sun had climbed almost to the center of the cloudless sky. She could see the Chiagio winding far below, muddy from the rain two nights before, and on its banks the towers of Santa Maria di Valfabbrica and the castle of Coccarano. This was country she recognized from rides with her mistress.

She guessed the friar would steer well clear of Valfabbrica, another abbey of the black monks, and very likely avoid the castle too. Sant'Ubaldo had been more excitement than he could handle. Conrad, no doubt, would feel safer sleeping among the wild things of the forest. Well, she wouldn't mind that herself, as long as they kept a good-sized bonfire going through the night. And good things could happen in the darkness too. She resisted the temptation to steady herself by leaning forward with her hands resting on Enrico's shoulders—and the temptation to tweak Conrad one more time by doing so. *Patience, Amata. Let's see how the play unfolds.*

Was it the thought of wild things that caused her to stop on the path and stare, first into the shade of the trees, then back along the path? She had a fleeting intuition they were being watched, but the trail twisted too frequently to let her see more than a short distance in either direction. She shivered and jogged down the footpath until she'd caught up again to the others. All of a sudden she had no desire to lag behind.

She hoped Conrad would stop to open the food pouch at a widening of the trail, but of course he wasn't the kind to notice hunger either. He seemed anxious to press on. Something at the abbey *had* stirred him up. She just hoped it had nothing to do with her. Not that his opinion of her mattered after tomorrow. She'd be back in San Damiano and he'd be off to solve Leo's riddle.

Jesu Christe! Returning to Assisi was weighing on her too, much more than she'd expected. She'd miss being free of the convent walls, miss being on the road, in spite of its unknowns and hazards—maybe miss the unknowns and hazards most of all. They were the spice lacking in the daily fare of San Damiano.

As she guessed, Conrad marched them past Valfabbrica that afternoon. Enrico and Jacopone droned on about civil law, as if they knew what they were talking about, but the friar had wrapped himself in his own thoughts.

He kept them tramping almost until nightfall, by which time Enrico's stomach rumbled too. Jacopone gnawed at the bark of a twig he'd broken off along the side of the road, but seemed otherwise as immune to hunger as Conrad. He could probably live like a fanatical prophet on locusts and honey—or air, if it came to that.

Deep inside a forest thick with cork oaks and pines, Conrad relented at last. "We can rest here," he said. "I know of a cave just off the road. We still have time to gather firewood before dark." He beamed proudly at them. "We've done well today. We'll be in Assisi before midday tomorrow."

"I'LL BEGIN," Conrad said after they had eaten. The four travelers clustered around the fire. Outside the cave a pair of owls hooted a duet. "My example of virtue is a saint of Poverty . . ."

What else, Amata thought.

". . . not a friar minor as you might expect, nor any member of a religious order," the hermit said. "Donato the banker puts to shame even those of us who have taken formal vows of poverty. He was once a wealthy man, but he became so filled with compassion for others out of his love for God that he gave all his possessions to the poor. Had he then joined our Order, he would only have followed the example of Fra Bernardo, the first son of San Francesco. Instead, this banker went even further. He sold himself into bondage and gave the whole price of his slavery to the poor also. I've yet to hear of his like."

"I've heard of one, perhaps" Jacopone murmured, "the Tuscan money-lender, Luchesio da Poggibonsi."

The penitent bowed his neck. The smoke from the fire drifted toward his slumped figure, but he gave no sign that it bothered him. He appeared to Amata to be immovable as the rock on which he sat. But, she reminded herself, she had seen the fissure in that rock once today already.

"I'm ashamed to admit, friends, that in my former life I was a usurer," he began, "loaning money at exorbitant fees against the laws of God and the Church—among other sins. Like Luchesio in his younger years, I threw myself wholeheartedly into climbing the social ladder with my money—and the money of others—as the rungs. I advanced high enough to became one of the leading guildsmen of my city." He looked up with a wry grin and shook his ragged cloak. "Hard to imagine, isn't it?

"But Sior Luchesio had one advantage I didn't. While he was still fresh on this path of foolishness, he met San Francesco and was moved to penitence by the saint. He sold all he owned to benefit widows, orphans and pilgrims. Then he left for the plague-ridden marshlands, his donkey laden with medicines. His own wife derided him at first and called him an idiot—as you might expect when a once-wealthy woman finds herself impoverished overnight by her husband's generosity. But once she understood his purpose, she joined his work and herself earned the title '*buona donna*.'"

And how came you to be so impoverished? Amata wondered. *That's the story I want to hear.* Her curiosity died unsatisfied, however, for Jacopone lapsed into silence once more. He stared dully into the fire until gradually the pain she had seen on the road flickered in his eyes again.

"I have an example of Justice," Enrico said. He waved his hand like a schoolboy to gain their attention.

Go ahead, Conrad motioned.

"My father once worked as a gatekeeper in Genoa. He told me how the city fathers hung a plaintiff's bell outside the walls. Any man treated unjustly could ring the bell and the magistrates would look into his case. Over the years, the bell rope wore out and someone strung a vine in its place.

"It so happened that a certain knight didn't want to pay for fodder for his old warhorse, and turned it loose outside the city to forage where it would. The horse was so hungry he chewed on the vine, and the bell began to ring. The judges arrived and decided the horse had claimed his right to be heard. They investigated his case and ruled that the knight, whom the horse had served so loyally in its youth, was duty bound to provide for its old age too. The king also agreed; he even threatened to torture the knight in his dungeon should he ever starve his horse again."

Jacopone raised his deep set eyes from his reverie and chuckled. "Well narrated, boy," he said. "And here's another tale of Justice, a riddle for you really. Tell me how you'd rule in this case.

"A famous cook once brought a fellow servant—a rather large-nosed servant, I might add—brought him to court for having consumed, through this enormous nose of his, the aroma of the cook's exquisite fare, and for having paid nothing for the pleasure. Was he entitled to damages, or no?"

"They should have tossed the cook in prison for wasting everybody's time," Amata offered.

Enrico threw up his hands. Conrad waved off the question also. "I would never presume to understand the workings of a civil court," he said.

Jacopone looked around the circle with a knowing wink. "Which is why some men become judges, and others not. This particular judge proved to be most wise—much wiser than I when my master first posed the question to me. He settled the case in favor of the cook."

"No!" Amata objected.

"I tell you *yes*," Jacopone grinned. "And as his penalty, he ordered the large-nosed servant to pay for the smell by clinking his few coins loud enough for the cook to hear."

Enrico and Conrad applauded. "Well judged," the hermit said. "The man was a Solomon."

"Have you been a judge too, Sior Jacopone?" Amata asked.

"A notary, brother, but never a judge. Granted, we were all members of the same honored guild of jurists, but I can't say I carried the honor well." He changed the subject quickly. "But what of yourself, have you no tale for us?"

She glanced at Conrad, then decided she'd do better to fix her eyes on Enrico while she talked. "Mine's an example of Stupidity."

"Stupidity?" Conrad's voice had a nervous edge to it, which pleased her.

"Yes. The stupidity of a traveling merchant. It's a tale I heard from Fra Salimbene."

"Salimbene?" The friar echoed again. He sounded *really* nervous now.

She plunged ahead before he could stop her. "There was once a traveling merchant who went on a long voyage. He returned two years later to find a new suckling child in his home. 'Ho, wife,' he cried, 'whence came this infant? He is surely none of mine.'

"'Oh, dear husband,' said she, 'Forgive my carelessness. I allowed myself to become stranded all alone in the wintry mountains one afternoon. The Snow King took me by surprise and forced himself upon me. This boy, I'm afraid, is the result.'

"The merchant said not a word, but when he sailed to Egypt on business some years later, he took the child with him and sold the boy into slavery. When he returned home his wife asked, 'Where is my son, husband?'

"'Alas, my faithful wife,' he wailed, 'we sweated in those tropic regions full many a week, until we were all near delirium. But your poor boy, being the son of the Snow King, suffered most of all in the heat and finally simply melted away.'

Enrico guffawed. Conrad grumbled: "And what did Fra Salimbene say was the moral of your tale?"

"That the merchant was stupid to leave his wife unattended for two years."

Conrad grumbled: "You were supposed to give an example of virtue." He broke off in mid-sentence. Across the fire ring, the penitent was sobbing with his face buried in his hands. Amata touched his shoulder. "What troubles you, Sior Jacopone?" she asked. "Did I tell my story *so* badly?"

He shook his head and wiped his eyes with a corner of his cloak. "Pardon, brothers," he said when he had regained his composure. "I was thinking of Umiliana de Cerchi, who was to be my example of Penance."

His words came in spurts. "She lived in a bare room at the back of one of the richest banking houses in Florence where she led a life of hidden penitence ... fasting and weeping ... to atone for the dishonest dealings of her rich brothers next door." He looked around the group again with those grief-stricken eyes, nearly moving Amata to tears herself. He fanned only half-heartedly at the smoke swirling around his face.

"Such a woman was my own dear wife, a saint in her own right. While I collected huge sums through my usury, while I managed the properties and accounts of my clients ... always to my own interest, while I gambled away my gains and my family's good name at dice ... all the while forcing that pious woman to decorate herself in the vainest frippery and behave like a foolish ornament to my prestige—she was doing penance, hoping to win back my lost soul from the Prince of Evil."

"And why aren't you still with her?" Amata asked. "Where is she now?"

"Gone, child. Dead these four years. One evening I sent her to represent me at a client's wedding feast. I told her I would join her later, preoccupied as I was with my ledgers and counting my wealth. But before I arrived, a loggia overburdened with revelers collapsed as she fanned herself beneath it.

"They carried her broken body to our home. When her maidservant and our baby's nurse removed her expensive gown to wash her for burial, they found she wore a rough hairshirt underneath. The whole year of our marriage, she'd tortured that delicate skin of hers because of my sins. I had never seen that side of her. I never even imagined she did such things."

He closed his eyes, as he had in the Piazza del Mercato that morning, and began to sing softly: "I remember a woman with olive skin, soft raven hair, and splendidly dressed. The memory of her, it torments me still; so much do I long to speak with her."

Amata shifted closer to the penitent. She wanted to put her arm around his shoulder, a comforting, womanly gesture—but she couldn't. Only Conrad knew she wasn't Fabiano, one of these stoic males. She could only murmur her sympathy: "I'm so sorry for you, Sior Jacopone." No one else spoke until the hermit finally broke the painful silence and the spell of the man's grief. He murmured softly, respectfully: "We should retire now, but one of us must stay awake to keep watch and stoke the fire. We can stand guard in shifts."

Amata's body yearned to rest after Conrad's forced march, but with the mood of the evening disrupted, her earlier daydream—one final night in a secluded clearing beside Enrico's hard body—came again to mind. "I can't sleep yet," she volunteered. "My stomach still aches. I'll take the first watch." Her fantasy would have been twice as sweet had she seen but a trace of Jacopone's passion in the boy.

At a safe distance from the sparks that kicked outside the fire ring, the travelers spread the pine boughs they'd gathered for matting. Amata arranged her nest, then crawled across Enrico's mat toward the cave entrance. "Try to stay awake," she whispered as she passed him. "I have another tale to tell, but it's not one these old men should hear."

X

ORFEO ROLLED OUT of his bunk just before dawn. The sky had the dull sheen of a pewter tray, hardly light enough to isolate the ship's features. The sleeping quarters in the aftercastle that he shared with the pope-elect and the rest of Tebaldo's entourage had been heavily perfumed to counteract the stench rising from the oarsmen's deck. In contrast to the Venetians, who hired freemen like him to row their galleys, the Anglos followed the Genovese custom and powered their warships with Turkish slaves. Chained to their oars by day and to the sleeping decks by night, they wallowed in their own ordure, welcoming any wave that crested the deck railings. That King Edward's mariners could tolerate such a reek only confirmed Orfeo's low opinion of northerners.

He nodded groggily to the steersman, who kept his watch beneath a canopy on the ship's stern, then tiptoed among the slaves. He traversed the length of the man-of-war and climbed up to the platform at the highest level of the forecastle, where the wind blew unobstructed against his face. The fresh sea breeze cleansed his lungs, calming and revivifying him. He sat down at last with his back to the parapet, his knees pulled up to his chest.

For the past two hours Orfeo had pitched and turned on his bed, his fists clenched, soaking his bedding in sweat. He labored to breathe. When he did lapse into sleep, he dreamed he was besieged by a horde of faceless, hooded figures who charged from the cover of a thick fog, then disappeared as quickly back into the mists, frustrating his efforts to defend himself. And now that he was awake, a foreboding of danger still pressed in on him. Yet the sea could not be calmer, with not a single cloud in the sky. The wind blew just hard enough to keep the square sail billowed. The convoy remained intact, three warships and their provision galley. A seafarer couldn't wish for a more tranquil dawn.

A slit of light struck the railing opposite him. He looked abaft the stern where the rising sun rimmed the eastern horizon. The first rays shimmered in the ship's wake. He held his hand up to the sunbeam, watched his skin shade from pink to coral to orange, as though his fingers still dripped with the dyes of his father's woolworks.

Orfeo stretched his legs and braced them against the iron mass of a grappling hook. He closed his eyes again, trying to recapture the dream. Was he truly in peril? Perchance God meant to warn him about someone else—maybe that bloated murderer he had once called his sire. Had his father gone at last to eternal damnation? He tried to picture the old man's features, but the image refused to focus. The faces of his brothers replaced his father's one after another. But no, these faces were neither the substance nor the subjects of his dream either. He fixed his imagination on Marco, trekking across Armenia into the unfamiliar, but again his gut didn't react. The likeness of a girl followed—a child really and not one he even knew. This memory started his pulse racing. *Her* again!

He'd seen the girl only once, standing on one of the towers that framed her family's castle gate, watching him through dark almond-shaped eyes, her hair twined over her shoulder in a long black plait bound with a leather thong. While their fathers quarreled over the toll the castellan charged, Orfeo untied a yellow silk cloth from his arm and knotted it into a puppet. Then he put his finger inside the puppet and bent his finger in an elaborate bowing gesture. She'd ducked from sight when he followed the puppet's courtesy with a bow of his own.

There might lie the source of his nightmare. As he sailed each day nearer to his native soil, the cause of his leaving kept haunting him. He'd often pictured in his mind how the castle looked after the raid: its walls battered, wooden outbuildings in flames, the inhabitants slaughtered or begging for death in their terminal throes, the winsome girl-child among them. His father's man, Simone della Rocca, was as thorough as he was ruthless.

Must I face all that again? he wondered. *Is that why You deprived me of my hope, Lord—my ambition?* He shivered and curled again into a ball, for the salt air blew suddenly cooler.

But he had only to sail with the pope to the isle of Negropont, and thence to Venice, he reminded himself. The Holy Father had asked no more of him. After that, he could hire onto a galley returning to the Levant.

His head snapped up as the gong sounded to waken the slaves. Chains scraped and clanked against a chorus of grumbling. As an oarsman, Orfeo could relate to the slaves' early morning stiffness. Passenger life bored him, and he envied the slaves their work, if not the misery of their servitude.

Poor brutes! They loathed the oar. It symbolized their degradation, while he saw release from his past in the same tool. Orfeo would study the rowers hour after hour as they stood in unison, shoved the grips of their nine-stone oars as far forward as they could stretch, then pulled back with slow control, falling as one being onto their benches. He loved that dance to the rhythm of the steersman's gong.

He would be back at sea before the new year, he reassured himself. Afloat once again, doing his man's work day-in and day-out, he'd enjoy the sleep of utter exhaustion and be quit at last of this fractious dream.

THE OLDER MEN made no noise as they slept. Enrico's mamma and papa always kept him awake with their snores. The bed he shared with his brothers lay an arm's length from his parents, in the same room where the family cooked and ate. Some nights, the snoring grated so loudly he would stumble through the low gate that separated the family's half of the cottage from the stable and snuggle down in the straw among the animals.

He peered into the darkness beyond the mouth of the cave. Fabiano wandered out there alone somewhere. The novice's bravery impressed him. His brothers had often dared him to spend the night in the woods outside their cottage to prove his courage; he always chose instead to put up with their jeers.

Enrico was willing to stay awake and hear the other boy's story, but he didn't know how much longer he could fend off his drowsiness. His eyelids grew heavy and had just closed when he heard Fabiano calling softly. "Fra Conrad? Sior Jacopone?" Then the novice knelt beside him, placing a finger against his lips. Enrico rolled over and rose up on one elbow. Fabiano motioned for him to follow. "You wait here," he said outside the cave. "I'll put another branch on the fire and be right back."

The nearly full moon and the firelight from the cave cast a twilight effect through the trees. Leaves rustled, but gently, stirred only by a light breeze. Enrico listened for the footfalls of wild animals, scanning the bushes for any movement or eye shine. He was glad when Fabiano returned. The boy took his sleeve and led him away from the cave.

"Shouldn't we stay near the fire?" He found himself whispering too.

"I found a glade on the other side of the road. You aren't scared of the dark are you?"

Enrico avoided answering. "You said you'd keep watch."

"We'll be close by. It's not a very long story."

Enrico's steps grew unsteady as they moved from the light into the dark shrubbery. At one point a dead branch cracked beneath the weight of his foot. Fabiano stopped short and glanced back at the cave. "Be careful. We don't want to wake them."

In the clearing, the novice turned and faced him. Fabiano seemed much shorter than he did in the faint moonlight. They stood so close together, the novice had to lean back his head to look up at him.

"This is the story of a young hermit named Rustico and a beautiful girl called Alibech."

"Not hermit *Conrad?*"

"No, definitely not hermit Conrad!" Fabiano chuckled.

"While barely in her teens," the novice resumed, "this Alibech ran away from her home, having no desire to be given in marriage. She only wanted to live a holy life of prayer in the desert. She wandered from cave to cave, asking the hermit living in each to instruct her in the ways of God. Every time, the wise old men, knowing that even they weren't secure from temptation, would give her roots and herbs, wild apples and dates, and send her on to seek help from the next hermit. At last she came to Rustico's cave.

"In his youthful pride, Rustico decided to put his constancy to the trial, and received her into his cell. He soon found, however, that he couldn't withstand her beauty or her innocence, for he discovered that she knew absolutely nothing of men. After several days, he yielded at last to the fire that raged in his loins. He asked the girl to kneel before him that he might teach her how to put the devil in hell."

Fabiano tugged at the chest of Enrico's tunic. "Kneel down," the novice said. "You must play the part of Rustico."

Enrico did as he was told and the other boy knelt in front of him. Dry leaves crunched beneath their knees, but Fabiano said nothing about the noise this time. "'First,' Rustico told the girl, 'we must remove our robes and undergarments.'"

"Do I have to do *that?*" Enrico complained. "It's cold away from the fire."

Fabiano hissed: "Look, if you're going to whine about everything, you'll ruin the story."

"I'm sorry. I haven't done this sort of thing before."

The novice smiled. "I understand that."

Enrico pulled his shoulder-cape and tunic over his head. He could hear the rustle of fabric as Fabiano did the same. The night air made him shiver and he hesitated to toss his clothing aside. He looked imploringly at the novice.

What he saw caused him to suck in a deep draught of the frigid air. He'd seen his younger sister naked before, but her breasts were only buds, nothing like the full fruit that bobbed before him now, nearly as large as his mamma's when she nursed a new baby. His eyes traced her slim silhouette down past the curve of her hips, across her thighs, to the heap of thick black curls that invited exploration, and her navel, deep as a vortex in the obscure light. He reached out toward the soft flesh of her abdomen, but stopped short of testing her reality by actually touching her. He started to speak, but the girl put her finger to his lips again. Then she picked up the thread of her story as though nothing unusual had happened.

"'Rustico,' cried Alibech, 'what is this thing you have that I have not, which rises like a dome before you!'"

"'Alas, daughter' he said, 'It's *il diavolo*, that very devil I mentioned. God has afflicted me with this beast, which has caused me to suffer all my days, so that I've often thought the pain of him must kill me. But now, in answer to my prayers, He has sent you to me. For He has given *you* something that *I* have not, a hell into which this devil can be plunged and my pain eased.'"

The girl began to fondle Enrico. "You *must* be cold," she said. "I'm freezing too, but it affects me just the opposite." She guided his hand toward her chest and placed his fingertip on the firm, protruding knot of one of her nipples.

"I can't go on with my story unless you cooperate. You heard what Alibech said. You must rise like a dome." Her voice encouraged him. "Are you nervous? You must relax. Remember what the men said? You should experience life. Even the nights with pale-skinned ladies."

He pressed her nipple between his thumb and forefinger, curiously, gently, so as not to hurt her. He breathed hard now, in short gasps, and his pulse throbbed in his temples. He blinked against the dizziness.

"That's better," she said as she continued to rub him. "It's all right, you know. You've taken no vows yet. Oh yes, that's *much* better. I should nickname you 'big Rico.' And you can call me Amata, which is my real name."

He laughed softly, and with both his hands began massaging her breasts. "Big Rico. Like Sior Jacopone," he said.

She placed her free hand across his and held them in place for a moment. "Jacopone? Why do you bring him up at a time like this?"

He opened his eyes again. "*Jacopone.* It's a nickname, not his real name. He told me it means 'big Jacopo.' His townsmen called him that because he's so tall."

She stopped rubbing. Her fingers tensed and squeezed him tightly.

"Ow. What did I say."

She let him drop.

"What townsmen? His townsmen in Gubbio?" she asked.

"No. Not Gubbio. He said he's from Todi, in the farthest corner of Umbria."

The girl sank back on her heels, breaking contact with his hands. She wrapped her arms around her stomach and began to groan. "Why, God?" she whimpered. "Why do you take everyone who's dear to me?"

She brought her fist to her mouth and bit down hard on her knuckle. Her mouth opened wide, as though she wanted to scream, but her distress came from a place so deep it defied sound.

"What's wrong?" Enrico asked.

But she'd forgotten him. She rolled over onto her side, thrashing in the forest litter, still gripping her stomach and moaning. Her fists lashed out at some invisible enemy.

"Oh, my precious cousin, what a horrible way to die."

She's raving, he thought. He began to worry that the noise might waken the others. He pulled on his clothes again. He didn't want to be caught with her like this. He considered slipping back to the cave, but just then she rolled over onto her back.

Ah. Che bella! Che grazia di Dio! Her skin glowed in the moonlight, perfect and unblemished, and her tear-filled eyes glimmered like gemstones. She seemed a faerie creature, a wood nymph, stretched out on the black humus. He began to stroke her stomach.

"Don't." She removed his hand. "I can't do this now."

"What happened?"

She didn't answer at once. Enrico became fearful that they'd be missed. Finally, when he thought he could stay no longer, she spoke again.

"*Signore Jacopo dei Benedetti da Todi*, the famous notary." She uttered the name slowly, in a deferential tone. "That's what they called him when he was still sane. The tallest man in Todi. At the time I was carried away from my home, he was betrothed to my cousin Vanna. I never saw him in person before this day.

"Enrico, that was my own sweet cousin crushed beneath the balcony. She was like an older sister to me—the most-beloved sister a girl could have, the one person who understood me best."

She sat up and listlessly regathered her clothing. Enrico watched in silence while she dressed, intrigued, not so much by her garments as by the objects she strapped beneath them—something white and crinkly against her abdomen, a dark sheath on her forearm. She glanced up and caught his stare.

"This scroll's a chronicle of the friars' history," she said. Her voice assumed an air of importance. "I'm taking it to San Damiano tomorrow. Several of the sisters there can write. I'm going to have it copied as a surprise for Fra Conrad, so say nothing about it."

She held out her arm for his inspection. "And this knife is to ward off danger." Again she spoke proudly. "The last man who touched me without my willing it can no longer count to ten on his fingers."

She was fully clothed now. She looped the cincture around her waist and took the boy's hand. "I'm sorry, Enrico. This wasn't the ending I planned. Maybe I can finish the story for you another day. At least you will have the memory of Suor Amata and what you saw tonight." She managed a melancholy smile.

"Amata," he said. "The Loved One. It suits you. I know *I* love you."

"Don't even think it. It's bad luck to love me. I mean that." She stared grimly into his face and her smile had vanished. "We have to get back," she said at last.

He followed her toward the road and the wavering glow from the cave. Unexpectedly, she stopped dead and motioned to him to be silent. He imitated her example as she crouched behind a tree.

She cursed softly and whispered. "There's a gang of men on the road."

AMATA COUNTED FIVE murky figures. She thought of Dom Vittorio's hunting party and their quarry—the thugs hired by the Perugians to terrorize travelers. Had they been followed from Gubbio? She remembered her premonition on the trail. She prayed to God this wasn't the same gang or another like them, but knew in her heart that was wishful thinking. Only thieves and cutthroats had reason to be on the road in the black of night, looking for campfires. The fire that protected sleepers from animals and cold lured outlaws like these.

The men stopped near the tree where she and Enrico hid, making their plan in low, gruff whispers. They spread out, about ten yards apart, across the road, meaning to approach the cave from several angles. Amata could see that they carried clubs and pikes, and guessed they also concealed other, smaller weapons.

"They'll murder Conrad and Jacopone," she said, her lips right beside the boy's ear. "I have to warn them. You wait here."

The back of her neck tingled as she crept out to the edge of the road. Her eyes opened wide and she took several deep breaths, delaying the inevitable moment when she must try to dash between them and give herself away. She thought of Conrad and how he'd risked his life to help her across the mountain face, and that memory finally impelled her to her feet.

"Brothers, wake up!" she screamed. *"Banditi!* Wake up!"

She raced as hard as she could for the woods on the other side of the road, but one of the men caught her sleeve. He spun her around and raised his club above her head. Instinctively, she dove against his chest, so that the weapon flailed harmlessly behind her. He grunted, then bawled in pain and dropped his cudgel to the ground. With both hands he grabbed her wrist, trying to push her away, while she twisted her knife in his belly, struggling to reach his heart with the point. Warm blood spurted over her fist. The man finally released his grip with a shudder as Enrico landed on his back.

"Run, Amata!" he yelled as two of the men dragged him off. Her assailant weakened and she drove her dagger home. With a look of infinite sadness, he dropped to his knees, then fell forward onto his face. She stooped to snatch up his club. In the confusion of shadows, Enrico shouted for help.

She almost failed to see the man bearing down on her with a pike. At the last instant she jumped back. She heard her robe tearing in front and the ripping of Leo's scroll as she barely escaped being disemboweled. The brush crashed behind her and as the pikesman drew back his arms to thrust again. Conrad's hurtling body bowled him off his feet. The friar regained his balance first and positioned himself in front of Amata.

"In the name of God, leave off," he shouted at the men.

"These aren't God-fearing men." Amata screamed. "Take this club and fight, or commend your soul to heaven." She shoved the cudgel into his hand.

The pikesman hesitated. "To me, brothers," he called.

The two men who had dragged off Enrico rejoined their leader. A bad sign, Amata thought. They no longer worried about the boy. The last of the gang also came back to the pack and now all four faced Conrad and the woman. The hermit stood motionless. The weapon Amata had forced upon him hung at his side. A fleeting standoff followed as the pikesman sized up the situation.

"This is our man. Finish what we came to do, and let's get out of here," he said. Amata backed toward the trees. She grabbed a fistful of Conrad's robe and tried to pull him after her.

He resisted her tugging and held his ground. "Why am I your man? Do you know me? I'm not an Umbrian."

The explosive blare of Jacopone's trumpet from the direction of the cave shattered the tense standoff. Seeing the startled look on their faces, Amata tried again to drag Conrad away. Jacopone, meanwhile, barged noisily through the trees, shrieking and roaring as he closed the gap between them.

"Aiee! God's angels protect them!" the leader screamed. "*Un drago*," shouted another. Amata turned to see two great flaming eyes charging down the hillside.

The gang froze for an instant as the apparition raced nearer and in that instant of delay Jacopone leaped among them. He shoved a firebrand into the face of the pikesman while, with the second torch he carried, he raked the man's clothing. The bandit howled and bolted—blinded and ablaze—into the forest. The other three scurried back up the road toward Valfabbrica with the dragon bellowing in pursuit. Jacopone managed to set another cloak aflame before he gave off the chase.

With the gang out of sight, Conrad knelt by the man who had attacked Amata. He rolled the body over and placed his hand on the blood-soaked chest.

"Too late for final absolution," he said. "His soul is already gone to its eternal home."

"To Hades, I hope," Amata said.

"Was it you killed him?"

She appreciated the tinge of awe in his question. "He wasn't much of a fighter," she answered. She left Conrad kneeling beside the outlaw and ran a short distance down the road in the direction of Assisi. Then she backtracked to the fight scene.

"Enrico," she called. "Enrico." As Jacopone headed back with his torches, Amata spotted the motionless heap at the edge of the brush. She couldn't bring herself to touch it, but it was clearly human. Her stomach spasmed and she began to gag.

Amata dropped to her knees beside the figure. "No, Rico, no!" she wailed. "Not you too!"

XI

CONRAD BRUSHED PAST AMATA. He felt Enrico's chest, as he had the dead man's. Then he leaned his face close to the boy's. Amata squeezed her hands together helplessly, at the same time praying and despairing.

"He's still breathing, but barely. Where's Sior Jacopone?"

"He's coming, padre," she said. "We're over here," Amata called down the road. "Hurry!"

The penitent raised his torches high into the air and gave a roar of triumph as he approached them. "I haven't fought so since we ran Benedetto Gaetani and his Ghibelline crowd out of Todi," he said.

"You saved us most certainly, brother," Conrad said. "But we may be too late to help Enrico. He's almost perished. We have to move him before the *banditi* return." He gestured toward the woods. "Leave one of your torches with Fabiano, Sior Jacopone. Find some saplings we can use for litter poles."

Jacopone stared down at the boy for an instant, then crashed again in among the trees. Conrad buried his forehead in the palm of one hand, thinking, then he began to cast around. "Follow me, sister," he said at last. "It grieves me to strip a corpse, but we need the outlaw's robe to carry Enrico. We can run the poles through the sleeves."

She stumbled after him in a daze. She could only think that, but for her, Enrico wouldn't be lying half-dead on the road now—although she might be dead herself. She'd prefer that. God had surely placed His scourge on everyone she cared for.

Conrad ordered her to turn her back while he undressed the body. She did a slow pivot and faced into the darkness until he cried out, "*Dio mio*, sister! What have you done? This was a friar you killed."

Conrad had removed the outer cloak. She saw that the dead man wore a grey robe belted with a cord like their own. Knotted to the leather thong bunched at his throat was a crude wooden cross.

"He tried to *kill* me." Her body drooped and her words were little more than a hoarse whisper. She hadn't the strength even to defend herself. The torch in her hand dipped until it burned just above the man's bald head and rigid, agonized features.

"Padre! I know this one! I saw him this morning!"

"In Gubbio?"

"Yes. In the piazza. He stood at the back of the crowd with several of our Order. He had his hood off and I remember thinking he seemed to enjoy the cold."

"But why *attack* us?"

Amata raised her hands. "The one said they were looking for you." She stared across the road at Enrico's motionless form and gripped Conrad's sleeve. "I'm afraid for you, padre," she said. "Please don't go to the Sacro Convento. You're walking into a death trap."

"That decision is mine," he reminded her, "and for now I see no other choice." He studied the dead friar for a moment. "Besides, is a life so important? If these men had killed me earlier, I'd already be rejoicing with Fra Leo and San Francesco." He smiled, patting his chest, and added, "*And,* I'd already know the meaning of this letter."

"But Leo wants you alive to publish what you learn. I'm sure of it."

Jacopone emerged from the brush dragging two thin sturdy trees with the branches snapped off. He laid them beside Enrico and rejoined Conrad and Amata.

"We have to bury this brother first," Conrad said.

"Bury him?" Amata cried. "We don't have time for that! We have to get Enrico out of here."

"The man was a friar. He should be buried like a Christian, not left as food for scavengers." Conrad removed the cross from around the dead man's neck and handed it to her. "Hold this to mark his grave. Sior Jacopone, help me take off his robe. We can wrap him in his cloak and heap a burial mound over him."

"Give his cincture to me," Amata said. "I can use it."

She waited on the road, torch in one hand, cross in the other, while the men dragged the friar's remains into the trees. She kept her eyes on the bends where the trail disappeared in each direction, fearing the return of the gang. Three of them had run off toward Gubbio, but the pikesman might be anywhere. His screaming had long since faded to silence in the cold night air. She strained to hear past the scraping in the underbrush where Conrad and Jacopone scooped leaves and pine needles and dirt on the corpse. She also cupped her ear toward Enrico, hoping for some moan or cry of pain or any sound of life. The silence in all directions magnified her dread.

After an interminable interval, Jacopone stepped from the darkness and exchanged the rope cincture for the cross she held. Amata hurried to Enrico's side of the road and bundled an armful of branches into a faggot. She transferred the waning flame from her firebrand and, as the fire spread from twig to twig, scrutinized the boy's face. Scrapes and bruises blotched his fair skin and dried blood matted his yellow hair into a sticky thatch. So young, the same age her brother Fabiano would have been by now. She sat on the ground next to him and stroked his forehead, running her fingers through his hair to free the gummy tangle.

The boy's eyelids fluttered, then opened wide as he recognized her. "Amata," he murmured. "You're still alive."

"Oh thank God, Rico," she said, "so are you."

"I'm not so sure. I hurt all over. And I feel so weak."

"You did a brave thing, jumping on the man's back."

He tried to smile. "The first brave act of my life and it's done me in."

"Hush. Don't talk like that. We're almost to the Sacro Convento. The friars there will patch you up."

His eyelids closed again. He rolled his head from side to side, fighting to stay conscious. She heard the men coming. "Remember, I'm *Fabiano*, not Amata," she whispered, but he'd lapsed again into insensibility.

Conrad and Jacopone formed a stretcher of the poles and robe. The boy remained limp as the men lifted him onto the robe and raised the litter to their shoulders. Amata stepped in front to light up the cart ruts and potholes.

"Now may the grace of God protect him and us," Conrad said. "Let's move." The road, although rough, ran level for nearly a league, until they passed the Porziano crossroads. The facade of a tiny country chapel loomed in a clearing to their right, a place where they might find sanctuary. Conrad paused long enough to set down the litter and poke his head into the doorway. Then he motioned to Amata to follow with the torch and went inside.

The light triggered a flurry of rustling as some small animal scuttled along the wall. Overhead the air filled with the whirring of wings and a swarm of bats escaped through a hole in the ceiling. Amata stood immobile in the doorway until the noise subsided, then followed Conrad toward the altar. The air reeked of burned flesh. She'd heard stories of Jews who butchered animals on their altars and offered them as a burnt sacrifice. Their temples must smell like this all the time, she thought.

The hermit brushed a layer of dirt from the altar stone and opened the tabernacle door. "It's not safe. It's no longer used as a church. There's no Eucharist to protect us."

"Even so, we could stop for a while. All this jostling could kill Enrico."

"We can rest at daybreak. It's too dangerous to stop in the dark."

A groan rose from the darkness behind the altar. Conrad snatched the faggot from Amata and held it high above his head. "If you are man and not beast, identify yourself," he said.

"Damn your zealot soul, Conrad da Offida," a voice grated. "We never meant to harm you. Our orders were only to take you prisoner."

Conrad inched his way around the altar until he could make out the figure slumped against the wall. The man extended his pike toward them, but appeared too feeble to do them serious harm.

"Throw aside your weapon if you want our help."

"Help? He nearly ripped out my stomach!" Amata said.

The man held his defensive pose.

"Throw it aside, I say." Conrad waved the torch in a large slow circle. "Do you wish the fire again?"

The pike thudded to the dirt floor. Conrad stepped forward, but Amata placed her rigid arm in front of him.

"Be careful. He might have a knife."

"Then take his weapon and cover him. I think he'd prefer to live."

Amata found the pike in the shadows and pressed the point against the man's chest. Conrad held the light closer.

"Do you know him too?" Conrad asked.

"I can't see his face. Pull back his cowl."

The man yelped as the priest's hand brushed his face. This was the stinking flesh she'd smelled. His charred features were indistinguishable, an oozing mess from which one malevolent eye glared at her. Conrad eased back the hood. The man's hair was the color of straw, and cropped in a religious tonsure.

Amata leaned closer, steadying herself against the altar. "I think he's one of the friars who directed me to Monna Rosanna. At least his hair looks the same."

"That's impossible! Weren't they on foot?"

"No. They rode donkeys. I told you, the other one was very old. They could have reached the friary in Gubbio yesterday. Thank God we didn't sleep there last night."

Conrad held the flame close to the man's face again. "Do you know the meaning of Fra Leo's letter?"

"No." He coughed, and bloody phlegm spewed onto his chest. When he spoke again, his voice rasped and the words formed with difficulty. "My companion said only ... that the minister general ... would be pleased to have it—and you." He tried to lift his hand, but it fell back onto his chest.

"Your companion's name!"

The man's lip curled into a sneer. "Amanuensis."

"That's not a name," Conrad said. "It's an occupation."

"Amanuensis," the man repeated steadily.

Conrad frowned. "And he likely spoke the truth. Bonaventura thinks of me as a troublemaker. He would *not* welcome news of my return. That's hardly a reason to imprison me, though."

The man choked again as mucus caught in his throat. "For the love of God, help me," he begged. "Hear my confession. I need to unburden my soul."

"That I will, brother," Conrad said. "Wait outside, Fabiano, and don't worry. I promise to keep a safe distance between us."

Amata carried the pike to the doorway, but close enough to hear the undertone of the two voices. She saw Jacopone in the moonlight, squatting beside the litter, and her anxiety rose. *Jesu Domine!* Why did Conrad put everyone else's needs before theirs? She watched the penitent's outline fade into the darkness, then reemerge, as a long cloud crossed the moon. All the while, Conrad droned on to the injured friar. At last the torch passed around the altar again. "Rest now in peace, and keep your mind free of sin," she heard him say. "I'll send some brothers to help you as soon as we reach Assisi."

The priest handed her the torch and he and Jacopone wrestled the poles back onto their shoulders. She tried to hold the fiery bundle with one hand, but her fingers started to cramp and she reluctantly hurled the pike into the woods.

A short distance beyond the chapel, the path climbed toward the No-cigliano Heights, the last hill they had to scale to reach Assisi. The mud was firm and almost frozen beneath Amata's sandals, and she wondered that the barefoot men seemed not to feel the cold in their toes as much as she did. The strength of the two ascetics impressed her too. With the shorter Conrad leading the way, the steep ox-cart path hardly slowed them. She remembered her father's tales of the Spartan warriors of ancient days, the most grim and fearsome fighters in memory, whose regimen centered on their wretched mess halls and diet of organ meat, oatmeal pudding and other such miserable fare. Like these two, they also shunned women. She didn't even *want* to probe the implications of *that*.

The moon dipped behind the western mountains, but the trail ahead, up toward the crest, grew lighter. Amata saw the outlines of the trees on the summit and rejoiced to hear the sporadic twitter of waking birds.

"All the way to the top, Sior Jacopone," Conrad urged. "We can rest there."

At last, where the road opened on the basin of the River Tescio, they set down their load. The faint daylight spread beyond the encircling mountains and Amata saw the plain laid out like a small universe below her with its distant villages, solitary hamlets and groomed fields extending to the distant hills. Nearest of all those towns lay Assisi, and a flush of hot anger surged through her as she picked out the main tower and crenellated fortress walls of the Rocca Paida brooding over the city. She ground her torch into the mud, wishing she might snuff Simone della Rocca and his sons as easily.

The men stretched and shook their arms. Jacopone selected a suitable bush and reached into his loincloth to relieve himself when Conrad grabbed him by the cloak.

"A little further into the woods, brother. I'll go with you."

Amata grinned. Conrad meant to keep up their charade—and his dilemma—to the end. Something stirred behind her and she turned to see Enrico tossing and flailing his arms in the air.

She rushed to the litter. "I'm here, Rico," she said. "We're almost to Assisi." She grasped his wrists and brought his hands down across his chest.

Conrad returned before the boy could answer. "We're *all* here, little brother," he said. He put his palm to Enrico's forehead and stared into his face. "I've just heard the confession of one wounded man, and will hear yours also if you so wish."

"I do, padre. Please shrive me. I know I'm dying."

"But can't you wait until you've reached the friary?" Amata asked.

The youth rolled his doleful eyes toward her. "I'm sorry. I need to confess. Now. The friary may be too late."

"Enrico's right," Conrad said to her. "We shouldn't risk the delay. Go down the road a bit and wait with Sior Jacopone. Let the boy confess in privacy."

Amata turned her back on the pair and walked away. She felt her sinking heart could hold no more—not one more death of a loved one, not one more enemy—and prayed it might finally break. Surely Conrad would hate her after he'd heard Rico's confession.

She fought the urge to tears. Jacopone came up beside her, cupping her shoulder in his huge paw. "The fitful breathing of the dying. The sinning, and the forgiveness of sin. It's all the patchwork of poetry, brother. All of life is but a never-ending epic poem."

LORD JESUS CHRIST, Son of God, have mercy on me, a sinner. Lord Jesus Christ, Son of God, have mercy on me, a sinner.

Jacopone's lips moved noiselessly, over and over the same prayer he'd uttered how many millions of times these past four years? It had become as natural to him as breathing. He waited with his legs dangling over the edge of a large rock, hands folded in his lap, eyes half-closed. At the edge of the road, a shiny black beetle struggled in a puddle.

The priest Conrad strode toward him. "Where's Fabiano?" His face twisted with anger. He bellowed his question like a dyspeptic judge Jacopone had known in Todi.

The penitent motioned with his thumb down the road toward Assisi. The friar's grey eyes filled with tears then, and he wiped his arm across his bearded cheeks. He spread his fists and looked up toward the heavens. Then he let his arms drop and dropped his head.

"Enrico's gone." The friar bit off each word as he spoke. "Because that selfish, perverse Fabiano didn't mind the watch, this good boy is dead."

"Children throw stones at frogs in sport, but the frogs die in earnest." Frog-like Jacopone hopped from his perch. "He called me *Cuz*."

"Who?"

"Your novice. '*Farewell, Cuz*,' he said. '*I share your grief*.' I don't know what he meant. My wife had a cousin named Fabiano. He is no grey-friar novice, though. Vanna mourned for her cousins, many, many months. We delayed our wedding. I wish we'd *never* married. I wish our parents had *never* arranged for us to meet. She'd still be living, poor girl."

He raised his head to look at the priest, but his sight clouded. "All tangled, all full of knots. You're a clever man, Fra Conrad. Do *you* understand what any of it means?"

XII

CONRAD *DID* UNDERSTAND, of course. He knew exactly why Amata had called the penitent *cousin*, and why she mourned the death of his wife as deeply as he. But what he knew of their connection, he had just learned from Enrico's confession and he could not violate the sanctity of the Sacrament of Penance.

The friar wished he could feel greater pity for the young woman's loss of her cousin, but his fury at her behavior burned so hotly it suffocated any softer compassion. He tried to remind himself that Amata was little more than a child herself, barely older than Enrico, but the rationalization didn't help. Conrad wanted to scream. He wanted to weep—for the dead boy, for Jacopone and his lost Vanna, for Amata—for all of humankind who groped so wildly and misfortunately toward final judgment. And for his own impetuosity. None of this grisly night would have happened had he refused to be drawn into the labyrinth of Leo's secrets, had he stayed in his hut. *Chi non fa, non falla*, Rosanna's practical father used to say. *Who does nothing makes no mistakes.*

But for now, he and Jacopone had to deal with the worst outcome of his choice. They had to dispose of Enrico's body.

He patted the penitent on the back. "Come, my friend. Let's finish our duty here." He kept his voice business-like, denying for the moment the sorrow that weighed on his spirit. "The boy should be buried at the Sacro Convento. The friars can notify his family."

The two men picked up the litter and resumed their march, the taller Jacopone taking the lead now that they were pointed downhill. Trees arched over the path into the city, creating a tunnel so dim Conrad felt they had stumbled into one of the subterranean channels to the nether world. In his imaginings, the underbrush became the fabled asphodel infected by the black venom that dribbled from the maw of three-headed Cerberus—the plant magicians gathered to prepare deadly philters. Like the ancient poet Orfeo bearing his lyre, they descended into the very bowels of Hades, searching for the lost . . . lost *what?*

The legendary poet at least had his Eurydice, a reason to confront the terrors ahead of him, but Conrad had no one so tangible to look forward to—a few nebulous answers at most. Still he felt he was being dragged just as ineluctably toward the catastrophe of his personal tragedy.

The hermit worried, too, for the skeletal poet trudging down the trail ahead of him. Since his passionate sermon in the piazza, Jacopone had slipped steadily into a confused melancholia, rallying only briefly to fight off the attack on their cave. What would become of the penitent once they entered Assisi? If the city accepted him as a remorseful sinner, he wouldn't be harmed; but if they considered him a madman, the same laws that governed lepers caught within the walls would apply to him. The people could stone him—or worse. Even the urchins in Gubbio understood that.

Conrad wondered what would become of *him,* for that matter? If the friars at Gubbio were waiting for him, wouldn't his brothers at the Sacro Convento be ready also? But he also knew that only on the other side of the friary door had he any chance to find the answers to Leo's riddle.

He berated himself for his fear. He repeated the passage from the *Pater Noster* that had echoed through his mind so often since he'd left his hut: *Thy will be done, Father. Amen, amen.* He reminded himself too that the worst the friars could do would reunite him with those he loved most—Fra Leo and San Francesco.

He and Jacopone cleared the forest at last and came out onto a bare, rocky hillside. Below them, the friar saw the gate leading to the northeastern sector of the city. That would be their most direct route into Assisi, but the spectacle of a tattered hermit and a lugubrious penitent carrying a dead child through the streets would be sure to draw a curious crowd in their wake. "Take the footpath to the right," he called out.

The trail, narrow and twisting as a rivulet, snaked across the hillside above the city's fortress and the northern walls. When they reached the westernmost corner, where the Basilica di San Francesco and the Sacro Convento jutted away from the city in splendid isolation, they started down, bracing their heels against sparse tufts of grass thrusting through the loose shale. Jacopone's head rose and his grip on the poles strengthened noticeably as they approached the Porta di San Giacomo di Murorupto. *Into the wolf's mouth*, Conrad thought with resignation.

"God's peace be with you, brother," the hermit called to the civil guard as they passed through the gate. The gatekeeper reached for his pike and approached them warily, jabbing at their lifeless burden.

"What's happened here?"

"We were set upon in the night," the friar replied. "Several men attacked us and mortally wounded our companion. We're taking his body to the Sacro Convento." The guard's jaundiced eyes narrowed as he sized up Jacopone. Perchance he looked for lesions on the penitent's rough skin. He paced around them, scratching his rib cage thoughtfully, in the same way a more philosophical man might stroke his beard. Finally, we waved them forward.

"I'll be watching that you do so," he said. From his gatehouse, the guard had an unobstructed view across the piazza to the upper church of the basilica and the steps that led down to the lower church and the Sacro Convento. Conrad fairly pushed Jacopone across the square. The penitent's prolonged silence made him nervous and gained them no trust from the guard.

The face that appeared at the grille after Conrad pulled the bell rope at the friary looked equally skeptical. The hermit's tension lessened all the same. He didn't recognize the porter and the unfamiliarity seemed mutual. Moreover, judging by the curl of the young friar's upper lip, he was put off more by the ragged dress of the strangers than by the corpse lying in the dirt between them.

Conrad told again how they'd come under attack. "We've brought the boy for burial," he said. "He should have been one of us. There's a letter tucked in his belt, addressed to Fra Bonaventura from the Bishop of Genoa."

The friar ignored his explanation. "Do you plan to shelter here?" His words dripped icily, cold as the ground under Conrad's feet.

"Not I. At least not today." He didn't know how his poor patched robe would be viewed, although the porter's disdain seemed a good clue. If the other brothers felt Conrad rebuked them by flaunting his poverty, he could end up in the friary dungeon again without so much as a glimpse at the library. Now that he had finally arrived at the door of the Sacro Convento, he found himself hesitating to cross its threshold.

"I can't speak for my companion," he added. He turned to Jacopone, but the penitent had slipped away as silently as the dew evaporating from the tiled rooftops.

He spread his hands feebly. "Please help me get the boy inside," he said to the porter. "My companion..." His words trailed off, for he had no explanation for Jacopone's disappearance.

The door opened with an angry moan. Without a word, the younger friar bent over the nearest end of the litter and dragged Enrico's body inside; he didn't wait for Conrad to lift the other end. The traveler was proving a royal nuisance, his manner said, and the sooner he continued about his business, the happier the porter would be.

Conrad gazed one final time after the would-be novice, at the crooked furrows left in the soil by the saplings—and at the robe that formed the bed of the litter. He had almost forgotten the dead friar and the pikesman in his distraction!

"Another brother still lies injured," he said, "in a ruined chapel near the Porziano crossroads—a Fra Zefferino."

The porter looked at him sharply. Clearly he knew the name. "You left the wounded brother behind and brought us this corpse?"

"Both were alive when we left the chapel. I promised the friar I would send help. Surely you can spare two strong brothers for the task?"

The porter searched Conrad's eyes, trying to fathom how this beggar might be connected to Zefferino. "I'll see to it," he said finally. He put his hand to the gate, but again Conrad stopped him.

"One more question, brother. Do you have a Fra Jacoba living in this community?"

"Fra Jacoba? I know no *friar* of that name. Don't you rather mean *Suor* Jacoba? Jacoba is a woman's name."

That much was certainly true. Conrad suddenly felt like a dolt for having overlooked a point so obvious. Maybe he had misread Leo's tiny scrawl. He wanted to pull out the letter then and there and scan the message one more time, but cautioned himself to bide a while. The porter continued to watch him, as did the civil guard who had followed the strangers across the piazza and now stared down from the top of the stairs. Conrad wondered whether he'd been standing there when the penitent moved on. If so, he clearly found the friar the most suspicious of this odd pair of characters.

He pulled his hood up over his head. "Thank you, brother, for your help," he said. "I'd count it a kindness if you passed the bishop's letter to the minister general. It deserves an answer."

"Fra Bonaventura will decide that," the porter said and slammed the door shut.

From the maze of streets behind Conrad, a trumpet blared unexpectedly. He grinned. The penitent would be all right now. The fish had flopped back into his stream.

RELIEVED ON TWO ACCOUNTS—Jacopone's safety and, for the moment, his own—Conrad hurried from the Sacro Convento. He knew he'd have to return here soon, but for the rest of this day he wanted to savor being alone once more. He'd not had a waking hour to himself since he'd found Amata in his hut. Leaving the friary and the gatekeeper behind, he slowed his pace and wandered down the Via Fonte Marcella.

Once within the city proper, however, Conrad realized he'd have to settle for being alone with his thoughts only. The streets and alleys had come alive.

Children still too small to be apprenticed barged past him in squealing gangs, forcing the friar to squeeze up against houses to avoid colliding with them. The piazzas vibrated with the sounds and smells of commerce. Leather tanners and cobblers, silversmiths, wool manufacturers with their allied sheds of dyers and weavers, fullers and felters, fletchers, armorers, and saddlers—all worked feverishly. Conrad remembered then that the harvest fair would take place soon and the merchants would want to be fully stocked.

Assisi had grown prosperous in the six years of his absence. He passed several crews of masons transforming wooden houses into brick and stone. The main streets had been paved with cobblestones and guttered for filth runoff. He marveled at the new sewers, which he'd seen only once before, during his years in Paris. Such a logical concept. Why had it taken so long to reach Umbria? And towers! The towers of the nobility had multiplied like tall weeds as the castellans abandoned their country estates and swarmed into the city. They were so thick and so high that they shrouded the streets in constant shade.

He followed the natural incline toward the lower city and the Porta San Antimo. He had decided to spend the afternoon in the open valley south of the city and sleep that night below the walls, at the Portiuncola: the "little portion" where the Order had its humble beginning. At the small oratory where the first friars prayed, a few of the earliest cells were still intact; at least they had been when he left Assisi. In the morning, he would seek out the person most likely to have given Leo the vellum for his letter, the widow Donna Giacoma.

The air warmed noticeably once Conrad left the shadows of the towers and houses. He passed below the walls and wandered into a mature grove of gnarled olive trees heavy with fruit. He searched until he found a smooth-barked younger tree. There in a sunlit spot he sat down with his back against its trunk. He took a piece of bread from his food pouch and as he munched reread Leo's letter slowly.

Nothing new.

He held the vellum at arm's length, momentarily blotting out the sunlight. Fra Leo, with all his cunning, might have used an ink that showed only when heated or lit from behind. But there too his mentor disappointed him. The message contained no more nor less than he'd already read.

Read with your eyes, discern with your mind, feel in your heart the truth of the legends. Legends. Plural. There lay his probable starting point. But which legends? Bonaventura's version of San Francesco's life was certainly one. God had pointed in that direction by having him stop at Sant'Ubaldo on October fourth. He would find a copy of the *Legenda Major* easily enough inside the Sacro Convento.

"The first of Tomas" might have referred to a legend at one time

also—Tomas da Celano's original biography of San Francesco. But the provincial ministers had banned it five years before, along with all the memoirs
predating Bonaventura's sanctioned life of Francesco. Even if the library of
the Sacro Convento still owned a copy, he'd be forbidden to see it. And there
might be still other legends that Fra Leo wanted him to read, though the
letter offered no more clues that Conrad could see.

The question of the female friar troubled him too. Leo had clearly written "Fra Jacoba." But the porter was also right—Jacoba was a female name.
Maybe Leo had meant to write "Jacob*o*" or "Jaco*po*" or "Ja*com*o." He cringed
at the variety of possibilities. He'd so little to work with as it was. The last
thing he needed was a misspelling or a false lead.

At some point while the sun mounted up the sky, Conrad stopped looking for meaning in the letter. He repeated the words in his mind until they
became as rote and familiar as a childhood prayer. At length, he clambered to
his feet, rolled up the parchment, and returned it to the folds of his robe.

A gust of wind curled a spray of wet, withered leaves against his feet and
ankles. Conrad wound his way aimlessly through the orchard, stopping at
one point to scoop up a pruned branch. He studied the gall protruding halfway down its length, then poked the stick at a smelly mixture of grey-green
olive leaves, straw and manure heaped between two rows of trees. Prying
up large matted slabs of the decomposing midden, he let the humid air flow
underneath. All in due time the farmer would have his fertile soil; all in due
time he'd have his answers. For now, this compost and Leo's clues needed to
simmer.

He tossed the infected branch away. Then he remembered a trick his
father had taught him to start a midden stewing. He looked around to make
sure no one was about, then lifted his robe and pissed on the pile. He recalled
how grown up he'd felt when he and his father had urinated side-by-side in
their vegetable garden that morning of his fifth year.

If Conrad missed the comfort of his father's love, he wasn't one to reopen
doors on the past. He dropped his robe, and instead admonished himself
for failing to trust in his *heavenly* father's love. Surely, at the right time, he'd
receive the one ingredient he needed to start Leo's incongruous words meld-
ing and fermenting. His lips twitched in a near smile as he pondered what
form the Divine Piss might take.

The hermit sorely needed this day to himself. He spent the rest of it
meandering blessedly solo from one to another of the shrines sacred to the
brotherhood. He hiked first to the River Torto and the ruins of the crude
hovel where the original friars endured their harsh, wintry initiation. He
climbed Monte Subasio as far as the *carceri,* the caves where Francesco hid
when he wished to fast and meditate alone. Then, with the shade creeping
up the hillside, he descended once more into the basin below the city. While

the darkness deepened, Conrad ate the last of the food he'd brought with him and entered the oratory of the Portiuncola.

The hermit stood motionless in the aisle while his eyes adjusted to the faint light. He stared at the carved wooden Jesus suspended over the altar, writhing on His cross in the flicker of the chapel's single oil lamp. Conrad could almost visualize San Francesco at prayer, almost hear his words mingling in the draft that whistled through the room's narrow embrasures.

Leo had told him how the saint knelt weeping before that crucifix for hours at a time. Sometimes Francesco would prostrate himself on the dirt floor with arms outspread until his muscles throbbed, joining his own pain and loneliness to the sacrificial pageant, the blood-drenched solitude of his Victim God. The people had come to know Francesco as a joyful holy man singing on the high roads. They had heard also his stern calls to penance and renunciation. But no one knew as well as Leo the depths of his self-propitiation, how he starved and abused *Brother Ass* (as he called his body). He drove his beast through sleepless vigils, ignoring illness, fatigue, depriving it of the thinnest blanket on flesh-numbing February nights. He subsisted on horribly unappetizing food and mixed even that with ashes, until, small wonder, the weakened beast had collapsed, unable to keep pace with his soaring imagination, with the soul that, having in rarefied moments slipped its cage halfway to the heavens, had finally gone on alone—free at last of plodding *Fra Asino*.

While Conrad focused on the crucifix, he felt a tingling heat rush up his back. It coursed through his spine and shoulders, then out through his arms, floating them up from his sides until his pose mirrored that of the dying Christ. His head slumped to one side and in that position he remained transfixed until all the fear and hesitancy he'd felt at the gate of the Sacro Convento siphoned from him—until he knew in the certainty of his innermost being that he stood ready and never alone.

"Yea, Lord," he whispered aloud. "Whatsoever you ask of me." And this time, his heart and his lips moved in unison.

XIII

THE MOMENT THE SKY lightened enough for Conrad to climb the path to the city without stumbling, he left the Portiuncola. His brief retreat among the shrines of his Order had revitalized him and balanced to some extent the jarring events of the last several days. The hazy outline of the city walls, barely visible through the early morning fog, softened his mood even further.

The mist grew thicker as he neared the olive grove where he'd rested the day before. He slowed his pace, not wanting to lose the trail. As he advanced, a murmur of sleepy male voices seemed to spring up all around him until it became a grumbling crescendo. The friar could also hear the soft nickering and jittery stamping of horses and the jangling of metal. A few more steps and he found himself standing beneath an open pavilion, returning the startled stares of several half-dressed warriors—for such he assumed they were from the weapons and armor piled around their bedrolls.

"God's peace be with you, brothers," he said to relieve the oddity of the situation. "I seem to be turned around in the fog." He was only a friar after all, no cause for alarm, and the men resumed strapping on their gear.

The ancient Roman highway to the northern states passed below Assisi's walls, very close to this orchard. Conrad remembered Leo's description of the triumphal passage of Otto IV in the winter of 1209, after Pope Innocent III had crowned him Holy Roman Emperor. Innocent, with his usual temerity, ordered Otto to leave Rome and return to Germany the day after the coronation. The pope meant to discourage any mischievous notions on the parts of the Emperor and his six thousand knights camped in the eternal city.

Despite Innocent's curt dismissal, the citizens of Assisi, good imperial Ghibellines for the most part, cheered Otto lustily as he passed beneath the city. In that age of shifting domination, the wise city supported all parties, paying equal homage to pope and emperor. The townspeople created such a rumble and shout that they disturbed Francesco and his small company, who then shared the shack on the River Torto. Francesco, characteristically, ignored the fanfare of the latest Caesar with his enormous retinue and freshly-vested glory. Instead, he sent one of the brothers to lecture Otto on the frailty of earthly gain.

But Otto's successor, Frederick II, had died in the Year of Our Lord 1250, and Charles D'Anjou beheaded the last of Frederick's sons in 1268. The back of the Empire had been fractured once and for all, the friar thought. The papacy had won.

Or had it? The presence of this many soldiers bivouacked beside the high road, mumbling and joking in the Roman dialect, made him wonder. Had the German princes resolved their destructive squabbles and reunited under a new leader?

He glanced around the group. "Are we at war, friends?" he asked.

One of the soldiers laughed. "Not this side of the Land of Promise, brother. Haven't you heard the news? The new pope is sailing from Acre to Venice. We've gathered the sons of every noble family of Rome to meet him there and escort him back. There'll be big excitement in this village of yours when we ride through here on our return trip."

The man turned away and bent again to his chores. Then as an after-thought, he turned and knelt before Conrad. "Bless our journey and pray for our safe return, godly friar." The other knights, hearing their comrade's request, stopped their activity and knelt also.

"So I shall." Conrad said. He took the breviary from his pocket and paged through the back until he found the prayer for wayfarers. Raising his right hand over their lowered heads, he implored, *Hear, oh Lord, our supplication and keep the path of your servants in safety and prosperity...*

For good measure he added the oration *pro navigantibus*, "for those at sea." The men crossed themselves at his final "amen."

The city walls had totally disappeared in the fog as the hermit stepped outside the pavilion. He was close enough to Assisi that he didn't need to see them, though. He had only to keep moving uphill and be alert for dropoffs.

INSIDE THE CITY AGAIN, Conrad had no trouble locating the home of the noblewoman even in the mist. The townspeople were out early, hammering and sawing, framing stalls for the upcoming fair, building display shelves or arranging planks on trestles, and every few cross streets someone pointed him closer to his destination.

As he expected, the house lay in the upper city, midway between the Church of San Giorgio and the basilica. From the Via San Paolo, a serpentine stairway wound upward to the alley that fronted Donna Giacoma's house. The stone quadrant of the compound facing the alley was solid as a fortress, its slate roof sloping into lead gutters from whose corners fearsome gargoyles leered down at the hermit. Their mouths gaped wide, and during a downpour waterfalls cascading through those maws likely drenched passers by. Narrow arrow-slits formed the only openings in the upper story, in contrast to the shutters of the street-level windows that hung open to the morning light. A scarlet shield embedded in the rock lintel above the doorway portrayed a pride of golden lions poised for the hunt, eagles with their claws outspread, and a tangle of vipers whose tongues flicked ominously at anyone approaching the door.

Conrad hunched his shoulders. He knew something of the owner's history from Fra Leo: a daughter of the Norman princes who had subdued Sicily in decades past; married for eight years to Graziano, eldest son of Rome's murderous Frangipane clan who manhandled popes like they were children at the family's personal beck. The heiress of warriors and widow of one of Rome's most powerful barons, she had abandoned her palace and the eternal city when San Francesco died, moving to Assisi to be near his tomb.

Conrad had never been in the home of such a grand personage and tried to imagine how she might appear—maybe stooped with age but otherwise regal, her hair and ears covered by a veil held in place by a golden diadem, her purple satin gown embroidered with jewels or decorous buttons trailing behind her as she swept about the management of her household and servants, her hands clasped across her stomach to hold up her long flared sleeves, the latest rage among the nobility. He glanced once more at the menacing shield, then swung the heavy brass knocker against the door. The metallic thunk echoed down the alley. Conrad expected to see another suspicious eye at the grille, as he had at the Sacro Convento, but instead the door opened wide. The youth who greeted him proved the very antithesis of the compound's exterior, in manner sweet and gentle, and so comely that Conrad thought this must be how angels looked when they took on human form. Dark hair, cut in straight bangs across his forehead and curled under where it touched his shoulders, framed the boy's unblemished face. He wore pale blue hose, felt slippers, and a short blue overtunic trimmed in white—the livery of the Virgin Mother of God. Someone had stitched the Latin command AMA, *love*, repeatedly around the hem of his bliaut.

"The Lord's peace and welcome to you, brother," he said. "How may we serve you?"

"I wish to speak to your mistress. I'm Conrad da Offida, a friend of Fra Leo."

The youth bowed. "*Madonna's* still at chapel." As he spoke, Conrad's stomach rumbled aloud, for he'd arrived fasting. Without a pause, the page added, "Perhaps you'd like to wait in the kitchen?"

Conrad nodded gratefully and followed the boy through the foyer. The house smelled warmly of burning pine and he could hear fires crackling in several chambers off the hall. Tapestries covered the walls and fresh reed mats softened the tiled floors. Rush lamps glowed in the corners where sunlight couldn't reach. The heavy carved chairs lining the walls were cushioned with scarlet pillows. All in all, Donna Giacoma's home spoke of comfort and hospitality.

"Mamma, a visitor," Conrad's guide called to the cook as they passed through the scullery into the aromas of fresh-baked bread and drying spices and bubbling farina. A mound of unbaked dough waited in its kneading trough beside an oil kettle. The woman looked up at Conrad from the table where she sliced a cream-colored cheese. She appeared not much older than himself, and shared the boy's clear complexion—no doubt from years spent leaning over steaming cauldrons—although patches of dusky down on her cheeks and above her upper lip darkened her otherwise fair skin. Soup and juice stains spotted her white apron and her bare forearms were powdered with flour.

"The bread's just cool enough," she said. "Please seat yourself with Maestro Roberto, brother."

An older man, in the same pale blue livery as the youth and wearing a round blue skullcap, gestured to the bench across the table from himself. He displayed some of the openness and curiosity of the other two, but Conrad also noted a tinge of suspicion in his stare.

"I don't believe we've seen you here before, brother," he said after Conrad scraped his bench into position.

"It's my first visit."

"He knew Fra Leo," the boy interjected.

"Ah. Then you're *most* welcome. I'm *madonna's* steward, so it's my duty to worry about strangers. Our mistress can be too softhearted for her own welfare sometimes. She's let herself be fooled by many a charlatan looking for an easy meal and lodging. And the religious ones are the worst, impressing her with tall tales of visions they've seen, angel voices they've heard, trying to sell her an eyetooth of John the Baptist or a plate used at the last supper. We've been offered enough of those to feed all the apostles and two score dinner guests besides. I know you understand." His eyes narrowed, underscoring the not-so-subtle warning in his voice.

"She must be grateful to have a cautious man like yourself guarding her affairs," Conrad said.

The cook laughed. "Nay, brother. Nobody guards our lady's affairs but herself alone. She tells us what she wants and we do it with good cheer."

The woman set a wooden bowl full of the thick farina porridge, a mug of milk and a piece of bread covered with cheese in front of each of the men. The steward bowed his head.

"Please lead the benediction, brother. We make our friar guests earn their meals by praying for the good of our souls." He spoke his request with the same earnestness as his warning, and Conrad gladly complied.

When he had finished the farina and mopped his bowl clean with the last chunk of bread, Conrad became aware of another scent, sweeter than the cooking smells. He inhaled deeply and his nostrils tingled with pleasure.

"Frangipani—of course," the steward said. "The perfume of the red ginger flower." He rose as he spoke and looked past Conrad. "*Buon giorno*, Giacomina.*"

"*Buon giorno*, everyone." The woman spoke in a husky voice that wavered ever so slightly. The friar staggered to his feet, almost falling over his bench, flustered because he hadn't heard Donna Giacoma enter the kitchen.

He saw the reason immediately. The old woman moved noiselessly on bare feet, supporting her weight on a cane as she limped across the kitchen. She wore the grey-brown tunic of a friar. Conrad then recalled that Leo once said she lived as a tertiary. Donna Giacoma was large, matronly—predictably enough for the descendant of heroes and heroines—but the surprise, for Conrad, was the lack of wrinkling in her full, round face, marred only by a scar on her cheek. She might pass for a woman of fifty. Her white hair surprised him too; she wore it uncovered and cropped in the manner of a bondwoman, but modestly combed to cover her ears. Beneath her bangs, green eyes glittered bright and intense as a cat's.

The noblewoman's manner struck Conrad immediately as both charming and rare. It explained the easy grace with which her servants received him, for she exuded a gentle power that had to influence those who lived in daily contact with her. A word came to mind—*gentilezza*—a gentility that went beyond nobility inherited through birth or wealth. He began to understand how Francesco and Leo had come to love and revere their woman friend.

Conrad introduced himself once more and explained the cause of his visit. He had some questions about a letter he'd received after Leo's death, and would be pleased if *madonna* would favor him with a few moments of her time.

She brightened as he spoke. "You did receive it then? I was so worried that the task was too much for Mother Prioress."

"She entrusted it to the most—obstinate—member of her congregation."

Donna Giacoma motioned to the boy. "Pio, lead Fra Conrad to the courtyard, down to the sunny end. The fog is starting to burn off." Then, to the friar, "I'll join you as soon as I finish my business with Maestro Roberto."

The hermit followed the page once again into the hallway and through an arcade that formed a cloister around the lower level of the courtyard. A wooden loggia hung from the upper story, while the side farthest from the alley soared high above the rest of the compound—the *keep* to which the household could retreat in case the city came under attack. The boy pointed out a stone bench where Conrad could bask in a patch of sunshine and enjoy the gurgling of the marble fountain in the center of the court while he waited.

Donna Giacoma followed close behind. The hermit took the letter from his robe when he saw her coming and unrolled it before her as she sat down.

"I hope you could read my handwriting," she said. "I learned to read and write as a child but haven't had much occasion to do either. Fra Leo insisted he dictate the letter to me, though, rather than to my secretary."

"He had his reasons, though for the present I'm at a loss to understand what they were." With his finger he traced the border around the message. "Did he tell you what any of this meant, the part he wrote himself?"

Donna Giacoma looked curiously at the frame. "I didn't know it was part of the letter. Leo's fingers had become so crippled and he took so long to fashion this that I left him to finish it alone. He had such a peaceful and simple expression while he worked, like a child decorating a love note to his mother. I thought it to be just that—decoration." She squinted where he pointed, but finally shook her head. "Please read it to me. My eyes don't see as clearly as they used to."

"It begins 'Fra Jacoba knows much of perfect submission.'"

The color rose in her cheeks. "He wrote that?"

"Here it is. It stumps me. In my fifteen years in the Order, I've met no Fra Jacoba. Maybe you know of him? You've been as close to the Order as anyone, from the very beginning."

"Oh, that sweet man. I haven't heard the name in years."

"Then you knew Fra Jacoba?"

Her green eyes grew watery. "I *am* Fra Jacoba. Or *was*. San Francesco christened me an honorary friar more than fifty years ago—for the *virility* of my virtue, he said." She laughed. "He compared me to Abraham and Jacob and the other patriarchs of Israel. I know he meant it as the highest compliment, but with two young sons racing around my home at the time, I felt anything but *virile*."

She dabbed at her eyes with her sleeve and smiled. "Pardon my foolishness, brother—my *lack* of virility. Your question unleashed a flood of memories." She worried the folds in her robe for a moment, alternately creasing and smoothing them, working to regain her composure. Conrad took advantage of the pause to recover his also. Leo had tossed another wonder into his lap.

"Well then, teach me about perfect submission," he said in turn.

Her busy fingers settled again on her lap. She stared at them briefly, thoughtfully. "Fra Leo spoke to me of submission—he even *emphasized* the word—during his last visit, the same week he composed this letter. I'd asked him, for the hundredth time, to tell me what he saw on Monte LaVerna the night the seraph impressed the wounds of Christ upon our blessed father's flesh. In all the years I'd known him, in all his letters to me and in our talks, Fra Leo always kept silent about the stigmata—even though he'd been with San Francesco when it happened. This time proved no different. As before, he said nothing, but only repeated the words Francesco used when people asked about his ecstasies: '*secretum meum mihi*,' my secret is my own. What he did confide to me, however, and this for the first time, was that he kept silence *out of holy obedience*. He said Fra Elias took him into his office immediately after our master's death and forbade him ever to discuss the matter."

She twisted on the bench so that she faced Conrad and tilted her head. "Do you make anything of that? It struck me as very odd. Fra Elias spoke so often of the wounds himself after San Francesco passed away."

Again, her eyes brimmed with tears. "Elias fetched me in person and led me into the small hut where our master's soul had just left his body. Francesco's head rested on a pillow I'd brought from Rome, but they hadn't yet wrapped him in his burial shroud. He wore only a loincloth, like Christ come down off the cross, and I saw for myself the nails protruding from his hands and feet and the mark of the spear in his side. His wounds were always bound while he was still alive, so that no one ever saw them but Fra Leo, who tended him and changed his dressings.

"Fra Elias lifted his body off the mat and said to me, 'He whom you loved in life you shall hold in your arms in death.' Miraculously, the body wasn't at all rigid; in fact it seemed suppler than when Francesco still lived, for his members were often contracted and cramped with pain during those last years. I held him easily; he was light as goose down from years of fasting. I understood in that instant how the Magdalene must have felt when she received her dead Lord to her breast—and all the while Fra Elias stood beside me, like the apostle John."

Donna Giacoma's last remark caused Conrad to start. "You draw a very different picture of Elias than Fra Leo did."

"Sadly, Elias changed after the funeral. He loved San Francesco and, while our master yet lived, hovered over him as a mother cares for her ailing child. But our saint had also been his conscience. When his conscience died, he became obsessed with power and greatness, both for his own person and for the Order as a whole."

"The popular tale would have it that he even dealt in the black arts."

"A popular *fiction,* I hope. But you're right. I've heard it said he sought the Philosopher's Stone. When the Order's Protector, Cardinal Ugolino, became pope, he built himself a palace in Assisi, where he might stay when he visited the city. This palace has many hidden chambers and lodgings."

"I've seen it," Conrad said, "but only from outside."

"As the story goes, whenever Fra Elias learned of brothers in the Order who, while they were yet in the world, had delved into the alchemical arts, he sent for them and kept them as virtual hostages in the papal palace. Not only did he force these brothers to continue practicing alchemy, but he had others he consulted—diviners and interpreters of dreams."

Conrad grimaced. "Which is as much as to trust in pythonic oracles." *Such a man wouldn't shrink from a pact with the Evil One*, he thought.

Donna Giacoma frowned. "One incident I can relate to you as fact," she said, "for I was a part of it. Elias infuriated me so that I refused to speak to him thereafter, or to several of our city fathers, except to vent my anger." She fidgeted again with the folds of her habit.

"What did they do?" Conrad asked.

"They betrayed us," she said, "all of us who wanted nothing more than to worship at San Francesco's tomb. For years we made our donations and waited patiently for the lower church of the basilica to be finished, for the day when we could enshrine the sacred relics. When the day came at last, friars converged on Assisi from every province and dozens of cardinals and bishops traveled here besides. We all marched in procession from San Giorgio, and I was even privileged to walk with the brothers of the Sacro Convento.

"We had just entered the piazza across from the upper church when a phalanx of knights charged our ranks. At the same instant, the civil guards snatched the coffin from the brother pallbearers."

Conrad nodded. "Leo told me of this kidnapping. I'd like to hear your version of that dark event."

"What followed was total chaos: Giancarlo di Margherita, our mayor in those days, yelling commands to his guards and knights; the friars at the front of the procession shouting for help, screaming and even cursing the soldiers. Far behind us, I could hear other brothers chanting, for they knew nothing of what was happening at the front. When the friars, including Leo, tried to defend the body, the guards knocked them to the ground. They wounded several, while the knights' horses trampled or kicked many others. I tried to pull off one of the guards myself and caught a gauntlet in the face for my trouble."

Conrad stared anew at the scar on her cheekbone. "Were you injured seriously, Giacomina?" Without thinking, he'd used the diminutive form of her name, just as her steward had. He blushed at his familiarity.

Her faraway expression showed she took no offense. "My cheek bled, opened to the bone in fact, but what hurt me most was seeing the coffin carried off by the guards. They barred themselves inside the church and kept the door blocked while they hid the body. It's never been found. I feel so cheated, not knowing even where to kneel to be close to my master."

"But surely the prelates objected."

"They did, but to no avail. Even the Holy Father, as friendly as he'd been with Elias during his years as Cardinal Protector of the Order, condemned the thieves as insolent barbarians. He compared Giancarlo to the sacrilegious Uzzah, whom God struck down for daring to touch the Ark of the Covenant."

"And all this was Elias' doing?"

"His and Giancarlo's and others. I asked them once, long after that day, *Why did you do this thing?* Giancarlo claimed the procession had gotten out of control and he feared the body would be ripped to shreds by relic seekers. Elias said the Perugians wanted to steal our saint. Their excuses were pure nonsense! Our procession could not have been more peaceful. It was as calm and devout as Sunday mass at the convent of Poor Ladies. And the Perugians had every chance to kidnap San Francesco's body when it rested at San Giorgio for four years. Besides, they'd have had a holy crusade raised against them if they tried. They'd have had to kill every man, woman and child in Assisi before they could escape with the coffin."

"But you said other friars were involved?"

"Not friars. The *signore* of the Rocca and his sons led the knights. I also saw San Francesco's brother Angelo standing with a nobleman inside the church door."

"One you knew?"

"No. I'd seen him once before, when Bishop Guido blessed the building site—before work began on the basilica. Elias pointed him out to me, and described him as a great benefactor. He said the man owned an estate in Todi commune."

"Ah." Conrad closed his eyes and leaned his shoulders against a pillar behind the bench. He laced his fingers on top of his head and pressed down hard while he tried to recall a comment Amata had made at his hut. Something to do with the hillside, the Colle d'Inferno, where the basilica and Sacro Convento now stood. The image of her dark eyes, staring ingenuously into his, interfered with the words, however. He couldn't remember.

Well, no matter. He'd found Fra Jacoba. He'd come a step closer to understanding what Leo meant by *secretum meum mihi*, and that secret had something to do with San Francesco's vision of the seraph on Monte LaVerna.

XIV

SEATED BENEATH THE AUTUMN foliage of Donna Giacoma's courtyard, Conrad rested his open breviary in his lap. The lady hadn't given him any more answers, but she had proved herself more than willing to help in other ways. No sooner had he explained that he must continue on to the Sacro Convento, than she grasped the significance of his shabby appearance. She sent at once for the servant woman who trimmed and shaved the men of her compound, but Conrad wouldn't allow the woman near him. He understood the lesson of Samson's downfall, the danger should a woman touch his head. He also understood the need to reestablish his tonsure, however, and submitted when she offered to hire a male barber from the city.

The man did his job thoroughly, shaving the friar's head and neck, shaping and accentuating the tonsure. Conrad remarked to Maestro Roberto and Donna Giacoma afterward how carefully the barber had even cleaned up the hair clippings from the floor, every single strand so far as the friar could see. The steward burst out laughing.

Donna Giacoma explained. "The man heard you were a close friend of Fra Leo, whom we all revere, and that Leo often praised your sanctity. Now don't blush, brother. Leo thought the world of you.

"This barber, being a person of modest means, merely collected some potential income against the cares of his old age. Should you die and be canonized, those clippings could support him for many years."

"He'd deem it a great favor if you didn't tarry overlong," Roberto added. "Canonization can be a slow process. Our barber has shaved many a friar's head. He saves all your clippings, just in case, and collects them in separate little pots, labeled with markings that only he understands."

The breeze through the inner court where Conrad now read blew cool against his bare neck and cheeks. He closed his breviary, smiling at the man's simple faith—and opportunism. From the shadows, the noblewoman limped toward him, a roll of grey cloth tucked beneath her arm. Apparently, she'd been waiting for him to finish his daily office.

"The townspeople often bring gifts for the brothers to me," she said. "They know you're not allowed to handle money. A lady gave me two *soldi* yesterday, and with them I've bought material for a new robe for you. In return, she asks only for your prayers for the salvation of her soul."

She waited for his response. Conrad shrugged and raised his hands. "I suppose I must have it, and I shall pray for her." He grasped his worn robe by the chest. "But please, Donna Giacoma, keep this old friend here in your house that I might reclaim it when I return to the mountains." He stroked a stitched-up rip on his sleeve with the tenderness of a mother soothing a child's wound.

"Only if I have your permission to launder it. With all due respect to your spiritual disciplines, Fra Conrad, vermin aren't as welcome in this house as they are against your skin."

Conrad nodded and forced a smile. Could this be the same woman San Francesco had praised for her virility? Her concerns could have come from the lips of any common housewife. He rubbed an arm, feeling the prickles and scabs of a hundred tiny bites and sores, those constant chastisements so salutary to the mortification of his flesh.

"Do as you deem best." He tried to relax the tightening in his jaw that had come with each new suggestion for change. His heart rebelled, even as his mind recognized the need for all this camouflage.

Donna Giacoma hesitated before she spoke again. Her tone was almost timid, a marvel in itself, but he understood why when he heard the idiocy of her offer. "The robe should be finished tomorrow," she said. "If you wish, at that time I'll have the servants fill a washtub with warm water for you."

This time she had *really* crossed the line! "*Madonna*, surely in all the time you sat at our master's feet, you must have heard him speak of the depravity and corruption of bathing." Conrad blushed at the nude image of himself that came to mind. "Not only is one exposed to his own nakedness, pardon me for even saying the word, but a weak soul might be tempted to luxuriate in the warm water, give sway to the sensuality of its flow against his skin . . ."

"Say no more, brother. You answer as I thought you would. It would grieve me as much to expose you to temptation, as it would grieve you to expose your insect friends to extinction."

She may have smiled in the shadows, but before he could see her face clearly she had turned and shuffled back down the hallway. She was a good and charitable lady, to be sure, kinder than any he'd known since Rosanna;

but how disappointing that she remained so caught up in the vanity and cleanliness concerns of lesser, more frivolous women.

ON THE FEAST OF Dionysius the bishop and Eleutherius the martyr, the third morning after Conrad arrived at Donna Giacoma's, the harvest fair began in the streets of Assisi. The friar decided to test his altered appearance on the world-at-large. In his new robe and sandals, beardless and nearly bald, he fidgeted like a foreigner in a strange land. Mingling among the people, he might get used to the transformation himself before he moved on to the Sacro Convento.

The fair would last twenty-one days, but the curious of every class already milled through the streets, as thick as stars on a cloudless night. Everywhere Conrad saw serfs in their cleanest tunics, their families huddled wide-eyed around them, dodging the tumbrels and handcarts and donkeys loaded with trade goods, gawking at the wonders displayed through the open fronts of the merchants' stalls. Stewards and reeves would be hard pressed these next several weeks to keep the bondsmen at work on post-harvest chores: repairing harnesses, sharpening scythes and mattocks, hauling firewood and mending roofs.

The serfs would have their excuses ready. Didn't they need salt to preserve their meat? Didn't their wives need to go along, to buy dyes for the little ones' wool cloaks? The women wouldn't be stitching or carding wool or making candles for their mistress' nightstand during the fair either. And somewhere among their small purchases, the peasants would find time to touch a peacock feather or a pink phoenix skin, howl at tumblers and the dancing bear, weep with the balladeers who peddled their rhymes to such as could read. The stewards, who watched it all, could only bemoan the inevitable lost work as they wandered the fair too, loading in supplies for the women's workshop: vermilion and madder for the master's garments, sheep shears, wool combs, spindles, teasels and grease.

While the serfs might shirk their duties these several weeks, the civil guards would be busier than usual. In the shops and pavilions where wine flowed from daylight to dark, brawls inevitably erupted. A loud argument from an open tent just ahead of him reminded Conrad that this was the nature of fairs too.

He peered through the opening, where the wine merchant held up a coin for the others to see. "He sits here and drinks my wine all morning and gives me *this* for payment? It's clipped to but a sliver of its new size. Either you fork over a real denier or by San Niccolo I'll clip *you* upside the ears with this jug."

"*Vaffanculo!*" the peasant slurred. "Your wine's half water anyway, the weakest *vino di sotto* that never slaked a gullet. Half a drink gets half a coin."

The burly man pushed himself to his feet and placed one steadying hand on the table. He aimed the other at the vendor, and to Conrad's horror pointed his index and little fingers in the form of devil's horns. Sighting between the horns, he intoned, "May them that waters wine be manacled in the deepest rung of hell with brimstone smoke blowed in their eyes and be chased by all the fire-eyed curs of Satan across the plains of Hades with a blacksmith's anvil strung through their nuts."

An outcry burst from the other patrons, most taking the side of the wine vendor, for their own drinking had been interrupted. "Crack his skull and throw him out," the man nearest the drunk shouted.

But the peasant had more to say. He raised his voice to drown out the other drinkers, and jabbed his finger at the merchant's supporters. "And may all as has any word of praise for wine thinners be chained with their heads up the devil's arsehole, and the chain locked, and the keys to the lock lost in the deepest bog, there to be retrieved by a blind man with no limbs..."

His curse ended there for the wine dealer leaped at him and shattered the empty jug against his forehead. The man tumbled backward over his bench, doing as much damage to the rear of his head against the pavement as the jug had done to the front. While the others roared approval, the vendor grabbed him by both ankles and dragged him outside the tent, his head bumping along the cobblestones with each jerk and trailing a trickle of blood. "*Proprio uno stronzo*," the wine vendor muttered. "A complete asshole." He left the man groaning in the square at Conrad's feet with his tunic pulled up above his slops, too dazed even to sit.

Conrad bent down for a closer look at the grimy, blood-smeared face. The peasant squinted at him dumbly, trying to block the sunlight with his hand. His eyes bulged open suddenly and he tried to crawl away. "Aiiee! Here's the church already. I'm a dead man for sure."

"I think not. You're in for a miserable headache, but you'll live. Your skull looks hard as a crusader's helmet!"

The man let his body drop and again cracked the back of his head against a paving stone. He winced and closed his eyes.

Conrad knelt beside him and his lips twisted in a sardonic smile. Maybe he *had* been mistaken to withdraw for so long into his wilderness. Maybe Amata *had* been right—anyone could be a saint on a mountaintop. Real saints tested their beliefs helping people like this man from the fair, "serving Christ's poor ones," as Leo had commanded him. For an instant, he glimpsed the prospect of a different vocation for himself, laboring among and preaching to the masses, himself the poorest of the poor. His heart warmed at the image. He could do that—once he'd finished his business at the Sacro Convento. He could say "yes" to, even embrace, the details of so-called real life: the drunken peasant's jerkin spattered with wine and blood, the way Roberto's bushy grey eyebrows met over the bridge of his nose and shadowed his serious face, the ivory bird's beak carved into the grip of Donna Giacoma's cane, Amata's...

There his mind balked, for the thought that came to him was "Amata's long legs," pale, well formed and sturdy, as he remembered them from the morning on the scree, as Enrico must have seen them—and more besides—his last night on earth. There Conrad had to draw the line. If he said "yes" to those legs, or even to the memory of them, he was doomed as surely as the boy from Vercelli.

XV

ONRAD SLEPT RESTLESSLY that night, and long after sunrise his mind still recoiled at the thought of Amata. He paced the great room, stopping to peer out at the new day through the open slats of a shutter. Maestro Roberto strode away through the wall of narrow houses and finally disappeared down a stairwell.

"*Buon giorno, padre*" Donna Giacoma whispered behind him. Once again she'd surprised him, padding silently down the hallway on her bare feet. It was a trick of hers actually, he'd discovered, her little private joke. She had to place her cane very carefully not to be heard. When she didn't care whether she snuck up on him, the tapping of the stick told him she was coming.

She studied his expression. "Are you wondering how you'll be received at the Sacro Convento today?"

Conrad turned to face her. "No, actually, *madonna*. I suppose I was grieving—mourning for a soul who is surely damned. I recently met a ... a clever young woman. Too clever really for her own good." He felt a surge of his former anger again. "A sister whose religious habit in no way interferes with the licentiousness gnawing at her heart." He fairly spit out the last words.

Donna Giacoma's eyes widened and she raised her eyebrows. "A *woman* friend, brother? You must feel a strong concern for her, to speak so heatedly."

"I never said she was a friend!" Conrad objected. "Fortune joined our paths for several days. Actually, she was the servant sister who brought Leo's letter to me."

The noblewoman continued to gaze at him with those large green eyes. She waited to hear more, and the friar realized he wanted to talk just as eagerly. Donna Giacoma motioned him to a high-backed armchair. When she had settled herself, Conrad related as much as he knew of Amata's background.

"I won't speak of her misdeeds, for some was confided in the Sacrament of Penance. Nor will I speak of my suspicions surrounding our night at Sant'Ubaldo, for they're *only* suspicions. But from what I've seen, I feel I can say with certainty that Suor Amata has lost her footing on the slippery path to perdition."

The lady smoothed her lap, a gesture that Conrad had come to recognize as a sign of uneasiness. "My poor brother. How she must have disillusioned you, especially after you two had begun so well."

You *two?* Conrad hadn't thought of Amata and himself as a twosome, but his benefactress had a point. Donna Giacoma had, as it were, reached her hand into the murkier recesses of his spirit and dredged up disenchantment he hadn't recognized himself. It was true. For a time, Amata had literally *enchanted* him. He recalled his feelings when he held her on the ledge of the cliff.

The noblewoman sighed and rested one hand against her chest. "And that hapless child. What she must have suffered the last five years to be so tormented today. She misses her mother so sorely."

Conrad's head snapped upright. He hadn't expected Donna Giacoma to respond with sympathy for the "child," as she called her.

Donna Giacoma pursed her lips at his reaction. "Dear Conrad, I don't doubt for a moment Leo's high opinion of you. Your dedication is rare, even among the brotherhood, and only an extremely presumptuous old lady would try to counsel a man of your spiritual understanding. But, you *have* been much removed from the world. I'm not sure you can fathom how the mass of men and women struggle each day just to survive to the morrow.

"Can you even *begin* to imagine how your Amata must have been brutalized in her captivity, living at the whim of that cruel murderer and his sons? I know such men. I was married to one, and shared a villa with his brothers. These overgrown boys let their pet leopard roam freely in our home, and laughed when it killed and partially ate a serving woman. That woman had four small children who played with my own sons."

Conrad grimaced. "I know Suor Amata conceals a knife beneath her nun's habit."

"And why do you suppose that is?" The noblewoman answered the question herself. "Because she *needs* to! Because she has no one to protect her. Because she's had to learn, from the age of eleven, to defend herself."

"That still doesn't excuse her other behavior."

"Take care how you judge her, brother. Your Amata had her childhood ripped away, cruelly and abruptly. She was denied the normal, carefree affection of a child for years. Mightn't she be forgiven if she's become misguided in her search for that affection now? If our Blessed Savior could forgive the Magdalene, who was older and sinned with full understanding of her actions, if He could forgive the woman taken in adultery and even defend her against the stones of the village men, don't you think you could forgive this poor, deluded girl also?"

Conrad squirmed in his chair. He knew he was on shaky ground and could only worsen his position by trying to rebut the lady.

"Women need love," Donna Giacoma continued. "We need to be held and touched and told we're special among all other women. Yes, you should hear these things, even though your own life is far removed from them. We can't feed on theory and speculation as you men with your stronger intellects do. My lord husband, at times, could be a monstrous man. He left me widowed these sixty years since, and after he died I consecrated my life to God. Yet, after all this time, I sometimes lament the emptiness of my bed. I still miss the proud father of my children as much as I do my sons themselves."

The noblewoman dabbed at her eyes with a handkerchief she pulled from the sleeve of her friar's robe. Then she squared her jaw again and actually managed a chuckle when she saw Conrad's expression. "Close your mouth, *padre*. You'll be swallowing gnats. You miss my meaning, I think. I'm not speaking of carnality. At my age, I hardly remember those moments. I mean companionship, the bond that enables us women to love and forgive the worst of men—which, I believe, we must have learned from our Blessed Savior Himself, for He does no less. You won't find such love described in your theology books, for theologians have no experience of that feeling. It would be like my trying to describe a satyr, which I've neither seen nor touched, although I've heard that such monsters exist."

She took a deep breath and fanned herself briefly with her hand. "You should know too that even the rare independent woman who has the freedom and means to seek out love on her own, rather than have marriage forced upon her, has no guarantee of choosing wisely—especially when she hasn't been steered in her youth by a good, caring, forceful mother. The prospect frightened me half to death after Graziano Frangipane died; I think I chose our heavenly Father to be my next great love from fear as much as from devotion."

Conrad's chin sank against his chest. Donna Giacoma, like Amata, amazed him. Most likely *all* women would *always* amaze an inexperienced man like himself.

And once again he'd been humbled for failing to take into account the weakness, whether one deemed it "carnality" or "love," that made women (and young women particularly) so vulnerable to the lures of the Evil One. As he saw it, the deadly sin of Lust held Amata fast, as it had snared Francesca Polenta before her. What did Amata say during their journey, when they talked of Francesca and her Paolo? "*Is it such a sin to love?*" Dear God, maybe she really didn't know the difference between Lust and the love bond that Donna Giacoma described. But he *shouldn't* judge, either. The lady was right about that. Rather, he should bear in mind that Satan used the deadly sin of Pride as the particular stumbling block to trip up those who presumed to read the consciences of others.

Conrad could sense the hopelessness in his eyes as he returned Donna Giacoma's intense gaze. Had it been only ten days since his life had been all simplicity? "You've given me much to ponder," he replied weakly. "God reward you for opening your home—and your memories—to me."

He hesitated, then asked in a voice that quavered ever so slightly, "If you don't hear from me within two weeks, would you please inquire of the minister general on my behalf?"

Donna Giacoma smiled. "Courage, brother. By now Fra Bonaventura knows you've been my guest, for the friars miss little that passes in this city. He respects me, and would never let harm befall a friend of mine within his walls."

CONRAD HARDLY RECOGNIZED the Piazza di San Francesco. As in every other square of the city, booths and merchandise covered each inch of available space. Well above the clutter of the piazza he could make out the bell tower of the upper church and the delicate stonework that traced the petals of its rose window—the only distinguishable landmarks. He skirted the northern edge of the congestion, passing near the gate through which he and Jacopone had carried the boy the week before. The guard waved as he passed.

"A good morning to you, brother," he called. "Keep us in your prayers today."

Conrad returned the guard's salutation. The man obviously had not recognized him. He continued past the upper church and down the steps to the Sacro Convento. Although a thick layer of clouds blotted the sun, he grew hot beneath his new robe. He began to sweat and the muscles in his calves and thighs became inordinately tired, as though he were back slogging through the quagmire toward Sant'Ubaldo alongside the farmer's cart. He sat down on the steps, contemplating the friary arcade below.

The guard's deferential greeting had left him melancholy, rather than pleased at his respectable appearance. This was not *perfect joy*; nay, rather its antithesis.

Leo must have told the story a half dozen times, of the night he and San Francesco trudged the road from Perugia to the Portiuncola in the dark of winter. Their robes were wet and muddy, and so cold that ice had formed along the bottom hem, striking their bare legs at every step.

"Brother Little Lamb, do you know what perfect joy is?" Francesco asked unexpectedly.

As his mentor later confided to Conrad, they hadn't eaten all day and Leo, who did not share Francesco's gift for fasting, thought a hot stew might come close to the definition at that moment. He'd been wise enough not to admit his frailty to the saint, however. "You tell me, father," he said instead.

"Imagine, brother, that a messenger rides up to us on this road and says that all the masters of theology in Paris have joined the Order. This would not be perfect joy. Or that all the ultramontane prelates have joined, bishops and archbishops, along with the kings of the Franks and Anglos. This would not be perfect joy either. Or that my brothers have gone to the unbelievers and converted them all to the faith, or that I had such grace from God as to heal the sick and perform many miracles. I tell you, Brother Little Lamb, perfect joy would not be in any of these things."

"But what then is perfect joy?"

Francesco replied, "When we come to the Portiuncola, soaked by rain and freezing from the cold, and we knock at the gate of the place and the porter comes and asks angrily, 'Who are you?' And we say, 'We are two of your brothers,' and he contradicts us, saying 'No, you are two rogues who go around deceiving and stealing. Go away!' And he does not open for us, but makes us stand outside in the snow and rain, cold and hungry—then if we endure all those insults and cruel rebuffs patiently, without being troubled and without complaining, and if we reflect that the porter really knows us, and that God makes him speak against us—*Frate Pecorello,* perfect joy is there.

"And if we continue to knock, and the porter comes out in anger, and I insist, 'I am Fra Francesco,' and he says, 'Go away, you simple, uneducated fellow. Don't stay with us any more for we are so many and so important that we no longer need you. Go to the Crosiers' hospice and ask there.' And he takes a club rough with knots and grabbing us by our cowls throws us into the mud and beats us until he covers our bodies with bruises and wounds—and we bear all these evils and take the insults with joy and love in our hearts, reflecting that we must share the sufferings of the Blessed Christ patiently for love of Him—Brother Little Lamb, that is perfect joy and the salvation of the soul!"

CONRAD RUBBED THE fine stuff of his robe between his thumb and forefinger. He'd been much nearer to perfect joy the week before, when the porter at the Sacro Convento had treated him like a rabid cur. If Leo suffered from frailty, *he* was behaving downright cowardly. Wouldn't he do better to march back to Donna Giacoma's, return to the Sacro Convento in his old garment, and leave the consequences in God's hands? In choosing the *practi-*

cal path to gain access to the friar's library, wasn't he behaving just like those expedient brothers he so contemned, those who traded poverty for security, simplicity for scholarship, and humility for privilege? Hadn't Elias claimed *practicality* as his rationale for weakening Francesco's Rule?

Conrad steadied himself against the wall supporting the stairway and continued to the bottom of the steps. He found himself before the carved double doors of the lower church, set deep beneath their arches. A series of fluted columns angled toward the doors on either side to draw the passerby within. Conrad couldn't resist the invitation. He'd find Leo's tomb; his mentor would tell him what to do.

The lower church for the friars' use was darker and more austere than the public basilica that rested on top of it. The small, round-arched windows were designed in the old manner, while the Frankish architect of the upper church had chosen to follow the new, pointed-arch style. Not that the friars' church lacked adornment. Conrad's eye went immediately to the main altar at the far end of the nave, built to resemble a miniature arcade with the main stone floating on a circlet of ornately-columned arches. He'd start his search for Leo there.

He paced around the altar, scanning the tiled floor for signs of recent masonry. His hand rested on the smooth surface of the altar stone as he passed around it, when he encountered a disturbing curiosity. His fingers had traced across a rough spot, a design chiseled into the holy stone. Conrad thought some urchin must have desecrated it. The crude stick figure resembled a child's drawing of a man, arms and legs stretched out stiffly, the head a mere circle—a double ring of concentric circles, actually. A larger circle enclosed the entire figure. Above that outer circle, the vandal had scratched two arches. What a disgrace that children these days neither respected the city's greatest saint, nor even feared the wrath of God Himself!

The friar stared down the length of the nave. The artist Giunta da Pisa had layered events from Francesco's life face-to-face across the nave from corresponding frescoes from the life of Jesus, whom the saint had imitated more completely than any man. In the years since Conrad's last visit, great chunks from the bottom sections of the frescoes had totally vanished. At regular intervals, workmen had knocked out walls to make room for lateral chapels with individual altars. The increased emphasis on scholarship within the Order had created a vast number of priests, and priests needed altars to say their daily masses. Conrad himself had never felt compelled to say mass, believing he could draw nearer to God without the mediation of ritual, but his Conventual brothers predictably kept to the common practice.

He wandered from chapel to chapel until he came full circle back to the south transept and the Chapel of San Giovanni Evangelista. Inscriptions cut into the block walls identified several tombs. Here lay Fra Angelo Tancredi—Santa Clara's cousin—and next to him, Fra Rufino. This last was a surprise. Conrad hadn't heard of Rufino's death. The obituary date said he'd passed away within the year. The last time the friar had visited Leo, his mentor and Rufino shared a tiny cell at the Portiuncola.

"Rest in peace and joy, old friend," he said aloud. Then he saw the marker he sought:

Frater Leone
Qui Omnia Viderat
Obitus
Anno Domini 1271

The inscription was perfect, even ironical: "Brother Leo, who witnessed all." Or, as Conrad preferred to read the words: "Brother Leo, who didn't miss a thing."

He knelt before the marker and touched his forehead against the cold stone. He neither spoke nor thought any specific question, for surely Leo understood his dilemma without the intrusion of words. In this position he remained as the morning advanced, but no answer came. At one point, he caught himself recollecting Leo's assurance that Amata would be a help to him. Perhaps the instant of doubt that accompanied that memory caused Leo's silence now.

His mind drifted to the apostles on their way to Jerusalem with *their* master. They followed, bewildered, for Jesus had just told them He must suffer and die when they arrived in the city. They'd lost sight of their mission, troubled by incertitude and the seeming pointlessness of all that had happened up until that moment. And just when they felt most wearied and beaten down, Jesus appeared before them, transfigured, in the company of two prophets of the ancient days, and they remembered once again Who it was that led them.

Maybe, Conrad thought, he had expected too much. Did he imagine Leo would appear to him in glory, accompanied again by San Francesco—twice in two weeks? Even the apostles had seen the transfiguration but once.

He stumbled to his feet and stretched his muscles. He'd delayed long enough. Let these "three companions"—as Angelo, Rufino and Leo had affectionately been known by the other friars—enjoy their final rest together, even as they'd endured so many hardships together during the Order's infancy. The nickname had become so widely accepted that the brothers called their now-banned memoirs of their days with San Francesco simply the *Legenda Trium Sociorum*, "The Legend of the Three Companions."

The friar whirled suddenly and strode again to Leo's marker. Could it be possible that Bonaventura or some earlier minister general had tortured Leo or one of his friends? *Why was the companion mutilated?* Leo had asked in his letter.

"Please, little father," he prayed, "tell me who among your companions you referred to?" he asked. "How can I find out *why*, when I don't even know *which* of you it was?"

But again, only silence.

ONE OF THE GOOD FRIARS, Donna Giacoma had thought to herself when she watched Conrad head off through the alley. She regretted having upset him, although she also believed it was high time he came out of his isolation. He was so young—a baby really compared to her eighty-two years—so guileless. She'd seen the same naivete, and stubbornness, in San Francesco. Maybe those were the qualities that made such men saints: a divinely inspired single-mindedness that admitted no grey into their black-and-white world of right and wrong.

She pondered too his story of the young woman who'd been so abused. The old woman's vision blurred at the thought; she wanted to cry out in anguish for the lot of the girl-child, of all women, to shriek from pure rage and release the age-old knot in her stomach. Men possessed such power for ruthlessness and destruction, while their wives, children and servants were left to endure the outcomes as best they could.

By the time her steward returned from his errands, Donna Giacoma had decided what she must do. "Maestro Roberto, have Gabriella lay out my blue robe and my wimple. You and I are going to San Damiano. I have business with the Mother Prioress."

The man's forehead creased in surprise. She seldom left her home anymore. "I'll send for a litter," he offered.

"That won't be necessary," she said. "I feel very strong all of a sudden."

XVI

B Y THE END OF THE MORNING, Conrad had been assigned his cell in the priests' dormitory and taken his first meal with most of the other friars in the refectory. Most, but not all. Fra Bonaventura and the chief officials of the Sacro Convento apparently ate elsewhere—most likely at the more lenient table of the infirmary—which suited Conrad perfectly. He wanted to stay as inconspicuous as the limited size of the community allowed, and that meant avoiding direct confrontation with the minister general. The friars dispersed after the midday collation, and he headed for the library.

"Fra Conrad! What an agreeable surprise." A tall friar grasped him by the shoulders and placed a dry cheek against his own. "Peace be with you, brother."

"And with you, Lodovico. I'm pleased to find you're still librarian here. I've seen so many new faces since I arrived, I thought I'd wandered into the wrong friary."

"You'll find new additions to my collection also," the librarian said. Conrad glanced around the room at the stacks; they covered twice the area he remembered. He'd also noted Lodovico's use of "my," the possessiveness that seemed so prevalent in this place.

Despite his cordial welcome, the librarian's leathery brown face remained impassive as a flagstone. Conrad had forgotten the flat nose, the drooping eyelids and unusually high forehead, that made one think Lodovico's mother must have squashed his head while he was yet unborn. His face resembled a mask, an artist's conception of how a man might look, more than actual human features. "Fra Brutto-come-la-Fame," the novices called him behind his back, Brother Ugly-as-Hunger. Lodovico hadn't been in the refectory either, which might explain the girth he'd added during the six years of Conrad's absence.

Compared to the libraries of the larger monasteries of the black monks or the university schools, the chamber above the north arcade at the Sacro Convento seemed hardly more than an afterthought—which it probably was. It doubled as both library and scriptorium and each aperture had its own high writing desk and set of implements. But the tiny windows, made even smaller by the leaded panes criss-crossing them, offered inadequate light for either reading or copying. The writing desks were vacant now, and Conrad guessed the copyists did most of their work before the midday hour of Sext, after which the morning sun no longer struck the library's east-facing wall.

San Francesco hadn't disapproved of knowledge in itself, but he had discouraged learning for his spiritual sons, believing it to be both unnecessary and dangerous: unnecessary because a friar could save his soul without it; dangerous because it might lead to intellectual pride. Elias built the Sacro Convento soon enough after the founder's death that the saint's wishes still carried some influence. Even that worldly friar couldn't have predicted the Order would become one of the most learned institutions in Christendom within twenty-five years.

Conrad himself couldn't resist swelling his chest figuratively, recalling that the Order's lectors at Paris, Oxford and Cambridge, Bologna and Padua included the finest minds in the Church: men like Odo Rigaldi, Duns Scotus and Roger Bacon who could rival even those brilliant preaching friars, Albertus Magnus and Tomas D'Aquino. Not that the friars minor and preaching friars were rivals, despite the secular theologians' jealous attempts to pit the mendicant Orders against one another.

Distracted by his revery, Conrad had missed something Lodovico said. The librarian took his arm and led him toward a wall lined with locked, glass-covered cases, probably reliquaries for treasured manuscripts. Beyond the cases, in the farthest corner of the chamber, stood several tall wooden cupboards, also clasped with iron padlocks.

"Since you were his close friend, I'm sure the note will fascinate you," the librarian continued. "We found it concealed beneath Fra Leo's habit after he died. It was composed, apparently, just after the wounds of Christ were impressed on our blessed master's body."

Several sets of white gloves hung on pegs above the display cases. Lodovico pulled on one pair and gestured to Conrad to follow his example. Unlocking one of the cases, the librarian lifted out a worn sheet and cradled it in his hands. Decades of contact with Leo's body oils had darkened the rough parchment. His mentor apparently had folded it twice before placing it beneath his tunic, for it showed signs of damage along the creases and edges.

The librarian opened the note carefully. It was little more than a fragment, a *chartula* as wide, but barely longer, than a man's hand. Several different scripts covered its two sides in both black and red inks. When he saw that Conrad was having difficulty deciphering it, the librarian read the largest scrawl on the first side aloud:

"The Lord bless you and keep you:
The Lord make his face to shine upon you
and be gracious unto you:
The Lord lift up the light of his countenance
upon you and give you peace."

Conrad recognized the blessing from the Book of Numbers; the Bishop of Assisi had repeated the same words over him when he was ordained into the priesthood. Beneath the Mosaic formula, the writer had added a post-script, "The Lord bless, Frate Leo, thee," and signed the benediction with the Greek letter tau, a cross rising high between the letters of Leo's name.

Conrad held out his gloved hands toward the sheepskin parchment. "May I?" he asked.

The librarian laid the scrap in his hands as gently as one would set a bird's egg in its nest. Conrad carried it to the nearest window. He recognized Leo's minute handwriting on the opposite side. The message appeared to be a hymn of praise, probably dictated by San Francesco to his secretary.

"You are holy, Lord, the only God. You do wonders ... You are Three and One ... You are good, all good, the highest good ... You are love, You are wisdom, You are humility, You are patience, You are beauty, You are inner peace, You are joy, You are justice ... You are eternal life, great and admirable ... Merciful Savior."

While the lauds were magnificent and inspiring, they also disappointed Conrad. Neither message mentioned the vision of the seraph that had inspired this outpouring of praise. He turned the sheet over again, and Lodovico pointed to the series of notes written in a smaller hand with red ink. Two brief sentences above and below the tau testified that Francesco himself had written the blessing and symbol.

"Fra Leo must have added these comments later," the librarian explained. The script might indeed have been Leo's—if anything, even tinier than his mentor's. Lodovico then traced up the fragment with his fingertip, drawing Conrad's attention to the lengthier paragraph, composed in the same red ink and the same hand, above the blessing. Without waiting for a reaction, the librarian began to read aloud again over Conrad's shoulder.

"Blessed Francesco, two years before his death kept a forty-day retreat on

Monte LaVerna in honor of the Blessed Virgin Maria, Mother of God, and of the blessed Archangel Michael. And the hand of the Lord was laid upon him. After the vision and words of the seraph and the impression of the stigmata of Christ in his body, he composed these praises written on the other side of this sheet and wrote them in his own hand, giving thanks to God for the kindness bestowed on him."

Lodovico lifted the parchment from Conrad's hands and repositioned it in its reliquary. Conrad trailed behind him, pondering both the paragraph Lodovico had just read and the librarian's eagerness to show it to him.

"It's rather odd, don't you think, brother?" he said.

"What's that, Conrad?"

"The praises. They're in a different hand than the blessing of Leo. They're obviously dictated, yet the person who added this note said they were in San Francesco's own hand. It makes me wonder whether the friar who took the dictation, whom I should imagine was Fra Leo, and the friar who wrote in the red ink, weren't two different men."

Lodovico stiffened and leaned over the reliquary, his eyes close to the parchment. For the first time, Conrad thought he detected a twitch in the mask, a grimace that pulled down the corners of the broad lips into the slightest hint of a frown, a minuscule chink in the librarian's armor.

Before Fra Lodovico could reply, Conrad added, "Perhaps you'd direct me to the chronicles of our Order?"

HIS TRANSITION BACK into the Sacro Convento had gone smoothly—almost too smoothly, as Conrad remarked to Donna Giacoma two days later. They shared soup in the noblewoman's kitchen while he recounted the events of his return. He was grateful, both for the hot liquid and the large fireplace. The autumn days had become almost as cold as the nights, and the oilskin windows of Donna Giacoma's house offered only a scant barrier to the weather. Maestro Roberto had set the framed inserts into the window openings just moments before, but Conrad guessed the winter would be hard on the old woman despite the oilskins and tapestried walls and numerous fireplaces.

"The porter who was so arrogant to Sior Jacopone and me last week couldn't have been more gracious," Conrad said between swallows of broth. "Granted, he might not have recognized me. But none of the friars disturb me, or ask anything of me. I feel, how shall I say it—invisible. Something's false about the way they're treating me, or maybe I should say, *not* treating me."

"Nonsense," Donna Giacoma said. "I've told you, you worry too much, brother. Bonaventura won't trouble you. But have you learned anything that adds meaning to Fra Leo's letter? I've been puzzling it over in my mind since the day you showed it to me."

"Nothing yet."

He told her then of San Francesco's note to Leo, and added, "I also found a copy of the letter Elias sent to all the provincial ministers after our master's death," he added. "I copied passages of it." He took a roll of notes from his robe. "Even I must confess it's a beautiful message. It was too long for me to transcribe in its entirety, but this part I found particularly moving for it describes the effects of the vision on LaVerna:

"I take this occasion to communicate to you very joyful news—a new miracle. Never yet has anyone heard of such wondrous signs except in the case of the Son of God, who is Christ the Lord.

"For, a long time before his death, our Brother and Father Francesco was visibly crucified; he bore on his body the five wounds, the genuine stigmata of Christ. His hands and feet were pierced through as by nails; they retained these wounds and showed the black color of nails. His side was opened as by a lance and bled frequently.

"As long as his soul still was in his body, he was not handsome of appearance; his countenance was unattractive, and none of the members of his body was spared acute sufferings. ...But now that he has died, he is lovely to behold, he shines with a wonderful brilliance, and he causes all who look upon him to rejoice..."

Conrad's throat constricted and he stopped reading. He looked up as he cleared his throat, and saw that the noblewoman rubbed at her eyes with a fingertip. "That's just how I saw him the night I held him in my arms," she said, "skin as white as ivory." Then she added, "Do you hear the love in those words, brother? Elias wasn't always a monster."

She stood up, but motioned to the friar to keep his place. "I have a letter to share with you, too. Wait here where it's warm while I fetch it."

The noblewoman returned a short time afterward carrying a single sheet in her free hand while she worked her cane with the other. "This too was given to Fra Leo by San Francesco. He wanted me to have it, in thanks for the small favors I showed him. As you'll see, Leo's gift far outweighs anything I might have done on his behalf."

She laid the parchment on the table in front of Conrad. It seemed in better condition than the note at the library, although it was also soiled by brown finger marks. If anything, the letter confirmed—even more than the blessing —the saint's special affection for his closest companion.

"Frate Leo, wish your brother Francesco health and peace.

I speak to you, my son, as a mother. I place all the words we spoke on the road in this phase, briefly and as advice. And afterwards, if it is necessary for you to come to me for counsel, I say this to you: In whatever way it seems best to you to please the Lord God and to follow His footprints and His poverty, do this with the blessing of God and my obedience. And if you believe it necessary for the well-being of your soul, or to find comfort, and you wish to come to me, Leo, come!"

Here was a true love letter. Conrad could well imagine Leo's agony during some period of separation from his master, and how this message from San Francesco must have eased his bleeding spirit.

"Fra Lodovico would be ecstatic to have this in his collection," he said.

"I've thought as much. I know my time here is short, and I want this jewel mounted where it will receive proper reverence. I'm considering donating it to the Poor Ladies at San Damiano, though—in return for a special boon."

Conrad clapped his hands. "Ha! Perfect, *madonna*. That would surely be Leo's preference, if someone other than you is to have it. The Poor Ladies put today's friars to shame in their obedience to our Rule."

"I'm happy you agree, brother." She smiled as she rolled up the letter, and stared at him with a calm, green-eyed abstraction that left him baffled.

THE MUSTINESS OF THE LIBRARY made Conrad want to sneeze. What a contrast to the sea smells that wafted up the hillside from Ancona to his hermitage. Still, the odors of ink and bookbinder's glue, the soft touch of the manuscripts as he fondled their leather covers in his hands, the aisles of Latin titles divided neatly by category, made Conrad somewhat wistful for his student days. He appreciated the total silence of the library, too, where he browsed undisturbed and almost alone among the stacks.

Oddly enough, it was while he foraged in a bookcase sagging with eclectic groupings of guidebooks that Conrad found the first hint of anything pertaining to Leo's letter. Clustered with prescriptions for victory in the crusades were works like David von Augsburg's *De inquisitione* and Jacopo dei Capelli's *Summa contra haereticos*, describing the proper duties and behavior of those inquisitor friars who now numbered in the hundreds. Conrad thumbed through illuminated guides for preachers also: Servasanto da Faenza's *Liber de Virtutibus et Vitiis, Dormi Secure*, and numerous books of examples, all seemingly drawn from fables, bestiaries, and romances—generally vivid but, to Conrad's mind, hardly edifying. How could the sermonizers believe their parables of unicorns and dragons and antelopes raised their listeners' minds to God? San Francesco, like Jesus himself, preached with homely examples. "A sower went out to sow his seed," images common people could understand.

The shelf that most appealed to Conrad were the spiritual guides, however, for he discovered there two books by his university master, Gilbert de Tournai. Most of the manuscripts in this section focused on the crucifixion and appealed to the emotions, but some showed rational Germanic minds like von Augsburg's *De Exterioris et Interioris Hominis Compositione*. Lodovico had set aside two entire shelves for guidebooks authored by the prolific

Bonaventura himself and finally, among these, Conrad picked out a short treatise *De Sex Alis Seraphim*, "Concerning the Six Wings of the Seraph."

True to his logical mind and scholarly training, Bonaventura described how each of the six wings represented a stage of spiritual development. Conrad admired his clever use of a symbol that held special significance among the brotherhood. What startled Conrad was finding the same image used again and repeatedly in the next of Bonaventura's books that he picked up.

"While I was on Monte LaVerna . . . there came to mind the miracle that occurred to blessed Francesco in this very place: the vision of a winged Seraph in the form of the Crucified. . . . I saw at once that this vision represented our father's rapture in contemplation and the road by which this rapture is reached."

The image of the seraph clearly held a special fascination for Bonaventura. But what had he meant when he used the verb *effingere* when he wrote, "this vision *represented* our father's rapture in contemplation?" Hadn't San Francesco experienced an actual vision? Was the entire story only a symbolic representation? Surely not, but...

Coming from another author, Conrad might bring himself to ignore such a seemingly trivial blurring of distinctions, but Bonaventura had an extremely legalistic mind. He too had served for a time as lector at the friar's school in Paris, the contemporary and friend of Tomas d'Aquino. He did *not* select words carelessly. Conrad carried the book to a writing desk and took out his notes. He wondered how many Ave Marias he might pray this time before Lodovico strolled by. He'd discovered during his first day in the library that scribbling on scraps of parchment drew Lodovico to his elbow as swiftly and powerfully as iron to a lodestone.

And pat he comes, Conrad thought. The librarian's sandals skimmed the tiles behind him. "Ah, the *Itinerarium mentis in Deum*," Lodovico said as he scanned the desk with apparent disinterest. "An excellent work. Fra Bonaventura would be pleased to know you've become such a student of his writings."

Which I'm sure you'll report to him at supper, Conrad mused. He felt a sudden need to reread the minister general's biography of San Francesco. He wanted another look at this seraph. Should he, in the process, come across the blind man mentioned in Leo's letter, so much the better.

XVII

AT THE FIRST GLIMMER of dawn, Conrad hurried with the copyists to the library. The hours of available sunlight dwindled with each passing day as the calendar sped toward Santa Lucia's Eve, the longest night of the year.

The friar steered directly to the shelves that held the chronicles of the Order's beginnings. To his disappointment, they contained but a few brief lives of the Order's uncanonized saints, Thomas of Eccleston's history of the first friars in Anglia, and a similar chronicle by Giordano di Giano describing the Order's expansion into Germany. Nothing about Umbria, the cradle of the entire movement, a gap that Leo's hidden manuscript would fill perfectly.

Copies of Bonaventura's *Legenda Major* took up the rest of the shelf space. The scribes working at the tall desks duplicated the same work—a side effect of the infamous edict of 1266. Besides banning the earlier legends, the provincial ministers had decreed that each house of the Order should have at least one copy of Bonaventura's history. Periodically, the motherhouse sent out Brother Visitors to friaries in the provinces, and each Visitor led a pack mule carrying these copies. From what Fra Leo had told Conrad, the Visitors in Elias' day should have been called "Brother Extractors," for they came back to Assisi with their sumters burdened with treasures extorted from those provincial ministers who wished to keep their positions—everything from golden goblets to precious salt fish bound in canvas.

Lodovico had pasted a copy of the edict to the *Chronicles* bookcase. Each time he passed it, Conrad simmered with indignation for all those first-generation friars who, in effect, had been rebuked for their honesty.

"The General Chapter orders under obedience that all the Legends of the Blessed Francesco which have been made should be deleted, since the Legend made by the Minister General has been compiled as he received it from the mouth of those who were always with blessed Francesco and had certain knowledge of everything."

From the mouth of those who were always with Francesco? Certainly not Leo's—nor Rufino's, nor Angelo Tancredi's, nor any of the inner circle of intimates.

Conrad first learned of the edict four years after its publication when he visited Leo in 1270, the year before his mentor died. Leo thought Bonaventura's official Legend a disaster, a portrait of a plaster saint remote from the real world, perched high in an inaccessible niche where the people no longer could touch him—a distortion of the Francesco he had followed. This was not the vital being who in his youth led the spring revelries through the streets of Assisi as King of the Tripudianti, who frittered his indulgent father's money to keep current with the latest fads and fashions. The wastrel, the troubadour, the jester had been "deleted;" only the miracle worker remained.

"They've sucked his blood and his spirit," Leo ranted. "They've leeched him like physicians, as if his humanity were some deadly poison that must be drained to preserve his sanctity. All the Spiritual brothers are in mourning."

But they weren't *just* mourning. Leo confided that many of the exiles had hidden the manuscripts in their possession; the Poor Ladies of San Damiano had done likewise. That was when he asked Conrad to preserve and copy his own chronicle of the Order. While Leo's manuscript did not contain the answers Conrad sought now, it was clearly an important link to the Order's past. Conrad shuddered now, recalling that only he and Amata knew of the scroll's existence. He must tell Donna Giacoma at his next opportunity, in case some harm should befall him and prevent his return to the hermitage. The girl couldn't be relied upon and, in any case, she was confined once again (thanks be to God) to her convent.

With all these conflicts swirling through his brain, Conrad opened the *Legenda Major*. He prayed to the Holy Spirit for the grace of wisdom and understanding, and turned directly to the thirteenth chapter, the chapter of the seraphim.

CAPUT XIII

ON HIS SACRED STIGMATA

"Two years before he gave his spirit back to heaven, Francesco was led apart by divine providence to a high mountain called LaVerna. There he began a forty-day fast in honor of San Michaelo Archangelo. ...

"Through divine inspiration he learned that if he opened the Gospels, Christ would reveal God's will for him. After praying with much devotion, he took the Gospel book from the altar and had his companion, a devout and holy friar, open it three times in the name of the Blessed Trinity. Each time it opened at the Lord's passion, and so Francesco understood he must be conformed to Christ in the affliction and sorrow of his passion. ...His body had already been weakened by the great austerity of his past life and continual carrying of the Lord's cross, but he was inspired more than ever to endure any martyrdom. ...

"About the feast of the Exaltation of the Holy Cross, while he prayed on the mountainside, Francesco saw a seraph with six fiery and shining wings coming down from the heavens. The vision descended swiftly and came to rest in the air near him. Then he saw between the wings the image of a man crucified, his hands and feet nailed to a cross ... Francesco was dumbfounded ... overjoyed at the way Christ looked upon him so graciously under the appearance of a seraph, but the fact that He was fastened to a cross pierced his soul with a sword of compassionate sorrow.

"As the vision vanished, it left in his heart a marvelous ardor and impressed miraculous markings upon his body. ... His hands and feet appeared pierced through the center by nails, the heads of which were in the palms of his hands and on the instep of each foot, while the points stuck out on the opposite side. ...His right side seemed as if it had been pierced with a lance and was marked with a red wound that often bled, staining his tunic and undergarments.

"When Christ's servant realized he could not hide the stigmata imprinted so visibly on his body, he was thrown into an agony of doubt. ... He called some of the friars and asked them in general terms what he should do. One of them, who was called Illuminato, was enlightened by grace and realized some miracle had occurred because the saint was still dazed. He said to him, 'Brother, remember that when God reveals divine secrets to you, it is not for yourself alone, but also intended for others.' The holy man often said, *Secretum meum mihi, my secret is my own*, but when he heard Illuminato's words, he described the vision in detail, adding that the one who appeared to him had told him a number of secrets which he would never reveal to any man as long as he lived."

Conrad glanced up from his notes to see Fra Lodovico puttering in the bookcase nearest his desk. "Can you tell me, brother," he asked, "why the name '*Illuminato*' rings familiar? Did he have an important role in the early history of our Order?"

"I think you'll find your answer in the ninth chapter," the librarian said. "Fra Illuminato accompanied San Francesco when he sailed for Egypt. He traveled with our master when he tried to convert the Sultan and as he made his way back home through the Land of Promise."

"Where San Francesco contracted the eye disease that caused his blindness?"

"So I've heard said. The bright sun of the Holy Land must have struck his eyes directly."

Lodovico drifted back to his bookcase. Conrad added to his notes a sentence from Leo's letter. *"The first of Tomas marks the start of blindness,"* he wrote, and underscored it three times. He chewed on his thumbnail and tapped his quill on the desk. Could it be that Francesco himself was Leo's "blind man?" But where did his blindness begin, if not in the East?

While he stared at the single sentence, the scribe at the desk in front of him, a friar no older than he, swung his immense haunches around on his stool and blinked at Conrad through watery pink eyes. "I heard you ask about Fra Illuminato," he said.

The man wiped his eyes, which seemed constantly irritated, while he spoke. "Just last week, I overheard some of the older brothers talking about this Illuminato. One mentioned that he served as Fra Elias' secretary after Elias was elected minister general."

Conrad's breathing almost stopped. In Elias' day, the role of secretaries like Illuminato—and Leo before him—was still described by the antiquated term "amanuensis." The age of Zefferino's road companion, as Amata had sketched him, and the name by which the pikesman identified the man, seemed to connect.

Lodovico, who hadn't moved more than a few steps away from Conrad's desk, hurried to rejoin the conversation. "The brother is right. I'd forgotten that fact about Fra Illuminato."

Perhaps Illuminato had also been the friar whom Bonaventura consulted to create his Legend, Conrad thought, one of those who were *"always with the blessed Francesco and had certain knowledge of everything."* How curious that Bonaventura should mention *him* by name in this chapter, but not name the friar who opened the scriptures for Francesco, who'd surely been Leo.

"Is Fra Illuminato still living?" Conrad asked.

"Yes, although naturally he's quite old," the librarian said.

"Old enough to need a donkey when he travels?"

Fra Lodovico smiled benignly. "I doubt he goes anywhere anymore."

"Not so, brother," the younger friar interrupted. "He passed through Assisi just a week ago and stopped to confer with Fra Bonaventura. That's how his name came up in the brothers' conversation. It's too bad you missed him, Fra Conrad."

"Yes. Too bad," Conrad said. "But my thanks anyway to you both for your help."

"That's enough idle gossip, brother," the librarian added. "You keep Fra Conrad from his work and shirk your own with your prattle."

The chastised friar lowered his eyes. "Yes, brother." He swung around again on his stool and bent once more over his desk.

Then this Illuminato does travel still, despite Lodovico's doubts. And if he is the old man Amata met, which now seems more than likely, Bonaventura already knows as much as a trained secretary could remember of Leo's letter.

With the conversation disrupted for the moment, the librarian went back to his tasks, still keeping an eye on the talkative scribe. Conrad turned again to his notes on the vision of the seraph. He underlined a single word from Bonaventura's long passage: *Illuminato.*

XVIII

*A*VANTI! *A VANTI*, YOU STUBBORN *ciuco.*" Illuminato prodded his donkey with his sandals and switched at its rump. The higher they climbed above Lake Trasimeno and the placid valley of the Chiana, the more recalcitrant the animal became. Up ahead Illuminato saw the proud Etruscan citadel of Cortona. Sinister in its arrogance, isolated and menacing among its glacial mountains, Cortona had been an apt backdrop for Fra Elias' last years as an outcast. Despite Illuminato's warnings against overreaching, Elias had exalted himself like a worldly prince with his fat, big-boned palfreys, his secular youth in multicolored livery who waited on him like bishops' pages, his delicate meals prepared by a personal cook. Aided in his ambition by the torturing skills of his dungeon master, he had grasped for absolute power over the brotherhood. A decade later, the brothers, with help from the pope, had dragged him to his knees.

While Illuminato lurched to the jerky rhythm of the donkey, he reflected that Bonaventura could have taught Elias much about tempering ambition with patience. The current minister general would rise higher in the Church hierarchy than any friar ever had, but when he was elevated, maybe to the papacy itself, it would be at the insistence of the princes of the Church.

Illuminato too had waited, while the wheels of the years ground slowly and ever more finely. *My reward shall be equally secure.* Bonaventura had promised as much when the old priest told him of Leo's message to Conrad.

In the city's main piazza, Illuminato dismounted and waved to two boys hopping about the square. They seemed oblivious to the wind flapping their ragged tunics. *"Fratellini,* I need help up the street," the priest called. "God will reward you if you get me and my donkey up to the church."

The urchins eyed him with curiosity and one addressed him in an inarticulate gibberish. Illuminato responded to the local dialect with a series of gestures, holding his back, pointing up the steep street, and repeating *"Chiesa, chiesa,"* At last they understood, and approached him shyly.

Above the city Elias had constructed a smaller version of the basilica he'd built in Assisi. Even after the pope banished him from the Order, even after he'd gone over to the side of the Empire and shared in Frederick's excommunication, Elias persisted in wearing the grey tunic of the friars, as did the dozen or so brothers who remained loyal to him. When he retired at last to Cortona, he tried to reproduce a particle of his past glory, building a friary and church bearing the same name, even the same facade, as the famed basilica. He also built a stone hermitage for himself. Somehow, he'd managed an act of deathbed contrition, been absolved by the local priest and been buried in that church. Illuminato reflected: *I might be the first pilgrim ever to seek out the tomb of a fallen minister general.*

Coming to Cortona hadn't been his idea. He'd agreed, however unwillingly, to Bonaventura's suggestion that this outpost would be an ideally remote spot for him to wait for his appointment. It wouldn't do to have Conrad questioning him. One more grinding revolution of the wheel before his ambition could be fulfilled.

But what a prize it would be: *Bishop of Assisi.* Stationed in the bishop's palace close to the Sacro Convento, he could still satisfy his hunger for involvement in the Order's politics and the insider information that went with it. He'd seriously believed for a time that he'd been sent to die of boredom at his previous post: father confessor to a convent of Poor Ladies, nodding gravely (or nodding half-asleep) while those innocent souls recited their litanies of peccadilloes. But through a stroke of luck—his chance encounter with the boy on the road outside Ancona—he'd thrust himself into the center of a potential whirlwind. He could feel the blood pulsing with renewed vigor through his aged veins. Bonaventura had grasped at once the import of Leo's letter, the danger it represented to the credibility of the Order. Initially, the general reacted to the news with characteristic *sang-froid.* "Let Conrad come," he said, unperturbed, while he slowly twisted the ring on his finger. "He'll leave knowing as little as when he arrived."

"And if he somehow stumbles onto the truth?"

"In that case, he'll not leave at all."

But then Illuminato had to tell Bonaventura the rest of his tale, how he'd taken the liberty of ordering Conrad's detention should he pass through Gubbio. His heart sank momentarily when he saw Bonaventura's forehead ripple. But then the high brow smoothed again. The minister general tapped his fingertips and rang the bell on his desk. His secretary, Bernardo da Bessa, must have been waiting just outside the room, for he entered immediately with his wax tablet and stylus in hand.

"Fra Illuminato, repeat what you just told me. Give Fra Bernardo also the notes you made at Fossato di Vico, your recollections of Leo's letter."

After the secretary had finished, the minister general repeated his thanks and stated that Illuminato's quick action would not go uncompensated. The Bishop of Assisi had recently gone to his reward, and the position remained vacant pending the coronation of the new pope. Bonaventura already had on his desk a letter to the pope requesting that one of his own friars be installed in this secular post. "Tebaldo Visconti da Piacenza is a personal friend. We share the same view of the shortcomings and corruption of the secular clergy. He would prefer to see more friars in these positions of power." Illuminato's heart soared when the minister general implied that he, with his years of wisdom, not to mention his patent understanding of the need to quell disharmony within the Order, would be the perfect friar to fill the vacancy. As minister general, he would be pleased to state as much in a postscript to his letter.

But Bonaventura had made his promise before the dead boy showed up at the front gate of the Sacro Convento. The incident might have passed, unexplained, had not a group of friars carried in Fra Zefferino later the same day, parched with thirst, half-blinded and raving about a vengeful angel with flaming eyes. The boy had some connection to that wrathful spirit. The wounded friar also babbled that Conrad, thanks to the miraculous inter-vention, had evaded capture. Then, worse still, two more brothers arrived from the Order's house in Gubbio looking for a missing brother.

"He's dead," Zefferino said flatly when Illuminato led the two friars to the infirmary. He glared at Illuminato with his good eye. "Murdered by that harmless little courier who carried the letter to Conrad. Thus are we paid for our efforts this week, eh brother?" Illuminato chose to say nothing of Bonaventura's promise.

All the following week the old priest steered clear of the minister general. Bonaventura hated any disruption in the smooth operation of the Sacro Convento, and that included the death and mutilation of postulants and friars. Finally, though, Illuminato couldn't avoid his superior. Bonaventura sent for him.

"Conrad is in Assisi," he said. "He's staying with the widow Frangipane and we expect him to show up here any day. Your donkey is well rested. I recommend you pay your respects at the tomb of your late master. No doubt he could use your prayers."

"But what of the bishopric?"

"I'll send word to you in Cortona when the time is right."

Illuminato had no choice but to genuflect, kiss Bonaventura's engraved ring, and take his leave. As he rose from his knee, however, he tapped the lapis lazuli, gleaming in its golden setting.

"I'm sure you understand that Conrad's at least an indirect threat to the Brotherhood of the Tomb?"

"I've considered that," Bonaventura replied, "although the letter, as you've repeated it to me, doesn't point in that direction."

Now, as he neared the end of his journey, Illuminato felt more like an exile than a future bishop. Leaning for support on one of the small boys while the other led his donkey and kept up a steady jabber in their wild dialect, the priest climbed the twisting streets to the church. He repeated the blessing on his helpers as he tied up his animal, and went inside to find someone who could guide him to Elias' tomb.

The nave of the church loomed cold and dark and empty as a cavern. He shuffled through the dank interior toward the single oil lamp burning in the transept and rapped on the side door that connected to the friary. The sloe-eyed brother who answered looked as worn and musty as the church itself.

"*Per favore*, brother, show me the tomb of Fra Elias," Illuminato asked.

The friar shrugged. "*Un momento.*" He disappeared back into the friary, then returned with a lantern. "Follow me."

The man led Illuminato behind the main altar and into a back room that appeared to be used for storage. Choir stalls had been pushed haphazardly against the walls. Piles of musty manuscripts covered and overflowed a table in the middle of the room. The friar kicked aside a mound of sheets beneath the table, raising a thick cloud of dust. Finally he went down on all fours and brushed at one of the large stone tiles. The square was inscribed with Elias' name.

"Here," the friar said.

Here? This doddering fool of a friar had nothing more to say than *here?* How could it be—the masterful ruler of men whom Illuminato had served for a dozen years, whose political skill and architectural genius the entire civilized world had once admired—gathering layers of dirt beneath a table? The priest's stomach roiled at the indignity of Elias' end.

"Does no one even guard his bones?"

"Ha. That'd please his conceited soul, to think his bones worth coveting. No, they aren't here anyway. After he died, a brother *custode* hauled them from the church and threw them onto the hillside out back. They were carried off by wolves." The friar chuckled grimly. "If you want to find his unholy relics, seek out the white powder in the nearest heap of rotting wolf turds."

The man gazed up at Illuminato. Neither his face nor his voice betrayed the slightest emotion as he added, "*Sic transit gloria mundi.* Fame is fleeting, Brother."

"I CAN'T SAY I EVER KNEW Fra Illuminato," Donna Giacoma answered Conrad. "There were so many friars, even in the early days. I don't remember hearing his name among those who came with San Francesco to Rome." She sat before the fire in the main hall of her home, a wolf-skin lap robe across her knees, her face content in the dancing firelight.

"But later," the friar asked, "when he served Elias?"

"As I told you, I hardly ever spoke to Fra Elias after he hid San Francesco's relics."

Conrad held his notes toward the light while he continued to fumble through the sheets. He glanced up as Pio entered the room carrying a plate of pastries. "Mamma insisted I bring these while they were still hot, *madonna.*"

The noblewoman smiled and gestured toward her guest. "Our master's favorite," she said as the servant boy extended the plate to Conrad. "Marzipan. I carried a small chest of these cookies with me to Assisi when I heard of San Francesco's condition, along with the material for his burial shroud. He loved the almond flavor, and for him I baked them in the shape of a cross." The cat eyes sparkled joyfully at the memory. "Today, cook baked halos, in honor of the upcoming Feast of All the Saints."

Conrad took one of the treats and allowed the sugar to melt for a moment on his tongue before he began chewing. He'd much to learn about true asceticism if a saint like Francesco saw munching cookies as no slackening of his fervor. For his own part, he had to admit that cook's endless variety of delicacies might have as much to do with the frequency of his visits to Donna Giacoma's home as the noblewoman's trove of memories. He liked the notion that his cravings might somehow link him more closely with San Francesco. He brushed the crumbs from his notes into the fire and continued searching until he came to another section of Bonaventura's Legend.

"Here's a second description of the stigmata, from the time of Francesco's death. Bonaventura writes of a knight named Giancarlo. I wondered if he might be the mayor you mentioned, the one who helped Elias carry off the saint's body." He translated the Latin:

"In his blessed hands and feet could be seen the nails miraculously formed out of his flesh by God ... so embedded in the flesh that, when they were pressed on one side, they immediately jutted out further on the other. ...The wound in his side, which was not inflicted on his body nor the result of any human action ... was red, and the flesh contracted into a kind of circle, so that it looked like a most beautiful rose. The rest of his skin, which before inclined to be dark, both naturally and from his illness, now became a shining white, prefiguring the glory of the bodies of the saints in heaven. ...

"One of those allowed to see the body of San Francesco was an educated and prudent knight named Giancarlo. Unbelieving like the doubting Apostle

Tomas, he fervently and boldly, in the full sight of the friars and many towns-people, did not hesitate to move the nails and to touch the saint's hands, feet and side. As he felt the marks, the wound of doubt in his own heart and the hearts of others vanished."

Donna Giacoma nodded. "That would be Giancarlo di Margherita—a brazen man, even before the people named him mayor. I remember the scene well; he stood out in his scarlet toga and ermine cloak." She closed her eyes. "Yes, and he wore a cap of vair—a banty cock among cat birds, all preened and puffed out among the friars in their grey tunics. For years afterward, he talked of this experience. He became a tireless champion of the stigmata against all doubters."

"*Doubters?* There were doubters?"

"Oh yes, many. Doubt, not unmixed with jealousy, especially among the other Orders. But of course they hadn't seen what we had."

Conrad caressed his naked chin. "I missed my chance to talk with Il-luminato. Do you know if this Giancarlo still lives?"

"That I can't say. He retired to his country estate in Fossato di Vico almost two decades ago. I've not seen him in Assisi since, nor heard any word of him."

Conrad collected his notes and clutched them with both hands against his chest. He closed his eyes, waiting for inspiration, while the red flicker continued to dance through his eyelids. Nothing. Still nothing but questions, as puzzling as ever.

"I want you to safeguard these notes for me," he said finally. "Someday, these fragments will speak to me with one voice and all will be clear, but not yet. Tomorrow I plan to ask Fra Lodovico for 'the first of Tomas,' and I don't know how he'll respond. I may be treading on swampy soil or standing on top of an earthquake. Or, God willing, I may somehow bridge the void that remains here."

Maestro Roberto tiptoed into the hall while Conrad spoke. "*Scusami,* Giacomina. The room's ready for your inspection as soon as you're free."

"Excellent. *Grazie,* Roberto."

She turned her serene gaze on Conrad. "I don't know whether I told you that both of my sons died childless. I never had grandchildren. It's a sorry fate to outlive your offspring.

"All this time I've left their old room unopened and untouched. For me, it became a maelstrom that sucked the joy from my own breast each time I entered. That's about to change, however. I've had it cleaned and whitewashed."

Conrad waited for her explanation, but she was evidently in an enigmatic humor. She said only: "We all have our voids to fill."

"THE FIRST OF TOMAS? Certainly, brother."

Conrad sank onto his stool, dumbfounded, while Lodovico went to fetch the text. This was too easy. The librarian reacted as though he heard the request every day.

Lodovico returned lugging a massive tome. As he set it down in front of Conrad, the desk creaked and swayed on its spindly legs. "I can't imagine how you knew I had this, but you're welcome to see it. It's my newest acquisition. We received one of the first copies only because of Fra Bonaventura's personal friendship with Tomas when they both taught in Paris."

The explanation perplexed Conrad. Was the minister general old enough to know Tomas da Celano? *Possibly.* But Conrad hadn't heard that Tomas ever taught, or even spent time, in Paris. He smiled vaguely as the librarian turned away, then raised the leather cover of the book and scanned the title sheet:

SUMMA THEOLOGICA
auctore Tomas de Aquino
and beneath the title, in smaller letters: *Liber Primus.*

The *first book* of Tomas d'Aquino's *Summa.* Conrad groaned. That fox Lodovico. No wonder he'd been so accommodating. He'd been prepared for Conrad's request. Apparently Fra Illuminato had remembered well and had passed on that part of Leo's message.

The friar spread his fingers, measuring the thickness of the work. Reading the entire book could take the rest of the autumn. *But I can play your game,* he thought. *I have time. And patience.* And who was to say this *wasn't* the Tomas whom Leo meant him to read? He surely had heard of d'Aquino's work before he died. Maybe it was spiritual or theological blindness he meant, not a blind *man* at all. With a protracted sigh, he turned to the text and began:

FIRST PART
TREATISE ON GOD
Question I
The Nature and Extent of Sacred Doctrine
(In Ten Articles)

Conrad stared through the leaded panes of the window. Despite the haze filming the ocher fields far below, he located the fork where the River Chiagio joined the Tiber winding its way toward Rome. His mouth opened in a wide yawn. In two months there'd be no question about the identity of the blind man. That man would be himself!

XIX

"IC VOBIS, AQUATILIUM *avium more, domus est.*"

"Holiness?" Orfeo turned to the pope, who stood beside the ship's captain under a white silk awning. Tebaldo Visconti lowered the scented pomander that partially hid his face.

"Do you know the poets, Orfeo?" Tebaldo asked.

"Only such as I learned in childhood."

"Cassiodorus wrote of this city, '*floating on the waves like a sea bird.*'"

The mariner shaded his eyes and peered beyond the swells hissing past the prow to the city on the horizon. He didn't see the resemblance. If Venice must be compared to anything, he thought it should be a moored treasure chest that refused to sink despite the repeated efforts of emperors and neighboring powers to stave it in. When Charlemagne's son Pepin once threatened to cut off the Venetians' food supply, the scornful citizens answered his warning by slinging loaves of bread at Pepin's troops.

"The beginning of your welcome," the captain said, pointing out over the water. A flotilla of galleys, racing before the wind with squared spars and fully billowed sails rushed to close the remaining leagues between the pope's convoy and the harbor behind them. Thick as anchovies they sliced through the chop and as they sailed closer Orfeo could hear the crescendo of the crews' chanting, "*Vi-va Pa-pa! Vi-va Pa-pa!*" The high-masted men-of-war, with their tiers of decks and castles, moved like ponderous mountains through the flotilla as the Venetian galleys parted to clear a path for them. Stepping from beneath the awning, the pope raised his arms to acknowledge the mariners' cheers, still clutching his pomander.

"So it begins," he said quietly.

And so it ends for me, Orfeo thought. He'd come to admire Tebaldo in the course of their weeks together, but he also chafed to be quit of his obligation and to be his own man again.

As they entered the harbor, the galleys gave way to lesser craft: the small *grippi* that brought wine from Cyprus and Crete to Venice; flat-bottomed *sandoli;* fishing barges and the sail-fitted *braggozzi* used by the fishermen of Chioggia. Even the rafts the dockhands used to unload the large merchant ships sat low in the water under the weight of crowds of shouting workmen.

Orfeo peered over the railing, grinning at the sheer, rabid excitement all around them. Venice boasted a hundred thousand inhabitants, and every one of them seemed to be either on the water or lined up along the pier. The pope's ship crept toward the quay of San Marco, where a fanfare of trumpets, cymbals, and drums boomed in competition with the cheers. A rhythmic slapping joined the clamor as *gundule* emerged from the canals and the gondoliers began to beat their oars on the water. The slender ferries flaunted gilded and richly carved prows and painted decoration; luxurious coverings draped their *felzi,* the cabins that protected the passenger benches in bad weather. The gondolas, Orfeo could now see, were escorting the Doge of Venice's *bucintoro,* and there, in the center of the state barge, stood the doge himself. He dropped to his knees as the man-of-war bobbed near. The two vessels floated close together and Orfeo made out the features of Lorenzo Tiepolo. The Dogate hadn't changed hands during his time in Acre.

The fanfare gave way to the pealing bells of the Basilica di San Marco as the pope and doge debarked from their respective vessels. The crowd parted like the Egyptian sea to let a procession of church canons and archbishops through to the quay. Tebaldo whispered to Orfeo as the clergymen approached. "Stay with me. I need the comfort of my familiar through this uproar."

Orfeo bowed and stepped in line just behind the pontiff. The thousands of pairs of eyes focused in their direction left him feeling suddenly conspicuous, and he wished he might melt into the throng. Tebaldo turned. "No. Not behind me. *Beside* me," he said.

The prelates led the pope and doge and their retainers between two gargantuan standards painted with likenesses of San Marco and raised on pine poles as tall as the man-of-war's mast. Beyond the standards, Orfeo spotted the basilica's five leaden cupolas capped by their onion-shaped lanterns. Mosaics encrusted the exterior of the church while marble reliefs of saints and angels and mythic heroes crowned each of the five arched doorways and filled the spandrels between the arches. A forest of statues by long-dead stonemasons sprouted from every level surface of the facade.

The pope nudged Orfeo and nodded toward the four horses above the main portico, their rippling bronze muscles poised to spring at any moment from their terrace like the Pegasus of legend. In a low voice Tebaldo said, "I hope to return those one day. The price will be small, if it reunites the Churches."

Orfeo well knew the pope's ideas on this subject. At sea through night after starlit night, Tebaldo Visconti had opened his mind to the young oarsman, like a clan elder passing on the lore of the ancients—or maybe out of respect for Orfeo's late, sainted Uncle Francesco. "Two things I hope to accomplish," he said as they reclined on the ship's deck and stared up at the heavens. "I want to reunite the eastern and western Churches; and I want to reform the abuses among the secular clergy. I plan to use your uncle's friars to accomplish both, should God grant me the time and strength. Their present general, Bonaventura, shares my feelings in this matter. He thinks the new Orders, united with the universities, can reform our Holy Mother Church, extirpate heresy, and take a giant step toward realizing God's kingdom on earth. That's the kind of man I need beside me in this work."

He talked of the sack of Byzantium. Although the raid had happened even before Tebaldo's birth, the pope knew the story well. He'd read the horrifying eyewitness report of Niceta Choniates, and recounted to Orfeo how Enrico Dandolo, the blind Doge of Venice in 1202, subverted the fourth crusade for his city's benefit.

"When these so-called *Christian* crusaders seized Byzantium, they burned more houses than you can find in the three largest cities of Lombardy," he said. "They threw the relics of holy martyrs into latrines, and even scattered the consecrated body and blood of Our Savior. They tore the jewels from the chalices of the Haghia Sophia and used them as drinking cups. After destroying the high altar of the church, they led horses and mules inside to carry off their loot. Niceta says that, when some of the beasts slipped and fell, the crusaders ran them through with their swords, fouling the church with blood and ordure. Then these knights placed a common harlot on the Patriarch's throne and made her dance immodestly in the holy place. Nor in their lust did they show any mercy to innocent maids, or even virgins consecrated to God."

A heavy silence followed, while the pope gazed off to the East. "Much of the decoration of San Marco came from that raid, including those marvelous horses facing the piazza. These heralds of the Anti-Christ even stole the arm of San Stephano, the head of San Filipo, and bits of flesh from the body of San Paolo. More importantly to the doge, they seized trading concessions throughout the Eastern Empire, and were able to block Genovese and Pisan merchantmen from the region. It's safe to say your Venetian friends would barter their souls for profitable trade routes."

As the procession advanced to the main portico of the basilica, Orfeo's attention passed from the horses to the doge and his men. The mariner knew that Enrico Dandolo's successor, not to mention the merchants who strolled the Rialto, would not hesitate to poison a certain pope-elect had they heard his remark about the statues. Judging from their glowing faces, though, they hadn't, having drowned out his muffled words with their own enthusiasm. For the moment, the Venetians were content to honor their guest with a high Mass at the basilica before Tebaldo retired to rest at the doge's palace.

ORFEO FINALLY BROKE FREE of the papal entourage as nightfall settled on the Piazza di San Marco. Leaving behind the glittering candles and brilliantly-garbed Venetian courtiers and more rich courses than his stomach would normally encounter in a year, he escaped into the nearly empty square. The sheen of a light drizzle on the paving stones reflected the glare from the windows of the doge's palace. He followed the path along the waterfront until he came to a familiar street lined with shops and intersected with alleys. At the far end of one of these, a small banner marked his favorite *ridotto*. His felt no urge for cards or dicing this evening, but the possibility of a cup with an old shipmate drew him into the tavern. He wanted to be working again and could learn of openings for an oarsman in this place as quickly as at the harbor.

He ducked through the low doorway and peered through the smoke and shadows. Here were none of your shopkeepers or craftsmen or guild fathers. Mariners like him, rag and bone pickers, chimney sweeps, crab catchers who, for a tip, helped you climb out of a *gundule*—these were the patrons of Il Gransiero. They talked in low murmurs now, but would grow boisterous as the night advanced, until the tolling of the toper's bell closed the taverns and sent them stumbling to their homes and sleeping mats. The men in the room wrapped themselves in simple cloaks, with cloth bands wound for warmth around their legs. The women who drank with them wore plain grey shawls; about their necks hung chains of tiny rings, the decoration reserved by Venetian custom for women of the poorer classes. From above the low ceiling Orfeo could hear the giggling and groaning of other male and female voices. He smiled: good to be home, good to be free for the moment of the grandiosity that had swallowed up his pope.

In the corner farthest from the door he spotted what he'd come for. Two men he knew drank with a third, a stranger to him but also a mariner, judging from his dress. One friend looked up with a start as Orfeo grabbed a nearby stool and approached their table.

"Orfeo, bless my soul! What are you doing here? Are the Polos back already?"

"No. They're on to Cathay as planned. I docked this morning with the pope."

"*Il Papa?*" The man flicked his hand rapidly and whistled softly. "Better and better for you, is it?"

"I'm bored stiff, Giuliano. I haven't touched an oar in two months. I'm getting soft as Cecilia, here." He reached out toward a plump young woman passing their table with a small wine cask balanced on her shoulder.

"You welcomed this softness the nights you were hard," she shot back. Her full lips curled upward as he wrapped his arm around her waist. "Are you in port for a while?"

"Don't know. That's what I hope to find out tonight."

"Well, if y'are ..." She tousled his hair with her free hand then spun out of his arm, laughing. He liked Cecilia. A good and cheerful soul, he thought, as he watched her swing away. He had a host of new tales to share on her pillow later.

"D'ye hear the doge's getting up a war party against Ancona?" Giuliano asked. "Nothing like a sea battle and pulling the cork on a few merchantmen to cure boredom. We leave the day after All Saints and the main ballyhoo with the pope. The guilds'll be marching for a week, but we'll be long gone. Two hundred ships. They're hiring on all the crew and archers they can get."

"What's the pay?"

"Twelve *libbre* of biscuits, twelve *oncie* of salt pork, twenty-four of beans, nine of cheese, and a cask of wine. We'll eat and drink well." He laughed.

"I meant ducats, something I can jingle in my coin purse when I return."

"Coins? He wants coins. Still the practical one, eh Orfeo?" Giuliano winked at the other men. "Can you hear the son of the wool merchant in him? D'ye not see the naked ambition glittering in that Hebrew-like eye?"

He reached beneath the scarred table. When he opened his hand, it held a gold piece. "Two of these lovely portraits of Lorenzo Tiepolo, *amico*. And better still, all the booty you can carry back on board. It's not to be sneezed at. The Anconans are doing well these days."

"Too much wealth—for their health," the stranger rhymed with a disagreeable smirk.

Orfeo looked around the table at the expectant faces. This could be a good opportunity, and they'd be home from the raid within the month. Strangely, however, he found himself hesitating.

He returned their stares with a small frown. "I'll sleep on it and meet you here tomorrow," he said. "I need permission of the Holy Father. He asked me to come with him only as far as Venice, but he's yet to release me entirely." He grinned sheepishly. "I'm his good luck talisman."

"Ah. No wonder you're gone soft," Giuliano said. "We need more wine," he yelled. His two comrades rapped their cups on the table until Cecilia reappeared with her cask.

Her red hair trailed against Orfeo's cheek as she bent over the table. The long tresses had been freshly scented, and if he doubted she perfumed for him, the pressure of her knee against his thigh as she poured dispelled any uncertainty. He stroked the back of her leg and gave it a squeeze as she pulled away to serve the next table. This would be the last cup with his mates.

Most Venetian women had red hair, although few let it hang freely the way Cecilia did. Some churchman, no doubt, had decided that displaying hair or ears was immodest, but Cecilia trafficked little with churchmen—or, if she did, they weren't such as faulted her lack of headdress. Orfeo pictured in his mind the grand ladies of the city who paraded each day across the marble steps of their palaces on their stilt-like *zoccoli,* dressed in brocaded gowns and loaded down with enough jewelry each to buy the entire city of Assisi. Their long braids and rice-whitened skin were as false as their hearts, and on neither account could they equal the plain-dealing Cecilia. He looked up to see where she'd gone. He caught her eye across the room and the desire that flashed back from her glance sent an exquisite pain shooting through his groin.

"I CAN WRITE my name now," Cecilia said. "A friend showed me how." She pushed up on one elbow to better see his face. Orfeo returned her sleepy smile and stroked her hair as she traced the letter "C" around his right nipple and continued across his chest. "E - C - I . . ."

The feeble light straggling through holes in the tattered window covering nagged at his exhaustion like the buzzing of a mosquito. He wanted to guide the woman's head to his shoulder and close his eyes again, but he knew he should return to the palace soon. A ripple of depression washed over him. Cecilia stopped printing and furrows of concern creased her forehead.

"You've gone sad again, Orfeo."

"And I don't even know why," he said.

"Don't you? I could tell you in a second."

He grasped her chin between his thumb and forefinger and pulled her face toward him for a kiss. "Then tell me, O wise woman, that I too may be enlightened."

"Don't poke fun." She pouted, and her face became pensive. "Women understand things." She stretched out full length beside him again and slipped her head into the crook of his arm.

"Don't you remember how you told me about running away from your home? You'd just been brawling, and I cleaned you up. 'I'll fight any man for the joy of it,' said you, 'but the Devil take me before I'll kill for money.' If you was to go with them others against Ancona and scuttle their ships, you'd be little better the man than your papa what burnt the castle. If I was you, I'd stick with my pope a bit longer. And my Cecilia."

Orfeo brushed her cheek with his lips, then let his head sink back into the pillow. "My Cecilia," he repeated. "The sagest woman in Christendom. I'm damned if you're *not* the last of the oracles."

"That's good, is it?"

"Oh yes. In the ancient days, men traveled for months across the entire world to seek out the priestesses and oracles. They knelt down before them and showered them with gifts."

"I'd like a *little* of that. Why don't they do it anymore?"

Orfeo laughed and wrapped her in a tight hug. "Because, woman who doesn't know *everything,* you're not allowed to be priests anymore. Those days are passed forever, more's the pity." He kissed her again, softly, on the throat just beneath her chin, and nipped her with his teeth. "But when *I* need wisdom, I'll still come to you."

Another time, another situation, he *might* stick with his Cecilia, like she said. He knew she'd always be here for him, in any case, but *his* was the life in motion. And Cecilia, with her warm and generous heart, would never lack for some man's comfort.

STILL NO ANSWERS, Conrad fumed to himself. There are no answers here. I'm wasting my time with this Tomas d'Aquino.

His patience hadn't lasted nearly so long as he'd expected. After a week of reading, his new stack of parchment remained nearly empty. He'd jotted down but a single article describing the defective nature of woman, and that only because he hoped he might read it one day to that mouthy Suor Amata, who so clearly misunderstood the position of the female in the Great Chain of Being. He drew some grim solace from the passage, realizing that the brilliant theologian, and even Aristotle the Greek, confirmed his own instincts.

Question XCII, Article 1, Reply to Objection 1
For the Philosopher says, 'the female is a misbegotten male.' For the active force in the male seed tends to the production of a perfect likeness in the masculine sex, while the production of woman comes from defect in the active force or from some material indisposition, or even from some external change, such as that of a South wind which is moist, as the Philosopher observes in his *Generation of Animals.*

Despite his personal distaste for dialectic and systematic theology, Conrad had to admit he envied Tomas' deep comprehension of natural matters. He also wished he'd paid closer attention to Aristotle in his student days. Even though he'd had limitless occasions to observe the wild creatures that roamed near his hermitage, he'd never achieved that breakthrough to the next level of understanding, the deeper insight that pierced through merely external perceptions. Who'd have imagined, for example, that moisture in the wind could affect reproduction?

Conrad slid off his stool and glanced covetously at the locked cupboards ranged like sentinels alongside Lodovico's reliquaries. If the Sacro Convento still possessed copies of the banished biographies, and Celano's first history of Francesco's life in particular, they'd be in those cabinets. He stretched his back and dipped his knees several times. The librarian seemed preoccupied on the other side of the room.

Conrad strolled in among the stacks, browsing and occasionally pulling a book from the shelves. As he replaced each book on its shelf, he glanced down the aisle. He was out of sight of Lodovico and the copyists by the time he'd worked his way next to the cabinets. The iron padlocks hung large and daunting, but standing this close he saw that the cupboards themselves were made of soft pinewood. He stooped and pressed one of the side boards with his fingertips. The wood bowed slightly. With the proper tool. ...

He jerked his hand away. Dear God! Am I *so* desperate? *Yes, nearly so*. The more pertinent question was whether he possessed the nerve to act on his desperation. Gaining access to the library at night would be no problem. Lodovico never locked the door. Once the friar had the manuscripts he wanted, though, he'd have to escape the friary despite the porter and the barred gate. Then he would still have to elude the two-legged hounds Bonaventura would be sure to send after him. He might get away, though, if he could avoid capture as far as the mountains. The wilderness would work to his advantage. On the other hand, if he didn't escape, his life would be forfeit to the minister general.

The scuffing of sandals in the next aisle put a temporary end to his inner debate. He crouched and found himself staring through the shelves at Lodovico's knees. As the librarian continued toward the end of the row, he hurried quietly back to his desk. By the time Lodovico had completed his circuit, Conrad had his nose buried so deeply in the *Summa* that he could have used it for a blotter, were the ink still wet. When he did look up, he glimpsed the downturned corners of Lodovico's mouth before the librarian pivoted away again.

In two days, on the first of November, the friary would celebrate the Feast of All the Saints. By the end of the long day of prayer and liturgy, the brothers would be exhausted and eager for the warmth of their pallets. If he *were* to muster enough resolve to break into the cabinet, that would be the night to act. It was also the night of the new moon. With the grace of a cloudy sky to cover even that slim crescent of light, he could move about the friary unobserved.

XX

ON THE MORNING of the pope's official reception, Orfeo left for the basilica ahead of Tebaldo to help with the arrangements. While a small army of Venetians attended to flowers and carpeting, he lent a hand to the crew carrying a massive throne into the Piazza di San Marco, where the pontiff would receive the doge and other dignitaries. The workers brought a smaller throne for the doge, then Orfeo helped fence the pope's albino donkey. As a precaution, the men also raised a tent canopy over the two thrones; storm clouds billowed to the south and west.

All around Orfeo, the townspeople elbowed their way into good viewing positions. A troop of knights had ridden all the way from Rome and now formed a protective ring around the piazza to keep the crowd at a safe distance. At the hour of Terce the bells of San Marco tolled and within the basilica a chorus of male voices responded with the *Te Deum Laudamus*. The voices grew louder as the church canons emerged and crossed the square the short distance to the doge's palace.

Orfeo fidgeted as he waited for Tebaldo. The Venetians loved ostentatious display. What kind of entrance would the pope make? He'd only seen Tebaldo at ease, on board the ship and relaxing in the palace. Had he even brought sufficient wardrobe in his chests to match the sumptuous Lorenzo Tiepolo and his dogaressa? Appearances meant everything to the rich citizens of this city.

A murmur of excitement buzzed through the crowd closest to the palace. Orfeo craned his neck and smiled to see Tebaldo approaching his throne with bowed, uncovered head, barefoot and wearing the plain black cassock of a country priest. He seemed unaware of the onlookers as his lips moved in silent prayer. When he finally raised his head and caught sight of Orfeo standing behind the throne, his expression said: "The reform begins here."

The doge, meanwhile, had arrived at San Marco quay after spending the night at his family *palazzo*. The state barge tied up against the piazza and the humming, interspersed with cries of wonder and approval, commenced anew as Lorenzo climbed ashore. He'd replaced his round hat with a circlet of gold embedded with precious gems. He, too, wore a cassock, shorter than the pope's, but his was white and lined with ermine. He displayed purple hose underneath, and a cloak of gold cloth over, the cassock. The dogaressa and her female attendants stepped off the barge behind him. She glided across the piazza in his wake in a trailing dress of scarlet samite with tippets of ermine at the cuffs. A long veil, secured by a small ducal crown, hid her face and head. Behind her, her ladies followed in indigo gowns and scarlet cloaks, their heads covered with hats and turbans of jewel-studded velvet and veils of a gossamer weave.

When he reached the pope, Lorenzo threw off his golden cloak and prostrated full length on the pavement. He rose in stages, kissing first the pontiff's feet, then his knees, then rose to his full height. Tebaldo stood in turn. He grasped the doge's head with both hands, then kissed his cheeks and embraced him. "Welcome, beloved son of the Church," he said. "Sit thou at my right hand." The doge took his own throne to the cheers of the crowd.

The bells pealed again and the chanting of the *Te Deum* resumed. Tebaldo took the doge by the hand and led him into the basilica where the pope would officiate at the high Mass honoring all the saints. To Orfeo, every movement of the pontiff-elect bespoke humility and the solemn responsibility he felt toward his new duties. His dress, as well as his actions, matched the words he'd spoken during their journey. Orfeo felt a sudden rush of pride to be in the entourage of such a man.

The Mass lasted until almost midday. Then Tebaldo mounted his donkey while Lorenzo held the stirrup. The doge led him to the quay. The sailors destined for Ancona had already boarded their ships, which now passed, one by one, along the waterfront. "A blessing for the success of our fleet, Your Holiness," Lorenzo asked.

The pope responded softly, although loud enough for Orfeo to hear. Unfortunately, that meant some of the others closest to the pair could hear also. "I will pray for the safe return of your men and ships," he said. "I cannot pray for the success of an enterprise I consider piratical. The Anconans are my children too." Lorenzo's face flushed as Tebaldo turned, raised his arms toward the ships, and formed a large sign of the cross over the convoy.

Orfeo was suddenly ill at ease, despite the cheers of the passing navy. He wished the ceremony were over and they were already on the road in the company of the Roman knights. It occurred to him then that the organizer of the armed escort might have had more than a ceremonial interest in bringing his warriors all the way to Venice.

After the last ship had sailed from the harbor, the doge led the donkey back across the piazza where the pope's throne had been repositioned for better viewing. The parade of the guilds and the presentation of gifts would begin soon and, as Giuliano predicted, would probably be prolonged over several days. As Tebaldo settled himself, the doge whispered to one of his men. The message probably had nothing to do with the pontiff's rebuff on the quay. Still, as the scarlet-robed guild of glass blowers entered the piazza, hoisting their banners and flasks and goblets to a trumpet flourish, Orfeo slipped into the crowd and shouldered his way toward the captain of the Roman guard.

THE NIGHT TURNED OUT to be pitch dark—ideal for larceny. Black clouds hung low over Assisi throughout the day, an early harbinger of the winter storms that would bury the mountains in snow in coming months. A slightly paler shading along the edge of one cloud hinted at the position of the new moon.

The stone floor of the dormitory chilled Conrad's bare soles, but he welcomed the discomfort. A plank floor might have creaked and betrayed him, in spite of the vociferous snoring of the friars. His pocket sagged with the weight of the small iron bar he'd found near the blacksmith's forge. He planned to pry off one or two boards from the cupboards, then tap them back into place, leaving no trace of damage. Even so, he'd have to get away from the Sacro Convento. The theft might not be noticed, but he had nowhere to read, or even conceal, Celano's manuscript once he'd found it. If he could hide the fact of the robbery, though, he might buy himself enough time to walk away casually, in the full light of day, with the stolen manuscript under his robe.

He still couldn't believe he was attempting this theft, even as he slipped out of the dormitory and tiptoed down the main arcade. Would Leo and Francesco approve his method, even knowing and encouraging his purpose? He clung to the wall where the shadows were deepest, feeling with his fingertips the smooth chisel marks the builders had left on the granite blocks. A strange sensation came over him, as though he retraced the Order's history with his hands. He could picture the stone masons sweating under Elias' direction as they dug their foundations, shaped the great blocks arriving daily from the quarries, raised the stones and timbers skyward with their huge winding wheel. Wasn't that also why he was breaking into the cabinets: to recapture the origins of the Order that Bonaventura and the provincial ministers essentially wished to erase?

When Giovanni da Parma served as general, he had made a real effort to accommodate the Spiritual brothers. Those who wanted to adhere to the primitive rule of poverty still felt themselves to be part of the Order. But Bonaventura had a different vision of his friars. No longer would they be wandering evangelists who begged or mucked stables for their meals, nursed the sick and leprous, slept in cow barns, abased and subjected themselves to every man.

Seven years before, when he'd banished Conrad from Assisi, the minister general had tried to justify the growing opulence of the Order: "In the beginning, the friars were simple and unlettered," he said. "This is what made me love the life of blessed Francesco and the early history of the Order—the fact that they resembled the beginning and growth of the Church. As the Church began with simple fishermen and afterwards grew to include renowned and skilled philosophers, so must it happen in our Order. In this way God shows that the Order of Friars Minor was founded not by the prudence of men, but by Christ Himself."

Bonaventura's friars would be educated, university-trained preachers, men the general public could value and respect. That should silence the grumbles that the Order had deteriorated from its former ideals. And in the process of creating his new friar, he'd also silenced the intransigents. An idealized Order needed idealized friars and an idealized image of its founder. Conrad preferred to think that these plain granite walls represented more of the Order's true history than all of Bonaventura's magnificent prose.

He had just groped his way around a corner to the final passageway leading to the library when a flash of light stabbed at his eyes. In that instant, he'd seen the library door ahead of him as clearly as in broad daylight, which meant anyone who might be watching could have spotted him just as easily. A low rumble rolled across the valley and up toward the friary.

He sucked in a cool draught and waited for the pounding in his chest to subside. Then he hurried the remaining steps to the library before the lightning split the darkness again. Lightning would prove dangerous to his mission, but thunder could be good. Once he knelt beside the cabinets, he could wait for a flash, position his bar, and pry at the boards under the masking noise of the thunderclaps.

Conrad used the intermittent streaks of light to find his way to his desk, where he'd left an oil lamp the day before, using it conspicuously to read late into the afternoon when the light in the library dimmed. A clever touch, he thought, until he felt across the surface of his desk and underneath it. The lamp had been removed. Surely, he'd given Lodovico no reason to suspect his plan. The librarian had probably tidied up, taking no chance that spilled oil might discolor one of his precious manuscripts. Fortunately, God in His providence had given him another means to see.

With each crash of lightning, Conrad moved closer to one of the cabinets, and finally knelt to his work. He quickly evolved a system, prying during the rumbles, glancing about him during bursts of illumination. The odd shapes of the library's shelves, piles of books, desks and stools cast unexpected shadows, not at all the shapes their daytime forms suggested. Some appeared to shift with each lightning bolt.

The thunder boomed again, louder and closer now as the storm swept toward the city. With a fierce push of his lever he freed the base of a board. He swung it up with one hand and groped inside with the other. Scores of manuscripts filled the cupboard. He pulled one through the opening and laid it across his knees, waiting for the next flash to disclose its title. The opportunity proved brief, barely time for him to read the single word, *Sociorum,* and to see that two of the shadows now loomed directly over him.

THE FRIAR WHO led him away remained silent and hooded, although Conrad assumed the tall figure who stayed behind to replace the manuscript and repair the cabinet was Lodovico. Outside the library a boy waited with a lantern. The light flickering on his face showed him to be the Sacro Convento's newest novice, a child who'd introduced himself only the week before as Ubertino da Casale. Conrad and the boy had crossed paths several times, and Ubertino always seemed eager to talk, staring at the older friar in rapt hero-worship. Conrad had been amused, remembering his own infatuation with Fra Leo when he wasn't much older than this child. It dismayed him that Bonaventura involved one so young in this dirty business; maybe the minister general wanted the boy to witness firsthand how he dealt with disobedient friars.

The silhouette of old Fra Taddeo was also unmistakable, with its stooped shoulders and humped back. Another lightning bolt lit up the recesses of the friar's cowl, the sad, watery eyes and sagging jowls of the minister general's aged hound. Bonaventura must have known Conrad wouldn't resist, to have sent an old man and boy to fetch him. Nor did he *feel* combative. He'd been caught in a wrongful act, stealing from the library, trying to circumvent the interdiction on the early legends; he could only resign himself to God's will and accept the justice of whatever punishment he received.

The tapers in the minister general's office faltered in the draft of the open doorway. A glum Bonaventura sat behind his desk, a drowsy veneer shrouding his usually serene features. Conrad noted that his tonsure and thin brows had turned a silvery pepper-and-salt in the years since their last confrontation and stress lines radiated from his brown eyes. He had grown portly too. Fourteen years before, Bonaventura had been elected minister general at the tender age of thirty-seven. The years hadn't treated him well, and Conrad knew that recalcitrant friars like himself played a large role in the general's worries. A strange glow that played like a halo about Bonaventura's head fascinated Conrad also, until he realized it was nothing more than the torchlight reflecting from his sleek cranium.

Bonaventura leaned back in his chair and tapped his fingertips while he surveyed the friars standing before his desk. His eyes grew keen at last. "Leave us alone, brothers," he said. "Wait in the arcade." The minister general rested his steepled forefingers against his lips while the others left the room. Then he rotated his gaze to Conrad.

"So it's come to this," he said with an air of easy aplomb. "And what am I to do with you *now*?" The friar lowered his head like a guilty child and said nothing.

"Conrad, Conrad, you continue to disappoint me. Your behavior isn't totally surprising, for I know how Fra Leo corrupted you, but it disappoints me nonetheless."

"You're hiding something," Conrad snapped suddenly.

"Am I?" Bonaventura was fully himself now, shielded by his wonted calm. "Even were that true, it should be no concern of yours. As a dutiful friar, you need know only that I will let nothing disturb the holy reputation and credibility of our Order."

An overwhelming urge seized Conrad: to fire blindly with every piece of information he had. "Why have you banned the first of Tomas?" he blurted. "Why was the companion mutilated? Whence came the seraph?" He felt himself trembling in every fiber as he spoke.

"Serve Christ's poor ones," Bonaventura replied with a mocking smile. "Seek out Fra Jacoba." He twisted his ring as he spoke. "I know all about Leo's message."

"Because Illuminato met the messenger."

The smile continued to play on Bonaventura's lips and his eyebrows arched slightly. "Quite true. But again, that letter is of no import here. What should matter to you is that the Council of Paris, the provincial ministers, and not I, in their wisdom, and for reasons that they understood best, banned the legends of Tomas da Celano as well as the Legend of the Three Companions. They made their decision, and our duty, as obedient sons of San Francesco, is to abide by their judgment. Those who don't, we must punish as an example to the others."

Bonaventura had stunned him into silence, not by the threat of discipline, but by something else he'd said. Conrad reacted like a baker who suddenly remembers a loaf left in the oven. *Idioto*! You had it right there before you, plain as your nose. The mutilated companion was never a person—not Angelo, Rufino, Masseo, nor any of the friars buried in the basilica. Leo meant the *history* they'd compiled together, their memories and stories of Francesco, which apparently had been altered like a gelding horse. He'd held the manuscript in his hands in the library moments before—the *Legenda*

Trium Sociorum. That close he'd been to another piece of Leo's puzzle!

Bonaventura still droned in his passionless monotone. "But, brother," he said, "because Donna Giacoma in the kindness of her heart has seen fit to befriend you, I spare you this once, and this once only. You will leave the Sacro Convento immediately. I wish never to see you in this friary or even in the basilica again, nor hear of your speaking to any of the brothers from this place. You would act wisely to return to your mountain cell and forget this vain pursuit. Should I learn that you've not done so, and should you come once more within my grasp, you will experience the full burden of my authority. Take care that you never test me again."

Bonaventura touched his cheek with his index finger, just below the eye, pulling his lower eyelid down every so slightly. "*Ci capiamo, eh?* We understand each other?" As the minister general slowly rose and walked around the desk, Conrad recalled his words to Amata about the cruel claws of the gryphon. The image had barely reentered his mind when the beast spread its cloak wings bat-like and held out a jeweled hand for him to kiss.

Conrad's neck stiffened. He recoiled from the extended fist. "Kiss the ring, brother," Bonaventura said in a portentous voice. "In gratitude for your freedom, which may yet be rescinded, and as a mark of that humility you so sorely lack—kiss the ring."

A horrendous thunderclap rattled the walls of the room. The tapers struggled to stay alight, rustling and fluttering like wind-lashed pennants. Conrad bowed his head. He dropped to one knee, took the general's hand, and brought the lapis lazuli to his lips. His lowered eyes widened abruptly when he saw the inscription in the stone—a stick figure enclosed in a circle beneath a pair of arches.

XXI

S O *THIS* IS PERFECT JOY, Conrad mused. He managed a smile in spite of
the raindrops trickling off his nose. He huddled in a recess in the wall
near Donna Giacoma's front door, waiting for daylight, while the wind
whistled in icy spirals up the stairwell to her alley. He'd taken a roundabout
route through the city streets, avoiding the Piazza di San Francesco and the
night watch. Fortunately, the pelting rain had left the guards less eager to
make their rounds.

He knew he'd been lucky to escape unscathed from Bonaventura. But
he also knew he couldn't return to his hermitage now, not when he'd just
received another clue from the minister general himself. Somehow he had
to get his hands on those old biographies.

His eyelids drooped from weariness. He decided to risk sitting down,
although this pushed his feet almost outside the recess. He curled his arms
over his knees as a pillow, fell asleep in this position, and remained sleeping
until a woman tugged at his sleeve.

"Come inside, brother," she said. "We've a fire going. The neighbor saw
you from across the street and signaled over to me."

How long had he been drowsing? Through bleary eyes he saw that it
was dawn, although storm clouds still darkened the sky. Through the hiss
of the rainfall he could hear the tolling of the *Angelus* from the Basilica di
San Francesco. The woman led him to Donna Giacoma's door. She wasn't a
servant he'd seen before. She threw off her cloak in the doorway and shook
the raindrops from it. Beneath, she wore an ankle-length blue gown and
white wimple—the colors of the noblewoman's livery. She was also unshod,
in the manner of her mistress.

"This way, brother," she said as she led him toward the kitchen. "Have you stayed here before?"

So the woman *was* new to the household, or else so many friars passed through that she just hadn't noticed him earlier. Nor did he remember her. Although she had her back to him, her young voice had a familiar ring. "I have," he said as she pointed him to the table. There sat Maestro Roberto, waiting no doubt for his bowl of hot porridge.

"Fra Conrad," he called out. "You look like a drowned cat. We thought you'd forgotten us."

The woman whirled around at the mention of his name, and Conrad's heart leaped halfway into his throat. *Amata!* Her face, framed by the wimple, seemed a little changed, scrubbed and beautiful, if somewhat wan. He couldn't mistake those black, almond-shaped eyes, though, despite the fearful look he'd never seen there before. Her cheeks flushed pink as he returned her stare.

"What are *you* doing here?" the friar asked. "And where is your nun's habit?"

Roberto laughed. "Didn't you recognize him without his face hair, missy?"

"*Scu-, scusami,*" Amata stammered. She ran from the room, hiding her face in her cupped hands.

Roberto chuckled again. "Skittish little filly. But you probably know that. Madonna says you two are the best of friends."

"She said *what?*"

"Didn't you tell her to give the prioress San Francesco's letter and bring the girl to a proper home?"

Conrad sank down across from the steward, trying to remember his last conversation with Donna Giacoma. "Is *that* what I said?"

"A blessed, rainy morning, padre," the cook's voice sang out behind him. "I got a special treat here I been saving until you got back." She set a plate of dried figs in front of him. "They're stuffed with almonds and rolled in sugar, but you're not to touch until you've somewhat hot inside you."

Conrad hoped he didn't look as dazed or bewildered as he felt. Between lack of sleep, the brutal thundering weather, and the events of the last six hours, he felt he'd been plunked into a world tipped on edge. The kitchen fire warmed him though, cook's porridge fortified as always, and the savory figs she finally allowed him to eat diminished some of the trauma of his morning. He'd just licked the sugar from his fingers when Donna Giacoma limped into the room.

"Fra Conrad, I heard you were back. But, oh dear, look at you! I'll have your old tunic dredged up at once before you're taken with chilblains. Wait for me in your room when you're finished eating." And before he could give any explanation or ask about the change in her household, she left the kitchen.

Conrad turned to Roberto, who only shrugged and threw up his hands. "I've work to do, padre. You're on your own," he grinned. Then he too was gone. The cook retreated into the pantry. Conrad scratched his head, popped one last fig into his mouth, then went to rendezvous with his old, companionable, swaddling robe.

He didn't see Amata anywhere as he wandered through the house. Once he'd changed into dry clothing, however, Donna Giacoma led him to the great hall. Near a fire at the farthest end, half-hidden behind an ornate screen, sat the young woman.

"You two need to talk," the noblewoman said. "And Conrad ..." She paused, and added in a grave voice: "Be gentle. Mother Prioress said she hasn't been herself since she returned from Ancona." His chest and shoulders tightened as Donna Giacoma left the hall. How these women protected one another! All the anger he'd felt at Enrico's death, at the image of Amata laid out naked before the boy or rutting in Dom Vittorio's copious bed with the lewd monks of Sant'Ubaldo flooded once again to the surface. Outside, the storm raged, hail mixing with the rain and clattering on the tiled roof. He thought how, at his mountain hermitage, all that wet fury would be blanketing the rough pines with peaceful snowflakes. Why he'd traded that blessed quietude for this tempest that knotted his gut, God alone knew.

Amata lowered her head and stared at her lap where one hand massaged the other over and over. Conrad advanced stiffly toward the fireplace, ignoring the chair placed opposite her. For once she could look up to him, defer to his priestly rank, rather than face him eye-to-eye on the same level, like some sort of equal.

"The boy is dead, you know." He addressed the top of her bowed head.

"I know."

"That's all you have to say? I know?"

"What do you want me to say?" Her voice fluttered. "Shall I tell you how the pain of his death stabbed my heart soon after I left you, how I sensed the exact moment his soul fled his body, how I've cried night and day since?"

"Remorse won't bring him back. If you hadn't led him away from the cave in the first place ..."

Her head shot up. Pain contorted her features, and the glistening dark rings beneath her eyes startled him. Her voice managed a tinge of its former sarcasm as she replied. "Do you speak of something you heard in the privacy of confession, Padre?" Anger flecked her black eyes. "You know nothing, Fra Conrad. *Nothing!*"

She meant to offend him—and she succeeded at one level—but at the same time, he found himself strangely relieved at the old fire in her tone. She was right about Enrico's confession, but at the same time, he believed he understood more than she gave him credit for. She'd grown up in the country, in a *castella* no doubt surrounded by a primitive village—he in the trading port of Ancona and the rarefied atmosphere of Paris. But he knew something of the villages, too. He'd traveled once through the backward country south of Umbria, when he debarked at Naples on his return from Paris.

For two months he'd criss-crossed the hot, narrow valleys on foot, working his way northward toward Assisi. As he passed through one tiny hamlet after another, the dull black eyes of the women followed him from open doors with a downward glance, as though they measured his manhood. If he turned to scowl, they buried their faces in their hands and peeked at him through their fingers. "Don't take anything to drink from those women," the old men of the villages warned in awed tones, "no wine, not even a cup of water. They're all witches and they slip in love potions." The men would lean their yellow, diseased faces closer to his then, and sputter into his ear, "Menstrual blood, stirred with herbs." They also warned him not to sleep in the caves outside the villages, which were inhabited by gnomes, the souls of local children who had died unbaptized. Every man hoped to catch one of these creatures by its red hood, of course, and force it to lead him to hidden treasure, but the young friar Conrad would be safer sleeping in the local church. He'd stopped in many such towns, and the women rushed to the church to confess their sins in their various dialects, claiming they couldn't trust the local priest with the intimate burdens of their souls.

As well as he understood them, these women considered carnal love to be a natural force that no amount of willpower, good intentions, or chastity could resist. If a man and a woman found themselves alone in a sheltered spot, no power in heaven or earth could prevent their copulation, swift and unspoken, as when a male animal encounters a female in heat—and these women seemed to be eternally in heat. He felt the barely suppressed desire in their words even as they confessed, in their slow exhalations, with every breath ending in a prolonged sigh. He suspected that they *did* confess to the village priest—and often—but that they sought out the priest, as they now came to him, for more than forgiveness of their hopeless urges. Might it be that Amata had grown up in a similar atmosphere of uncontrolled passion, with the same primitive urges, in a world where even the most fundamental moral code did not apply?

Not likely, he decided. She was the daughter of minor nobility and she'd already spoken of her parents' piety. But something had happened to shatter the innocence of her childhood.

He sat down, finally, in the chair opposite her. He pushed his spine against its hard back and perched stiff and upright. The girl curled in upon herself on her own chair, ankles and arms crossed, her head turned toward the fireplace. "I'd like to understand," he said finally. "Will you talk to me?"

AMATA PULLED HER dark blue shawl around her shoulders. Her eyes took on the faraway look he had seen on the mountaintop, the day she told him of her murdered family.

"I played alone in the stable one afternoon, with a litter of newborn kittens—about two months before the raid. My body had started its changes that summer, and I suppose I already had babies on my mind. I'd seen the prettiest boy from our gatehouse tower just the day before, the day the wool merchant argued with my father. Between him and the kittens, I'd spent much of the morning daydreaming about being married and having my own babes nursing at my breasts—well, the breasts I'd have one day—just like the kittens nursing on their mother.

"I heard a horse trot through our courtyard toward the stable. My father's Uncle Bonifazio had ridden from Todi for a visit. He hadn't been to the Coldimezzo for almost two years, and when he got off his horse he eyed me strangely, as though he'd never really looked at me before. He asked what I was doing and I told him—including my silly fantasy. He looked me up and down very seriously and asked if I'd started bleeding yet. I hadn't, I told him. Then he wanted to know if I still had my maidenhead. 'Yes,' I said. I know I must have been blushing furiously because his questions embarrassed me. 'That's very fortunate,' he said. He told me that if a girl gave her maidenhead to a man of the Church, like himself, she could be sure of a happy marriage and many healthy children."

Conrad felt his skin beginning to itch as he sensed where the woman's story was leading. "Your father's uncle was a priest?"

"He was, and still is, the Bishop of Todi."

"The bishop!" He shook his head, trying to absorb his growing disgust at her information. "And you believed his nonsense?" he asked.

"I was eleven years old, Conrad! What did I know about anything? Wouldn't you have believed anything a bishop told you at that age?"

The friar nodded. "Yes, of course I would. Please. Go on."

"Anyway, he kept talking like that, and said what a pretty little girl I was, while he tied up his horse and pulled off its saddle. And his eyes—I remember they had a wild look. By the time he finished with the horse, his cheeks were flushed bright red and he said, 'Come with me,' very firmly, in such a way that a child couldn't possibly refuse. He took my hand and led me behind the stable where the hay was piled.

"He said he wouldn't hurt me, Conrad. But he hurt like hell, so much that I cried out in pain. My father must have been outside the stable, coming to greet his uncle. When he rushed to see what had happened, Bonifazio jumped off me, his fat prick as ugly as a grub worm still poking through the buttons of his cassock. He jabbed at me with his finger. 'That child's possessed with a devil,' he said. 'See how she has seduced me, even in my bishop's garb.' He tore at his cassock until it ripped and threw his skullcap into the straw and trampled it. He scratched his face until drops of blood ran down his cheeks.

"I was crying and frightened because I hurt so and my gown was all dirty and bloody, and Great-Uncle Bonifazio was acting more insane each moment. I tried to look at my papa, but he wouldn't meet my eyes. 'Calm down, Uncle,' he said. 'She won't behave so again, if I have to beat the demon out of her.'

"He took off his belt and, without a word, grabbed my wrist and rolled me onto my stomach on the hay. He began to whip me and raised such welts on my back and legs that it pained me to sit for days afterward, and all the while Great-Uncle urged him on and cried for the demon to come out of me."

Amata cradled her forehead in one hand. The tears streamed freely down her cheeks now, but she made no attempt to stem them. In the profound silence Conrad noticed for the first time the raindrops, like the tears of angels, hissing in the fireplace as they trickled down the chimney.

Her voice quavered as she spoke again. "Worst of all, my papa wouldn't speak to me or even look at me after that, and mamma feared to comfort me because of him. This silent torture lasted until the day he died. The raiders murdered him with the wall of his rage still raised between us. I never heard forgiveness from the man I loved more than any in the world."

"His shame kept him from facing you, Amata. He knew he'd acted unfairly. He beat you because he couldn't beat his hypocrite of an uncle. Tacitus once observed that it's human nature to hate those we have injured." The words came in a husky, thick-throated voice he hardly recognized as his own. "Did no one take your part?"

"Only cousin Vanna, but she left for Todi soon afterward. She was to be married to Sior Jacopo. By Bishop Bonifazio, no less. She was my only friend during those weeks, except for my brother. Fabiano knew I'd been punished for doing something wrong. Exactly what, he didn't know, but it hurt him to see me so sad."

"And when you were carried off by the murderers? How were you treated at the Rocca?"

Amata swiped at her eyes with her sleeve. "I tried never to be alone with the men of that place, but that wasn't always possible. I finally stole a knife from the scullery, the one I wore beneath my sleeve on our journey. I swore I'd kill Simone della Rocca and his sons one day—or maybe myself."

"Simone della Rocca Paida, the guardian of this city?"

"Yes, that's where they held me captive, in that grotesque fortress. Simone swung the sword that cut down my father; his son, Calisto, killed mamma. I actually tried to stab Calisto once. He cornered me the day before my mistress and I left for San Damiano, one last chance for him to abuse me I suppose. I only succeeded in slashing his hand, but I sliced it deeply enough that he needed tending. We escaped before he recovered; otherwise, I'm sure he'd have killed me."

Again she lapsed into silence. Her voice had steadied by the time she spoke once more. "I swore that no man should ever know me again except on *my* terms. I guess my mothering fantasy isn't totally dead, although I'm approaching seventeen now and nearly past marrying age." She stared into the fireplace, at the haphazard wavering of the flames.

"I became a little crazy out on the road, Conrad. My heart still aches, knowing Enrico paid such a price for that craziness. I so wanted to experience truly joyful lovemaking, just once."

She looked up into the friar's face. "If it helps you to hear it—either as a priest or, I hope, as my friend—I've vowed to Our Lord and His Blessed Mother that I'll never take love lightly again."

Her eyes were cheerless, though she forced a miserable facsimile of a smile. Finally she said: "Have I helped your understanding?"

For the first time since he'd learned of Rosanna's betrothal, Conrad regretted his friar's tunic. In that instant, he wanted nothing so much as to be a normal man, free of the yoke of celibacy, to take this enchanting womanchild into his arms, to speak the forgiveness and apology she never heard from her father, the words of enduring love she never heard from Enrico—to kneel before her and beg her pardon and acceptance of him in return.

But that, he knew, was an impossible fantasy. His vows were his reality, as real as his worn robe. He rose from his chair and patted her shoulder softly. "I'm so sorry, Amata." he said. "And my vow will be to pray daily that God will heal your injured body and soul. I'm going to *madonna's* chapel now to begin that vow. You're welcome to come pray with me, if you will."

With the dike of prayer raised between them, he hoped he would never have to face the waves of this particular fantasy again.

XXII

R AINWATER CASCADED OFF the roofs, flooding through the gutters and piazzas of Venice and into the canals—a rare prolonged deluge in the delta of the Po River. For two days the parade of the guilds had been postponed.

A restless Orfeo prowled the city from the Rialto, where traders fretted and prayed for the safe arrival of their cargoes, to the marketplace, where gloomy merchants had most of their wares under wraps and buyers were the lone scarce commodity. Bargaining even slowed in the market for pagan slaves and for the "little souls," the Christian children from the Levant whose parents had sold them into indentured servitude.

Only in the Jewish quarter and among the craftsmen's sheltered workshops could he find any activity. There, labor never ceased. Tradesmen continued to fabricate everything from playing cards to mosaics, porcelains to armor and glassware. Carvers and die sinkers decorated wooden chests, ivory hunting horns, sword hilts, leather belts, and gold and silver jewelry. *"Cavolo!"* the bored Orfeo muttered as he watched the industrious workers. He almost regretted not having gone with Giuliano and the others. At least he'd be doing *something*.

The third morning after All Saints Day, with the rain still pelting on his shoulders, he returned from a night with Cecilia to the doge's palace, wondering how best to while away the morning. He spread his hood tent-like above his head, recalling how the woman had draped her hair around his face as she mounted him in the predawn light, forming with her long tresses a red-streamered pavilion where they gazed undisturbed on one another, closed off from the rest of the universe. What deep understanding glowed in those ageless grey eyes, in that ambiguous smile that reflected no judgment, no blame or compassion, that accepted him as no more nor less than her friend, Orfeo the oarsman.

Cecilia knew everything that stirred in her corner of Venice, the intimate dealings of every man, woman, and child, and the hidden wellsprings that fed those actions. Sometimes her plain wisdom made her seem thousands of years old—a spirit of the earth like the all-knowing beasts, a spirit of the underworld like some sorceress of old. She had no fear of time or events. She could do the work of any man, shoulder the heaviest wine cask with the firm sure steps of a powerful ox.

To his amazement, Orfeo was to her even more wondrous than she was to him, possibly because of his dreams of travel and success on the grand scale or his second-hand stories of the Orient. She treated him as though he had greater than natural powers and in her patient way accepted entirely his goings and comings, even though they both knew that someday he would go away and not return.

A capricious notion struck him as he reached the palace. He should recommend Cecilia to the pope as a private counselor, adding her natural wisdom to Tebaldo's deep spirituality. But no. That would never do. Placing such luscious fruit before the would-be reformer of the clergy would no doubt prove disastrous. The salt might lose more than its savor. Still grinning at the possibility, though, he saluted the Roman knight who lounged in the shelter of a column near the main entrance. At Orfeo's suggestion, the band of knights now stayed with the pope-elect at all times. "How fares our Holy Father?" he asked. "Slept he well in the doge's bed?"

"Nay. Fitfully, *signore, una notte bianca*, from the reports I've heard. Nightmares woke him several times. He's still in bed, having breakfast. He left word you should come to his chamber immediately on your return from the city."

"Something boiling in the pot?"

The guard shrugged. "I've relayed the message as I heard it. Now you know as much as I do."

"Let's hope he wants to take to the road. I don't like the way things are dragging on here." Orfeo strode through the cavernous entry and bounded up the marble stairs two-at-a-time. The men stationed on either side of the chamber door stepped aside when they recognized him.

"Your Holiness," he said as he crossed the room and knelt beside the bed and waited for Tebaldo to extend his hand in blessing.

"*Buon giorno*, Orfeo." From the mass of pillows propped around him, the pope waved a strip of smoked eel. "Don't stand on ceremony. Just stand."

Orfeo rose and waited silently.

"Have you eaten?"

"I'm fine, Holiness." Had his mariner friend Giuliano posed the question, Orfeo's reply would have been more detailed, but one didn't dwell on *belli fichi* and other such earthy flavors with a pontiff.

"Well, taste a piece of this eel anyway. It's too delectable not to share."

Orfeo dipped his hand into the pope's bowl. Imitating Tebaldo, he nipped daintily at the oily meat with his front teeth.

"I had a miserable dream last night. My coach mired down in gigantic snowdrifts. You were up front, astride the back of an ox, crying out to your uncle to save us. All of a sudden, the animal began to bellow and scream and a pack of wolves as huge as horses appeared on the mountaintop behind us. The oxen pulled with all their strength, but in their panic they veered off the road and into a gorge. I could feel the carriage flying through the air."

"And then?"

"And then I woke. One of the guards said I screamed in my sleep." He held out the bowl to Orfeo again. "I'm from Piacenza. I can read the signs of the weather in the Po Valley. But you grew up in the Apennines. Is my dream prophetic? What's this downpour doing in the mountain passes?"

"It might be snowing, Holiness, although this is our first heavy storm of the winter. At best, the rain will make a quagmire of the dirt sections of road. The old Roman highway's mostly paved with stones, though." He paused, and asked: "Do you feel obliged to endure the full hospitality of the doge?" He knew the phrasing of his question was impolitic, but his own patience had already burst its limits.

The pope didn't reply at once. Perchance the newness of his role made him unsure how far his duty and the bounds of protocol extended. Orfeo wandered to the window and pushed open the shutters. The wind blew wet and cool against his face, bracing and refreshing him as he strained to see beyond the harbor. He cupped his hands around his eyes, shielding them from the spray.

"*Sangue di Cristo!*" he swore aloud.

A lone war galley, minus its mast and top castle, limped under oar power toward the quay. Two specks, further into the distance, moved in the same crippled fashion in the wake of the first.

He ran to the bed and snatched the tray off Tebaldo's lap. "Get up, Holiness," he shouted. "Dress for travel as quickly as you can. I'll tell your men to pack your gear and ready the horses at once."

The proud fleet the Venetians had launched against Ancona with such fanfare, the fleet Tebaldo had publicly refused to bless with success, had foundered in the stormy Adriatic.

DONNA GIACOMA THRILLED at the change in Amata following her talk with Fra Conrad. The girl stood taller, head erect and shoulders thrown back as though they'd shed a mighty weight. The old woman thanked the friar for his part in hearing Amata out, but he refused any credit for the transformation. The girl's pleasure at having her old comrade in the house was plain to see, and Donna Giacoma believed Conrad felt the same, even though he spent hours at a time in the chapel and made no obvious effort to seek out the girl. As always, he cloaked his emotions in manly stoicism, unlike Pio, who trailed after Amata at every chance and suffered through the most blatant pangs of puppy love. The page made Amata laugh, and once, while they played at Naughts and Crosses, she inadvertently called him "Fabiano," the name of her own younger brother. How happy her childhood must have been, the noblewoman thought. Donna Giacoma prayed God that, with herself as the instrument, the girl might enjoy a home again.

Much of Donna Giacoma's amusement came from watching what she thought of as "Fra Conrad's secret affection," and his attempts to grapple with it. Because of his predicament, she knew the friar would balk at the next task she'd planned for him. She gave him several days to resettle into the routine of the household while she assembled her props and arguments, beginning with a bound collection of saint's lives her husband had given to her in the first years of their marriage. She knew right where to find it, although she'd not opened the book in almost sixty years. It lay wrapped in her lace wedding veil in a corner of the trunk she'd brought from her parents' home. Four days after Conrad's return, while the male servants returned to their post-supper chores and the women sat down to eat, she cornered the friar in the foyer, limping out from behind a pillar to block his escape to the chapel.

"Amatina wants to read and write," she said. She'd taken to using the diminutive when she spoke of the girl.

He chuckled. "Does she indeed? I hope you told her those are unfit aspirations for a woman."

"I did nothing of the sort." She fixed him with an unyielding stare. "You're the only one in this house qualified to teach her."

Conrad shook his head. "While I grant you the girl has a quick mind, I wouldn't want to be the one guilty of leading her into pride of spirit—which usually results when women overreach their bounds. As the saying goes, *non fare il passo più lungo della gamba*. Don't stride longer than your leg."

She ignored the jibe. "Come with me, brother," she said. She led the friar across the soggy courtyard. The rain had stopped at last, although water still dripped from the loggia. In a small room that could only be entered from outside stood a table, two plain chairs and several books. "Read this," she said, opening one of the books to a section marked with a purple ribbon. "It's the life of the holy anchorite San Girolamo."

Conrad's complacency irritated her. He sat down at the table, scanned the biography and looked up smugly. "If the saint wished to teach Roman noblewomen their letters while he served as Pope Damasus' secretary, well and good. Amata's not a Roman *nobildonna,* though."

"Her father was a count."

"*Country* gentry, *madonna.* I doubt that either of her parents could read. She told me herself that she hadn't begun her letters until she arrived at San Damiano."

"And what of Santa Clara, who *founded* San Damiano? Think how much poorer the Church would be without her letters to blessed Agnes of Prague—who could read and answer them herself, by the way. What of Hildegarde of Bingen and Abbess Jutta of Disibodenberg? No man ever described such visions and shimmering lights as Hildegarde."

"Oh yes, visions. I'm sure our Amata has many such experiences to share with the pious *literati.*"

Donna Giacoma ground her teeth. Her face warmed and she knew her cheeks must be glowing. "And what of Hroswitha of Gandersheim who three hundred years ago wrote plays and histories the equal of any male chronicler?"

"I tell you, I can't do it," Conrad said. "I *won't* do it." He set down the book with an air of finality.

Donna Giacoma banged her cane on the table, causing both the friar and the books to jump. "Conrad, you fool! She wants to learn to write so she can copy the chronicle Leo entrusted to you, the scroll you were too timid to carry to Assisi with you."

"What do you know about that?" His eyes bulged.

"I know the manuscript's safe at San Damiano, no thanks to you. I know Amatina risked her life on the edge of a mountain to bring it here, when the scroll wrapped around her waist caught on a rock and upset her balance. I know that, through Fra Leo's blessed intervention, it also saved her life, for it turned aside the pike aimed at her heart." The noblewoman drew herself up to her full height and rested both hands on the carved handle of her cane.

Conrad abruptly leaped to his feet and grasped the table with both hands. "You've answered my prayers, Giacomina!" he said. "Every day since I returned here, I've knelt in your chapel, asking one question of San Francesco and Fra Leo. How can I gain entry into the Sacro Convento again and get the manuscripts I need? I didn't even think of San Damiano and the copies hidden there." He gnawed briefly at one of his knuckles, mulling this new option. "Did Amata leave the Poor Ladies on good terms?"

"Of course. She has done nothing to lose their favor."

"And for love of you, and the deep respect she bore Fra Leo, Mother Prioress might entrust the girl..."

"Don't you dare suggest what you're thinking, brother. I won't place Amatina in further danger. Maestro Roberto says two friars station themselves every morning at either end of our alley, watching all who enter or leave this house."

"It's *my* movements they watch, *madonna*. Their vows require them to keep a chaste distance from secular women. Amata could deliver a gift—of linen, say—to the Poor Ladies. In a basket. She could return with the manuscripts—two in particular that I must see. If she concealed Leo's scroll on her person so cleverly that I failed to observe it, she could easily outwit Bonaventura's watch dogs."

Donna Giacoma was tempted to point out that few friars could match Conrad's naivete and lack of observation, but she held her tongue. Besides, his plan didn't sound totally preposterous. She was about to agree that it merited consideration, when she realized he'd distracted her from her purpose.

"What of her lessons?"

Conrad smiled like a satisfied ox trader. "I'll make a deal. If Amata can bring me Tomas da Celano's first life of San Francesco and the *Legend of the Three Companions*, I'll instruct her. Using appropriate sources, of course."

Donna Giacoma pointed toward the two remaining books on the table. "I studied these as a girl. One is a book of manners; the other instructs young wives in household management. They'll teach her ladylike deportment at the same time she's learning to read."

The friar snorted, an aggravating, supercilious grunt. "Talk about fashioning a trumpet from a boar's tail."

Her grip tightened on the head of her cane. "Well spoken by a man who straggled in here looking like a barbarian a few weeks ago. If I could clean *you* up, Fra Conrad, how much easier it will be to teach the girl. She'll be mistress of this house one day and must be able to handle herself and her affairs accordingly."

Donna Giacoma had succeeded in startling him again. "I have no heirs," she continued, "other than the men of my late husband's family, people I haven't seen in decades. Simone della Rocca despoiled Amatina of her birthright and proper upbringing, as well as her chance for a worthy marriage. When my time comes, she'll have my house and income as her dower, if she so chooses. A woman of her wit and charm and fortune would be an equal match for any man in Christendom—any man not bound by vows of chastity, that is."

Although she seldom spoke maliciously, Donna Giacoma couldn't resist the jab. Conrad had persisted in demeaning the girl and deserved to squirm a bit. She saw that her announcement hadn't set well with him, and she knew she'd rekindled the conflict in his mind. She had her own fantasy, one in which these two young people could come together and at least admit openly how much they cared for each other. Conrad could concede that much and still remain true to his vows. And she knew that true he'd always be, no matter how shabbily the Order treated him. If Conrad had any heroic qualities, they were his persistence and perseverance. She thought of Fra Leo, and how their lives kept intersecting the last fifty-five years of his life. Maybe Conrad and Amatina could at least recreate that pattern, which had brought her such comfort over the years.

To change the subject, Donna Giacoma used her cane to slide the books toward the friar. "While you look these over, I'll talk to Amatina." After a pause, she added: "She'd risk anything to please you, you know." With her business now settled, she allowed herself a smile.

"And brother, please say nothing to her of this last conversation. She believes I merely purchased her bond from the Poor Ladies. She doesn't know yet of my plans for her future."

AMATA STOLE THROUGH Donna Giacoma's front door under the cold, brilliant stars of the scorpion, the same constellation that marked the hour of her birth—how many lifetimes ago? The storm had finally passed into the mountains, leaving only a thin cloak of high clouds to the East. The wind roared up the stairwell near Donna Giacoma's house and blew in every direction through the narrow alley. It numbed her, even through her heavy cloak.

She looked in both directions down the alley. As she expected, the outline of a hooded figure huddled at one end. The friar who guarded the opposite corner had done a better job of concealing himself in the shadows, and protecting himself from the wind, but she felt certain he waited down there somewhere. She picked up her basket and balanced it on her head, arching her back in the graceful, erect posture of a serving woman. She started down the stairs, planning to reach the city's southeastern gate just as the guards opened it for the day.

The wind could be a problem. She wouldn't be able to stop around a curve in the stairs and listen for pursuing footfalls. Well, let them try to keep up with her. She welcomed the challenge of eluding them, just as she'd eventually learned to avoid her captors in the labyrinths of the Rocca.

She'd been disappointed when Giacomina told her Conrad had bartered for her help. Didn't he know she'd have gone for the manuscripts gladly, asking no favor in return? Hadn't he said they were linked in this enterprise, the day they intertwined their cinctures on the mountain ledge? Conrad confused her. Some days he seemed to be her closest friend; at other times he could be totally distant and cold. When she told him how Bonifazio had raped her as a child, she felt as though she had exposed herself naked before him. While he seemed to understand her hurt, he'd avoided her ever since. Maybe he'd heard too much. Maybe this business of the manuscripts preoccupied him. She hoped, as Giacomina told her, that he was simply as bewildered as she was about his feelings toward her and how to show them.

When she reached the end of the Via San Paolo, Amata turned to the northeast and picked up her pace until she came to the Cattedrale di San Rufino. She ducked behind one of the columns of the cathedral porch where she'd have a clear view of the street behind her, and set down her basket.

An uneven light spread through the piazza. The pale sun rose with difficulty over Monte Subasio, straining through the film of clouds. Amata saw a friar cross the piazza from the same direction she'd come. He continued on past the cathedral, still heading northeast. The woman grinned and picked up her basket. This was too easy. She entered the church, hurried down the length of the nave, and left through a door in the transept. She came out into an alley that twisted back toward the south gate of the city and the road to San Damiano.

XXIII

CONRAD KEPT VIGIL over the alley throughout the afternoon. He stationed himself at the shutters, while Donna Giacoma paced from the foyer to the kitchen and back. Each time she completed the circuit she'd glance at him, concern lining her forehead. Amata should have returned by now. They shared the thought, although neither of them spoke the words.

The lengthening shadows of the two-story houses at the end of the row already darkened the alley when Conrad finally saw the woman emerge up the stairwell. She appeared bit-by-bit: basket first, the hood of her cape, then her solemn, half-concealed face. She kept her eyes fixed on the steps, her shoulders and back straightened to balance her load. He rushed to the door before her foot touched the top step. Donna Giacoma's cane tapped rapidly behind him, reacting to the creaking of the door's hinges. Amata swept into the entryway and grinned broadly. She dropped to one knee as she set down her basket and threw back her hood. Then she stood again stiffly.

"Are you all right? Did everything go well?" the noblewoman asked. Conrad knelt and lifted the cloth that covered the lumpy contents of the basket. Bread. Only loaves of fresh-baked bread from the Poor Ladies. He stared up at the girl, making no effort to veil his disappointment.

The girl ignored his petulance. "Nothing to it," she said. "Thump my back." Donna Giacoma rapped at the girl's spine and chuckled at the solid echo.

"The manuscripts are bound," Amata explained. "I wasn't able to wrap them around my waist the way I did Fra Leo's scroll, and I didn't think they'd be safe in the basket. I figured the civil guards must be in league

with Bonaventura. They would have to know those friars stay in our alley
beyond curfew.

"Just as I expected, the guards at the gate searched my basket. Oh, that
basket was a clever idea, Fra Conrad. Because I had to keep it balanced on
my head, no one suspected I couldn't have curved my spine if I wanted to."

"We were so worried about you, Amatina," Donna Giacoma said. "You
were gone so long."

Amata smiled. "I had to wait for the bread to bake. The loaves might
be warm yet, though it's a cold wind that's blowing outside. The wait also
gave me a chance to visit with Suor Agnese. She was my best friend during
our novitiate." She looked down at Fra Conrad, who still knelt beside the
basket. "Do you know of her? She's Fra Salimbene's niece. She said her uncle's
returned to the Romagna and may be in Umbria before long."

She giggled, too excited to wait for his reply. "The stories he told us when
he came to visit Agnese on his last trip! I was so glad she brought me along
to the visitor's gate as her chaperon. I wouldn't have missed a moment. I do
hope you'll have him stay here, *madonna*, instead of at the Sacro Convento.
He'll have the whole house roaring." She sidled crabwise down the corridor
as she jabbered on. "I'll tell you the rest over supper. I need to get these
books off my back."

Conrad's face darkened as he stood, in spite of the good news about the
manuscripts. He caught himself thinking: *It's not my fault I'm not a storyteller. It
doesn't suit my nature. I've always been melancholic; Salimbene has a sanguine humor.
Besides, what a drain of one's spirit, titillating goose-brained little girls.*

Donna Giacoma grinned at the friar as Amata disappeared. "I'll have her
wax tablet and books in the great hall first thing tomorrow. Maestro Roberto
will go for parchment and writing tools as soon as you tell me she's ready for
ink."

"But what of my own work? Leo said these legends were urgent."

"And so they are. Just teach Amata until *mezzagiorno*, when the sun peaks.
Use the rest of the day as your own."

He agreed the arrangement was fair, but also itched to be at the manuscripts. He might begin after supper this evening. But in the past, reading
fine script by candle or torchlight had strained his vision and set his left
eyelid fluttering—a symptom his Paris master attributed to the pale grey
of his irises. Weak-eyed as he was, he'd do better to wait for the sun's next
passage. He picked up the basket of bread and followed the noblewoman to
the kitchen.

AFTER THE STORM passed, a stagnant mist blanketed the valleys of the
Apennines. The mountain peaks thrust above the pallor, floating islands in
a shapeless sea. The pope's ox-drawn carriage rumbled through the fog like

a ghostly, fantastic trunk while all around the high road, mud and clay oozed down the hillsides, a grey-brown flux in a liquefied world.

Several days had passed since the papal party fled Venice. The last of the Roman knights were still catching up to the main body. Tebaldo had bolted so abruptly that many of the warriors had been left behind, scattered through the city's brothels. Their captain had posted a rear guard at the doge's palace, to direct the stragglers on their way and to apologize as best they might to the doge and dogaressa. The laggards described scenes of growing chaos and violence in the city, as word of the disaster spread.

"People were struck dumb at first," one of the tardy knights shouted through a carriage window to the pope. "They gathered all morning on the quay, counting the ships and looking for friends and relatives among the surviving sailors. The city lost most of its two hundred galleys."

Orfeo, who rode beside the pope, prayed a silent blessing on Cecilia's head. She'd saved his life when she convinced him not to join the expedition. He prayed too that God had spared Giuliano, although some instinct in his bones told him his friend already lay at the bottom of the sea.

"The doge's barge arrived around mid-morning, just after Terce," the knight continued. "He stood with the crowd on the quay for a while, and then came to his palace looking for Your Holiness. His face was white as leprosy. Hearing you'd already gone did nothing to settle his nerves. I heard him dispatch one of his men to tell the dogaressa to stay home. Then he went inside the palace and I didn't see him again."

"Aye, by midday the mob'd lost hope of seeing any more of their navy," another knight added. "I passed among them in the square, just returning to my post, when the grumbling started—a lot of it directed against Your Grace, I'm sorry to say. That's when the two of us decided we'd done all we could in Venice."

Orfeo couldn't see the pontiff's face through the narrow slits of the carriage windows. He could hear his pained voice, however. "I did pray for their *safety*, if not their success. God willed the storm. No blessing of mine could have changed that."

Later stragglers recounted the rest of the drama over the next few days. When the Venetians found the pope had escaped them, they vented their despair against the doge. God continued to punish Venice, some wailed, for the sins of Enrico Dandolo and the sack of the Haghia Sophia. Inevitably, the blame came around to Dandolo's current successor, the unlucky Lorenzo Tiepolo (who'd ordered the raid in the first place) and to his Greek-born dogaressa.

The Bishop of Venice ranted and incited the people in front of San Marco's. "God can no longer endure the luxurious habits of this woman. Her rooms hang heavy with incense. Venetian air is not good enough for her.

She scorns to wash herself with our common water, but makes her servants collect the dew that falls from heaven. Nor will she deign to pick up her meat with her fingers in the ordinary fashion, but commands her eunuchs to cut it into small pieces, which she impales on a golden, two-pronged instrument and thus carries to her mouth. I have seen this vanity with my own eyes, for I have supped at their table. Is it any wonder that even the God of infinite patience finally cried '*Enough*' at such insolence?"

Most of the mob directed their fury at the doge himself. They'd seen him enter the palace next to San Marco earlier; thus, he was more accessible than his wife. They shouted abuse through the windows and demanded his life in exchange for the lives of the drowned seamen. Yet, he might have avoided further harm had he waited out their grief and rage. Surrounded by his palace guards, he remained safe despite the crowd's ugly mood. But the finale of the Venetian tragedy was yet to come.

At the end of the Roman company's third afternoon on the road, the last of the rear guard rode into camp. Unaccustomed to full days in the saddle, Orfeo stood massaging his backside behind the group of soldiers who ate with Tebaldo around the campfire.

"Get this man some food," the captain called to a servant as the knight dismounted. Tebaldo motioned the man to a tree stump near himself. Other warriors and their squires emerged from their tents and clustered around, some still half-dressed in their armor. The guard pulled off his bascinet and gauntlets. As the servant handed him a trencher and cup, he inhaled and began his story of the people's revenge.

"I can only guess Lorenzo panicked. He hoped to claim sanctuary in San Marco, but he knew the mob expected such a move. So instead, he fled through a rear door of the palace, making for the church of San Zaccaria across the Ponte della Paglia."

The knight drew out his tale between swallows of wine and mouthfuls of food. He chewed slowly, savoring the center of the stage as well as the hunk of roast that dripped from one greasy paw. "I watched from an upper story of the palace. God knows, the guards who broke out of the palace with the doge did their best to protect him. They struck with their swords in all directions. Blood flowed down both slopes of the bridge, but the people kept crowding in."

He drained off his cup and held it out for a refill. No one spoke while a servant poured wine into the outstretched cup. "Finally," the man concluded after another prolonged swallow, "in the Calle delle Rasse, a man slipped through the ring of soldiers and stabbed Lorenzo to death." The knight thumped his cup against his chest to show where the fatal thrust had entered and, as if the effect were planned, a splash of the red wine sloshed against his breastplate.

A murmur rippled around the ring of listeners. Then stillness settled over the camp again until Tebaldo said in a steady voice, "He was a decent man. May he rest in peace."

"Amen," the warriors responded.

After a respectful silence, the pope added, "We owe special thanks to our young Assisan friend. Save for his quick action, that might have been our own person bleeding in the Calle delle Rasse."

Orfeo found himself unexpectedly buffeted by cheers and a backslap from a beefy hand that sent a shock of pain through his spine and ribs. Until that moment, the haughty Romans had treated him as the Umbrian bumpkin; for his part, he'd cared too little for their opinion to try to convince them otherwise. Suddenly embarrassed, he cried out *Viva Papa!* to deflect the attention back to its source. The others took up the chant, while he escaped through the circle of knights.

In the shadows at the edge of the camp a horse whinnied. Orfeo spotted several pairs of orange eyes glimmering from the shrubbery. He picked up two stones and hammered them together as he stepped in their direction. The lanky, dog-like creatures scattered noiselessly back into the darkness. He recalled the huge wolves of Tebaldo's nightmare. The mariner shivered and crossed himself.

AMATA RACED THROUGH her morning chores, eager to leave as much time as possible for her lessons. Each day Conrad inscribed a new letter on her wax tablet, first in its small form and then its capital, and told her what sound it made. Then she retraced the grooves. After the first week she could write complete words. During the last hour of each lesson, he read a few lines from Donna Giacoma's book of manners or the lives of the saints, pointing to each word as he read so she could follow as she sat beside him. Then he had her read it back to him from memory, until the words began to look familiar.

"Understand that it is discourteous to scratch your head at table, to remove from your neck fleas or other vermin and kill them in front of others, or to scratch or pull at scabs in whatever part of the body they may be.

"When you blow your nose, you should not remove the excrement with the fingers, but in a handkerchief. Take care that no drippings from the nose hang there like icicles that one sees suspended from the eaves of houses in winter.

"Make sure your hair is well combed and that your headdress is not full of feathers or other trash."

Conrad concluded each day's reading with a few lines from his breviary, usually a verse or two from the psalms, and a brief homily pointing out that the spiritual training of the soul still had precedence over worldly wisdom. "The woman who has small understanding and fears God," he said, "is better off than one who has much wisdom and transgresses the law of the Most High." Amata found his stubborn consistency both amusing and reassuring.

The routine helped November pass quickly for her. In the afternoons, while Conrad pored over his legends, she had others who helped reinforce what she'd learned earlier that day. Wandering friars and threadbare clerics passed through the house for days at a time, and those who didn't disapprove entirely seemed fascinated by the novelty of Donna Giacoma's experiment. Imagine an ordinary laywoman being taught to read and write! Next the widow would be teaching her cinnamon-brown mouser to say grace before it lapped its bowl of milk!

Amata suspected that some of the younger men were fascinated for other reasons, although she did nothing to encourage them. Conrad must have thought so too, judging from his expression whenever he passed through the great hall and found her reading with one of these travelers.

With the little subtlety he possessed, Conrad reminded her of her recent, personal vow. When the friar was in such moods, the scriptural readings that ended their lessons came not from the psalms, but from Ecclesiastes: "Behold not every body's beauty, and tarry not among women. For from garments comes a moth, and from woman the iniquity of a man ... I have found a woman more bitter than death; she is the hunter's snare, and her heart is a net, and her hands are bands. He that pleases God shall escape from her, but he that is a sinner shall be caught by her."

Once, he interrupted their lesson to tell her point blank that one of the friars, a Fra Federico, extended his visit solely for the sake of her company. That day he quoted a poet with an unpronounceable name: "Would you define or know what woman is? She is glittering mud, a stinking rose, sweet poison, ever leaning toward that which is forbidden her."

Had she actually been interested in Federico, this fly on Conrad's nose might have offended her. As it was, she had trouble keeping a straight face at his stern indignation. The more he railed, the more consideration she heard behind his harsh words. It was far easier for him to compare her to "glittering mud," and call friars like Federico *un cane in chiesa*, a dog in church, than to say "I care for you and worry about you," but she never failed to hear affection in his scolding.

"I have a plan to protect you from such unprincipled brothers," he said one day. He sent a servant to find Donna Giacoma.

When the noblewoman joined them, Conrad suggested that Amata spend her afternoons repeating her day's lesson to the boy Pio. "Not only will Pio learn from Amata," he said, "the repetition will aid her own memory."

Pio was delighted when Donna Giacoma agreed, since the arrangement gave him one more excuse to hang around Amata. The thwarted Fra Federico moved out of the house, Conrad seemed satisfied, and Amata didn't mind

either. Lessons with the boy were more like play, because he found her book
of injunctions rather silly. She might read,

"If you are forced to belch, do so as quietly as possible, always averting
the face. If you spit or cough, you need not swallow what you have already
drawn into the throat, but spit on the ground or into your handkerchief or
napkin."

Pio would respond by forcing an exaggerated burp, being careful to turn
away his head, or hawk up a wad of phlegm and ask, through pursed lips,
to borrow her handkerchief. The writing lessons on the wax tablet usually
degenerated into more Naughts and Crosses, or a game of Six Men's Mor-
ris with the squares traced on the tablet and scraps of charcoal from the
fireplace used as game pieces.

Conrad said little of his own progress. Amata knew only that he read
Tomas da Celano's legend. He seemed dismayed early on by the biographer's
portrait of San Francesco's youth. The friar said Bonaventura's version had
only suggested euphemistically that the founder had been "drawn to earthly
things" as a young man. "How potent is the grace of God," Conrad added.
"Only His might could have formed a saint from such a beginning. Bonaventura diminishes God's mercy and power by downplaying the full magnitude
of Francesco's conversion."

Amata remembered enough and overheard enough to understand that the
real purpose of Conrad's search through Tomas had to do with blindness or a
blind man, and for a long time he seemed not to have found what he looked
for. That may have changed one afternoon in mid-December, however.

Conrad paced into the great hall where she sat sewing and chatting with
Donna Giacoma. "*In illo tempore*," he muttered to himself. "*At that time*." He
glanced their way, but seemed to stare beyond them. "Why is it significant,
though? In *illo* tempore." He strode to the far end of the hall with his hands
clasped behind his back, skirted the back wall, and stalked back past them
and through the doorway again without another look in their direction. The
two women turned to one another and giggled.

XXIV

B Y THE FIRST WEEK of December, winter had settled over Assisi in earnest.
The wind whistling through the covered windows of the room where
Conrad read became a ceaseless wail, with all the spirits of heaven and
earth joined in lamentable chorus. Monte Subasio and the surrounding hills
rested in turbulent sleep.

Only the gloomiest light filtered through the translucent linen of the
window frames, even at midday. Forced to read in the dim light cast by his
candle and the fireplace, Conrad progressed slowly. Savage gusts hurled
smoke back down the chimney, choking him with the bittersweet smell of
the juniper branches a peasant woman delivered on her donkey each day.

He could have carried his manuscript at any time into the brighter hall
where Amata and Pio studied, with its larger windows and chimney that
drew cleanly, but the many strangers who passed through the house and
the need for secrecy left him leery. On one occasion before he moved out
of the house, Fra Federico had even strayed into Conrad's room as he read.
Conrad did his best to distract the friar, telling him of the new work, Tomas d'Aquino's *Summa Theologica*, that he'd just read at the Sacro Convento,
casually closing Celano's manuscript behind his back as he chatted. Any
traveling scholar would be intrigued—understandably—to come across no
fewer than four books in the house of a lay woman, be she noble or not.
Books of any sort. Banned manuscripts would be *extremely* interesting. So
Conrad kept to himself, grappling with the smoke and poor light, rubbing
his stinging eyes in the privacy of his room.

He knew the history of Celano's legends from his talks with Leo. After
San Francesco's death, the brotherhood assumed that the saint's secretary

would be named to write the hagiography. No one had been closer to Francesco, and Leo's plain, unadorned style matched his master's austere life. But Elias and Cardinal Ugolino instead chose Fra Tomas da Celano for the task, even though the friar had never met Francesco and had spent most of his religious career in Germany. Tomas *had* composed a stately hymn of death and judgment, the *Dies Irae*, demonstrating that he could write eloquently. But as one who had no personal knowledge of Francesco, he'd had to rely for information on the head of the Order who commissioned his task—Fra Elias. Not surprisingly, Elias played a prominent role in Tomas' work—so much so, that after the minister general's disgrace and excommunication, a later general, Fra Crescentius, asked Tomas to write a second legend in which Elias wasn't mentioned once. To help Tomas with this second work, Crescentius asked all the friars who had known Francesco to write down their recollections—and thus the *Legend of the Three Companions* came to be.

Conrad started his search through Tomas with the first line of the first chapter. He wanted to take no chances of missing his clue, the words that marked "the start of blindness." He read a story of a blind woman whom Francesco had healed, but nothing in that account struck a chord with Leo's phrase. He still searched as the snows came. The hands of the peasant woman who brought the firewood turned red with frostbite and she wrapped a heavy black wool shawl over the hood of her cloak, while Conrad coughed his way through chapter after chapter of Tomas' life of Francesco. He read the account of Francesco receiving the stigmata on Monte LaVerna and the apparition of the seraph as Elias must have told it to Tomas. And then, in the chapter immediately *following* the vision, the simple opening words *in illo tempore*, "At that time:"

"At that time, Francesco's body began to be burdened with various and more serious sicknesses than before. For he suffered frequent infirmities inasmuch as he had chastised his body and brought it into subjection during the many years that had preceded."

That Tomas meant the Year of Our Lord 1224, the year of the stigmata, was underscored by the next sentence. Francesco's conversion had taken place in 1206.

"For during the space of eighteen years, *which was now completed*, his body had known little or no rest. ...But since, according to the laws of nature and the constitution of man, it is necessary that our outer man decay day by day, though the inner man is being renewed, that most precious vessel in which the heavenly treasure was hidden began to break up. ...In truth, because he had not yet filled up in his flesh what was lacking of the suffering of Christ, though he bore the marks of the Lord Jesus in his body, *he incurred a very severe infirmity of the eyes*."

There it was, in a single sentence. He *already* bore the marks of the stigmata when his blindness *began*. The eye disease hadn't come about as a result of his trip to Egypt in 1219 as Conrad had always heard. The friar continued reading:

"When the infirmity increased day by day and seemed to be aggravated daily from a lack of care, Fra Elias, whom Francesco had chosen to take the place of a mother in his own regard and to take the place of a father for the rest of the brothers, finally compelled him not to abhor medicine."

When Elias dictated this, he obviously had no reason to conceal the timing of the blindness, nor his own part in its treatment. Who then, later on, started the tale of the hot eastern sun searing the saint's eyes, if not Elias—and why? Tomas' biography didn't name San Francesco's companion when he traveled to the court of the Sultan Melek-el-Kamel. But Bonaventura's had!

Conrad thought back to Lodovico's answer when he asked the librarian why Illuminato's name seemed familiar. "He was with our master when he tried to convert the Sultan." Illuminato *again*! He no doubt had fed Bonaventura the details of Francesco's voyage to the East, just as Elias had fed his version to Tomas. Yet that didn't tell Conrad why Illuminato felt the need to create a different explanation for Francesco's blindness years after Tomas completed his biography.

The friar took out the notes he'd brought from the Sacro Convento and copied down the entire chapter titled, "*Of the fervor of Blessed Francesco and of the infirmity of his eyes*." One day, God willing, he'd reread these passages and understand exactly why his mentor considered this timing important enough to make it part of his letter.

He felt more certain than ever that Leo's mystery centered on events leading up to, or immediately following, the impression of the stigmata. Consequently, when he took out the other book Amata had brought from San Damiano, the Poor Ladies' copy of the *Legenda Trium Sociorum*, he turned directly to that incident in the saint's life. What he found there sent him racing through his notes again.

"IT'S A DISTINCT LACUNA, *madonna*," he explained to Donna Giacoma later that same evening. "A gap so wide you could drive a haywain through it. I now know *how* the Companion was mutilated, though I still can't answer Leo's *why*. Or by *whom*." He doubted the noblewoman could comprehend the details of his latest finding, but asked her to his room because he had to share it with someone before he burst.

"See here," he exclaimed as he ran his finger down the length of one page. "The sixteenth chapter of the Companion ends with events that happened in 1221. Then there's this brief summary of the stigmata—in the Year of Our Lord 1224—and after that the book jumps to San Francesco's death in 1226.

Where are the five years after 1221? So many important changes came about in those years, both in Francesco's life and within the Order. Leo and the other companions would never have glossed over every single event in so crucial a period."

"Save only the imprinting of the stigmata."

"Ah! That's the other thing I want to show you. Look at this description of San Francesco, just before the seraph appeared. Leo wrote clearly, but his style is simple, homespun. *Cum enim seraphicis desideriorium ardoribus: absorbed in seraphic love and desire.* That's elegant Latin, *madonna. Elegant!* And the writer also uses highly technical philosophical expressions, like this *sursum agere.* None of our three companions wrote this. Such a phrase could only have sprung from the mind of a Paris-trained theologian."

Conrad realized he'd been talking faster and faster in his excitement. He took a deep breath and exhaled slowly before he turned to his notes. Donna Giacoma's look meanwhile implied that all this concern for Latinity had gone over her head already, although she'd try her best to keep pace. "Bear with me for yet another moment, *madonna*," he apologized.

He spread out some of his notes beside the manuscript. "Here's Bonaventura's description of the same scene." He pointed out specific passages as he talked. "The identical phrasing occurs in each—here, and here, and here—except that in this passage, *when the vision passed*, where Bonaventura writes *disparens igitur visio*, the Companion has *qua visione disparente*, the ablative absolute—the choice of a less mature mind, in my judgment. The similarity's remarkable considering Bonaventura compiled his *Legenda Major* seventeen years after Leo and the others completed the Companion."

"What do you make of it then?"

Conrad folded his arms across his chest. "I believe we have answered Leo's question: *Whence the seraph?* I make out that this seraph in the Companion came from Bonaventura, whom I know to be fascinated with that particular image—a fascination no doubt stimulated by the story Elias told Celano. I believe the man who served as minister general in 1246, the year Leo submitted the Companion to him, asked a younger Bonaventura to write this insert. That man, who also deleted the five years from the manuscript, was Crescentius of Iesi; Giovanni da Parma, who succeeded him, would never have condoned such a mutilation and forgery. When Bonaventura came to write his own legend years later, he needed only to copy his earlier study of this scene with a few grammatical improvements."

As he unraveled his theory, Conrad had a fleeting intuition that Giovanni's incarceration may have had as much to do with the mutilation as with his "heretical" Joachimism. Donna Giacoma interrupted his train of thought. "But why?"

"But why?" he repeated her question in a puzzled whisper as he regathered his notes. "That's the question I keep coming back to myself. But *why?*"

He stacked the sheets of notes on top of the Companion and stooped to put both books away. The slap of sandals in the arcade speeded his action. He was still doubled over when Pio appeared in the doorway.

"There's someone from the Sacro Convento here to see you, brother."

"One of the friars? They shouldn't be out at this hour."

"He wears a friar's robe, but he's only my age. I think he ran all the way. He was so out of breath he could hardly talk."

"Did he give his name?"

"Yes. Ubertino da Casale."

THE BOY'S CHEEKS and nose and ears glowed bright pink, a combination of the cold and his exertion. He shifted restlessly from foot-to-foot as he waited just inside the front door, his normally fair eyes dilated almost black.

"*Buona notte*, brother," Conrad greeted him. "What's wrong? Why are you still up after Compline?"

"I stole out after everyone else went to bed. I had to talk to you."

"How did you do *that?*" Conrad asked. Oddly, he found himself more curious about the *how* than the *why* of Ubertino's visit. He'd faced that dilemma the month before. As far as he knew, the friars locked the Sacro Convento tight once darkness fell.

The boy's face shaded a deeper red as Donna Giacoma joined them. He seemed shyer, speaking in front of the woman. "There's a crawl-through door that leads from the friary into the crypt beneath the lower church. It's never used and the lock's all but rusted away. One of the novices showed it to me the other day."

"Well, you're a little fool. Bonaventura will punish you severely if he finds out you came here. He has spies who watch this house constantly."

Some of the color drained from the boy's cheeks. "I saw no one in the streets," he said. He glanced nervously toward the doorway. Obviously, he hadn't considered the possibility of sentries. "I had to warn you."

Donna Giacoma touched Conrad's arm. "Hold your tongue a moment, brother. Don't scare the boy any more than he is already. Let him speak."

Ubertino smiled gratefully. "I served supper in the infirmary this evening," he said to Conrad. "The minister general had a guest, a Fra Federico. They were talking about you."

Federico! Was he another of Bonaventura's spies? Had he been trying to pry information from Amata all those afternoons while Conrad studied?

"Federico said you had books Fra Bonaventura should see. The minister general was furious! He said he'd have them—and you too! He plans to send Federico back here with another friar to steal them.

"He said you'd probably leave the house the day after tomorrow. A herald came to the friary this afternoon with word that the pope's just two days away. He'll be stopping in the city for several days and Fra Bonaventura said the whole city will turn out to cheer him. He told Federico he'd have you seized when you ventured out."

Conrad stood dumb as a doorjamb, until Donna Giacoma pounded her cane on the tile and jarred him from his trance. "Bonaventura's turned as wicked as the others," she said. "Power rots them all. I'd hoped for better from him."

Pio waited a discreet distance down the hall. The noblewoman motioned to him. "Amata should be in the chapel, saying her evening prayers. Wait outside until she's finished and bring her here."

As Pio hurried away, the noblewoman patted Ubertino on the shoulder. "You're a brave child. It's the young ones like you, and Fra Conrad here, who keep me hopeful for the Order. Would you like something hot to drink before you go back?"

The boy shook his head.

Conrad finally found his tongue. "Why did you risk this for me?"

Ubertino blushed. He seemed flustered now that he'd done the daring part of his task. "A lot of the friars say you're a holy man. They say that someday the minister general will lock you up forever. That doesn't seem right, if you've done nothing wrong."

Conrad managed a sardonic smile at the boy's innocence. "If you'll recall your scriptures, that's how the Church began, with the persecution of an innocent man." He took the boy's right hand in both of his. *"Mille grazie,* Ubertino. I hope I can repay you one day. For now, be careful when you leave the house. We don't want *you* locked up, or flogged either."

The door clicked shut behind the novice as Pio returned with Amata in tow. She looked quizzically into Donna Giacoma's face. "We've just had disturbing news, Amatina," the old woman said. Sarcasm withered her words like an arid wind. "Our minister general is bucking hard for preferment, maybe even sainthood. He's willing to sacrifice our godly friend Fra Conrad to maintain the fiction of harmony in the Order—just as he did with Fra Giovanni da Parma."

Her words jolted Conrad. They might have come from his own mouth! She turned to him, her face taut with concern. "You need to escape, back to the mountains," she said.

Her plan caught him off guard, as much as it did Amata. His shoulders slumped in disappointment, and seeing the same disappointment in the girl's eyes didn't let him down any easier. "This isn't the time for our little family to be together," the noblewoman continued. "The idyll we've enjoyed the past month was just that—an interlude." She stretched out her arms and took each of them by the hand. Conrad flinched, but didn't pull his hand away. "God willing, we'll come together again one day, and that in my lifetime."

She released their hands and turned to Amata. "Can you take the books back to San Damiano? We need to act before daybreak." The younger woman nodded. "I think you should leave the city together, by the closest gate, the Porta di Murorupto on the north wall. You should be positioned nearby so you can leave as soon as the morning *Angelus* rings and the gate opens." Donna Giacoma spoke with the precision of a military captain deploying her troops, worrying the handle of her cane as her mind worked through the details.

"How long is your hair now, child?" she asked. Amata lifted a corner of her wimple.

"Good. Not too long yet. It's time you became a friar novice again. The civil guards will be less wary of two brothers leaving the city than of either of you traveling alone."

Her green eyes flashed. "Bonaventura doesn't know we're aware of his plan, so surprise is on our side. We can act while the brothers sleep. I doubt the minister general has notified the city guards yet, either, but the friars posted in our alley may be more alert than usual. Amata, stay on a day or two at San Damiano before you return here. Once Bonaventura discovers Fra Conrad's gotten away, he should call off his sentries."

She turned from one to the other, her face reflecting the pride and fear, anger and sadness she felt at this abrupt rupture in her household. She looked spent, but determined. Again she reached out to them and closed her eyes. Lifting her face toward the ceiling, she prayed: "Dear God, please don't make me give up my children again."

XXV

AMATA CROUCHED BEHIND Conrad in the portico of a house that
bordered the Piazza di San Francesco. The night smelled of snow and ice
and slush. In the crisp air the slightest noise—rats rustling through
the open sewers, wind creaking the chains of a free-hanging signboard—
echoed eerily through the deserted streets. She wished she might lean
against the friar, to draw heat from his body, but she knew Conrad would
rather see both of them frozen first.

To her left she had a clear view across the piazza to the basilica; to the
right, the barred gate of the Porta di Murorupto blocked their escape. She
and Conrad had risen in the early morning darkness, when the bells of the
basilica summoned the friars to Matins. They slipped from Donna Giacoma's
house with the manuscripts strapped to Amata's body again. At the time
they had seen no sign of Bonaventura's sentries, but each moment the gate
remained closed increased the woman's nervousness. She shivered, both
from anxiety and cold, as the wind nipped at her toes and ankles and calves.
A bead of cold sweat traced a winding path down the ridge of her spine. In
spite of her clenched jaw, her teeth clacked together, causing the friar to turn
and frown.

"The *Angelus* should have rung by now," he whispered. Time must be
passing slowly for him too, Amata thought. Although the sky would remain
dark for some time, every pounding heartbeat measured the passage of an
eternity.

Suddenly, Conrad muttered something inaudible. She craned her neck
to see over his shoulder. Two lanterns swung from the direction of the Via
San Paolo, the way they'd just come, and were headed directly toward them.

A few steps closer and she could see the outlines of the friars who carried them. She felt a sudden urge to urinate; fear squeezed her lower abdomen and melted her insides.

"Wait here," Conrad said. He set down the food Donna Giacoma's cook had packed for his journey. "Be ready to move as soon as the gate opens. I'll catch up to you on the road." Before she could reply, he stood and walked in full view across the piazza, increasing speed until he almost ran when he reached the basilica. *What's he up to?* The lanterns veered toward the church, too. She kept her eyes fixed on the dark side wall of the basilica, hoping to see him re-emerge through a different door, as she had the day she brought the manuscripts from San Damiano.

Conrad had dashed off before she could tell him the thought she'd been harboring. She'd wanted to speak to him before now, but had been afraid to talk or even whisper, to create the slightest noise that might disclose their hiding place. She'd decided to wait until they were outside the city, and now he was gone.

She had already composed (and recomposed) the speech in her mind. The sum of it was: would he let her go with him into the mountains after she returned the manuscripts to the Poor Ladies? Her life at Donna Giacoma's was the best she'd known since Simone della Rocca dragged her from the Coldimezzo, but she still needed to be totally free. And while she knew she wouldn't be able to say these particular words, her feelings for Conrad had grown stronger too. She'd never before known a man who seemed so intent on her good, although he didn't use the kindest words to say so, and who asked nothing from her in return. She remembered the softness of his lips when they brushed her forehead on the mountain ledge. "A kiss goodbye in case we die." Amata needed such a kiss now. She knew she could never hope for anything more than friendship from him. But she had a resourcefulness he lacked. She'd be a help to him, once she learned the ways of survival in the mountains. She could even free him from his chores, so he could spend more time in contemplation. She'd build her own hut apart from his, and they'd live together, but separate, like two holy hermits, and he could be her spiritual director.

The friars with the lanterns disappeared into the basilica and fear scattered her fantasy. *Conrad! Where the hell are you?*

The bell in the campanile of the basilica tolled three times, the *Angelus* at last! She mouthed the prayer, as sincerely as she had ever prayed, as she rose to her feet, keeping an eye on the porter as he stumbled from the gatehouse:

"The angel of the Lord declared unto Mary,
And she conceived of the Holy Spirit.
Ave Maria, gratia plena, Dominus tecum..."

The bell rang three more times, and the gatekeeper hoisted the heavy wooden bar that spanned the gate. Still no sign of Conrad outside the church.

"Behold the handmaiden of the Lord.

Be it done unto me according to thy word.

Ave Maria, gratia plena..."

She should move now. The bell would ring three more times, while the Word became Flesh and dwelt among us, followed by a third silence for the last *Ave Maria* and antiphon, and then a sustained pealing while the bleary-eyed faithful all through the city rolled from their mats.

Amata stepped from the shadows and padded toward the gate, but the third set of chimes never came. She'd walked halfway across the piazza when she saw the porter stop and look up at the campanile with a puzzled expression. She realized now why Conrad had left her. It was he who pulled the bell rope and the friars with the lanterns had chased him off—or worse, captured him.

The guard glanced from the basilica to her. He still held the crossbeam in his arms. He turned his back momentarily to reposition the beam across the gate. A lantern emerged from the main door of the basilica and moved toward the gatehouse. She was trapped in the city!

Above the northernmost fringe of homes, an undeveloped, scrub-covered hillside rose toward the Rocca. The city's ramparts swung out and up the hill to enclose the citadel, so that the north wall of the Rocca also formed a section of the city wall. Amata plunged into the brush. She hoped she could work her way between the houses and the fortress, then around to the lower city, before the friars alerted the porters on that end. She also hoped the friar and guard wouldn't pursue her. She knew she couldn't hide in the brush. With the lantern, they could easily track her footsteps through the hillside's thin coating of snow.

She was still within hailing range of the piazza when a sharp voice called after her, "You there, friar! Halt!" Without looking back, she started to run, but her sandals slipped on the uneven surface and the icy scrabble beneath the snow. She lost her footing and cried out as she skidded a short distance down the hillside. Her heart throbbed in her temples while she regained her footing and set off again. "I'll give chase," the voice behind her shouted. "You cut through the city and keep a watch below."

She forged on through the brush, hoping she could outrun the older man pursuing her, or at least that the going would be equally slow for him. She grabbed at the bushes as she passed, feeling the branches tearing the skin of her hands and arms, but also holding her upright as she used them for handholds. The crashing to her rear subsided enough that she knew she gained on the guard. He still followed though, occasional curses or the clattering of metal pinpointing his location when he slipped. Ahead of her, the first grey light of day silhouetted Monte Subasio.

Midway across the hillside she came upon a cleared strip winding its way upward through the bushes. Even covered with snow as it was, she recognized the road to the Rocca. She paused, thinking she might shake the guard if she headed uphill first, then continued across. He seemed to be laboring, and the steep hill might discourage him enough that he'd give off the chase. She'd only climbed a few paces, however, when she stopped again, startled by an irregular staccato on the path above her. Too late she recognized the sound of cautious hoofbeats, for the rider appeared from the darkness almost on top of her. Had he been galloping at normal speed, the enormous warhorse would have run her down.

She darted for the cover on the far side of the path, but the horseman blocked her escape. "Hold, friar," he said. "Providence has placed you in my path." She recognized the guttural voice of Calisto di Simone and froze in her tracks.

For one wild instant, she imagined the night watch had alerted him, but then realized he had no way of knowing her plight. She lowered her head beneath her cowl and tried to remain motionless, even though she could hear the crashing in the shrubbery drawing near.

"Are you a priest?" Calisto asked. "My father's dying and needs shriving."

She had to decide quickly, trapped as she was between the rock and the whirlpool. The guard would burst from the brush any moment. "Yes, *signore*," she replied, making her voice as deep as she could. She hadn't spoken since she'd left Donna Giacoma's house, and the raspy, early-morning roughness of it aided her charade. "Give me a ride. We've no time to waste."

Calisto kicked his foot free of his left stirrup. He held his hand out to her as she placed her own sandaled foot in its stead. Although most of his fingers curved around her hand, his index finger remained upright, unable to bend. She smiled grimly beneath her hood as she swung up onto the horse's crupper. It was a small vengeance, but she knew he'd never forget one girl he'd tried to rape. For just an instant she considered finishing the job—sliding her knife between his ribs and taking his horse. She'd still be trapped within the walls, though, and a friar riding a warhorse would definitely attract attention.

"Grab my belt," he said, as he spurred his horse. She did so gingerly, wishing she might grab his throat instead. She gave the horse an extra swat on its rump to urge it on. She was thankful now that Donna Giacoma had suggested strapping the books around her waist, one in front and one behind her. Not only did this afford her more flexibility, but the front book now acted as a buffer between her body and Calisto's. She probably looked older too, with the added girth around her waist.

She saw the pitch-black entryway of the castle ahead of her, outlined with torches and yawning like a voracious maw. *Prepare to enter again into hell*, a small voice mocked inside her head. She knew she trembled entirely from fear now, rather than cold, for sweat began to trickle down her sides and under her breasts in spite of the icy air.

What if Calisto discovered her identity? If he didn't decapitate her with his broadsword or battle-ax, she'd be imprisoned and brutalized forever. She felt a sudden urge to slip off the horse's croup and bolt for cover again, but she didn't need a determined warrior on her heels too. She had to play out the role she'd claimed. She'd seen Extreme Unction administered only once, when her grandfather, *Nonno* Capitanio, died. She knew it involved holy chrism, and she had no oil of any kind with her. Could she use the household's olive oil and mumble some kind of blessing over it? Maybe she could claim the urgency of the situation as an excuse to skip the ritual. She decided she'd offer to hear Simone's confession and pray God to inspire her actions from there.

"Duck!" Calisto yelled as they clattered across the courtyard. The front door of the Rocca swung open and he continued on horseback into the castle. He negotiated several corridors until they came to the great hall. She slipped from the horse while he dismounted and tossed the reins to a servant. Several people holding candles gathered around a bed in the middle of the room.

Amata could scarcely believe that the shrunken figure buried among the pillows was her old tormenter—this shriveled, powdery-white moth with wings and antennae plucked, and tiny black caverns where his eyes should be. Except for one arm that rested outside the covers, the bedding enclosed him from the neck down like a winding-sheet cocoon. She walked directly to his side, keeping her cowl over her head. "Please clear the room and close the doors that I may hear his last confession," she said.

"He can't talk," Calisto said. "He only mumbles gibberish."

She hadn't considered that possibility. She stared down at the motionless form. "Is he paralytic? Can he move his hand, even a finger?"

"He's paralyzed, but on one side only."

"Then I'll recite the litany of sin to him, and he can respond 'yea' or 'no' by moving his finger up-and-down or side-to-side."

Calisto nodded and herded the others from the room. When the door closed behind them and she was alone with Simone, she addressed the insect on the pillow. "Can you hear me, you miserable sinner?" she began.

A look of terror rose in Simone's sunken eyes as they rolled in her direction. "Yes, you're dying. I've been asked to pluck your soul from the flames of hell. Have you ever sworn false oaths or taken God's name in vain?" His hand moved slightly. "Yes, of course you have, thousands of times, for I've heard you with my own ears. And have you not dishonored the Blessed Mother and your lady wife with your adulteries, abusing your male and female servants and even your own daughter in the lust of your heart? Do you not deserve to burn through a million eternities over for your crimes?"

The terror mingled with pleading now in the hollow sockets, but she wouldn't relent. "Did you not murder Buonconte di Capitanio while he prayed in his chapel at the Coldimezzo, along with his son and his wife Cristiana? Did you not enslave his daughter and subject her to the vilest abuse? Don't try to deny your sins, Simone, for God sees into the deepest recesses of your evil soul."

The old knight tried to twist away from her, but she grabbed his shoulder and held him in place. She pulled back her hood. "Look at me closely," she said. "See that I am that same Amata, Amata di Buonconte whom you ruined, and no priest. I have no power to unburden your soul, even if I wished to do so. This very night you shall dance with the devil in hell, and every night after this for all eternity. You're damned, Simone! *Damned and doomed!*"

With his last strength Simone stretched his unparalyzed hand toward the bell on his nightstand, but Amata caught his wrist and held it suspended in mid-air. She could feel the power drain from him. "When I lived as a captive here," she said, "you were like a leech that had fastened onto my heart and sucked my life blood. Now, at last, the filthy creature has dropped away and returned to *your* heart, where I pray it will gorge itself until you're too rotten to nourish it."

The knight began to cough, and saliva dribbled down his chin. The choking worsened as he struggled to free his hand, and the blanched face first turned a pinkish-blue, then shaded to deep purple. As his face darkened, a stubble of white whiskers appeared on his cheeks. To Amata, the whiskers resembled stars emerging in a darkening sky. The novelty of the image captivated her, even though part of her mind also registered that Simone couldn't breath. In this state of dream-like fascination she held his wrist firmly until his exertions ceased. Then she laid his arm across his chest. She took his other arm from under the covers and placed it on top of the first.

"You bastard," she said as she dropped the hand. She wiped her eyes with the heel of her hand to stem the hot tears that unexpectedly welled there. "You even stole the ring *Nonno* Capitanio gave my father." She tried to wrest the lapis lazuli from his finger, but his hand was too cramped. "Cowardly, thieving bastard," she hissed. She fumbled for the knife strapped to her wrist, thinking to cut off his ring finger, but just at that moment the door cracked open. She covered her head with her hood again and said in a somber voice, "He's gone. May his soul now receive its just reward."

She waved her hand over the corpse, being careful not to form an actual cross and accidentally bless it, and walked to the door. In the corridor, Calisto straightened in a pose befitting the new *signore* of the Rocca Paida. "Stop in our kitchen before you leave, padre." He motioned to a servant, and Amata followed the woman.

Amata knew quite well the way to the kitchen, just as she knew where every other corridor in this labyrinth led. How often had she and her mistress played hide-and-seek in these hallways? How often had she used them to escape Simone and his sons? At one point where two hallways crossed, she allowed the servant to continue straight ahead, while she slipped her feet from her sandals and tiptoed quickly to the right. She had to make it to the next turn before the woman realized she no longer followed. A left, another right, down a flight of stairs, and she came to the sally port in the castle's north wall. She removed the bar and shoved it open.

She was safe, outside the castle walls, outside the city! She could skirt Assisi easily now, staying a cautious distance from the ramparts and using the shelter of surrounding groves as she made her way to San Damiano. She'd return the manuscripts and then, if her good fortune held, she would find Conrad. Had he escaped, he'd flee to his hermitage; she would follow him there and tell him her plan.

The sky had lightened, white and clear except for a solitary rain cloud as black as a charred cinder that hung directly above the Rocca. As she watched, it began to drift, slowly at first, then with greater speed as it blew southward. Amata thought: there goes his dark, unredeemed soul, along with the million sordid images that fed it. She pictured Simone writhing in a lake of flame, screaming with pain while legions of demons prodded him with glowing-hot pikes and hayforks. *Thank You, Lord*, she prayed, *for letting me play a part in his unredemption*.

She'd avenged her parents' death—if only in part. Someday, in some manner, she'd visit equal vengeance on the house of Angelo Bernardone, the wool merchant who hired Simone and his bloodthirsty son.

XXVI

THE FIRST DAY, Conrad stayed in an isolation cell, waiting for Bonaventura to decide his fate. Two friars searched him, taking his breviary and Leo's letter, his flint and his eating knife. His notes he'd left behind at Donna Giacoma's house. He'd also memorized the letter from his mentor long before and actually felt a sense of relief to be rid of his other possessions. Now he owned absolutely nothing but the clothing demanded by modesty. The friars left him both his robes—the old threadbare tunic *he* insisted on wearing when he left Donna Giacoma's, and his new robe that *she* insisted he wear over it. She believed the gatekeeper would be more likely to let him pass in the garb of a Conventual brother. The friars did take his woolen cape, however, and tore off the hoods of both his robes to signify his dishonored state.

The dank, underground cell had the scent of freshly-opened soil. He welcomed the extra robe, as he couldn't move to keep warm. An iron manacle anchored in the wall fettered one ankle and a leather neck band restricted motion in his upper body. Within a few hours in the windowless room, he lost all sense of time. He didn't know at what point in the day or night the friars returned. One released his ankle, and the other led him out of the room by a chain attached to his neck band. He recalled a harvest festival where he'd seen a bear led by the neck and chained to a stake where it had to duel against a pack of snapping hounds until it finally bled to death from its numerous bite wounds. Perhaps it was that memory that aroused the foreboding in his heart.

The brightness of the room they finally entered forced Conrad to clamp his eyes shut for an instant. As he reopened them little-by-little, he saw a fire roaring in one corner and a frightening collection of pincers and pokers and odd-shaped iron tools piled near it. A third friar bent over the fire. His captors had brought him to a torture chamber!

He had a sudden premonition that Bonaventura meant to brand his forehead before releasing him—a warning to other disobedient brothers. As Conrad entered, the brother torturer extracted a poker from the flames and blew on its glowing tip. Tiny sparks shot away from the metal and the tip throbbed a vibrant orange. *And now comes the claw of the gryphon*, Conrad thought.

The two friars led him to a wall, where they shackled his ankles and wrists. One of the manacles pinched the skin on his leg as it snapped shut and he yelped involuntarily. Without looking around, the man by the fire said: "As the kite said to the hen when he carried her off, '*You may squawk now, but this isn't the worst.*'"

Conrad knew that voice, but the last time he'd heard it, the speaker had been the one in anguish. The man turned slowly, and in the flickering glow of the fire the friar saw the straw-colored tonsure and the scar tissue that covered half his face. The mouth twisted in a perverse smile as Zefferino fixed his good eye on him.

"Not a pretty sight, is it, brother? You can see why I asked to be gaoler here. Above ground, this face brings only repulsion and mockery upon me." He signaled the other two to leave the room. "Torture's a new occupation with me. I don't want to sicken them if I botch it," he explained to Conrad.

"What do you mean to do?"

Zefferino turned away again and spoke into the flames. "I mean to observe the ancient law: an eye for an eye." He twisted his head and shot Conrad a look of pure malice.

"But *why?*"

"For looking into that which concerns you not. Did you think you could ignore the general's warning without penalty? *Quando si è in ballo, bisogna ballare*. When you come to the dance, you must dance."

"Zefferino, for God's sake!" Conrad pleaded. "I shrove you when you feared you were dying. I sent help to the chapel for you." The friar didn't respond, and Conrad said: "Christ did away with the law of the Old Testament. He replaced it with a new law of love and forgiveness. Forgive your enemy seventy times seven."

Zefferino straightened and blew on the poker one final time. "He also said, 'If thine eye offends thee, pluck it out.' And thine eye, thine unimpeded sight, offend me exceedingly, Fra Conrad. It's on your account that I am what I am, and where I am, today."

As the friar crossed the room, Conrad's mind raced through an episode from San Francesco's life, a time when the doctors tried to cure his blindness by cauterizing the veins from his jawbone to his eyebrow. Fearful though he was, Francesco besought his Brother Fire: "Be kind to me in this hour. Be courteous. Temper your heat that I may bear it when you burn me." Conrad repeated the appeal, addressing the inanimate poker.

The smell of hot iron near his face seared his nostrils and he clamped his eyes shut. Crimson pain exploded through his eyelid as the fiery claw scorched his flesh. He screamed in spite of the stoic image of San Francesco he held in his mind.

"Be glad I lost but half my sight, brother!" Zefferino shouted above the shrieks of pain, just before Conrad slumped, unconscious.

ORFEO NEVER IMAGINED the walls of Assisi would appear so welcome to him. The last week of their journey had been horrendous, as the snow deepened and the wolves that scavenged in the wake of their convoy grew bolder. The Romans lost two horses in one night when the frightened animals jerked free of their tethers and ran from the camp, drawing the wolf pack after them. The wolves didn't show up again for two days.

The many hours on horseback had beaten him down. If he'd learned nothing else on this trip, it was that he much preferred the hard wooden bench of a galley to a leather saddle. At least the bench stayed in one place. The elderly pope had been battered even more than he as his carriage jounced over the paving stones of the high road, careening from side to side in a continuous jostling. Tebaldo welcomed the overnight pauses at major villages and towns, when he could get out and stretch while he acknowledged the cheers and good will of the townsfolk and could sleep in a real bed.

The papal entourage had reached Assisi's southeastern gate. The townspeople ranged all along the south wall, leaning out and waving from the openings of the crenellated ramparts, and hundreds more spilled outside the city. As at every other stop, the surrounding mountains resounded with cries of "*Viva Papa!*"

Down the hillside to his left, Orfeo saw the convent where Uncle Francesco's nuns lived. A solitary female, wearing a half-length black cloak over a grey robe, ascended the path from San Damiano. She climbed toward the high road at a rapid pace, rushing to be part of the spectacle.

Orfeo dismounted when the pope's carriage stopped before the gate. The crowd parted to allow a richly-dressed civilian and a friar to approach. The pontiff stepped out to meet them.

Orfeo guessed they were the city's mayor, one that he didn't recognize, and Fra Bonaventura, the minister general Tebaldo praised so highly. Only Assisi's bishop was missing to complete the tableau.

The young man walked his horse nearer while the secular and religious leaders dropped to their knees before the pope and kissed his ring. When they rose again, Tebaldo spoke mostly to Bonaventura, of church reform and of a General Council he intended to convene once he'd settled into his new role. The minister general replied in turn that the unoccupied bishop's palace had been prepared for Tebaldo's visit and that he wished to discuss the vacant bishopric with the pope. He had an excellent candidate in mind, one of his own friars. The two men then backed away as Tebaldo motioned Orfeo to draw near.

"Let us bless you, my son, before you go your way. Know that we are eternally grateful for your help, and if ever you have need of papal favor, you have but to ask."

Orfeo knelt in the slush before the pope. Tebaldo placed both hands on his head and prayed quietly. Then he took Orfeo by the shoulders and helped him to his feet. "Remember what I said. Enmity between father and son distresses the natural order. Go now and make your peace at home. May your days be many, may they be filled with bounty and joy, and may Our Lord welcome you into His bosom at the end of your time. We shall ever remember you."

The crowd had hushed during the pope's blessing. As Orfeo looked around him, he saw a respect akin to reverence in the eyes of the onlookers. Doubtless, they didn't recognize him as one of their own, but only knew him to be a special favorite of the Holy Father.

At the front of the crowd stood the woman in the black cape. She was young, pretty, and seemed faintly familiar, although most of the women of this district had the same dark, almond-shaped eyes. She regarded him curiously, too. He tried to picture her as she might have looked six years before, but gave up when he realized she'd have been no more than a child—as he himself was then.

Others of the leading citizens came forward to receive the pontiff's blessing. Orfeo tugged at his horse's reins and made his way through the throng toward the gate. He noticed that the woman followed at a short distance, maybe wanting to hear what he said to the porter. She seemed interested. He'd use the opportunity to introduce himself.

The porter saluted him. "Do you plan to stay with us a while, *signore?*"

"I've come home. For how long, I don't yet know." He laughed at the guard's puzzled look. "Don't you recognize me, Adamo? I'm Orfeo di Angelo Bernardone."

"My God, how you've grown," the guard said. "You were just a stripling when you left here. Look at you. You're a filled-out man now."

Orfeo smiled and glanced casually toward the woman. The ferocity of her glare as she hurried past him into the city left him bewildered.

AS SHE CLIMBED through the city, Amata pictured Bernardone's son again, the vaguely familiar man at the city gate who called himself Orfeo.

Her imagination churned. How the elderly Angelo would suffer at the destruction of his child, probably more than if she attacked him directly. She'd find out from Maestro Roberto where the clan lived. She'd invent a pretext to go there, some market day perhaps when the Bernardones were out in force displaying their wares. For her own safety, she should destroy the whole family, branch and trunk and root, but if she avenged herself only on this Orfeo before someone snatched the knife from her hand, she could die satisfied.

The euphoria that had sustained Amata the last two days since she'd dispatched Simone della Rocca to hell melted within moments of her return to Donna Giacoma's.

"Bonaventura has him," the old woman said as soon as Amata entered the house. Her listless green eyes reflected her distress. For the only time since Amata had come to know her, the noblewoman seemed to have lost heart and to show her age.

"The boy Ubertino came again last night. He said the friars captured Conrad in the basilica and took him to the dungeons."

Amata needed a moment to absorb the shock of this news. Her mind still swam with images of revenge on Angelo Bernardone and his son. When she finally spoke, her voice was as flat as the noblewoman's mood. "I came back to tell you I wanted to go with him."

The old woman tilted her head and sighed. "*Amor regge senza legge*," she intoned. "Love rules without rules." She took Amata's arm. "It could never have worked, child. Wherever he lives, free or captive, Conrad is God's alone." She added: "But stay here with us and be patient. He may be freed yet."

Amata nodded, although she scarcely heard the words. She withdrew her arm and walked in a daze to her chamber. She stretched out on her bed and curled her arm over her face. She touched the weapon under her sleeve, fighting back depression and the desire to weep. *There really is nothing left to me but the vendetta*, she thought.

Her mind returned to the Coldimezzo, and from the parapet of her tower she overheard once more the quarrel between her father and the wool merchant. She remembered how Angelo Bernardone's sons had rallied around their father while he ranted and threatened. All except one, that pretty boy who had started her dreaming of babies. The boy ignored the commotion. Instead, he'd fashioned a puppet from a yellow scarf and turned in his saddle to smile up at her—*the same complacent smile he'd just turned toward her at the gate*.

She could stem her tears no longer and they fell freely onto her pillow. "Not *him*!" she murmured. "Oh papa, mamma, Fabiano . . . does *he* have to be the one to pay?" She wept until all the sorrow had ebbed from her heart. Then she sat up on the edge of her bed and wiped her face with her sleeve. While her emptied heart petrified in her breast, she whispered her vow, "So be it. Even *he*."

CONRAD TRIED TO BEAR his laceration instant-by-instant. *I can deal with the pain this long, if no longer*, he repeated to himself. *This long, if no longer. This long...*

He stumbled behind the light of Zefferino's torch, shielding his mutilated eye with the palm of his hand. He heard a key click in a padlock and the gaoler lifted the grate to a cell. Still trembling from shock, Conrad followed him down the cold steps. In the torture chamber Zefferino had attached bands like falconer's jesses to his ankles and he now linked a chain through the loops in the manacles. Darkness black as mortal sin settled around him once the guard replaced the grate and the torch faded back along the shaft that served as a corridor to this nether world. He fought to stay conscious, but finally succumbed and slid once more into the void.

Sometime later—whether minutes, hours, days he couldn't say—he struggled to his feet. The trembling had settled, but the sting in his eye was excruciating.

This wasn't the same cell where he'd waited earlier. This room sloped away from the steps toward its furthest corner, and the silence here wasn't total either. Water trickled down the wall to his right. He groped along the stones with one hand until he came to the damp area and leaned his eye socket gratefully into the cold spring. Even as it soaked, the irony of the situation struck him, how through the labyrinthine workings of the Mind of God, both he and Zefferino had lost an eye, and neither was the wiser for it. Both had been thwarted from completing their missions. He'd become an actual prisoner, while Zefferino was virtually imprisoned. Yet, with all this commonality, Zefferino insisted they were enemies.

He became aware of a stench rising from the lowest corner of the room. The water must pool there, he realized, and form the latrine for this cell as it flowed out through a hole in the wall. But if the latrine stank, it must be in use. He turned and scanned the thick air with his remaining eye. "Is there another prisoner here?" he called.

A metallic clink echoed back from across the room. A weak voice crackled like a death rattle. "Why do we stay here, mamma? Why can't we go away?"

"Tell me your name, brother," Conrad said.

The voice dipped into a singsong melody. "A hedge of trees surrounds me, a cuckoo's lay sings to me."

Conrad leaned his face against the wet wall again. The spring gushed down his cheek and robe like a font of despair. He knew that many friars had been arrested over the years as schismatics and heretics, condemned to perpetual imprisonment, deprived of books and the sacraments. The ministers so dreaded their influence that they forbade even the friars who brought the prisoners food to speak to them. Every week the hebdomedary reread their sentences in the chapters of the various friaries, with the clear implication that any brother who reflected aloud on the injustice of these sentences would share an equal fate. Conrad knew himself to be no heretic, but Bonaventura might consider him schismatic and use that pretext to make *his* imprisonment perpetual also. How many months or years did he have, he wondered, before he turned into the pitiable fool across the cell?

The man sang again, a poem Conrad remembered from his own boyhood:
"The ship sails tonight
In the bright moon light,
With her sails a-billowing white.
The ship sails tonight..."

Conrad had a sudden, unsettling glimmer of his cellmate's identity. He raised his voice to a higher pitch and called out tentatively, "Giovanni. Giovanni. Time to come inside."

"*Vengo, mamma*," the man replied in the voice of a small child. "I'm coming."

The shuffling and clinking drew nearer as the man slowly closed the space between them. When he stood but a few steps away, Conrad finally saw the nearly-naked, cadaverous creature, wavering pale and spectral in the darkness. The prisoner might have been a sea-washed skeleton, but for his shoulder-length white hair and the scraggly beard that reached almost to his waist. Conrad stretched out his hand and touched the man's exposed ribs. "Unhappy boy," he said. "You've lost your cloak."

Salt tears stabbed his mangled eye while he peeled off his outer robe and helped the creature slide it over his arms and head. Then he enveloped the shriveled manchild in a bear hug and rocked him as he'd rocked the frightened Amata on the mountain ledge, swaying to the rattling of their fetters. "*Mettisi il cuore in pace*, Giovanni. Put your heart at peace. Mamma will look after you now."

"Why can't we go away from here, mamma?" the man asked again. "I don't like it here."

"Someday," Conrad soothed. "Someday."

Willing as he had been always to see God's hand in all circumstances, the creature who shared his cell set the friar quaking once more. Such was the unnerving effect of his lamentable reunion with the hero he idolized as much as he had Fra Leo: the universally revered, deposed minister general, Giovanni da Parma.

XXVII

A WEALTH OF FAMILIAR sights opened before Orfeo as he rode into the mercato: the Roman Temple of Minerva, the Chiesa di San Niccolo that stood before his family home. The marketplace had been paved with bricks in his absence, half burying the steps leading up to the temple and creating an unexpected resonance of his horse's hooves. To the left of the church, he saw the permanent market stall reserved by his family. Their home and business were ideally situated in the heart of the city; the marketplace opened only a few steps from the warehouse where his father's laborers worked the fleeces that arrived from all over Umbria.

Orfeo guided his horse around the church to the stone house where he'd spent the first fifteen years of his life. The place seemed strangely quiet. Most likely the household and workers had gone off with the rest of the town to gawk at the pope.

He rode into the courtyard, tied up the animal and took a deep breath. Even his knock sounded weirdly hollow in the silent city. An unfamiliar servant opened the door, a tall, broad-chested man who had to stoop to look out through the opening. He seemed better suited to be a man-at-arms than a domestic. The servant confirmed that Orfeo's brothers were gone.

"Then I'll wait inside until they're back," Orfeo said. "I'm Sior Angelo's youngest son."

A shadow of suspicion darkened the servant's face. "I thought I knew all the *signore's* sons. If it's your father you want, you can find him in his counting room. I'll show you the way."

"No bother. I know where it is." How like his father to pass on his one chance to see a living pope while he counted his money. Orfeo was relieved, actually, that he'd have a chance to talk to his father alone before his brothers returned. This reunion would be difficult enough without an audience.

"I'll go with you just the same," the man replied in a firm voice. He crossed his arms and partially blocked Orfeo's path into the house.

Orfeo shrugged and spread his hands. "Of course. He wouldn't want a stranger sneaking up behind him." His attempt at a smile drew no response.

The man stepped aside and together they walked through the house to the work area. Orfeo's heart raced as the servant held the door open for him. He wiped at his tunic with clammy hands.

His father sat at a table under the light of a window, his back to the door and sheets of parchment spread in front of him. Absorbed in his work, he didn't give Orfeo or the servant so much as a cursory glance.

At one time Angelo Bernardone had been solid and stocky, like his youngest son, but too many decades at his desk had left him obese in his old age. The plump hand that held a quill poised over the sheepskin flashed gemstones on each fat finger—intended, no doubt, to ward off pain in his joints. He wore a black armband around his sleeve.

"Working on your books, papa, with the pope at the gate?" Orfeo hoped his cordiality didn't sound too forced.

His father growled, his nose still buried in his work. "It's this damned double-entry ledger system the Florentines devised." He seemed about to expound, but paused and swung around ponderously on his stool. "*Who* the hell are you?"

"Have I changed so much? It's Orfeo." Again he compelled a smile to his lips, despite the discouragement that gripped him. He sensed already that his attempt at reconciliation would fail utterly.

"I know no one of that name. Leave my house."

The servant reached for his sword, but Orfeo stopped him with an upraised hand.

"Papa, this isn't easy for me either. I've traveled all the way from Acre with our new pope and I'm here today because he personally insisted I make my peace with you."

Angelo's Bernardone's layered chins turned pink as the skin of a scrubbed pig. "The pope himself you say? And should that move me to forgive an ungrateful child who turned his back on his own father and brothers? Remember that I grew up sharing the household of a lunatic whom all Assisi proclaims a second Christ. I'm obviously less impressed with holy men than you are. No, here's my peace to you, Orfeo late-of-the-Bernardone, and hear it well.

"You shall never more be part of me or mine. If you be married, I declare your wife a widow and your children orphans. Your inheritance I give to your brothers. The only shelter I offer you is the four winds. I commit you to the beasts of the forest, the birds of the heavens, and the fish of the sea."

He turned back to his ledgers. "There's your peace. Now, quit my sight."

Orfeo had heard, and held back, enough. "Don't you fear hell itself, you old murderer? First, you and Simone della Rocca butcher the people of the Coldimezzo; now you pronounce your own son formally dead? Even the father of the prodigal butchered the fatted calf, not his son."

His father's flushed complexion suddenly paled. "They weren't all killed. Simone spared the daughter." For the moment, the bluster in his voice weakened.

"The child is still alive?"

"I don't know. I'd tell you to ask Simone, for he took her as a household slave, but he died two days ago." He pointed to the black band on his arm.

"Ah. No wonder you look so frightened. Your sins do weigh on you." And indeed, his father's frame seemed to droop somewhat inside the shell of its own massive flesh. The old man's hand trembled as he set down his quill. Orfeo found himself hoping that fear of God's judgment, if no other reason, might yet lead to a measure of reconciliation.

Then his father spoke again, in the same muted voice. "You've heard my wish for you." The large head sank for a moment to the old man's chest, then rose again almost in afterthought, the eyes fixed on Orfeo through thick lids. "One token I did intend to leave you. I'll give it to you now, for I hope never to see your traitorous face again this side of hades."

Angelo fumbled with one of his rings. He twisted it off his finger and tossed it in Orfeo's direction. It clattered across the floor of the workshop. "Give that to him, then show him out," the elder Bernardone ordered his servant.

The man picked up the ring and handed it to Orfeo. Orfeo turned the gold circlet and ran his thumb curiously over the blue stone. He slipped it onto his finger, where it turned loosely. He bowed slightly in the direction of his father, then without a word trailed the servant back through the house to the courtyard.

The young man shook his head as he walked his horse through the mercato. He stared at the brick paving, wondering how his day had twisted so badly after Tebaldo's blessing. First, the woman near the city gate; now his father who'd exiled him forever from his home and even refused to recognize him as a living being. For the first time he felt the full impact of his decision made in youthful haste six years before. He hadn't realized when he slammed the family door behind him, that his father would turn a key in the lock.

The only good news he'd heard since leaving the pope's entourage had been the possible survival of the girl from the Coldimezzo. If the new *signore* of the Rocca still kept her as a slave, he might partly atone for his father's crime by buying her freedom.

He grimaced at his own dismal humor. He had barely enough money to support himself for a fortnight, let alone ransom a slave child. His seaman's bag held mostly clothing and his coin pouch little silver. If he didn't find work soon, he'd have to beg his meals like a mendicant friar.

The townspeople filed back into the city. Tebaldo must have moved on to the bishop's palace. Orfeo wished now he'd stayed with the pope. He'd be fed and he'd eventually have ended at a seaport. Perhaps his best course would be to rejoin Tebaldo and the caravan of knights. He'd made friends among the bodyguards who could be helpful when they reached Rome too.

Piccardo, the brother closest to Orfeo in age, spotted him first. He even astonished Orfeo by recognizing him immediately, calling his name from across the mercato. Then he ran to greet him while the rest of the clan kept to their measured tread. As they approached, Orfeo noted that little had changed in six years: Dante still dominated the younger men.

"Orfeo," the oldest brother acknowledged with a curt nod as he came abreast. He made no effort to hide his disdain. "Adamo told us you passed through his gate today. Don't expect us to receive you with hugs of joy, in spite of Piccardo's childish display."

"I've already talked to *your* father, Dante," Orfeo said. "I'm sure you mirror his sentiments. As always." He looked his brother steadily in the eye. He hated what he had to say next, but he'd try—without begging or flinching. "I'd hoped to get some money, enough to get back to Venice, or even a job in the shop until I've saved enough."

"Then you'd best find work. *Elsewhere*." Dante bowed again and resumed his march, drawing the other men of the household in his wake. Piccardo alone remained behind, uncertain which way to turn.

Orfeo spread his fingers for his brother to inspect. "Papa gave me this. Too bad the stone's so scarred. Some rich *padrone* might have given me something for it. You see, Piccardo? Nothing but bones for the one who goes out to piss in the middle of the banquet."

His brother shook his head from side-to-side. His brown eyes followed Dante until the bulky figure disappeared around the church.

"What's going on?" Orfeo asked.

"Don't wear the ring," Piccardo said. "It marks you for death."

"At whose hand?"

"I don't know. The thing has a history. Only members of papa's confraternity can wear it. That's all I've heard. Should anyone else be caught with it, the brotherhood is sworn to kill him on the spot. But I don't know who the others are."

Orfeo chuckled at Piccardo's solemn air. "That could be serious." His lips twisted in a cynical smile. "A fine gift from the old man, eh? I wonder he didn't just poison it."

"Don't laugh, Orfeo. This *is* serious."

Orfeo dropped the ring into his coin pouch. "Thanks, brother, for your concern. It's safely out of sight now. It's too big for my finger anyway." He swung up onto his horse and his jaw tightened. "I'll see you in the *mercato* if I don't starve first."

Piccardo seized the horse's bridle. He seemed reluctant to let Orfeo go. "The cloth merchant Domenico wants someone to lead a buying expedition to Flanders. You like to travel, and you know the difference between samite and damascene."

"Papa's old rival? That would be fitting." He leaned forward and clapped his brother on the shoulder. "Don't worry, Piccardo. I won't hang around to embarrass you or anger our father." He held out his arm. "God's peace be with you, as Uncle Francesco used to say."

Piccardo released the bridle and gripped his brother's forearm. "And with you, Orfeo. I mean that."

IN A MATTER of weeks, the world above ground seemed to fade, as though sucked into the past, into the distant swamp of Conrad's memory. Like the dying man whose life passes before his eyes, he'd been flooded the first days with recollections of Leo, Giacomina and Amatina. He smiled wryly when the familiar names of the last two invaded his thoughts. He'd kept such a careful distance from them above ground; now they seemed closer than ever. And every day he recited Leo's message to himself lest he forget it, though its relevance began to escape him.

Most often he thought of Rosanna. Swarms of boyhood memories crowded his mind, but soon he couldn't be sure which were true and which merely suggested by his imagination. He wondered whether she would even know he'd been imprisoned, whether they had finally been parted forever. Donna Giacoma didn't know Rosanna existed, and Amatina had no way to contact her, even if she'd managed to escape Assisi herself. To Rosanna, it would seem that he'd slipped off the edge of the earth.

He counted the days from his meals. The food seemed to be leftovers from the friars' midday collation, and he guessed the guard lowered it into the cell after None each afternoon, although the room remained dark as ever. The day's fare for the two prisoners consisted of ten chunks of bread, an onion, two pails of thin broth that sometimes contained a vegetable or so, and an apple or handful of olives each. Conrad stashed the onion and part of the bread for later, placing the food in a basket on the wall, out of reach of the rats that swam into the dungeon through the latrine. Then he and Giovanni drank their broth. Conrad would take a few small bites from his apple and give the rest to his fellow prisoner. The younger friar grew thin, but he hoped Giovanni gained thereby.

One afternoon, soon after his incarceration, each pail contained a cube of pork. "What's this largesse?" Conrad called up through the grate. He expected no answer. The gaoler never spoke. But this day Zefferino muttered, "*Buon Natale*," before he moved away to feed other prisoners.

Christmas? So soon? Conrad had more or less counted his days in the cell, but he'd lost track of *dates*. The friars at Greccio would be in their cave today, kneeling before the nativity scene. He pictured the townsfolk of the little village climbing the rugged path, candles in hand, to view the donkey and the ox and the live *bambino* lying in the straw. The friars and people united with the magi in presenting some small gift to show their devotion to the Christ Child.

Conrad sighed, disappointed that he'd no gift to offer this year. He glanced at Giovanni, curled into a dark ball on the chilly earthen floor. He recalled Christ's words: *I was hungry, and you gave Me food*. He did have one thing to offer. He picked the piece of meat from his pail and put it into his cellmate's. "*Buon Natale*, Giovanni," he said, as he set the bucket on the ground beside him. From that day forward he began to gouge holes in the wall to mark the progress of the days.

Each morning, or what he guessed must be morning from Zefferino's shuffling overhead, Conrad recited aloud as much of the office as he could recall. Gradually, Giovanni began to repeat fragments of the psalms and prayers with him, as the repetitions touched long-unused corners of his memory. Conrad took heart. After each meal, he said, "Now we must pay our Divine Innkeeper, in the only currency we have." Together they prayed five *Pater Nosters*, or ten *Ave Marias* or *Gloria Patris*, or other familiar prayers that Conrad knew must be lodged somewhere in the minister general's head.

Sometimes, to ward off the cold, they ended their meals and thanksgiving with a dance. They minced like hobbled horses, clapping their hands and clanging their chains and Conrad led the singing. He deliberately avoided children's songs of the sort Giovanni sang their first day together. He might sing a popular Latin parody from his university days or one of the livelier hymns from the liturgy. He hoped to lead Giovanni, step-by-tiny-step, back through the recollections of his young adulthood. With God's help the old man might actually catch up to himself one day, or at least catch up to the point where memory had ceased to matter for him.

About two weeks after Christmas, Zefferino spoke again. It wasn't much, just enough to startle and encourage the friar. He and Giovanni had been dancing and singing San Francesco's *Canticle of Brother Sun* when he heard a third voice join in softly overhead. When the canticle ended, Zefferino walked off. Conrad shrugged at Giovanni, who returned an impish grin, then covered his lips with his fingertips and rolled his eyes. The minister general no longer asked when they'd be leaving.

The pain in Conrad's eye had subsided for the most part, although it occasionally flared hot and throbbing. As far as he could tell, though, it hadn't become infected, and for this he prayed his thanks. On the nights when the pain returned, he writhed on the ground. His dreams, if he slept, were monster-filled nightmares of torturers and flaming infernos and roaring sea storms.

On one such night near the end of January, the noise of the water flushing through the latrine reverberated in his ears like a mighty waterfall. Rain likely pelted the world above or maybe the snow had begun to melt, swelling the spring, or maybe his distorted perspective somewhere between sleep and waking exaggerated its force. The cell seemed to rock, and he dreamed he clung to the mast of a ship tossed by mountainous waves. Screams of fear rose from the helpless crew. All about the ship leviathans and other colossal sea creatures leapt into the air, eyeing the puny humans hungrily before they vanished. Suddenly they massed and flew at Conrad, a pack of slithery phantoms with flaming sockets, teeth gnashing in frothing mouths. They knocked him to the ship's deck and swarmed over him, biting at his ankles and face. As he tried to fend them off, it was no longer he who struggled, but rather his drowned papa. He sat bolt upright and cried out in terror. A pair of rats scuttled away toward the latrine.

Giovanni started too, and began to weep softly. "I'm all right," Conrad said once his heartbeat subsided and he'd caught his breath. "The devils beat me badly tonight, but they're gone now. Go back to sleep, little one."

On good days his eye didn't hurt so much and the chill seemed tolerable. Giovanni slept much of the time, and Conrad spent such quiet moments in contemplation. With the need to feed himself, to solve Leo's riddle, to confront emotions that tugged him hither and thither all removed, his prayer went deeper even than it had at his hermitage. No sound or sight distracted him; the darkness without and within seemed to merge, with his body little more than a filmy curtain that fluttered between them with each inhalation and exhalation. At times, even this slight motion ceased as his breathing stopped for long spells.

On the first day of February the Church celebrated the ritual purification of Jesus' mother required of all Jewish women after childbirth. Conrad meditated on old Simeon, who'd waited for years at the doorway of the synagogue for the Messiah to arrive. Having held the Christ child for a moment in his arms, Simeon praised God and said, *"Now, O Lord, let Your servant depart in peace, for my eyes have seen Your salvation."*

What sweetness the ancient prophet must have felt. Moved by the image, Conrad began to pray intently to the Virgin, asking that she obtain from her Son this grace: that he might experience just for an instant the same delight Simeon knew when he cuddled the newborn Messiah.

As he prayed, the darkness gradually yielded to a soft blue light. Brighter and brighter it spread until it glistened more dazzling than sunshine. He seemed to be back on his mountain, for he found himself in a grove of white-barked trees, surrounded by the music of songbirds. Through the woods a barefoot peasant girl carried a baby. She walked with careful steps directly to Conrad and without a word offered the infant to him. His outstretched arms trembled, but a reassuring smile from the woman steadied him. He took the swaddled child and hugged it to his chest. Ever so softly he pressed its warm cheek with his lips. It seemed his soul must dissolve, so torrid was the ecstasy that coursed through him. As at the Portiuncola, a fiery vibration surged upward through his spine, but this time it rose unimpeded to the base of his skull and there erupted in a burst of golden light that spread outward through his head. Energy pulsed behind his eyeballs and although he tried to open his eyelids, he could not. The golden light continued to spread, beyond the confines of his body, commingling with the blue light outside him. The curtain of his flesh, the trees, the twittering birds, all melted in its glow. Nothing but light, within, without, then finally, no within-without at all. His strength ebbed and he sank back onto his heels, feeling he must surely faint from joy.

When he finally regained his senses, he still rested on his knees. The girl and the child were gone. Darkness filled the room as before, but a lantern flickered overhead. The grate swung away and slow footsteps descended the stone stairs. Then the gaoler came to the friar and knelt in front of him.

"Forgive me, Fra Conrad," Zefferino said. "I didn't know you were one of them. The light that spilled from your cell into the corridor ..." He fell silent, unable to express his contrition further.

Chains scraped across the floor behind him. Drawn by the lantern and the voices, Giovanni crawled toward the other men.

Zefferino set his lamp on the ground and held out his palms. In the sputtering light, they clasped hands, completing their circle. For several minutes they knelt so in silence, three battered cards shuffled from the turbulent deck of the *Duecento*: the creased and dog-eared beggar king from Parma, flanked by his tattered, one-eyed knaves. "Let us give thanks," Conrad offered at last, "for the events that have linked our fates."

With such joined support, he knew they could endure.

PART TWO

IL POVERELLO DI CRISTO

XXVIII

NENO SAT UNMOVING on the worn bench of his ox cart, silent and solid as a chunk of ice, hunkered over the traces with his back to the savage winds that swept down from the Alps, shoving him toward Umbria and home. As lead carter, his wagon forged ahead of the caravan, a plain enough job late in the day when many wheels marked the road's direction clearly. Mornings were another story, especially after a night of snow buried the ruts of the clay plains beneath fresh drifts. On such days the trader himself would ride ahead on his horse, crisscrossing the white expanse in careful diagonals, outlining the edges of the path with hoofprints.

The cloth merchant did well to hire this Orfeo, Neno thought—a man who understood hard work, who drank like a Turk with the carters, fearless on the road but ever mindful of the men and beasts entrusted to him. And a regular hawk's eye for a bargain! In two months at the fair of San Remi at Troyes, he'd not only sold all of Sior Domenico's goods, but also reloaded the pack mules they'd started with and added two laden carts besides. Many a Flemish trader had swallowed the toad trying to haggle with him.

As the caravan passed beneath the fortress city of Cortona early in the afternoon, the trader rode up beside Neno and pointed toward the citadel on the mountaintop. "Another place famous in my uncle's history," he said.

"That's where the exiled minister, Fra Elias, went to die. It's also where Assisi's Bishop Illuminato lived before his elevation."

Neno nodded without comment. Church matters interested him far less than the countryside his oxen now trundled through, headed for the tiny village of Terontola where they planned to shelter for the night. He shivered as he squinted through the blowing snow at the ruined smallholdings. Not only had the harsh winter frozen many of the tenants' animals, but the combination of wind, snow, and heavy rime had also left grape vines frostbitten and fruit trees with shattered limbs. In some places, the force of the ice and hoarfrost split tree trunks from top to bottom; sap oozed from their wounds and many trees had dried up altogether. *"Porco mondo!"* Neno muttered. His breath scattered down the wind in horsetail puffs of white. *Thanks be to God, they'd but a few days more to reach Assisi.*

As the wheels of his cart crunched into the town square of Terontola later that day, Neno saw a dozen rigid carcasses strung up and swaying in the wind like so many grey pennants. The sight was common throughout Tuscany. Driven by hunger, wolves ventured into the smaller, unwalled towns by night in search of domestic animals and children. The citizens trapped them and hung the scavengers in the piazzas like human looters as a warning to their pack brethren.

The caravan finally ground to a halt and the men-at-arms fanned out around its flanks. "Another day behind us, Neno," a voice sounded behind him. "I promise you, we'll bathe our throats until we drown when we reach home."

Neno spotted the trader's dark beard from the corner of his eye. He flicked the icicles from his own growth. "Aye, Maestro Orfeo," he agreed. "The civil guards will have to pull us from the gutters in the morning, for we'll never make it to bed."

AMATA DREW HER CHAIR close to the fire. To ward off the frigid midnight, she still wore all her daytime clothing and wrapped herself besides in her heavy winter cape. She tucked her slippered feet beneath her and, for what seemed like the hundredth time, allowed her mind to wander back to the morning Conrad sat facing her at this same fireplace, listening to raindrops hissing in the flames as the melting snow did now. Her friend had been imprisoned for more than two years, despite Donna Giacoma's persistent pleas to Fra Bonaventura. Worn out with begging, the haggard noblewoman finally had to give up when the minister general left Assisi to attend to his new duties as Cardinal Bishop of Albano and advisor to the papal consistory studying clerical reform. The friars reported that Pope Gregory had also asked him to help with the General Council to be held in Lyons the coming summer.

Summer would be a welcome visitor. In her nineteen years, Amata couldn't recall a season so cruel and severe as this winter had been. Pilgrims to Assisi, frequent guests at the house, told in frightening detail how travelers who exposed themselves to blizzards did so at the risk of fingers and toes, and sometimes life itself, should they be stranded far from shelter. The pilgrims had touched with their own hands the stiff unburied corpses of horses and riders alike. One group stacked bodies like firewood in their wagon and carried them, coated with snow, to the next monastery. The rock-hard ground kept the pilgrims from burying them on the spot, nor would good Christians have wished to be interred in unhallowed graves.

On one particularly bleak January evening, with her entire household gathered around her bed, Donna Giacoma died. As she neared her end, her muffled prayers for eternal rest turned into a death rattle; the rattle burbled weaker and weaker during her body's final resistance until it finally ceased altogether. Amata wished heartily that Fra Conrad could have been there to close the lids over her lifeless green eyes, and ultimately Amata performed the sad task herself.

The men of the house backed noiselessly from the room so that Amata and the servant women could begin their lamentation. Those docile females tore away their sky-blue wimples and yanked at their hair. They ripped at the seams of their black wool gowns and gouged their faces and arms with their fingernails. Forming a circle, they wheeled listlessly around the room, pounding their fists against their heads and keening the tale of Donna Giacoma's death through a low, prolonged wail. That agonizing wail overwhelmed Amata; a suffocating knot lodged in her heart and gorge and pain churned her entrails. The women pried loose the window covering and with each round of the circle one would poke her head into the frigid night, broadcasting the death to the entire city and to the heavens. The dirge continued two days, until the morning of Donna Giacoma's funeral.

The friars of the Sacro Convento honored the noblewoman by entombing her beneath the pulpit of the lower church. Amata asked that, in death, Donna Giacoma might rest close to her dearest friend in life, Fra Leo. She also commissioned a plaque of red marble, to be placed above the tomb. At the suggestion of Fra Bernardo da Bessa, who acted as Bonaventura's spokesman in his absence, she had the plaque inscribed simply, *Hic jacet Jacoba sancta nobilisque romana*: Here lies Jacoba, a holy and noble Roman woman. As a final tribute, she'd donated funds for a fresco that would depict the lady in her tertiary's robe. Fra Bernardo informed her that a fine artist, the Florentine Giovanni Cimabue, had been commissioned already to decorate the apse of the lower church.

Meanwhile, Amata faced other decisions, decisions that left her sleepless and caused her to stare into the fire while the rest of the household slumbered. She slid down from her chair onto the floor to be closer to the flames struggling to heat the room. *Her* room, in *her* house.

The notary's reading of Donna Giacoma's letter of manumission, releasing her servants from their bond obligations and willing Amata a sizable inheritance ("for the good of my soul and for a pious end, and because it would seem meritorious before God") hadn't come as a surprise. The shock had come several weeks before, when the noblewoman called Amata to her room and explained her intentions. Even now, as she recalled the old woman's generosity, she came near to weeping again and the firelight blurred to an orange shimmer. She felt she had lost her mother twice, once to assassins and once to old age.

The weakened Donna Giacoma had also whispered a warning to Amata. "Unmarried noblewomen have little control over their destinies," she said. "Were you a powerful, widowed queen like Blanche of Castile, or a craftsman's wife inheriting a shop, tools, and apprentices, or even a peasant women taking over your dead husband's fields, you might be allowed to live and work in peace. But the men of my husband's family won't afford you that luxury. As soon as word of my death reaches Rome, they'll try to confiscate all that I give you. They only left me alone because I had male heirs and, after my sons passed away, because of my age." She managed a feeble chuckle. "They were hoping I'd accommodate them and be dead long before now."

The old woman then clutched at Amata's sleeve, her mottled fingers gripping the cloth with surprising strength. "In a few weeks, the whole countryside will know of your good fortune. Suitors will swarm to you like bees to the honeycomb. You must marry soon, Amatina, if you would protect your inheritance from the Frangipani."

LISTS! How odd that so simple an exercise as listing—anything, everything—should prove the last restorative to Giovanni da Parma's mind. Since the Feast of the Presentation two years before when the wondrous light that flooded their cell, Fra Giovanni had gradually, but undeniably, rejoined the living. With all the wonder and delight of a toddler learning for the first time the names of things and movements, colors and scents, he'd begun to recover his memory. To Conrad's enjoyment, he'd also become extremely verbose, with frequent detours through long-abandoned caverns of recollection.

The first time he surprised his cellmate with one of his litanies, they'd just drunk their daily soup. "I was just remembering a meal, Fra Conrad, as clearly as if I'd just eaten it yesterday. Many brothers and I dined with the King of France. We'd gone to our friary in Sens for a Provincial Chapter.

"But this meal ... the fare included no fewer than a dozen courses: first, cherries, then a most delicious white bread; a choice wine worthy of the king's royal state; fresh beans boiled in milk; fish; crabs; eel pastries; rice cooked with milk of almonds and cinnamon powder; more eels baked in sauce; and finally, trays loaded with tarts and junkets and fruits of the season."

The old friar glanced at his pail of broth and shrugged. Then he tapped his forehead, trying to joggle other details of the visit to Sens.

"The morrow happened to be a Sunday," Giovanni continued. "At dawn King Louis came to our church to beg our prayers, leaving his fellowship hard by in the village, save only his three brothers and a few grooms to hold their horses. When they'd knelt and made obeisance before the altar, his brothers looked around for seats or benches. But the king sat in the dust, for the church was unpaved. And after he commended himself to our prayers, he left the church to go his way. But when a servant told him his brother Charles still prayed fervently, the king was pleased to wait patiently without mounting his horse. When I saw how earnestly Charles prayed, and how willingly the king waited without, I was much edified, realizing the truth of the Scripture: 'A brother who is helped by his brother is like a strong city.'"

Twelve and seven became the favored numbers of Giovanni's reflections because of their Biblical significance. Occasionally he'd diverge from the pattern and throw out a list of six, as when he recounted the six sins against the Holy Ghost or the six tempers controlling human action.

Conrad encouraged the mental drills. With a sharp-edged potsherd, he etched the lists on the wall of their cell—not that they could be read in the gloom, but for the sake of the exercise. Thus he scratched out the seven deadly sins, the seven healing virtues, the seven charismatic gifts of God, the seven spiritual works of mercy, the names of the twelve apostles, the twelve beatitudes. Day after day, the illegible scrapings spread across the mossy surface, like verb declensions traced by a Latin student.

In one scenario that usually began while they ate, Fra Giovanni would say nothing but would grunt occasionally, a mannerism Conrad had come to recognize as a kind of meditation. Then, as the younger friar gathered their pails, the minister general would suggest a new list. "We should reflect on Christ's seven last utterances. Seeing how Our Lord faced death, we can learn how to welcome our own end."

Conrad picked up the potsherd and positioned himself at the wall as Giovanni dictated: "*Eli, Eli, lamma sabacthani*—My God, my God, why have you forsaken me?"

Conrad paused as Giovanni added: "Even Christ knew desolation, loneliness, and uncertainty as His hour approached. He will understand and comfort us when our time comes."

One after another Giovanni called out the phrases, adding to each a brief exposition, down to the final "*Consummatum est*. It is done, Father. Into your hands I commend my spirit." The old friar concluded: "Death ends our time on earth, but also lends significance to our earthly actions. Death is the time to make of ourselves a gift to God."

"What do you think, brother?" Conrad asked. "Will we end our lives in this underground hole? Have our earthly actions already come to an end?"

His cellmate nodded.

Conrad's arm dropped to his side. "Forgive my wavering faith in God's design, Fra Giovanni, but why should our Holy Mother Church be denied a talent like yours? Even should you work outside the Order, many secular rulers and prelates could benefit from your spiritual counsel. What if you promised Bonaventura to speak no more of Abbot Joachim and his heresy? Surely he'd have no further cause to keep you fettered."

Conrad hobbled closer to Giovanni and sat down clumsily. Movement had become more difficult for him with each passing month; Giovanni hardly stood at all, save to totter down to the latrine. Even then Conrad had to help him back up the slippery incline.

What dim light existed in the cell reflected from Giovanni's eyes as he stared at Conrad. "Do you really believe I'm kept here because I cling to Joachim's teachings? The Church never condemned Joachim, you know—only Gerardino di Borgo San Donnino's interpretation of his prophecies. Gerardino was jailed here for that interpretation shortly before my own imprisonment.

"No, I'm here—as I suspect you are—because I sought to emulate our founder. I wanted to lead the Order as San Francesco himself had. I traveled on foot through country after country, personally visiting each of our friaries, trying to lead by example rather than through written counsel. But those who wanted to disregard San Francesco's *Rule* and his *Final Testament* to his friars considered me a threat to their comfortable lives. So here I stay, here *we* stay, in this *dis*comfort."

Conrad was suddenly alert. He had nearly forgotten about Francesco's *Testament*! He began to sway from side-to-side as he searched his memory. Somewhere in his message Leo had written that the beginning of the Testament would shed light—*shards of light* were his exact words—on his puzzling letter. Conrad, oddly enough, had almost stopped wondering about the quest that landed him in prison

He turned again to the former minister general. "Father, even though we may never leave this place, I do think God has restored your mind to some beneficial purpose. Do you remember *exactly* how the Testament begins?"

Giovanni lowered his head for a moment, mulling the question. "Why, it starts with San Francesco's account of his conversion. He wrote: 'The Lord granted me to begin to do penance in this way: While I was in sin, it seemed very bitter to me to see lepers. And the Lord Himself led me among them and I had mercy on them. And when I left them, that which seemed bitter to me was changed into sweetness, and afterward I left my life in the world.'

"Our holy founder had a special fondness for lepers. Not only did he work among them himself, feeding and clothing them, bathing and kissing their wounds, but he required the same service of many of the first friars. He called them the *pauperes Christi*, Christ's poor ones."

Conrad's fingers curled into a fist in his lap. "Did Fra Leo work among the lepers too?"

"More than likely."

Giovanni chuckled. "Thinking again of my visits to the friaries ... I wore out *twelve* secretaries in the process. I always made my secretary my traveling companion, as San Francesco had with Fra Leo. My first secretary, Fra Andreo da Bologna, later became provincial minister of the Holy Land and penitentiary to the pope. Then came Fra Walter, an *Anglo* by birth, an *angel* by temperament; and third, one Corrado Rabuino, big and fleshy and black—an honest man. Never met I a friar who could devour *lagano* and cheese with such gusto ..."

Conrad sat unmoving, half-listening to Giovanni's reverie. *All this time Leo had meant for him to serve in a leprosarium, as he himself probably had.* He remembered too Leo's reference to the dead leper's nails. Conrad thought: had I carried out that part of the message first—*servite pauperes Christi*—rather than returning to the Sacro Convento, I'd not be rotting in this cell now. He shivered as his mind conjured up the other, awful possibility: his limbs might instead be undergoing the putrefying transformation of leprosy had he entered a lazar house. And how would he garner wisdom from *that*?

"...The last friar came to me from Iseo, ancient both in age and in the Order, rich in wisdom; yet I felt he played the duke above measure, seeing that all men knew his mother had been hostess of a tavern ..."

Lord, should You ever grant I be released from this place, Conrad vowed, *I will offer to serve at the Ospedale di San Lazzaro outside Assisi, learn what the lepers there have to teach me, pursue Leo's trail (if it comes to that) to its worst possible finale.* In his heart of hearts, he tried to believe that God had merely been waiting to extract this promise from him before letting him wing free of his cage.

"AMATINA, WAKE UP. You have a visitor."

Amata rolled over with a groan. She'd had another restless night, burdened by her new role as head of household, as well as by the impending choice of husband that loomed over her like an executioner's ax. Just as Donna Giacoma had predicted, the weeks since the old woman's death had seen a regular procession of men eager for marriage, or at least eager to take possession of Amata's house and the rental lands the noblewoman left to provide her with an income. The suitors ranged from country aristocracy with rundown fortunes or seeking to add to their holdings, to aged merchants and widowers, but she'd seen no fish she wished to catch, none she'd cheerfully lie beside these cold winter nights. Pio, sixteen now and thinking of himself more as a man every day, was as smitten with Amata as ever, and had grown increasingly surly as he admitted one after another of the callers.

Amata blinked up at the face leaning over her. Most of Donna Giacoma's former bondsmen and women, including (thankfully) Maestro Roberto, had stayed on as hired servants, enjoying both their new freedom and the security of position. The maidservant who stood beside her bed, a sweet-faced, buxom girl a few years younger than her, had grown up in Donna Giacoma's house and knew no other home. Amata had jokingly offered the girl in her stead to one of her suitors, and when he objected that the girl possessed no dowry, she quoted Plautus: *Dummodo morata recte veniat, dotata est satis*, "Provided her morals be upright, a woman has dowry enough." The man stared blankly, for he knew no Latin. Had he shown the slightest inkling of understanding, either of the quotation or of its substance once she'd translated it for him, she might have offered the dowry herself. Perhaps Donna Giacoma had *over*educated her with the string of tutors she'd hired after Conrad's confinement.

"There's a *signore* waits to see you in the hallway," the maidservant repeated while Amata flicked the grit from her eyes with her fingertips.

"What's the hour, Gabriella?"

"The morning bell rang but a short time ago. He must have been perched at the city gate, waiting for it to open."

"At the gate?" The girl's conclusion came too fast for Amata's drowsy head to keep pace.

"It's the suitor from Todi, the cardinal's brother. He says he must speak with you. Urgently."

XXIX

A MATA SLIPPED A cadmium-blue robe over her linen nightshirt. She curled her braid against the back of her head and tucked the loops inside a net caul. What on earth could Count Roffredo want so early in the morning? Even a nobleman of the powerful clan of the Gaetani should wait until a decent hour to present himself. Well, he wouldn't see her at her best; maybe the sight of her unscrubbed complexion in the unforgiving light of daybreak might scare him off. That at least would be equal compensation for interrupting her sleep.

Roffredo Gaetani had impressed Amata as the most odious of the suitors who'd called on her. Now she understood Jacopone's jubilant mood after the battle in the woods, why he exulted in comparing that fight to old victories over the Gaetani in the streets of Todi. From her brief contact with Count Roffredo, she could accept that her half-mad cousin, who had known the family from childhood, regarded them as detestable—over and above the Guelph or Ghibelline party politics that divided every Umbrian city.

Although only in his mid-forties, Roffredo was already thrice a widower. He refused to satisfy her curiosity about his former wives, however, but dismissed their deaths with a wave of his hand. "Plagues. Always there are plagues—and the malaria." His yellowed skin suggested he might be infected with the latter disease himself and lent some credence to his curt explanation.

Still, the calculation in the tiny, obsidian eyes that refused to meet her gaze, the cool aura heightened by his sallow, pockmarked complexion and balding head, led her to fear he might be capable of extraordinary cruelty, that he might be a man diseased within as well as without. Her own skin crawled just to look at him. Their conversation, or rather his monologues, focused on his family's powerful connections in Todi Commune and in Rome, particularly the lofty position of his brother, Cardinal Benedetto Gaetani, who Roffredo bragged would be pope one day. He twisted the gold chain that rested on his chest and a slight smile played around his lips while he spoke of money and estates, of the wealth he'd accumulated through his earlier marriages, to which Amata's would be joined in robust alliance. He'd been candid at least, not camouflaging his motives with the slightest artifice, and he ended his speech by telling her she could forget the other suitors, for he'd determined to have her, *per amore o per forza*—by love or by force. He smiled again at his own little joke, but the gold chain stretched taut in his grip.

She had taken a bath immediately after his call, feeling a need to cleanse the lingering malaise of his suit. That one will surely never "have" me, she swore to herself. I'd die first.

And now here he was, come at this indecent hour to pester her anew. Still in a stupor, Amata entered the long hallway. Roffredo waited with his squire at the far end, by the front door. Pio stood to one side, making no attempt to conceal his displeasure as the two men bowed.

"I had a restless night, *signore*, and had finally fallen asleep when you called." She hoped her voice betrayed a bit of the edge she felt. "What brings you here so early?"

His lips twitched with the same sly mockery that so irritated her at their previous meeting. "The man who sleeps, earns no profit," he said. "I've come for your answer."

She stared at him incredulously. Some sense of propriety told her she must try to moderate the anger welling inside her, but Roffredo didn't make that easy. "Even a fool wouldn't risk disappointment before breakfast, I think, *signore*. But as you confront me bluntly, I'll be equally frank with you. I do not love you, Count Gaetani."

Roffredo didn't seem the least bit nonplused by her reply, probably because love had never been the issue with him. "You disappoint me, *signorina*," he said. "My brother will be disappointed also. He waits in Todi to marry us this very evening." He assumed an expression of mock terror. "Your answer *worries* me too. It can be very dangerous to stand up a cardinal."

Amata decided she'd been as polite as she could with this banty cock. Her only wish was to have him out the door so she could return to bed. "You obviously have never seen *me* angry, *signore*," she replied, "or you wouldn't speak so casually of danger. You have my final answer. Now I must insist that you leave my house."

Roffredo bowed, but this time his squire did not bow with him. Instead, the man swung the door open wide, and two knights who waited just outside rushed into the hallway. Pio jumped at the men, but one caught his upraised arm. The other drew a dagger from his belt and held it to the boy's throat. Before Amata could react, Roffredo and his squire grabbed her wrists. The count smothered her mouth with his gloved hand. She tried to yank free, but they tightened their grips, and Roffredo gave her arm a painful twist. He curled his lip in a triumphal sneer.

"Come with us quietly, *signorina*," he said, "or your page will be grinning from beneath his chin."

Amata tried to yell out, but the leather glove muffled her cry. She couldn't believe this was actually happening to her. Could these bastard noblemen even carry off women from their own homes and force them to marry? Her eyes caught Pio's and the panic she read there mirrored her own sense of helplessness.

Again she tried to yank away, hating her vulnerability as much as she did the Count, but Roffredo held her firmly, gripping her chin and forcing her to watch as a thin trickle of blood started down the blade at Pio's throat. She stopped struggling and screamed into the glove. Roffredo lifted his hand slightly from her mouth.

"You said?"

"Let him be. I'll go with you."

THE ROAD TO TODI left the city through the Porta San Antimo in Assisi's south wall. Roffredo and his henchmen rushed the woman down the empty stone stairs leading from her house to the lower city, bundled in a winter cape with the hood pulled over her head. She darted her eyes from side-to-side in the dim light as they hurried past the still-shuttered houses, looking for any avenue of escape. The knight who'd threatened Pio held his dagger to her side now. She assumed she had no value to Roffredo dead; still the Count might think it no great matter to marry her *dying*. His knight had already proved he could control the point of his blade with meticulous skill. For that matter, the cardinal might marry her to Roffredo dead or alive.

All too speedily they reached the bottom of the last set of steps. Directly ahead Amata saw the triple churches of San Antimo, San Leonardo, and San Tomaso, and beyond that the city gate. A carriage waited in the shadow of an alley between two of the churches. Amata's legs buckled at the finality of that sight and she slumped to the cobblestones. Once outside the walls, she'd be totally at Roffredo's mercy.

She felt the knight's strong hand squeeze her arm as he tried to drag her to her feet, but the stones were slippery with frost and she fell again, face down this time. As she pushed herself up onto her hands and knees, she saw another figure crawling on all fours around the corner of San Tomaso, surrounded by a small cluster of jeering early risers—one more stroke of abnormality in this unreal morning. The crawling man wore a pack-saddle on his back and called out in a sonorous voice: "Is there none who would ride this lowly beast of burden?" He lifted his full sandy mane and stared plaintively toward the sky. A woman in the crowd hollered back, "I'll ride you, Jacopone, if you'll mount my saddle and ride me too."

"Jacopone! *Aiuto*! Help me!" Amata screamed. "Save me from the Gaetani!" Before she could say more, the knight lifted her bodily from the pavement and slammed the palm of his gauntlet over her mouth. Roffredo and his lackeys started to jog toward their horses. As they dragged her into the alley, she saw the penitent rising slowly to his feet with a querulous expression on his face. Then the knight shoved her into the carriage and slammed the door on her last hope.

Oh God, please, *please*! The wheels of the carriage began to move and gradually gain momentum. The swaying of her seat told her the team of horses had turned the corner toward the city gate when, just in front of them, she heard the shrill blare of a trumpet. The carriage tipped wildly as the animals bolted from the blast. She felt a bump, heard a cry of pain, and then all became pandemonium. Something heavy and unyielding exploded against the compartment, flipping it onto its side and shattering the wooden frame. Around her, the horses' frightened whinnies mixed with men's curses and the belligerent bellow of an ox.

Amata climbed from the wreckage. Her legs still weak with fright, her face and arms aching, she managed to force her way through the confusion and scurry down the alley. When no footsteps followed, she slowed and ducked into a corner where she could see what had happened. Jacopone lay curled on his side, motionless, in the street, his trumpet still dangling from in his fingers. A merchant's cart lodged in the debris of the carriage, while bolts of cloth were scattered all over the pavement. The horses continued to buck and rear, kicking out alternately with their front and rear hooves, while the lowering ox tangled in their traces swung his horns perilously near their bellies.

A furious Roffredo Gaetani, screaming at the top of his lungs, reviled the trader, a stocky, bearded man who returned him oath-for-oath. The Count and his retainers dismounted, but the trader only flipped his cape back over his right shoulder and drew his rapier. He wouldn't back down from a fight either if it came to that. The trader's own men-at-arms spurred their horses forward and even his carter reached into the wagon and pulled an ax from the upended goods. "Don't try to raise your broadsword," the trader warned one of Roffredo's knights. "Neno will have your arm off before it reaches full height."

The townspeople mocked both sides from a safe distance and a few rocks clattered into the melee. The two camps squared off, hesitant, weighing each other's strength and pondering what move to make next. Amata's eyes shifted from the quarrel to Jacopone and back again, and then to a pair of civil guards who finally raced up from the gatehouse, halberds in hand.

"What's the ruckus?" one called.

Again the two parties began shouting and gesturing, along with the onlookers who'd finally drawn close. The guard threw up his arms for silence. Amata stepped from her hiding place and tossed back her hood.

"These men of Todi tried to kidnap me," she said, "even though I'm a citizen of Assisi." Her words came out slurred and it hurt her to speak. The knight must have split her lip when he covered her mouth.

"It's Donn'Amata," a woman's voice said from the crowd.

"Their horses ran down this good and peaceable man," she continued, pointing to Jacopone's body. "But for him, their plan would have succeeded."

"They also collided with my cart and spoiled half my merchandise," the trader growled. "And I too am a citizen of this city."

At that the clamor resumed. Amata walked over to the penitent and knelt beside him. She heard the rage of the people around her, directed at Roffredo. "Out with you," a guard said. "You lied about your business when you entered the city."

"But what of my carriage and team?"

"Your carriage is kindling. Come back for your team another day, but don't expect to get them," the guard said. "There are Assisans to be compensated here, and we may have a charge of murder waiting for you."

Amata looked up in time to see the savage glare Roffredo directed at her. God willing, she'd never have to look on that hateful face again. The Count and his knights remounted and trotted toward the gate. The mob ran hooting after them and unleashed another volley of stones as the horsemen galloped out of the city.

The woman rubbed Jacopone's cheek and scraggly beard with the back of her fingers. "Cuz, poor Cuz," she whispered. "Can you hear me?"

One of the guards towered over her. "Did they kill him?"

"He's still alive, but he's badly hurt."

Someone knelt beside her on the stones. "My carter and men-at-arms will look after my goods. Can I help you bring this man to shelter?"

She looked directly into the trader's brown eyes. They didn't waver. "I'd be grateful," she said. "I'll see to it that he has a leech and chymist." She ran her fingers through the matted, filthy hair and added softly: "Or, if needs be, a decent burial."

The man folded his cape back over his shoulders again and easily scooped up the gaunt Jacopone in his muscular arms. "Lead the way. I'm at your service, *madonna*," he said. His voice vibrated with such tenderness that she turned to glance at him again. Could he possibly be flirting with her at such a moment as this? A warm grin glowed through the dark tangle of his ink-black beard. His eyes seemed, to her, to fix on the lower half of her face.

She touched her fingertips to her sore lips and blushed to realize they were swollen and bleeding. She must look a fright, she thought, disheveled to start with even before Roffredo's man battered her.

The trader smiled sympathetically, but said nothing of her appearance—only the single word, "A-ma-ta." He prolonged each short syllable, rolling it over his tongue like a taster of wines savoring a new vintage. His eyes met hers and sparkled with delight. "A felicitous gift of a name, *madonna*."

AMATA LEANED AGAINST her half-opened front door. The trader had finally gone to seek out his damaged cart. All well and good! He'd left just in time, stunned as she was by his parting words. But why, then, was she feeling this disappointment too?

The woman stretched over to the nearest window. She snapped an icicle off the shutter, pressed it to her bruised lips and went inside the house. She felt such a fool. What had come over her in the streets? Maybe she'd been giddy from fright after the near disaster with Count Roffredo. Maybe she spoke from desperation. In any case, she had jabbered nonstop all the way back home. She'd found herself wanting to tell this stranger everything about her situation.

"Just two years ago I wanted only to live a simple life as a hermitess in a forest hut, but the friars imprisoned my friend—my spiritual director, I should say. Then, for months I thought of nothing but avenging my family for ... for something that happened when I was a child, but the target of my revenge vanished from the city. Fortunately, through all this confusion, I lived with a kind noblewoman, as her servant, but she thought of me as a daughter, or a granddaughter, and now she's died and left me her house and money, and I'm besieged by greedy suitors like Count Roffredo. I'm told I need to marry to protect what I have, but at the same time, these suitors are all so awful and I've come to treasure my freedom, which is surprising in itself because once I wanted only to marry." She caught her breath, then blurted, "I mostly *dread* marriage, now. What do you think, *signore*? Do you have a wife and family?"

She blushed as soon as she asked the question, chagrined to realize how she'd been prattling, as well as by her own boldness—a boldness pressured no doubt by the decision she had to make, and soon. The man didn't mock her, however. He paused on the steps, shifted the burden of the penitent lightly in his arms, and turned to face her. He spoke evenly, with no shortness of breath or hint that he labored in the slightest. "No, *madonna*, I've had neither the time nor means to wed. I've no prejudice against marriage, though, and I'm flattered that you ask."

"Oh, I didn't mean ...," she started to protest, but she knew she'd said too much already. She *did* mean, and he'd been wise enough and forthright enough to do her the favor of cutting through the conventional roundabout. It was she who felt obliged to change the subject. "Aren't you tired? A tall man like Sior Jacopone must be very heavy."

The trader started up the steps again. "Pah. This one is a feather. I don't think he's eaten in three years. I worked as an oarsman on a Venetian galley before I turned to trading. Those years of hard work still stand me in good stead."

"Then you've traveled much?"

"I suppose you could say so. We've just returned from Flanders and France. And I've been as far to the East as the Land of Promise." He smiled, and his eyes brightened. "I could tell you such stories, *madonna*..."

A clatter of arms and bustling footsteps interrupted him as Pio, Maestro Roberto, and the other men of Amata's household came bounding down the steps toward them. "Amatina. Thank God you're safe," the steward cried. "We came as fast as we could when Pio told us what happened."

"Bless you all. I'm banged up a little, but Count Roffredo's been run from the city. I do need a physician for Sior Jacopone, though. He was injured rescuing me."

Roberto sized up the situation quickly. He ordered one man into the town to fetch the leech. He loaded most of the servants' weapons onto Pio. Then he and another man took the injured Jacopone from the trader.

"Put him in Fra Conrad's old room," Amata said as the men started back up the steps. "I'll be right behind you. I want to thank this gentleman who's been such a help to me."

As the servants scurried to carry out their tasks, Amata and the stranger resumed their climb. Pio used his burden as an excuse to climb more slowly than the others, but the woman slowed her pace even more, leaving him no choice but to move on ahead. "I'd like to hear those stories one day, *signore*," Amata said when she and the trader were alone again.

"Gladly, *madonna*," he said. "I'd hoped that I might call on you in a few days. Now that my employer owes me a sum of money, I have a family matter of my own to settle—a sort of reverse vendetta."

Some female instinct must have prompted her next question. Or maybe the same lightheadedness that had driven her entire conversation since they left the square. "Does it involve a woman?" She smiled at the trader as she asked, but she realized her heart beat a little too quickly for one intending only to tease.

This time the man did laugh. "Once again you flatter me, *madonna*," he said. "Yes, I suppose the target of my mission *is* a woman by now, though in my mind I still see her as a child."

And God grant that you continue to see her as such, Amata thought. She didn't want his mind dwelling on another woman just now.

They had come at last to her house. She offered the trader a warm mug and a moment's rest in her kitchen before he continued on, but he declined. "Another day, *madonna*. I should rejoin my men and tend to business." He was about to leave and she realized that, in all the whirl and commotion, she hadn't even learned his name.

"Orfeo," he bowed in answer to her question, "Orfeo di Angelo Bernardone." With a salute he turned back toward the alley. "*A presto, madonna*," he called over his shoulder.

He might as well have struck her between the eyes with the hammer edge of a hatchet. Amata froze, confused and immobile. All the past hatred and bitter feeling she'd conjured up against this son of her enemy came surging back into her heart. She pounded the heel of her fist against the portal as his footsteps faded down the stairwell and pressed her forehead against the cool oak. Why did he have to be so damned charming?

XXX

ORFEO GUIDED HIS HORSE up the steep path to the Rocca Paida, relishing the winter sun against his face. In a tree beside the path, a squirrel dashed from a hole to inspect the day more fully. The thin branch bent under its weight, nodding to a flock of geese that wedged and hooted northward overhead. The trader made a mental note to remove his beard and trim his shoulder-length hair before he rejoined Neno that afternoon. The icy winds of the mountain passes were behind him now; he no longer needed the protective covering on his neck and throat, nor was a face full of hair viewed with particular favor in his home city.

The jingle of coins in his pouch buoyed him too. Under the terms of his *commenda* with Sior Domenico, he'd received one quarter of the profits from his trip. He carried half a year's income with him, surely more than enough to purchase the freedom of the captive child—if she still lived at the Rocca. The townsmen he'd spoken to knew nothing of such a girl, even in this small city. The fortress seemed to have swallowed her up after the raid. They could tell him only that old Simone had died and that his son Calisto now played the *signore*. The knights of the Rocca lived in a world apart, exalted in their castle high above the houses of the general populace. One would be foolhardy to intrude into their affairs, they hinted.

But the offer of a nice sum—that might be a different matter. Orfeo hoped the new *signore* wouldn't drive too stiff a bargain; trader that he was, he expected he could get a fair price, certainly less than he'd have to pay for a female slave in the Venetian market. After all, he still had his own dreams to finance.

He thought again of the Assisan woman he'd just met, scarcely believing his good fortune. Beautiful despite her bruises, eager to evade her suitors but apparently as pleased to meet him as vice-versa—and newly wealthy besides. Although he'd spent two years bartering across the European countryside for what could only be called a "modest" salary, he still dreamed of trading someday on the scale of the Polos. Amata's fortune, added to his own savings, might be enough to afford him his breakthrough—especially if his dealings with the *signore* of the Rocca went well. He'd cause to smile, and the warming air reinforced his high spirits. It whispered of burgeoning springtime soon to come, of new growth, new enterprises.

Several guards watched Orfeo's progress from the castle's parapets as he rode up. The gate lay open, but the portcullis had been lowered as a precautionary measure. The porter lifted it just enough to let him ride underneath after he explained he had business with the *signore*. The man then took his horse by the halter and led Orfeo toward a group of knights gathered in the courtyard. He motioned to the trader to dismount and wait at a discreet distance. One of the men separated himself from the group.

The porter bowed. "My lord Calisto, this man would speak with you. He calls himself Orfeo di Angelo Bernardone."

Calisto della Rocca waved the servant away. The man took the reins of Orfeo's horse and led it to the stable. "Your name's familiar," Calisto said in a guttural voice as he walked ahead of Orfeo toward the great hall. "Why's that?"

"My father had dealings with the last *signore*, about eight years ago."

Calisto glanced back at Orfeo. The knight said nothing, however, as they entered the building. He seated himself in a large chair and motioned Orfeo to a nearby bench, picking at a carbuncle on his neck while the trader arranged his cloak.

Orfeo turned his head as two serving women passed through the hall. He judged that both were older than the girl he sought. The *signore* followed his eyes. "You like them?" His lips spread in a lascivious grin. "Were you staying here as my guest tonight, you could have them both."

Calisto baited him, Orfeo guessed. "Actually, they remind me of my purpose in coming here," he said. "I *am* looking for a woman, about eighteen-to-twenty years old by now I should guess."

Calisto's hand strayed nearer his sword hilt, although his voice remained jovial. "A relative?"

"No. I can't even tell you her name. Did you know of your father's raid on the Coldimezzo in Todi Commune some years ago?"

"Know of it? I was there! And a good, bloody business it was, too. They didn't know what hit them." His dark eyes glittered as he spoke.

Orfeo clenched his jaw. He'd like to take this gloating animal by the throat, right here and now, as he could never choke his own father, but he reminded himself that he'd come on business. The first thing a trader learned was to control his emotions. "There was a girl child," he said. "Your father took her as a slave, I believe."

Calisto jumped to his feet. "That bitch! Why do you look for her?" He held out his sword hand. "Look at this scar, where she tried to cut off my finger. I can barely grip a weapon any longer."

Orfeo rose as calmly as he could. He didn't like staring up at this man whose moods seemed erratic at best. Such lords lashed out on a whim. He didn't want to stay seated where he'd be vulnerable to the *signore*. He began to fear also that the girl might be dead. If she attacked such a man, she likely paid a heavy price.

"You punished her?"

"She escaped me, the miserable whore! She left within the day in the company of my pious sister. The devil screw both their miserable cunts, albeit they're shielded by nun's habits."

The pouch at Orfeo's side hung instantly heavier. If the child were safe behind the walls of a convent, he'd no need to haggle with this murderer's son. Still, he felt some curiosity about the girl's ultimate destination. "How might I find her, then, should I wish to see her?"

"Do you wish her well or evil?" Calisto's eyes narrowed to slits. "If you wish her well, I'd as soon sever your head on the spot and dangle it from my gate post."

Orfeo's breath shortened, though he remained outwardly composed. "That won't be necessary," he said. "She's in God's hands now, and no concern of mine." He smiled insincerely and bowed, keeping his eyes fixed on the *signore's* sword hand. As he did so, the chain around his neck popped free of his tunic, and the ring suspended from it swung away from his chest.

Calisto's eyes widened again as he followed the motion of the ring. "How came you by this?" he asked, tapping the stone with his finger. "A rather curious inscription."

"I had it from my father," Orfeo said.

Calisto stepped back. "Of course."

Orfeo tilted the face of the ring and studied the carvings in the lapis lazuli. Calisto's interest set him wondering. Perchance the ring had something to do with the business between their fathers. "Does it hold some meaning for you, *signore*?" he asked. "The thing's a riddle to me."

Calisto brushed aside his question. "Tell me where you're staying, Sior Bernardone—in case I remember anything more about the girl." His voice and manner became pleasant again, almost unctuous.

"I've just returned to the city," Orfeo said. "I can be reached at the house of the merchant Domenico." No sooner had the words left his mouth than he wished them back again. He remembered then his brother's warning. He bowed abruptly once more and turned for the stables as quickly as feigned detachment allowed. The hair bristled on the nape of his neck as he strained to hear the slightest shuffle of sound warning him that Calisto followed. Should the *signore* decide to attack him, he'd be helpless against the man and his score of knights.

SUNRAYS, SHADOWS, jousting on a cream-white wall.

Warm indoor air. House noises, besom brushing tile, logs thundering in a grate.

Faces. Hovering, bobbing, disappearing.

Pain. In his shoulder, ribs, knee, half his body. Throbbing pain in his head.

Now, Lord Jesus, let Thy servant depart in peace.

Vanna. I come soon. Wait for me.

Woman's whispering voice. "Is he better?"

Vanna?

"He drifts in and out of sleep, Amatina. He's got a fair knot on his head. The physician thinks he'll live, though. He's hardy as a forest beast."

Soft rubbing on his cheek. "I'm here, cousin. You must fight the demon. Don't let him take you yet."

Wrestling to stay with the voice. Shiny black beetle, thrashing in a murky puddle at the high road's edge.

Wanting to go, quit this vale of tears. Wanting eternal rest. With Vanna.

Whose the voice? Whose, if not Vanna's?

Cousin?

Face framed in black like a nun's, blurry, floating downward toward him.

Scent of frangipane. Cool dampness on his brow.

Shadows spreading. Distant murmur of words, blurring all together.

Darkness. Silence.

Lord Jesus Christ, Son of God, have mercy on me, a sinner. Lord Jesus Christ, Son of God, have mercy...

"I OVERHEARD YOU SPEAKING of Troyes." A corpulent, red-faced friar slid onto a bench opposite Orfeo and Neno and filled his cup from their jug. "A blessing for your generosity, friends," he said.

"All throats are brothers to one another," Orfeo replied good-naturedly.

The friar swirled the wine and held his nose to the rim. "The Franks are wont to say the best wine should have three B's and seven F's:

"C'est *b*on et *b*el et *b*lanc

Fort et *f*ier, *f*in et *f*ranc,

Froid et *f*rais et *f*retillant."

Then he sipped the wine and declared, "Need we wonder that they delight thus in good wine, for wine 'cheereth God and men,' as is written in the ninth chapter of the Book of Judges." He raised his cup aloft. "Wherefore of this wine we may rightly say with the wise King Solomon, 'Give strong wine to them that're sad, and wine to them that're grieved in mind. Let 'em drink and forget their wants, and remember their sorrow no more.'"

"Well quoted," Orfeo said. He raised his voice: "Let sorrow evermore be banished from this place." He and Neno hoisted their cups to meet the friar's. A smattering of hurrahs echoed from the dark corners of the wine shop.

Orfeo tapped himself on the chest when they'd drunk. "Orfeo, lately of the Bernardoni, and Neno, as strong and true as the ox he drives," he said.

The friar bobbed his hairless pink head. "Fra Salimbene, newly come from Romagna, at the service of God and all decent men ... and women too, be they decent or no." The friar laughed and plucked at his jowl.

Neno started to sing. The lyric ended in a muddle, however, as the carter leaned his arm on the table and slowly lowered his head to rest upon it. Orfeo gave him a shake and refilled his cup. "Wake up. Maybe this godly friar has a poem for us, or a song that *he* can carry to its *finis*."

Fra Salimbene nodded and rapped noisily on the table. He stood and looked around him as he addressed the room. "A rhyme of Maestro Morando, who taught grammar at Padua when I was a boy there. May God comfort his soul." He took another drink and intoned, as somberly as though he prayed the Mass:

"Drink you glorious, honey'd wine?
Stout your frame, your face shall shine,
Freely shall you spit;
Old in cask, in savor full?
Cheerful then shall be your soul,
Bright and keen your wit.

Is your liquor greyish pale?
Hoarseness will your throat assail,
Fluxes will ensue;
Others, swilling clammy wine,
Wax as fat as any swine,
Muddy-red of hue.

Scorn not red, though thin it be;
Ruddy wine shall redden thee,
So you do but soak;
But the cursed water white
Honest folk will interdict,
Lest it spleen provoke."

Orfeo slapped his hands on the table and pounded Neno's slumped shoulders. He signaled for another jug as Salimbene repositioned his broad haunches on the bench. "You've been to France, brother?" the trader asked.

"Not these twenty-five years," the friar said. "In the Year of Our Lord 1248, I journeyed to the convent of Sens to attend the Provincial Chapter of our Order in France. The Lord Louis, King of France, and his three brethren traveled thither, whom I sorely desired to see. The Provincial Minister of France and Fra Odo Rigaldi, Archbishop of Rouen, came as well, along with Giovanni da Parma, our minister general, and many custodes and definitores and discreti of the capitular body." He paused to take another drink, and stared heavenward. "Our minister general refused to thrust himself forward, according to the word of Ecclesiasticus, 'Be not exalted in the day of thine honor,' albeit the king invited him to sit at his own side. Giovanni chose rather to sup at the table of the humble, which he honored by his presence, and many were edified thereby."

"May we all learn from pious men," Orfeo said. He raised his cup in salutation. "And let us drink also to the health of beautiful women, especially one I met today."

"And to the many charming ladies whose director I have been," Salimbene said.

Neno began to snore lightly, while Orfeo and Salimbene swapped stories of travel. To Orfeo, it seemed they'd scarcely begun the serious business of drinking themselves into oblivion when a clanging sounded from a nearby campanile.

"Aiee! The fucking toper's bell is early tonight." He drained his cup and slammed it on the plank table with a noisy thud. He pushed himself up with great reluctance, shook Neno awake and helped the carter to his feet.

"*Addio, signori*," the friar called from the door. "I'll look for you here another night."

Orfeo waved his lantern to the friar in reply. The night breeze stung his cheeks, bare and still puffy from his recent shave. The cobblestones seemed unfairly slippery as he and Neno stepped through the doorway, lurching toward Sior Domenico's house and the attic where the hired men slept. The treacherous streets tilted dangerously. Neno stopped to steady and relieve himself against the wall of a house. He wanted to sing again, but Orfeo prodded him onward.

"The curfew bell rings next, *amico*. We have to reach Sior Domenico's before then."

Three men ambled toward them through the dark street, their faces screened from the lantern by the hoods of their shoulder-capes. Orfeo realized he still carried his coin pouch and instinctively put his free hand inside his cloak and wrapped it around the hilt of his rapier. Neno, oblivious to the men, staggered to the far side of the street, stretching his hand out toward the nearest wall for balance.

"That's him," the tallest of the men said as they drew closer. "The one with the beard." Before Orfeo could react, all three rushed the carter. Daggers glittered in the lantern's guttering light and Neno sank to his knees with a groan.

"Get the ring. It's around his neck."

"The devil it is! He's not wearing it. It's not on his fingers either."

"*Shit!*"

Orfeo roared and charged the men from behind, swinging his lantern and rapier wildly. The closest turned to face him, and received a slash on his neck. The other two yelled and sprinted down the street, not looking back to see who attacked them. The murderer who remained held one hand to his wound, menacing and carving the space between them with his knife. Orfeo thrust out his lantern as a shield and stepped toward him, sword upraised. The man tried to give ground, but tripped backward over the fallen Neno. Orfeo swung his lantern at the upraised dagger, sending it clattering to the pavement, and chopped furiously with the edge of his rapier as though he wielded an ax. He kept swinging until the screaming and movement stopped. He set down his light then, and leaned back into a doorway, panting and sobbing as he stared at his friend, crumpled in the black street like a heap of soiled clothes.

The trader wiped the back of his hand across his face and tugged at the chain around his neck until he'd dredged up the ring. He squeezed it in his hand, cursing his father and Calisto di Simone and the *signore's* assassins. Now *he'd* lost a comrade to a *signore* of the Rocca, just as the girl who'd fled to the convent lost her family. Even in the shock of his loss, he felt more bonded to her than ever. He swore that somehow, someday, he would avenge them both.

He wanted to snap the chain and hurl the damnable ring as far from himself as possible. He resisted, however, tucked it back inside his tunic, and sheathed his sword. For the second time that day, Orfeo dropped to one knee to gather up the casualty of a nobleman's unbridled violence. He whispered into Neno's unhearing ear, "Now, *amico,* are you finally free of this brutal and senseless world."

XXXI

JACOPONE BLINKED HIS EYES open, tawny and round as gold florins. In a hoarse whisper, he asked the woman sitting on a stool beside his bed: "Have you any scrap for a poor sinner?"

The woman motioned to a boy standing beside her. "Tell your mother our patient's ready to eat. Broth and bread for now, I think."

The penitent sniffed at his forearm, crinkling his nose.

"An unguent we rubbed on your bruises," the woman said. "The leech also left a powder for you to drink, to rebuild your strength."

"God save me from quack-salvers," he growled. "Spare me their restoratives, distilled from the crumbled dung of lepers. No ointments or palliatives or assuasives. Nature's the only leech I need." He grimaced and probed his fingers carefully through his sandy hair. "Are my brains spilt?"

"No, though you've quite a lump there. You must have cracked your head against the stones when the carriage knocked you to the ground."

The slightly-crossed, hazel eyes tried to focus on the woman. "I heard your voice before. Who are you?"

"I'm Vanna's cousin, Amata. Raiders took me from our home before you and I had a chance to meet." They *had* met on the road more than two years before, of course, but she saw no reason to confuse him just now by dredging up the novice Fabiano.

"Little Amata di Buonconte? Alive?" His forehead furrowed to a "V" above his nose. His eyes searched the room, groping for answers on the whitewashed walls. Finally, they rested on her face, scanning her features, until the heavy lids lowered again. "She missed you most of all," Jacopone said as his head sank deeper into the pillow. "She wondered what became of you."

Amata took his large hand, weaving her fingers through his. "It's a long tale, Sior Jacopone. Someday when you're strong enough to hear me out, I'll talk your ear off."

"It was you called for help in the piazza, was it?"

She nodded.

"But why would the Gaetani try to kidnap you?"

Amata crooked one corner of her mouth into a half-smile. "That was Count Roffredo Gaetani's notion of courtship. The man who marries me becomes lord of a fair fortune."

He continued to fix his gaze on her, and she was struck by the clearness of his eyes, unlike the crimson veins that webbed her own sleepless eyes of late. "Is there anyone you wish to marry?" he asked.

She laughed and shook her head. "None of those that have asked me so far. But I'm told I must choose one soon, some watchdog to protect myself from jackals like Roffredo."

Jacopone fell into a fit of coughing. "Not so ... necessarily. You've male relatives who could act as your guardians ... to oversee your property." He spoke with much effort, wheezing between phrases. "I've drawn up such writs for others ... in my former life."

The penitent began to roll his head on his pillow, wincing and grappling with unconsciousness. His simple suggestion had a mesmerizing effect on Amata. She found herself staring in fascination at this seeming lunatic, yet one so wise he could, with a quill and a single sheet of parchment, transform the tangle of civil law into a path of safe conduct for her.

Her list of male relatives had actually grown quite short. Grandfather Capitanio had died the year before her parents, leaving her papa the ring later stolen by Simone della Rocca. Great-Uncle Bonifazio would be the last man she'd turn to. He'd probably steal her blind and abandon her to beg on the streets—or shut her up in a nunnery where she'd have to live out her days as Suor Amata again. But one man, her Uncle Guido, Vanna's father, might be the solution to her dilemma. If her uncle were still alive, he would now be sole lord of the Coldimezzo. And if Jacopone spoke on her behalf ... surely the notary's father-in-law couldn't refuse, despite the old scandal involving Bonifazio and herself.

Jacopone's weather-cracked lips parted again. "Your brother."

"Fabiano?"

"If he wasn't vowed to lifelong poverty, he'd serve."

At the mention of her dead brother, Amata sucked sharply through her clenched teeth—a memory too painful to dwell on. But her cousin's allusion to Fabiano's vow of poverty also forced her to suppress a grin. Someday she'd divert Sior Jacopone with the tale of "Fra Fabiano."

A rasp of sandals sounded behind her, heavier than Pio's footstep.

The cook herself had brought the food. "Please let me serve our guest, *madonna*—in thanks for his saving of your life."

Amata smiled. "You see, *signore*, what good souls are here to care for you." She wondered if the fact that the pair were widow and widower had anything to do with the cook's special attention to the injured man.

She rose so the older woman could have her stool and drifted from the room to a window in the hallway. She peered through the shutters at the damp stones paving the alley, burnished to a faint grey luster by the wintry, midday sun. Amata also saw a beardless Orfeo Bernardone headed toward her front door, his head and shoulders drooping, his gait dispirited. How unfortunate for him, that he should show up just as she'd been thinking of her brother. If she suspected her resolve after his last visit, the timing of his return erased all doubt.

"I have a visitor," she called through the doorway of Jacopone's room. "I want to talk to you more later about your counsel."

A rough plan began to form in her mind as she strolled toward the foyer to receive the Bernardone. It would tie her revenge and her need for protection together. As soon as Jacopone strengthened enough to travel, they'd ride to the Coldimezzo—trusting that Count Guido still lived on the estate. She didn't even know if the castella had survived the raid, but Jacopone would know. She could continue to show interest in this Orfeo, ask him to accompany them for protection against marauders on the highway, and when they reached the Coldimezzo... the perfect place for the son of Bernardone to pay for her family's deaths! The rocky earth of the Coldimezzo would happily soak up her offering; it would become a sacrificial altar, like the flat stones flowing with blood where the Hebrew patriarchs butchered their goats and calves and pigeons to atone for their sins.

DESPITE THE FANTASY of final justice that buoyed her own spirit, Amata found Orfeo's dejection unsettling. What satisfaction would she have killing someone who already looked as though he'd be happily dead? The pallor of his newly-shaved cheeks only added to his dolorous aspect. He slumped into the chair opposite the stone fireplace from her, but couldn't face her. He fixed his gaze instead on the flames.

"Why such a long look, *signore*?" she asked. "Is this how you always appear beneath your whiskers? I thought you'd come to entertain me with tales of adventure."

"I shouldn't have come so soon," he said. "This was a mistake." He lapsed again into silence, twisting in his seat to face the fire, but he made no move to leave. His mouth gaped like that of an imbecile unable to remember what he wanted to say next.

Finally he spoke in a voice as dark as suicide. "I need to talk to *someone*.

And I *will* tell you a tale, of Ala-al-Din, the Old Man of the Mountain, a follower of Mahomet's uncle, Ali.

He stared into the flames as he began. "This chieftain dwells at Alamut, beyond the border of Greater Armenia. He's built there a garden filled with every fruit and every fragrant flower. Marble palaces furnished with works in gold, with paintings and silks, cover his grounds. Through conduits in these buildings, streams of wine, milk, honey and pure water flow in all directions. Within the palaces live elegant maidens, who sing and dance to lyres and lutes and are especially skilled in the art of allurement."

Amata smiled at the image. Why couldn't she have been born into such a pleasurable, pagan calling instead of this life of Christian hardship? She peered into Orfeo's face, but it remained dismal as before, a bleak contrast to his flowery descriptions. She closed her eyes, not wanting her daydream soured by whatever had put him in the doldrums.

"Few know of Ala-al-Din's earthly paradise," he continued in the same monotone, "for it lies hidden in a valley guarded by a strong castle, through which a secret passage leads to the entry. His purpose in creating this celestial setting is to pass himself off as a prophet, as one who can himself admit to the heavenly paradise such men as obey his will.

"At his court, Ala-al-Din entertains many youths from the surrounding mountains, selected for their martial skills and exceptional courage. After teaching them of paradise and boasting of his own power to grant them admission, he causes a certain opiate called 'hashishin' to be given to them. Then, when they're half-asleep with intoxication, he conveys them to the secret palaces where for many days they're further inebriated by excesses of every pleasure, until each youth believes he surely dwells in paradise."

Amata shifted to the edge of her chair. "And do these handsome boys ever leave?"

"Did I say they were handsome?" He tilted his head and glanced at her from the corner of one eye. "They don't leave by choice. The chieftain has them drugged again and returned to his court. He asks where they've been and assures them that if they obey his orders, he'll return them to the paradise they've just experienced.

"Thus the young men are happy to receive his commands and even to die in his service, for they believe they'll be happier after death than alive. Should any neighboring prince give offense to Ala-al-Din, he's put to death by the chieftain's warriors, none of whom fears losing his own life. No person, however powerful, being exposed to the enmity of the Old Man of the Mountain can escape his 'assassins'—for such they've come to be called because of the 'hashishin' they imbibe. From their murderous acts the word *assassino* has passed even into our language."

Orfeo paused, scraping at a speck on the back of one thumbnail. Amata clapped enthusiastically, but still couldn't get the trader to brighten. "A wonderful, frightening story, *signore*," she said. "Is it all true?"

"Too true," he said. He buried his face in his strong hands then. When he glanced up at her once again, the rims of his eyelids glistened wet and fiery red. "Assassins murdered my lead carter—my comrade—two nights ago," he said, "the man you saw holding off Count Roffredo's knights with his ax."

Amata felt the trader's sorrow. Yet she steeled herself against the urge to sympathy, closing off that corner of her heart. Instead she focused on one thought: assassins killed my family too, assassins hired by your father, Orfeo di Bernardone.

"Their daggers were meant for me," the trader continued, "but because I'd shaved and Neno hadn't, they mistook us."

Orfeo's chair scraped on the tiles as he rose and pushed it back with his calves. "I've come to say goodbye, *madonna*. I'm not sure why I incurred such enmity, but I know my life is forfeit should I remain in Assisi. I'm going to ask Sior Domenico to arrange another buying expedition. My sole regret is having to leave *now*, when I've just met you."

Oh no! You can't disappear again, Amata thought. "Isn't that just what these murderers would expect?" she blurted. "Won't they stalk you outside the walls?"

He paused and she seized the moment to intrude her own purpose. "I'm traveling to Todi Commune in a few days and need a man-at-arms to accompany me. I'd hoped to ask *you*."

She added quickly, "Your enemy wouldn't anticipate such a move, and you and I ..." *And you and I?* She stopped herself before she compromised her resolution, before she lied outright.

The gloom clouding his features began to disperse, even before she'd finished. She wondered whether the prospect of escape or the words she'd left unsaid appealed most to the man.

Orfeo took her hand. "I'm honored, *madonna*," he said. "Truly honored." An unexpected tingle warmed her inner thighs as he pressed his lips ever so gently to the back of her hand.

"GERARDINO'S LOSING GROUND. The grippe has settled into his lungs and he's stopped eating." Zefferino called the message through the grate as he lowered the day's food to Conrad and Giovanni.

Giovanni da Parma shook his head gravely as Conrad handed him a pail of broth. "Many believe Fra Gerardino di Borgo San Donnino to be the unwitting author of my own imprisonment. How long did you say he and I have been Bonaventura's guests? Sixteen years? It's been a tedious siege for one so young and amiable. You would have loved him, Conrad—a brilliant theologian: courteous, religious, temperate in word and food, helpful with all humility and gentleness."

"You describe a saint. What exactly was his offense?" the friar asked.

"Like me, he subscribed to the prophecies of the Abbot Joachim. But he pressed Joachim's theories to their antisacerdotal conclusion and the secular clergy at Paris turned on him. As minister general I should have punished him, for his claims truly bordered on the heretical, but I couldn't, for I saw the beautiful logic behind those claims. In fact, some of his writings were even attributed to me. Consequently, when he fell, I fell with him. It was just the excuse the Conventuals needed to replace me."

Giovanni submerged a chunk of bread in the lukewarm broth until it softened enough to chew. When he'd finished the bread, he raised the bucket to his lips. Conrad tried to draw his companion back to the topic.

"What then did Gerardino add to Joachim's teachings?" he asked.

Giovanni glanced up suddenly as Conrad spoke, a startled expression on his face, and the friar braced himself for one of his companion's frequent digressions. "Pardon, brother. I was reconstructing a song I haven't thought of in years. People say a babe in arms sang it first, as a warning of events to come.

"Once there was a Roman hit a Roman on the head,
And the Roman to the Roman, Roma offered him instead.
So the lion climbed the mountain and became the fox's friend,
But when he put on leopard-skins, he met a sudden end.

"I've never been able to puzzle out who were the Romans, or the lion or the fox, just as I don't know who is the Antichrist or the Abomination of Desolation in Joachim's prophesies. For years I believed the Emperor Frederick to be the Antichrist; his addiction to daily baths, even on Sunday, proved he regarded neither the commandments of God nor the feasts and sacraments of the Church. But when Frederick died with the rest of the prophesies unfulfilled, I began to doubt. When I asked Gerardino his opinion, he expounded on the eighteenth chapter of Isaiah, from 'Woe to the land of whirring wings,' and so on to the end, as referring to King Alfonso of Castile. '*Certainly he is that accursed Antichrist whereof all the doctors and saints have spoken,*' he said. As for the Abomination of Desolation, he believed with equal surety that it described a simoniacal pope soon to come."

"And was it for such interpretations that the ministers jailed Gerardino?" Conrad asked.

"Not entirely, although they brought ridicule enough on his head from the lectors of the University. Abbot Joachim divides all time into three: in the first state, God the Father worked in mystery through the patriarchs and prophets. In the second state, the Son worked through the Apostles and their successors, the clergy, of which state He says, 'My Father works until now, and now I work.' In the final state, the Holy Ghost will work through the religious orders, the friars, monks, and nuns, guiding the hierarchy into new ways. Not that the Old and New Testaments are to be abrogated, mind you, but men's eyes shall be opened by the Spirit to see a new revelation in the ancient Scriptures—an Eternal Gospel proceeding from the Testaments as its Author, the Holy Spirit, proceeds from the Father and Son. But before this happens must come the convulsions foretold in the Apocalypse, the Battle of Armageddon that must precede the reign of the saints. We thought the year of upheaval would be 1260."

"And why that year?" Conrad asked.

"It seemed plain from the story of Judith. Judith lived as a widow three years and six months, or 1260 days. She symbolizes the Church, who outlives Christ her spouse, not by 1260 days, but by as many years. The year 1260 must therefore be the great turning point in the life of the Church."

"But if Our Lord died in his thirty-third year," Conrad asked, "shouldn't the year of fulfillment come 33 years after the Year of Our Lord 1260?"

Giovanni raised his eyes to meet Conrad's, then rubbed his forehead with his fist. "Of course! That's why the events Joachim foretold haven't happened yet. Gerardino failed to take that into account. But there was more.

"He published an *Introduction to the Eternal Gospel*, containing Abbot Joachim's best-known works, with a preface and notes of his own. The sacraments are but transitory symbols, he claimed, to be set aside during the reign of the Holy Ghost. He also equated the papacy to the Abomination of Desolation, as I said, and with but a few years remaining to the year of fulfillment, the papacy wasn't pleased. *He further declared that San Francesco was the new Christ who was to supersede Jesus, the Christ of the second age.* The schools of Paris couldn't allow such a claim to pass uncontested and the matter came before a papal commission in 1255. The commission condemned Gerardino's work and torched all copies of it. Now it seems Gerardino must himself die, a heretic and excommunicate for his obstinacy, for he never retracted his unorthodox ideas."

They spoke no more of Gerardino until, some days later, Zefferino's husky murmur announced the inevitable: "Fra Gerardino's spirit left his body while he slept last night."

"May Our Lord and His Blessed Mother receive his soul," Giovanni said.

The grate creaked open and Zefferino climbed down beside them.

"Bernardo da Bessa used him as an example in this morning's chapter." Zefferino glowered and deepened his voice: "Behold this utmost folly, when a friar is rebuked by men of the greatest learning and yet will not retreat from his false opinions, but remains wanton and pertinacious, deluding himself."

"Does Bernardo now lead the chapter?" Conrad asked.

"That's my other news," Zefferino said. "Bonaventura's off to Rome. The Holy Father has asked him to address a church council in Lyons. He'll be gone at least through the summer."

Conrad bowed his head. He got up, wiggling his toes in the chill, damp earth of the cell. Dragging his leg irons behind him, he carried the leftover food to the basket on the wall. For two years, he'd nourished some hope that the minister general might relent and free both himself and Giovanni da Parma. Now, preoccupied with papal business, Bonaventura seemed less likely than ever to remember the meddlesome friars he'd left fettered deep beneath the Sacro Convento. They'd be stuck here for at least another half year.

Conrad studied the aged friar, drinking the last of his broth. Giovanni had been incarcerated as long as Gerardino. The friar glanced too at his own pale, skeletal hands, and squeezed one of the bony arms inside the sleeve of his tunic. Would he and Giovanni end their years in a prison cell like the rebellious Gerardino? Would he be unable to carry out his personal vow to work among the lepers? Pointless as it might seem, could this indeed be God's sum purpose in drawing them into the Order, that they should spend their days in subterranean darkness with none but rats as their companions? *Thy ways are indeed mysterious, O Lord*, he thought as he collected Giovanni's pail and handed it to Zefferino.

"Come, brother," he said when the gaoler had left. "Let us give thanks once again for our meal."

XXXII

AMATA MERELY BRUSHED at her cloak when Orfeo asked about their destination, pinching off splotches of drying mud. "We'll be there soon enough," she said.

He recognized the route through Todi Commune, of course, for he'd traveled it with his father as a boy. In fact he knew it *too* well, for he realized that unless they veered off at some fork within the next league, they'd pass directly beneath the Coldimezzo.

What dark whirlpool would he have to brave for accepting the woman's offer? Their tiny caravan skirted the edge of a vortex that could suck him into the dark heart of his worst nightmares and leave him shattered at its bottom. Sweat beaded and trickled down his temples and cheeks, belying the balmy air of March, as he imagined once again the conflagration he had seen in those dreams—people falling under the sword and the hooves of the warhorses—and freshly added to these, the image of the thrashing child roughly bound and carried off by his father's hired killers.

He allowed his horse to fall back to the rear of the group. His shallow breathing mingled with the twitter of birds calling to potential mates from the roadside cover. Even these birds mocked his changed mood. What had begun as a journey of courtship—his horse prancing alongside the lady Amata's while he talked of his friend Marco and she of Donna Giacoma, and of her one great journey into the Marches, his ardor rising like the sap in the surrounding trees stirring from dormancy—had been dampened by the reality of what he might confront at any turn of the road.

Amata seemed equally uneasy. She had turned cool and distant, and hadn't spoken to anyone for the past hour. She drew her hood up over her head, while the pace of her lead palfrey slowed. She didn't act like a woman intent on simple business, the reason she'd given for their trip. Even the boy Pio became discouraged and gave up riding abreast of her.

Orfeo spurred his charger forward until he drew even with Jacopone's wagon. The servants had filled it with straw and covered the straw with several layers of blankets. The injured man dozed peacefully, oblivious to the fly that hummed about his face, springing clear of his forehead as the wagon jounced up the dirt road. They climbed steadily after fording the Tiber River, the roadbed becoming more firm the higher they rose above the muddy river bottom. A carpet of new grass spread across each clearing they passed, and farmers tramped here and there, testing the fields for wetness. New leaves had greened up the brush and trees, and the first pink-and-white buds spangled those fruit trees that had survived the ruthless winter.

He trotted up finally behind Amata, just in time to catch her barely suppressed cry. She'd come to a full stop, facing dead ahead. When she pulled back her hood, the breeze lifted her dark curls from her face. Her hair was little longer than a man's, a holdover from her days in a convent, she'd explained. He forced his eyes away from her profile to see what had startled her.

That should be the place, he thought. Yet it had a different look. He remembered a dirt embankment circling the castle, a forest that grew nearly up to the ramparts, a wall whose only stone rose in the towers and arch framing its entrance. *This* Coldimezzo had tall block fortifications around its entire circumference. Only the keep in the castle's upper story showed above the battlements. The trees and brush had been cut back so an advancing enemy would be forced to charge uphill across a wide escarpment with no hope of surprising the occupants.

"They've strengthened it," Amata said quietly to no one in particular, "but the damage is already done." She swung the head of her palfrey and walked the animal back to the wagon. She leaned over the side rail and gave the sleeping Jacopone a shake. "Wake up, cousin. We're home."

Orfeo stiffened in his saddle, dumb as a tree, as the penitent struggled toward consciousness. He gazed as if for the first time at the woman, piecing together what he'd learned of her: her age, her friendship with the friar, her time as a nun, the generosity of the old woman who took her in (because she'd been orphaned?), a vendetta that yet festered in her heart (against the men of the Rocca?).

Here surely could be seen the hand of God, the hand that plucked him out of Acre, carried him back to Assisi and now to this place, with this woman. He studied the pale features framed by her black hair, straining to discover in Amata's face the child who'd peeked at him shyly from the gatehouse. How many years had it been? Eight, surely. The woman had once admitted, with some embarrassment, that she'd already turned nineteen. *Dear Lord, she had to be the one!*

His chest pounded like that of a man accidentally stumbling onto a valuable coin. And like that man, who would first cover the coin with his foot while he made sure no one watched, Orfeo decided he would hide his find for now. Someday soon, when the time and setting were right, he'd reveal the unhappy connection in their backgrounds. For the moment, he'd just watch, study her past as it unraveled in her present. He marveled at the woman anew, knowing how much she'd endured.

A still-groggy Jacopone rose up on the bed of straw and crawled onto the seat of the wagon. Amata motioned the troupe forward. Several additional guards had appeared along the top of the wall since they'd first come into view of the castle. Amata scanned the ramparts, as if searching for a familiar face among the warriors. A guard called down as they approached, commanding them to identify themselves and their purpose.

"Is Cleto Monti no longer gatekeeper here?" Amata shouted back.

"I don't know the name," the man replied.

"Dead these eight years, lady," another voice called down. "Killed in a raid on this castle."

"I didn't know," she said, but so softly only those in her own party heard her. Her body slumped momentarily, then she addressed the guards again: "Amata di Buonconte and Jacopo dei Benedetti da Todi seek the hospitality of her uncle, Count Guido di Capitanio."

"Then you are an impostor," the second man said. "Amata di Buonconte's dead too, killed in that same raid. And Sior Jacopo went mad and done himself in after his lady wife died."

Jacopone's head snapped up at the man's words. He thundered at the guard: "Go fetch her uncle, you blathering fool! Any idiot with two eyes can see we're neither of us ghosts."

Inexplicably, tears rose in Orfeo's eyes as he watched the guard disappear from behind the parapet. He wanted to laugh; he wanted to cry—all for Amata's and her cousin's sakes. He pressed his helmet tighter onto his head and lowered the visor so no one would see his emotion.

Several moments passed, with silence and no movement on either side. Then, from behind the wall, Orfeo heard an urgent commotion, mostly the shrill cries of women fluttering around a deep male voice that seemed to shout orders to everyone at once. Abruptly, the gate flew open and the voice cried, "Where is she?"

Amata slid off her horse and stood with her arm around its neck. "Am I welcome, uncle?" she said to the great bear who lumbered through the entry to confront the travelers. Several long strides and he was on her, swooping her up in his huge arms. The palfrey shied to one side as Amata's face disappeared

into his untamed grey beard. Finally her uncle set her down and held her by
the shoulders at arm's length. "Amata, darling child. We searched high and low
for you for months, but the earth seemed to have swallowed you whole. None
of the survivors of the raid could say who it was that attacked them."

"I was kept a prisoner in Assisi commune for many years. It's a long and
not very happy tale. But I'm here now and a free woman."

Count Guido took her hands and shook his head. "And I've missed you as
much as my own Vanna. We lost her too, about a year after we lost you."

"Sior Jacopo told me. It must have been awful for you."

The man glanced around and appeared to notice the rest of the caravan
for the first time. His gaze flitted from face to face, and Orfeo raised his
visor again. Finally, the reddish-brown eyes settled on the penitent, ragged
and ash-pale on the wagon bench. "Sior Jacopo?" he commiserated. "Have
you come to this?"

"*This* is *good.*" Jacopone managed a grin. "I've seen hell, *suocero mio,* but
now I'm back."

"A day to kill the fatted calf," the Count shouted to the people in the gate-
way. "Master reeve, get to work on a banquet at once." He grabbed the reins
of Amata's horse and wrapping his free arm around her waist, half carried her
toward the castle. Amata's shoulders quivered and she finally began to cry.

Orfeo dismounted also and fell in behind them. He picked up snippets of
their conversation as they walked.

"I wasn't sure..."

"Pah! Bonifazio's the fat turd of an ox. We all knew..."

At one point in their conversation, Count Guido stopped and stared into
her tear-streaked face. He said very deliberately: "Your father suffered every
day that he punished you. He did what he thought he had to, but it broke
his heart. To him, you were the most precious gift of a child in the world,
and he didn't know what to do when Bonifazio sullied his jewel. Uncle's the
one he never forgave."

Again Amata leaned into his arms, burying her head against his shoulder.
Looking past her and seeing Orfeo loitering nearby, the nobleman scowled
and waved his arm imperiously. "Take the horses to the stable, man. The
servants will show you the way. Don't be eavesdropping on your mistress's
affairs."

"But ... " Orfeo started to protest. He waited for Amata to say he was a
special friend, not just a hired man-at-arms, but she didn't even raise her head.
Finally, he noticed the wagon being guided away and a manservant helping
Jacopone toward the great hall. Orfeo took the reins of Amata's palfrey and
fell in behind the wagon. The count whistled to a wispy, sandy-haired child
of seven or eight years.

"Teresina, come along. Grandpapa has a huge surprise for you."

JACOPONE STRETCHED his sore limbs in his father-in-law's wide bed, near the fire in the great hall of the castle. The heat from the flames and his exhaustion from the jolting ride in the wagon made him drowsy.

He and Vanna had first met in this room. The penitent closed his eyes, picturing her as she appeared that day clothed in a plain green gown, a wimple covering her hair. She hardly looked at him, staring steadfastly at the floor while he directed most of his conversation to her parents, discussing the terms of the marriage. How different had been this modest country girl from the bold women he'd known in Todi. Her lack of refinement both pleased and discomfited him: he'd have to smooth those rough edges before he'd be comfortable presenting her in public. But her natural beauty, properly adorned and bejeweled, would be a glittering lodestone and asset to his career. The merchants of the city would flock to his home for the sheer pleasure of kissing her young hand as they heaped on their compliments, overly sun-browned though that hand might be.

Vanna *non vanitas*. He could have learned so much from her had she lived—had he been open to the truth she lived daily. Why had it taken a fatal accident to shake him from his delusions? He pulled Guido's heavy comforter, pungent with the odor of the old unwashed warrior, over his head. He begged: *When, O Lord, will you set me free? When can I see her shining soul and apologize in person?*

Outside the quilt, the room swarmed thick with whispers. A murmur deeper than the others urged: "Go on, now. He won't bite you."

Then the cherub came. Cautiously it pulled back the comforter, uncovering his arms and chest. He felt the hand, cool and tiny, grasp the rough palm of his own. He opened one eye. The slanting light of afternoon framed its head full of curls, adding a touch of dazzle to the shoulder and side of its white robe and the gold cord about its waist. The childlike face had the same mouth, the same chin as the Vanna of whom he'd just been dreaming. He welcomed the omen with all his soul.

"Is it time, then?" he said. "Have you come to take me to her?"

The cherub hopped like a small bird onto the edge of his bed. Its serious eyes stared silently into his face. He arched his eyebrows, alternately wrinkling and stretching the taut skin of his face and forehead. A tingling told him he still remained every bit alive.

"*Nonno* Guido says you're my papa."

Jacopone glanced around the room. His father-in-law stood with Amata near the entrance.

"Are you hurt?" the girl asked. "Grandpapa said you've been sick for many years, and that's why you couldn't come to see me."

He closed his fingers around the small hand. "Say your name, child."

"Teresa di Jacopo. Everyone calls me Teresina."

"It's a pretty name." He continued to hold her hand while his mind groped back through the fog of years. Again he pictured Vanna's crushed body carried into their sleeping quarters, the maidservants wringing their hands in their aprons, the wet-nurse keening with tears streaming down her cheeks even as she held the *bambina* to her breast. He'd scarcely been aware of the dainty presence in the house, so careful had Vanna and the nurse been not to disturb his business dealings. The infant couldn't have been more than two months old at the time.

He uncurled his fingers, but the girl left her hand resting in his palm. "The last time I set eyes on you, you were no larger than this hand of mine," he said. "Now look how big you are." He turned to Guido, who'd finally approached the bed. "May God reward you, *suocero*. You've guarded her well."

"Until today, she's been all I had left. To me, she's been a gift from heaven." The bear's growl had muted to a purr. He sat down alongside the girl, and the mattress sank under his weight. He ran his fingers through her curls. "See, you even have the same-colored hair," he said to the child, "though your face is definitely your mother's."

"*Deo gratias*." Jacopone laughed. "Thanks be to God."

"That laugh sounds a little rusty," Guido said. "I have a delicious wine will help oil it."

Count Guido stood again and hoisted Teresina off the bed. "We'll take good care of your papa and fatten him up, and soon he'll be strong enough to play with you," he said. "Let him rest for now. You two have many hours to get acquainted."

A FOUL HUMOUR curdled Calisto di Simone's gut. His men had thoroughly botched his plan to recoup the ring of the confraternity, and allowed young Bernardone to escape the city besides. Adding to his misery, the carbuncles on his neck had spread down both sides of his spine; he couldn't even sit comfortably in his high-backed chair.

He lay on his stomach across a trestle table while a serving woman lanced the filthy sores and spread hot compresses across his back to draw out the pus. One of the steaming cloths burned so hot it scalded him; he bellowed in pain and lashed out with his fist, catching the woman in the stomach.

"You did that a-purpose!"

The punch knocked the wind out of the woman, but she managed to gasp: "No, my lord. I swear." She whimpered as she fled back to the water cauldron, her arms wrapped around her midsection. "Upon my life, it won't happen again."

"Upon your life, it'd best not."

A tall, rangy man tramped into the room and bowed to the *signore*. His muddy boots, leggings and cloak showed he'd been riding hard. Calisto scowled. "You here again, Bruno? I thought you'd fled my face for good!"

The man smirked, less frightened by his disgruntled lord than the serving woman had been. "I've been tracking Orfeo Bernardone," he said. "I know where he's hiding."

"Then why didn't you finish him and bring me the ring? I don't want news, I want results!"

Bruno hunched back onto a bench and began scraping the mud from his boots with his knife, flipping it onto the floor in dirty clumps. He didn't bother to raise his head as he explained: "Can't do it alone. He's holed up in a *castella,* just over the border of Todi Commune. Place called the Coldimezzo."

Calisto rose up onto his elbows. "I know it. That's where we stole Amata the Bitch. Bernardone asked about her and the place when he rode up here the other day." He rubbed his scarred finger and asked: "What could he be doing at the Coldimezzo? My father and I left the place in ruins."

"Not ruined enough. It's lived in again." The messenger ran the blade of his knife along the edge of his sole to skim off the last of the mud and slid it back into his belt.

Calisto rolled onto his side and glared at the woman cowering in the shadows. "Get these damned rags off my back," he said. She rushed to the table and lifted away the compresses with her fingertips. It pleased him that she extended her arms full length to keep a cautious distance from his fists. When she'd finished, he sat up and eased his arms into the sleeves of his tunic, spitting out a string of caustic oaths. He strapped on his sword as he crossed the room.

Bruno watched dispassionately as his lord flexed and rotated his shoulders over him. Pain twisted Calisto's features. He narrowed his eyes in thought, and a glint of malice lit their black centers.

"It galls me to leave a job unfinished," he said. "Round up my knights. Tell them to get ready to ride. We can be at the Coldimezzo tomorrow. This time, we'll leave nothing but rubble—and no survivors."

"The men'll like that. They're bored for want of action."

As Bruno rose to his feet, Calisto abruptly swung his fist into the man's chest, knocking him sprawling backwards over the bench. The messenger's head slammed against the stone wall and a squirt of blood gushed from his ear. He struggled to his feet, holding one hand to his ear and groping for his knife with the other. The *signore* already had his sword out, however, and held the point to Bruno's throat.

"There's for allowing Bernardone to escape the first time. Be wary you don't fail me again, lest you suffer far worse."

XXXIII

ORFEO HARDLY KNEW WHAT to expect when Amata summoned him from the servants' quarters. Since their arrival, her *in*attention could only be called "icy." As he headed for the kitchen, he reminded himself that he really knew very little about the woman and her moods.

But Amata seemed pleased to see him. "I apologize for ignoring you, Sior Bernardone," she said. "Being back in my childhood home after so many years drove even basic courtesy from my mind. I hope you'll forgive me and accept this peace offering." The manservant behind her held a picnic basket and a folded coverlet. "I thought we might escape the bustle of the household for a few hours."

"I accept most gladly." Orfeo bowed. "And I hope never to incur your displeasure. A week of such cool behavior would be intolerable."

Amata laughed. "There's a glade where I used to play as a little girl," she said. "It's tucked in the woods a bit beyond the castle walls." She marveled at the calmness of her own voice. The Bernardone played the gallant jester intently; he showed not an inkling of suspicion. The more fool he, to be so blinded by his attraction.

She led the two men to the sally port. There, she caught Orfeo's eye and with a glance directed his attention to the basket. The trader nodded. "*Grazie mille*," he said to the servant. "I'll carry my mistress' basket from here." He grinned broadly, in lively spirits now that he felt secure in her good graces again.

The woman spoke little as Orfeo followed her into the trees, she merely responded to his small talk with brief smiles. She'd hardened herself for this day, and she wasn't about to let him distract her. She wouldn't let him catch her up in his gaiety.

The clearing she remembered had shrunk somewhat where the under-brush had encroached the last eight years. It was still used, however, judging from the flattened grass and the trampled condition of the path leading to it. Amata prayed no one moved abroad today; she scanned the woods and listened for voices or the rustling of other humans. Bird calls, the stirrings of bees, the feathering of new leaves in the breeze were the sole, soft intruders on the silence.

Despite his buoyant mood, the Bernardone strained at conversation while they ate their fruit and cheese and drank the first of the two jugs of wine she'd packed. Maybe she was being too reserved with him; she had to take care she didn't give herself away. Or maybe the trader was shyer, now that they were totally alone, than he normally let on. Several times his face became abruptly serious, as when a fleeting cloud snuffs for an instant the sparkle on a ripple. Whenever he seemed about to launch into a weightier subject, however, he caught himself and resumed his banter. *Santa Maria*, did he mean to take advantage of their isolation to propose marriage to her? She recoiled at the possibility. Amata had to see him only as the hated enemy of her family.

Perhaps he was waiting until he'd drained the second jug before he poured out his mind, drawing on the courage of wine. *She* would rather he napped by then. She refilled his goblet while he prattled of his travels through this part of the country as a boy. She smiled disarmingly as she set down the jug and loosened the sheath beneath her sleeve. She wished she knew what incanta-tions the Hebrew prophets chanted before their sacrifices of atonement. She would recite them to herself now. *Drink up, son of Lucifer*, she urged in her thoughts. *Prepare to balance the scale.*

She'd never killed a person in cold blood. The fight with the monk from Gubbio didn't make her present task any easier. That stabbing had been a reflex, a struggle for her life. The monk would've brained her with his cudgel had she not struck first. This time she'd be carving the soft flesh of a man's throat while he slept, the way the cook's helper lopped off a cock's head. Or the way Judith decapitated Holofernes, her people's oppressor, while he slept after making love to her. Amata had already decided she would pray sincerely over Orfeo's corpse with the deed done, for he wasn't an evil sort like Simone della Rocca, just star-crossed in his lineage. After that, she'd drag his body into the woods for the wild animals to dispose of and tell her uncle the scoundrel ran off after stealing her. . . damn, a detail she'd forgotten! She should have brought a piece of jewelry or something else of value—after flashing it about the castle for everyone to witness, of course.

The sun crossed the zenith while Orfeo drank, and stealthy shadows crept from the western edge of the glade. The trader yawned and stretched out at last on the blanket, his eyelids heavy from drink and the warm, humming air. The gold chain bunched around his neck probably held a crucifix, she realized, but even that sacred symbol couldn't protect him now. The muscles in her forearm tensed. Get it over with! Another moment and the chore would be done; she'd satisfy the vendetta at last and be free to get on with the rest of her life. Amata exhaled steadily, trying to relax the quivering in her limbs, and slipped the knife from its sheath.

An outburst on the path caused her to start. She tucked the knife quickly into the folds of her gown. A squealing of children, led by Teresina, tumbled helter-skelter into the clearing.

"Here she is! I found her!" Teresina cried. She plopped onto the grass at Amata's feet, while Orfeo sat up, rubbing his eyes and shaking the muzziness from his head. The servant children followed Teresina's lead and sprawled around her.

"Cousin Amata, tell us a story," the girl begged.

"A story about a prince and princess," added a second girl.

Amata panted from the fright the children had given her. She pressed her hand to her chest, trying to settle the rapid palpitation of her heart.

"I'll tell you a story," Orfeo said drowsily. He pulled a handkerchief from his sleeve and tied it over and around his little finger. "This is the prince," he explained. He turned to Amata. "We'll need your kerchief too, *madonna*."

The woman thought of the empty sheath strapped to her own arm. "I ... I forgot to bring one," she stammered.

"I have one," Teresina said importantly. The cloth was slightly soiled, but Orfeo thanked her with a chivalrous flourish of his arm. He had Amata hold up one of her little fingers and tied the kerchief around it. "You're the princess," he said.

He straightened her finger and began: "Once upon a time, a young prince traveled with his father and brothers to a faraway land." His hand bobbed along in front of the children with all the fingers raised. "One day they stopped before a castle and the prince saw a beautiful little princess, not much older than yourselves, standing on the ramparts. The prince waved to her with a puppet just like this one." Orfeo lifted Amata's hand until it stood higher than his own and stared into her eyes as he bowed his kerchiefed finger.

Amata avoided his gaze. What is he *doing*? And how long ago had he realized who she was? Was this what he'd been trying to tell her?

Orfeo's voice deepened as he continued. He knocked his index finger against Amata's. "Their fathers quarreled, however, and the prince and his family rode away before he had a chance to meet the princess."

"Oh," the children groaned in unison.

"The prince's father was very angry at the father of the princess. When he got back home he hired an evil knight to storm the castle. The knight killed the papa and mamma of the princess and carried her away to his dark fortress." Orfeo wrapped his free hand around the "princess" and pulled "her" slowly toward him. "The evil knight kept her as his slave for many years, while she grew into a beautiful young woman.

"The prince, meanwhile, became so sad and so angry at his father that he ran away from home and sailed to the Land of Promise. One day, many years later, when he'd grown to be a man, he met the pope. *Il Papa* told him: '*You must go home, young prince, and atone for your father's crime.*' The children's eyes grew wide at the mention of the pope, played by Orfeo's stout thumb.

"So the prince sailed back to his homeland," he continued. "He tracked the princess to the knight's castle, but when he got there, he found she'd escaped." His hand flew open, releasing Amata's finger. "'She's in a convent,' the knight growled, and that same evening the evil knight sent his men to kill the prince so he'd never find the princess. But, as fate would have it, the murderers killed the prince's friend by mistake."

Orfeo's voice broke and his hand started to tremble. The children glanced at each other and back at Orfeo.

Seeing how he wrestled with his emotions, Amata took up the tale: "The prince went to tell a lady he'd just met about the loss of his friend. She asked him to ride as her man-at-arms to her old home in the country, and he agreed. And do you know what?"

Amata looked around expectantly at the circle of girls and boys. "When they came to her home, it was the same castle where he'd first seen the princess."

Orfeo had regained his composure and his voice. "The prince realized the lady was none other than the princess he'd been seeking all these years." He placed his kerchiefed finger alongside Amata's.

"Did he ask her to marry him and live happily ever after?" Teresina asked.

Orfeo stared into the sea of hopeful faces. He glanced at Amata, and the question formed in his own eyes.

She shook her head. "It's your story," she said.

"Not at once," the trader said at last, "He first wished to make amends to the princess. He begged to serve as her knight and go on a quest for her." Orfeo paused and said: "But that's a story for another day."

"Tell us now," Teresina whined.

"*Now* I need to talk to your cousin," Orfeo said. "Alone." He waved the children to their feet. "Go see what you can find in the woods—but don't stray too far."

"Don't worry. We won't get lost. We play here all the time."

When the children were out of sight, Amata lay back on the coverlet with her eyes closed, more confused than ever. The blanket grew taut beneath her as Orfeo shifted his position. His chest pressed against hers as he leaned over her. When his lips touched her cheek, tears gathered in the corners of her eyes. She refused to open them and look at him, however. She wrapped her right arm around his neck and drew him down upon her, while her left hand sought the handle of her dagger. *Bernardone, Bernardone!* The name boomed like the devil's drums in her ears. She squeezed the knife hilt and raised her arm, but her hand shook so uncontrollably that the weapon dropped from her fingers. It bounced off Orfeo's shoulder and fell harmlessly to the blanket.

The man glanced at the knife and at the tears streaming down Amata's cheeks. He cupped her chin in his palm. "I'm not your enemy, *madonna*," he said. "My father was your enemy. Simone della Rocca was your enemy. His son Calisto would like to see us both dead. But I'm here to help you if I can." He stared into her eyes, a look of lingering sadness in his expression. "I love you, Amatina."

The intensity of his gaze consumed any last hatred lingering in Amata's heart. She clasped him with both arms and pulled him close against her. "What do you want of me, then?" she whispered.

His lips moved close to her ear, so close his warm breath tickled the lobe. "Do you really want me to say it, with the children playing so close by?" He raised his head and pulled away slightly, amusement dallying at the corners of his mouth. Then his face became serious again.

"I meant what I said about the quest," he said. "I want to repay, in small portion, the pain my family caused you. I have an idea how I might do so."

"And?"

"The 'prince' actually did meet the pope, and spent many weeks in his company. The pope promised to grant him any help within his means for his services."

The conversation had taken an interesting tack. Amata cocked her head, wondering where he led.

"You mentioned a hermit friend once," Orfeo continued, "one whose minister general keeps him in prison. If Count Guido can spare a few men to ride with you back to Assisi, I'll press on for Rome and ask the pope to pardon your friar. Unfortunately, I'd have to go at once. Gregory leaves for Lyons and his General Council soon."

Again, his eyes seared her very soul. "I ask but one favor in return, Amatina. Promise me you'll accept no suitor before I'm back with the pardon."

Tranquil warmth radiated through her chest, her entire torso—partly from his words, but also from relief that she'd been stopped in her revenge. She held one of his strong, callused hands in hers, remembering he also had a history as an oarsman. An interesting man, on so many accounts. "It's an honorable offer," she said, "and an honorable request."

She brought his hand to her lips. "Don't be like the ancient poet whose name you bear. You need not look over your shoulder to be sure I'm behind you. Accept my word that your Eurydice will follow you ever, on the darkest roads, in the busiest alleys, until you come back home. And when you return with the pope's pardon, I promise you will receive the just reward of your labors."

She rose onto her elbow. Leaning over him, she pressed her lips to his. "Take this seal of my fidelity and my patience," she said.

AS THEY LEFT the trees and crossed the clearing toward the castle, Amata thought how proud Fra Conrad would have been of her self control. Alone with a wonderfully romantic man who truly reciprocated her feelings, who in fact had loved her first, she'd acted with the greatest modesty and propriety. Conrad couldn't be more surprised than she was, though, albeit Orfeo had also shown courteous restraint. She must have gained maturity at Donna Giacoma's without even realizing it.

Her heart harmonized with all the hopefulness of early spring. Soon Fra Conrad would be free; soon Orfeo would return from the papal court. Finally she would be able to reconcile herself to happiness. Even the newly vibrant earth seemed to throb beneath her feet.

She stopped suddenly, listening. She'd felt the ground tremble like this once before, when Dom Vittorio and his warrior monks pounded up the incline toward Sant'Ubaldo. Orfeo spotted the dust cloud at the far side of the clearing at the same instant she did. The picnic basket dropped from his hand.

"Hurry! To the castle," he shouted, and grabbed her arm.

"The children!" she screamed. "They're still in the woods."

"I'll go back for them. You get inside the sally port!"

He gave her a shove and she ran so hard her chest burned. Voices yelled from the ramparts, and the door swung open. She twisted around just in time to see Orfeo dash into the trees and a lone horseman break away from the charge, galloping in his direction.

"Orfeo!" she screamed. "Behind you!" But her cry evaporated, too thin and fragile to withstand the thunder of onrushing hooves and the war cry of the riders.

XXXIV

INSIDE THE COMPOUND, knights and crossbowmen clambered up the ladders that leaned everywhere against the battlements. Amata spotted Guido on the ramparts. *Modesty be damned*, she swore as she grabbed her skirt and followed a man-at-arms up the ladder closest to her uncle.

Intent on the war party, Count Guido didn't notice her at first. Amata watched the horsemen come on like dusty hordes from hell. They slowed as they neared the wall. Finally they hauled back on their reins and brought their horses to a ragged halt as their leader raised his sword in the air. The charge dissipated before the castle like a wave frothing out against a beach. They appeared as surprised as she had been to find the place fortified and well guarded. None but a fool would storm a walled citadel; such a fortress could fall only to siege or treachery.

The attackers stared up confusedly at the row of bowmen waiting for the signal to release their shafts. The leader trotted from side-to-side along the line of riders, swishing his sword angrily. "Where the hell's Bruno?" he called. Amata guessed he sought the man who'd broken off from the pack to chase Orfeo. She glanced anxiously toward the woods and the screen of placid trees. She thought she heard the clash of metal against metal, but the distance of the thicket and the nervous whinnying of the horses made listening difficult.

"Identify yourself," Guido called down. "Why do you ride thus armed against us?"

The leader spurred his horse into the space between his warriors and the main gate of the castle and lifted his visor. He wore the new-style helmet with a hinged visor and light wooden crest. His limbs and torso were protected with richly-decorated squares of hardened leather strapped together at the sides, the light gear copied from the Saracens, newly fashionable among the Umbrian nobility.

Amata gasped aloud when she recognized the swine, Calisto della Rocca. The noise drew Guido's attention to the coif lined up alongside the burnished helmets of his fighting men. He glared at her sternly. She shrugged and walked along the rampart the remaining distance to his side.

"I am signore Calisto di Simone, lord of the Rocca Paida of Assisi." He swept his sword in a long semicircle, gesturing towards his men. "I'm sorry if we frightened your household, *signore*. We're looking for a thief, one Orfeo di Angelo Bernardone, who escaped our city headed in this direction."

A lame attempt to cover his predicament. Amata relished the red cast of Calisto's face, and the grumbling among his men as he attempted to justify his futile charge at the castle. Guido mumbled Orfeo's name, trying to place it.

"My man-at-arms," Amata said. "I assure you, uncle, he's no thief."

She leaned out through an opening in the crenellated wall. "I know you, you coward," she shouted. "Your father killed Buonconte di Capitanio of this castle while he prayed unarmed, and you, you mighty warrior against defenseless women, put his wife Cristiana to the sword as she covered his fallen body. You also abused their daughter when she was yet a helpless child."

The appeasement in the horseman's voice turned suddenly to rage. "And I know that harpy's voice. It's you the thief sought when he left Assisi. Don't try to hide him, you ice-hearted shrew, or it'll go hard for you and all in this place."

"*Frocio*! You *coward*! You don't have the courage, you prickless wonder," she taunted, "you so-called man with the testicles of a sparrow!"

The rider's face flushed nearly purple as a smattering of laughter spread through his own ranks. Guido followed their exchange open-mouthed, staring first at her and then at Calisto.

He'd listened long enough. "What do you say to her charges, *signore?*" he cried.

"I'm a warrior. I don't apologize for the victims of war."

Guido's face went hard as granite. He leaned out, exposing his great bulk. "I too am a warrior, *signore*, and a kinsman of the noblewoman you slew. I demand my blood-right to face you in fair combat, now, in this place."

Amata could imagine Calisto's mind working: the man's a greybeard—twice my age—but look at his size. Honor would be his last consideration, she knew. She smiled as he rubbed the knuckles of his sword hand.

Calisto's horse appeared to read his thoughts too, or perhaps the signore pulled back unconsciously on its reins, for the animal backed toward the line of knights. To her amazement, one man after another tilted his lance and pointed it toward their leader, refusing to let him slip among them. "Don't shame us, master," she heard one of the men say.

Amata whispered quickly into her uncle's ear. He laughed.

"Are *you* telling *me* how to fight, woman?"

"Just do as I say," she said. "He hasn't full strength in his right hand."

Guido straightened and called down again. "Tell your men to back off. I'll meet you alone before the front gate as soon as I'm armored. On foot, swords and shields."

Calisto bowed. He dismounted from his horse and removed the shield strapped to its back. His groom rode forward to take the animal's reins. At the same instant, a riderless horse trotted from the forest. One of the knights broke from the ranks and galloped after it. For a moment after he caught up to the animal, the knight hesitated, staring into the trees, then he led the horse back to the pack. Amata bit hard into her knuckle, but nothing moved in the direction of the woods.

"Off the wall. Now," Guido said beside her. "You don't need to witness this."

"I'm watching for Orfeo," she objected. "He ran back to get the children. One of Calisto's knights rode in after him. That's the man's horse just came out."

A tiny light of understanding flickered in the count's somber eyes. "I should get to know this Orfeo," he said, "if he survives. If we *both* survive." He crossed himself and started down the ladder.

As the sun sank lower in the sky, Amata watched the sweat beading on Calisto's face. Her eyes shifted from him to the trees and back to the armory where Guido had disappeared. The men on the wall and the men on horseback began to relax and talk in low drones among themselves, but no sound came from the forest. At one point, she leaned to the bowman nearest her and said, "If he kills Count Guido, put an arrow through him. Chivalry doesn't apply to such filth. I'll reward you handsomely." The man grinned and tugged at the stirrup of his crossbow. Amata paced down the rampart toward the corner closest to the forest, stopping at each bowman to repeat her order.

At last, Count Guido strode from the armory to the cheers of his men. He looked like a metal mountain, Amata thought, with a separate mail coif over his chainmail hauberk. Over all he wore a coat-of-plates, strips of metal inside a heavy leather surcoat. He carried an Anglo-style helmet under his arm, conically shaped to afford only a glancing surface to a sword blow. *Calisto will foul his slops at the sight of him.* His glittering shield had twice the span of the Assisan's and the crimson scabbard slung around his waist was longer by the length of a man's forearm than any she'd ever seen. She recalled that the women of the house always called him *spadalunga*, "long sword," during her childhood. She chuckled to realize, with her grown-woman's mind, that Uncle Guido might be endowed with other heroic qualities unknown to her little-girl world. If so, he must have particularly appreciated her calling Calisto a "prickless wonder."

She hurried back to her original position on the wall while the count again made the sign of the cross and nodded to a servant to open the sally port. She wished she might see Calisto's face, but he'd already lowered his visor. Guido's long strides ate up the space between them, and faster than she'd expected, he smashed his huge sword against his opponent's shield. The Assisan's knees buckled, but he recovered and returned a heavy blow of his own. They squared off evenly, and again Calisto swung hard, causing her uncle to give ground. "He's not doing what I told him," Amata shouted worriedly to the crossbowman beside her.

Back and back Calisto drove the slower, older man, to the cheers of the horsemen. The count seemed confused. He swung his sword in a wide sidewinding arc at his adversary's head, but Calisto, in his light gear, dodged the weapon easily. Again the signore of the Rocca responded with a flurry of blows, driving his foe into the shadow of the castle wall. Guido could only parry the shocks with his shield.

"Remember your kinsmen! Remember my mother!" Amata screamed down to him, but so many voices shouted at once that she doubted he heard her. She crossed and recrossed herself and folded her hands in prayer as her uncle sank to one knee, holding his shield over his head.

Surprisingly, Calisto did not swoop in on him, maybe suspecting a trick, and in fact Guido did take a swipe at his ankles. The older man regained his feet, swatting at his adversary's shield again, and triggering several more jolts from Calisto. These blows landed with less fury, though, and the count slid half a step to Calisto's left. "That's it," Amata urged. "That's it."

Canny, very canny, Amata thought, as she began to glimpse Guido's strategy. He'd lured the younger man into expending his arm strength while he held his own, older arm in reserve. Now he moved away from the weaker right hand of his adversary, forcing him to extend the arc of each swing of his sword. The next blow glanced feebly against Guido's shield as the sword twisted in Calisto's hand. The count answered with a tremendous wallop, crumpling the top-left quadrant of Calisto's shield. He circled another half step to the left while the Assisan jumped back to recoup. Calisto came forward again, but more cautiously than before, thrusting rather than slashing with his sword, but here the longer blade had the advantage and he couldn't close. The knights watching from their warhorses grew quiet as they recognized the shifting momentum in the duel. Guido stepped again to the left as his opponent backed off to rethink his tactics. Her uncle had maneuvered once more into the sunshine, and Amata noted anxiously that another sidestep could leave Guido staring directly into the slanting light.

The men on the wall became as silent as the knights in the field. The combatants feinted, but neither advanced. As the tension and anxiety built, every muscle in Amata's body strained along with the warriors'. At last, she could bear the suspense no longer and screamed shrilly, "Sparrow balls!"

A thunderclap of laughter exploded on both sides of the fight. Calisto roared something unintelligible, and charged Guido with his sword upraised. The old man rotated his shield ever so slightly so the beams of the sinking sun reflected directly into the narrow eye slits of the Assisan's visor. Again Guido slipped aside and Calisto's stroke missed him entirely. The sword flew from the Assisan's hand. As he stumbled off balance, the count shoved the point of his own weapon between the straps of leather protecting the younger man's ribs, then deeper, between the ribs themselves. The *signore* of the Rocca sank to his knees with a yelp of pain. Guido shoved still deeper, then finally withdrew his sword. Calisto's helmet twisted upward toward the rampart.

"Send for your chaplain," he pleaded. "I'm done!" The red stain on his side spread downward to his hip and thigh and stained the grass beneath his knee. He struggled to remove his helmet. The count stepped up behind him and lifted it from his head, and Amata realized that Calisto stared directly at *her.*

"I'll get you the same priest as shrove your father," she said. She pulled the hood of her cape up over her coif, folded her hands piously before her and chanted in the same, deep voice she'd used at the bedside of Simone della Rocca, "May your soul now receive its just reward."

Calisto's eyes rolled, wild and alarmed, as he slowly comprehended the sense of her charade. He fell forward, catching himself with his hands, digging at tufts of grass with his fingernails. "Bitch. Utter, evil bitch," he muttered, and with a moan collapsed onto the damp earth. His groom led the *signore's* horse to the body and, with Guido's help, hoisted his dead lord across the animal's saddle. Finally Count Guido, the master of the moment, swung his sword in a large circle. The file of riders wheeled and walked their chargers back down the clearing toward Assisi.

While Guido's men hailed him, Amata scurried down the ladder. She ran to the sally port and hugged her uncle as he stepped through. He lifted the helmet off his head. "You were right. He'd no grip in his sword hand."

Then she raced past him, through the portal and toward the woods. She'd just reached the abandoned picnic basket when Orfeo came out of the trees, surrounded by a cluster of children. She fell to her knees and clasped her hands together. He walked slowly, a bloodied sword dangling in his right hand, his left arm draped around Teresina's shoulder. She understood suddenly that the children weren't just gathered around him. They supported him as he tottered toward her.

Amata leaped to her feet and bolted forward. Orfeo fell heavily into her outstretched arms, his head almost touching her shoulder. As she struggled to hold him upright, he nipped her neck and whispered, "*Sparrow balls?*"

"THIS IS NO LIFE for a merchant," Orfeo said. He rested in Count Guido's roomy bed in the great hall, braced up next to Jacopone against a mound of pillows. "I'm not cut out for sword play." The child Teresina stretched on top of the quilt between the two men, toying with a kitten that had claimed a smaller pillow as its own. Amata sat on the edge of the mattress beside Orfeo, while her uncle sprawled in the master's chair beside the bed, scratching the ears of a yellow hound.

Amata squeezed Orfeo's hand. "I release you from your duties as my man-at-arms," she said. "Uncle Guido will escort me safely home. Besides, you've a petition to deliver."

"And every hour I lie here, the further I'll need to ride to catch up to the pope."

He groped for the chain around his neck. "That knight of Calisto's knew me. I think he was one of the men who murdered Neno. When he rode into the clearing, he said, 'Your ring or your life, Bernardone.' As it turned out he wanted both." Orfeo lifted the chain over his head. "Why would anyone kill for a scratched-up, worthless stone?"

Amata snatched the ring from his hand, quicker than Guido who'd also stretched out his arm. "Where did you get this?" she asked. "Simone della Rocca stole a ring just like it from my papa."

"I had it from my own father," Orfeo said.

Count Guido rose from his chair and walked to the *soppedana,* the trunk pushed up against the foot of the bed frame. He took out a small wooden casket and handed it to Amata. "I don't know what Simone showed you, but here's your father's ring," he said.

Bewildered, Amata lifted the lid of the casket. The ring inside matched that on Orfeo's chain: the same blue stone, the same puzzling engraving. "How did it end up with you?" she said.

"Your brother Fabiano passed it to me when he went to live with the black monks."

A log in the fireplace popped loudly while Amata shook her head, uncomprehending. "I've missed something. I don't understand," she said. "What do you mean, 'when Fabiano went to the black monks?'"

"Oh, God," Guido said. He closed both his hands around hers, around the ring she held in her palm. "You didn't even know, did you child? How could you? You were carried off before the monks found him on the rocks below the chapel."

"What are you saying? I saw him leap to his death."

"No, Amata. Not to his death. He'll always be crippled, but he survived the fall. He's assistant cellarer at the monastery of San Pietro in Perugia and soon to be ordained a priest."

"Fabiano a monk?" Amata murmured, stunned and light-headed.

"But no longer Fabiano," her uncle added. "The black monks christened him 'Anselmo' when he received the habit. The Benedictine custom is to give a new name to one who has left the world behind so no trace of their old life remains."

Guido again went to the trunk. He foraged beneath stacks of clothing and linens, and finally came back to his chair clutching a scroll tied with a piece of black ribbon.

"Seventy-five years ago, during the time of the communal uprisings, when armed mobs sacked and burned the homes of the nobility, the counts of the Coldimezzo placed this castle and its properties under the protection of the monks. The Abbey of San Pietro is powerful, both in arms and pontifical and imperial immunities." He unfurled the parchment and read:

"Should any commune, or anyone at all, attack the aforesaid castellans, the monastery promises to go out in their defense. And if they or their heirs or successors should fall into need, they may freely have recourse to the aforesaid monastery for whatever is necessary to life. And if fate should bring them to this extreme need, which God forbid, and they decide to put their nubile daughters, who are called by God, into nunneries, the abbot and the monks of San Pietro de Cassinensi obligate themselves, at their own expense, to provide them with dowries and to accommodate them in convents for women of the rule of San Benedetto. The principal members of the family shall ever be received and seated at the table of the abbot."

Guido put the agreement into Amata's shaking hands. "The monks rode as hard as they could when they learned of the attack, but of course they came too late. They saved what they could of the buildings, and then they discovered Fabiano, barely alive, with many bones broken. They nursed him back to health, and claimed God had spared him and delivered him to them that he might serve out his years in their company. Even your brother agreed with their logic. He settled in like a duckling into a pond."

"My brother, still alive all these years I've been mourning him." Amata turned to Orfeo, her eyes misty with joy. "We have a saying in this country, Sior Orfeo: 'Sister and brother, all to one another.'" She laughed and added: "Some even say, 'A husband is one thing, but a brother's something more.'"

"I hope *you* don't say such things," Orfeo replied. "I might become jealous." He reached out and rubbed her shoulder. "Why don't you visit Fabiano in Perugia before you return to Assisi?"

Amata glanced hopefully at Guido, who nodded, "Of course. I'd love to see the boy again myself."

She handed the parchment to Jacopone, knowing its legal aspects would intrigue the former notary.

"Did Fabiano say how he came to possess papa's—or should I say *Nonno* Capitanio's—ring?" she asked her uncle.

"Yes. Your father slipped it into his pocket when the murderers burst into the chapel. Buonconte told him to jump, knowing Fabiano would be butchered if he stayed in the room."

"But what is the carving on the ring, uncle?"

Count Guido shrugged. "Father may have shared that knowledge with Buonconte if he wanted its meaning passed down. He said nothing of it to me."

Jacopone had finished reading the pact. He rerolled the scroll and tapped it against his forehead, trying to free some memory. "I met a friar in Gubbio once who could figure it out. He claimed to understand nothing, this Fra Conrad, though he was truly wise. I think he knew the answer to every question. But even so, we became lost in the woods."

"You were never as lost as you imagined," Amata reassured him. "You were a hero in those woods."

The time had come to tell Jacopone of the other Fabiano—of Fabiano, the grey-friar novice—and of the brave and invincible dragon who'd saved the boy's life.

XXXV

IN THE HALF-LIGHT of their cell, Conrad scrawled the names of Giovanni da Parma's latest catalog, all the ministers general in the Order's brief history. Zefferino watched from the steps that led down into their cell, helping Conrad with the light from his lantern.

"The ministers of the ultramontane provinces deposed Elias in 1239 and elected Alberto da Pisa to succeed him. Unfortunately, Alberto lived but one year more. After him followed in succession Haymo of Faversham, Crescentius da Iesi and, in 1247, myself. When the ministers asked me to step down following my ten years in office, I nominated my own successor, Fra Bonaventura."

As Conrad scratched the final name across the stones with his shard, he thought again of Bonaventura's warning, the night the sky had seemed to split in twain while the minister general commanded him to bow and kiss his ring. The memory prompted another question he'd never had answered.

"Fra Giovanni," he asked, "doesn't the minister general wear a ring of office, a token that passes down through the succession?"

The old friar rubbed the bare fingers of his left hand for a moment.

"Yes," he replied finally. "A modest lapis lazuli. Why do you ask?"

Conrad held up his finger. He turned to Zefferino. "*Per favore*, brother, could you bring your light closer?"

Zefferino rose from the steps and raised the lantern on the side of Conrad's good eye. Conrad scraped the moss from a square of stone. Having cleaned a fair-sized area, he sketched a crude drawing, the stick figure surmounted by a double arch that he'd seen twice: carved into the altar stone of the lower church and engraved on the minister general's ring.

"Do you remember, or did you ever know, the meaning of these symbols?" Conrad asked. "The first time I came across them, I believed them to be a child's prank, but later I noticed them on Fra Bonaventura's ring, the same ring you must have worn when you were general."

Giovanni stared blankly at the wall. "That knowledge is privy to the office," he said in a flat voice.

Conrad nodded and set the potsherd on the ground. "I understand. You're quite right to reproach me. I merely wished to satisfy a lingering curiosity." He hesitated for a moment, then added in a faltering voice: "I grounded that wish in your conviction that we'll never leave this place anyway ... that anything I learn or that you share will be buried with us." He bowed his head, hoping Giovanni would respond.

"Fra Zefferino," the older friar said after a prolonged silence, "would you leave us for a moment? I want to confess my sins to Fra Conrad."

Conrad raised his eyes again, trying to read Giovanni's face in the shadows while Zefferino climbed the stairs and padlocked the overhead grille. In their more than two years together, Giovanni had never made such a request. In fact, so far as Conrad could tell, he'd never had need of confession.

"Padre, forgive me, for I have sinned," Giovanni whispered after the lock snapped shut. He drew in his breath slowly, then added: "For ten years I deprived the faithful of their right to pray at San Francesco's tomb."

"How so?"

"I know where he's buried. I knew the entire time I served as minister general."

"Are you trying to say the symbol carved into the ring is a map? Is the stick figure San Francesco himself?"

"We speak under the seal of confession—of sin, not the meaning of symbols."

"I understand, brother. I'll pry no further." Conrad made the sign of the cross over Giovanni and said: "*Ego te absolvo de omnibus peccatis tuis.*" He checked his tongue, before he could add the remainder of the forgiveness formula: "Go in peace and sin no more." Telling Giovanni to go in peace would be a cruel joke, given their situation.

After an interval, Conrad said: "I spoke with Donna Giacoma dei Settisoli once about the disappearance of San Francesco's remains. She witnessed the kidnapping as part of the procession that bore him to the new basilica. She could imagine no reason for the action of the civil guards beyond protecting the saint's bones from relic hunters—both the overly devout and robbers from other communes."

"I always heard the same. I can suppose no other motive myself."

Conrad limped stiffly to the wall. "Are there others besides Bonaventura who hold this key?" he asked, tapping at his drawing.

IL POVERELLO DI CRISTO 259

"No other friar that I know of," Giovanni said. "There was a group who called themselves the *Compari della Tomba*, the Brotherhood of the Tomb..."

"A lay confraternity?"

"Yes. All elderly or dead by now, I should imagine. These four men assisted in the entombment and each received the same ring as Fra Elias. They swore to defend the secret location of San Francesco's bones with their lives, to destroy anyone outside the confraternity who somehow learned or guessed the location, and finally to carry this secret, as well as its key, to their graves. The rings are to be buried with them, like the possessions of the ancient Pharaohs."

Conrad understood well the power of the confraternity. Even the tiniest village had its share of secret brotherhoods—unspoken webs spun out through ritual initiations to form symbolic kinships, *comparaggio*, among the men who made up these clandestine fellowships. Such kinships often proved stronger even than blood ties. They were sacred bonds. Fidelity to the point of death, or at least the promise of such fidelity, would not be unusual.

"You mentioned four laymen," Conrad said. "Do you remember their names?" He picked up the potsherd again and, as he hoped, Giovanni interpreted the movement as a challenge to his memory. He stretched out, rolled onto his back, and stared up at the grille as he reminisced.

"There was a man from Todi commune, Capitanio di Coldimezzo—the signore who donated the land for our basilica. San Francesco's brother Angelo. The guardian knight of the city, Simone della Rocca. And Giancarlo di Margherita, who served as mayor of Assisi that year."

"And Fra Elias."

"Elias oversaw the burial, of course. His secretary also served as amanuensis to the confraternity. If he lives still, he might be the only other friar who knows where the relics lie." Giovanni smiled. "Did I name all four?"

"Even better, you named six, the last being Fra Illuminato," Conrad said. He'd been given most of this list before, at Donna Giacoma's, but the names fell into place now. Giovanni had raised a seemingly important backdrop to Leo's puzzle—though Conrad still lacked Elias' motive in hiding the sacred remains in the first place. Surely such elaborate precautions, and the violence in the square, weren't needed to protect the saint's bones. As the noblewoman said, any would-be thief would have had a holy crusade raised against him. And the fact that Illuminato had tried to thwart Conrad's own mission made the friar more suspicious than ever. Might there be a fundamental link between Fra Leo's letter and this brotherhood?

A map! Fascinating! He felt an immediate, overwhelming urge to interpret the markings. Might he pry this last bit of information from Giovanni?

A noise behind him told him he could *not*, not this day at any rate. His cellmate had tucked his arm beneath his head and slipped into one of his frequent naps. He began to snore lightly as Conrad traced and retraced the double arches with his fingertips as though he might discover their meaning by touch alone.

WITHIN THE WEEK, the party of a swarthy merchant delivering casks of Tuscan wine to the Eternal City camped within the gates of the Coldimezzo. Orfeo, fairly rested and with his surface wounds already scabbing over, seized his chance to leave for Rome in pursuit of the pope. Moreover, he knew he'd ride more pleasurably alongside the merchant than when he'd traveled from Venice with Gregory's Roman bodyguard. They shared the languages of trade and young manhood.

Amata inhaled deeply of the cool, early morning air as she waved Orfeo out of sight, a final moment of calm before she and her uncle set off in the opposite direction for the full day on horseback to Perugia. They planned to take but a few men with them, knowing the road to Perugia would be well traveled and that they would reach the abbey guesthouse before dark.

She had hardly slept the night before, realizing she'd be face-to-face with her brother the next morning after nearly eight years of separation. And what a surprise she would be to Fabiano, like a spirit risen from her tomb! She grinned at a sudden playful urge to whiten her skin like some Roman *nobildonna* before their meeting, although the long winter had left her pallid enough.

Jacopone agreed to stay behind at the Coldimezzo, allowing himself more time to recuperate before he rode the haywain back to Assisi. Count Guido had invited him to stay on at the castella, of course, and he nearly accepted. But that was before Amata told him of her latest scheme, to construct a scriptorium in her home that would house as many trustworthy scriptors as she could find to make copies of Leo's manuscript. She hoped Jacopone would be the first. The urge to put pen to parchment again proved irresistible to the one-time notary and instead of Jacopone living indefinitely at the Coldimezzo, Count Guido agreed to return to Assisi with them after the side visit to Perugia. Teresina would make the journey to Assisi too, riding in the wagon with her father. The promise of several weeks at Amata's home already had the child bouncing with anticipation.

Today the girl had to remain behind, however. "Teresina," the knight admonished his granddaughter before they left, "keep your papa cheerful and well fed and let him sleep when he's tired." She nodded gravely, accepting the responsibility as seriously as though she were the castle reeve.

Amata was still cycling through her plans for the scriptorium as she and her uncle and their men-at-arms trotted through the castle gates. It pleased her that Jacopone seemed content to be rooted among family again, leaving Amata to wonder whether his days of wandering penance were done once and for all. She hoped with all her heart that he would finally accept the accident that had claimed their Vanna and allow himself to taste peace at last.

She quickly settled into the rhythm of her palfrey, her spirit buoyed by the warming breeze and spring growth that embraced the road from every side. She, too, was truly tasting peace for the first time in years, a taste sweet and satisfying as a honey mead. She was getting to know her uncle for the first time, or so it seemed, as an adult and not from the perspective of the small child who lumped all grownups together. She felt a swell of gratitude for this huge man who had with a single crushing hug restored her to innocence, to her family, to her past. And ahead waited Fabiano, the restored bridge to that severed childhood.

And the child! She pondered what it was that so attracted her to Teresina: her pure spirit, her limitless and joy-filled energy, the way she hummed as she traced scenes in the dust with a stick, her resemblance to her mother that again transported Amata back to her own time of innocence? The desire for children of her own that this *angelina* inspired? Whatever the source, her love for the girl added its unique flavor to this savory mug of peace that now seemed full to overflowing.

Between such musings that pleasured her mind like lingering wisps of musk incense, and the hours she spent trotting beside her uncle, listening to tales of the fury and clash of Frederick's crusade, the long day's ride sped by almost unnoticed. The enormous grey walls of San Pietro, the Benedictine monastery that served as southern outpost to the powerful city of Perugia, rose up before them almost before Amata was aware they'd arrived. The day was too far gone for them to see Fabiano, she knew, but perhaps after they'd settled in the black monks' guesthouse and dined, she'd get a glimpse of him. Most monastery basilicas had a section at the rear of the nave for visitors, generally sealed off from the monks by a grille. Maybe during Compline that evening she'd be able to spot him among the shadowy shapes bowing in the monks' stalls or pick out his voice from the ocean of chant.

The last impossibility made her smile. Fabiano's voice undoubtedly had deepened since she'd heard him last. She wouldn't know the sound of it. Her baby brother was now a seventeen-year-old young man.

FRATE ANSELMO PERCHED on a stool before a tall writing desk, alert as a marsh bird to the activity around him. One of his roles, as assistant cellarer, was to inventory everything produced for San Pietro on the smallholdings owned by the monastery, the cottager who produced it, and the amount and quality of the work. Today this meant cloth for the monks' robes, a yield of the long winter's indoor activity. The brother cellarer called out the details while the youth wrote.

His sallow face shone blissfully in the light of the candle that burned steadily in a stand beside his desk. He prepared a new sheet, beginning as he always did with the letters A-M-D-G: *Ad Magnum Dei Gloria*, for the greater glory of God. The Rule of San Benedetto referred to the chanting of the psalms as the *Opus Dei*, the Work of God, and Anselmo threw himself into his labor with that same conviction. He gripped the edge of his desk with his free hand to steady himself as he wrote and wrapped his good foot around a leg of the stool for added balance. He hardly glanced up when the guestmaster entered the storage vault, assuming the monk had come for supplies for the visitors' quarters.

The man conferred with the cellarer for a moment, who then called out to his assistant. "Anselmo, you have company in the guest courtyard. We can finish this business later."

The monastery allowed its monks visitors once a year, but even so the news caught him off guard. The first half of his brief life seemed ever more distant with each year he passed at San Pietro.

"My uncle?"

"Yes, Count Guido is here," the guest master replied. "And he brought a young woman with him this time."

Anselmo leaped from his stool, landing on the good foot, and grinning ear-to-ear. "*Amatina*! I knew she'd find her way here one day!" He snatched a pair of crude wooden crutches leaning against the wall.

"Your missing sister? Why do you think so?"

"You'd have to know her, brother. *No one* ever defeated her at *anything*! If you can picture one of our Perugian warhorses charging into the north wind as it blisters off the mountains, refusing to bend to the elements—or charging into a blizzard of arrows with no fear for its safety—then you'd have a small idea how stubborn my sister is."

"That *is* stubborn." The cellarer chuckled. "I pray you're right. Now go, enjoy your visit."

Even dragging one useless foot, Anselmo made it to the compound faster than the guestmaster would have thought possible. The older man, like all the monks of San Pietro, doted on the crippled orphan who'd come to live with them as a small boy. He was as much their pet as the abbot's greyhound and they spoiled him as shamelessly as the Rule allowed.

The guestmaster pointed to the man and woman waiting at the far end of the court, then backed away into the cloister. Anselmo saw his uncle nudge the woman as he hobbled across the courtyard. "Fabiano!" she cried as she fairly flew toward him and met him with such a fierce hug she nearly knocked him off balance. "I wouldn't have recognized you!"

"Anselmo," he grinned, a bit embarrassed. "I'm *Frate* Anselmo now. And I don't think I'm supposed to be hugging women. I might have to prostrate before the whole community and confess this at our Chapter meeting tomorrow morning."

"Oh, pooh!" she said. She stepped back and looked him up and down. "Are you all right? Do the injuries still pain you?"

"I'm all right that way. I'm alive and as happy as I've ever been, Amatina. If not for the raiders, I wouldn't be here today, and here is where I'm meant to be. And you survived too. I knew you would."

"Yes, I survived." Perhaps, when all was said and done, that was all her brother had to know.

"But who were the men who attacked us? A farmer who saw them carry you off said only that they rode away to the east. Uncle Guido looked for you everywhere. It was as if you'd disappeared into a mountain." He glanced at their uncle for confirmation.

Guido replied: "They were mercenaries, knights from Assisi hired by a merchant who quarreled with your father the week before."

"Because he had to pay a toll to cross our lands," Amata added.

Anselmo shook his head. "That's how it began, but there was more to it," he said. "I was there in the archway of the gate. Papa yelled back at the merchant. He said he knew the meaning of the merchant's ring, for he wore such a stone himself. He flashed it in the merchant's face and said if any in his household were harmed, he'd broadcast it's meaning to the world."

"I didn't hear that part." Amata blushed as she recalled her first glimpse of Orfeo. "A rather handsome boy in the merchant's train distracted me."

Count Guido interrupted: "So you think the merchant killed your father because of the ring and not because of the tolls?"

"It seems likely."

Amata turned to her uncle. "But papa had it from *Nonno* Capitanio. Grandpapa wouldn't have deliberately marked his son for death, the way Orfeo's father did."

"No, of course not," Guido said. "Knowing our father, he probably felt its meaning was too important not to be preserved—whatever that meaning is. It's clear now that Buonconte knew. Did he ever say anything about it to you, Anselmo?"

"I'd never noticed it before that day." he replied. "I didn't even know he'd slipped it into my pocket when he told me to jump through the window. The brother who returned it to you found it when they were tending my wounds. Whatever papa knew died with him."

Guido turned to Amata. "I'm thinking we should destroy the thing when we get home. And you should advise your Orfeo to do the same with his. These rings have laid a heavy curse on us all."

"Well, we can be pretty sure Simone's lies buried, if not on *his* finger, then on his son's. You saw to that," she smiled grimly.

Anselmo stared again at his sister and his eyes filled suddenly, allowing her to release her flood of tears also. They started to laugh at themselves, even as they wiped their eyes on their sleeves, as though they were nine and eleven again. Amata took her brother by the sleeve of his robe and led him to a bench where they began a round of childhood memories. Their uncle filled in with stories of the early days of the Coldimezzo, before either of them was born, when he and their father were children themselves.

Anselmo spoke at length of his joy-filled life at San Pietro, of his work in the monastery, how his ability to cipher led to his job in the cellarer's vaults, of his happiness to be of use to the community even with his limited body. He explained that Amata was the first woman he'd seen in almost eight years, a sighting as rare as an angel's visitation, and her wimple seemed a curious and outlandish headdress—just by virtue of his not having seen one in so long.

And then it was Amata's turn to tell him of her days at San Damiano and her current life in Assisi. Her brother seemed disappointed that she hadn't been thrilled to be a lay sister. How could anyone not prefer a life of dedication to God?

Amata had saved her best surprise for last. "But," she asked, "how could I be a nun and be married at the same time?"

"You're married?"

She beamed. "Not quite yet, but it could happen very soon. And when it does, we're going to name our first son Fabiano ... and the second Anselmo. We'll still have a Fabiano in the family, and two Anselmos." She wondered if she should explain that Orfeo was the son of the man who'd hired the assassins, but decided that would be to no point. She *did* tell him of Orfeo's friendship with the pope and of his trip to Rome, which she knew would impress her young monk.

At some point during the long day of lives shared, the guestmaster returned with food and drink so they wouldn't have to leave the courtyard. Then, inevitably, as the afternoon waned, the monks' bell rang the call to Vespers and Anselmo had to return to his cloistered life.

"Will you come again?" he asked.

"Every year," Amata said. "As often as we're allowed."

His next question startled her. "And have you forgiven our parents' killers yet? You know, you won't know peace until you do."

Amata swallowed hard on that one. "Most are gone now, and I was happy to see them die. I've carried the vendetta most of these years, for many reasons. But I'm almost there. Ask me again when I visit with my husband next year."

"Until next year then. Pray for me, as I do for you."

Anselmo stood and propped his crutches under his arms. Then, before he could protest again, Amata kissed him on the cheek.

"A kiss goodbye," she said. "Because we *didn't* die."

FRA GIOVANNI NEVER RETURNED to the subject of the rings. The former minister general seemed to regret having revealed as much as he had, and Conrad didn't press him. Instead, he listened patiently while Giovanni spoke of dreams and visions and apparitions.

In one dream he sat beside a noisy river and watched helplessly as many of his friars, burdened with heavy loads, entered its turbulent waters. The violent current swept them away and all drowned. But as he wept, other friars arrived carrying no load of any kind. These brothers crossed the river with no trouble.

"Truly, the Order needs your guidance more than ever," Conrad said. "The first friars are the Conventual brothers who burden themselves with all the baggage of this world. The second group are the Spirituals who adhere to San Francesco's Rule of poverty and remain content to follow Christ naked on the cross. You could easily have forded the river with them."

"I suppose I was aligned most closely to the Spirituals at heart," Giovanni conceded, "although I tried to rise above factions when I led the Order. The provincial ministers spied out my true sentiments, however—for which I now keep you company."

One night, Giovanni's chains clattered so noisily they startled Conrad from sleep. Fearing that demons tormented the frail old man, Conrad cried aloud for the protection of both their guardian angels and shook Giovanni from his nightmare.

"I dreamt of Fra Gerardino and his heresies," he explained when he regained his wits. "I fear for his soul. Yet he's no more to blame than the chroniclers of our Order's history. His claim that San Francesco's birth marked the second coming of Jesus is no more than a logical reading of the legends.

"I'm sure you've been inside the stable in this town where the lady Pica gave birth to Francesco—despite the fact her husband was Assisi's richest merchant. And, the stories go on to say, an old man proclaimed our founder's sanctity while he was yet a babe, just as Simeon did during Our Lord's presentation at the temple. Later, when Francesco traveled to Rome as a young man to obtain Pope Innocent's approval of the new Order, he had as his companions precisely twelve disciples. One of these, Fra Giovanni del Capello, eventually left the Order, unable to live up to the rigors of the Rule. The chroniclers branded him the second Judas. In such manner does the thread weave through all the stories of Francesco's deeds and miracles.

"In Giunta da Pisa's frescoes in the lower church, events from our founder's life are set opposite stories from the life of Jesus. This has never been done before in the church for any other saint. In any other basilica, you'll find scenes from the New Testament facing scenes from the Old. But in no wise has a human creature, even a great saint, ever been compared so directly to Our Blessed Lord."

Giovanni's vague cynicism disturbed Conrad. He'd never heard a friar express doubts about the literal truth of the legends, although Leo often suggested a deeper truth. He certainly didn't expect such skepticism from a former minister general.

"Yet there are the stigmata," Conrad interjected. "Donna Giacoma held Francesco's wounded and nearly naked body in her arms when he died. She told me he reminded her exactly of Jesus come down from the cross."

Giovanni grunted. "True. There are the stigmata, and for that miracle alone San Francesco might be considered a second Christ."

Conrad wasn't quite mollified. "There's also the testimony of the brother who in a vision saw Our Lord enter the cathedral of Siena, followed by a great throng of saints. Each time Christ raised His foot, the form of his foot remained imprinted on the ground. All the saints tried as they might to place their feet in the traces of his footsteps, but none of them could do so perfectly. Finally came San Francesco and set his feet right in Jesus' prints."

"I've heard many such proofs," Giovanni said. "Still I wish the Order's historians hadn't pressed the comparison so strongly. They might have spared Gerardino his heresy or, more importantly, the loss of his immortal soul."

XXXVI

STANDING BEFORE THE FIREPLACE of her great room, Amata squeezed Orfeo's unopened letter in her hand while the toothless Roman merchant prated on about his journey from the city. Her jaw locked in a frozen smile and her eyes focused on the hairy wart on the trader's nose. Did Pio never intend to respond to her summons? But at last the boy arrived and she had him lead the man away to the kitchen, repeating her gratitude as he tottered off.

She rushed to the courtyard, where she could bask in the midday heat and sit comfortably alone as she read. She clawed at the seal and uncurled the vellum.

"Cara mia,

"The days grow so long, less because the Solstice nears than because we remain separated. You are my constant thought. I dream of the child with the ebony braid, a woman in a glade with sunshine weaving through her hair. Is that not strange? Although you fret because your hair hangs only to your shoulders, I see blown strands floating over your arms, which are filled with flowers. I think it prophetic, the buds *bambinos,* fruits of our future love.

"My quest, I'm sorry to say, has failed, or is at least delayed. Gaining access to Gregory is nearly impossible. I'd almost despaired of ever seeing him, when I met a friend, a Fra Salimbene, who is part of the friars' delegation to Lyons. He introduced me to a second friar, Girolamo d'Ascoli, the Provincial Minister of Dalmatia and recently Gregory's legate to the eastern churches. I think this Fra Girolamo is no admirer of Bonaventura, for when I explained my purpose, he seemed to welcome the chance to embarrass his minister general. At any rate, he arranged an audience and helped me state my case.

The pope was heartily glad to see me, but didn't grant my petition at once lest he offend Bonaventura, his staunch support and ally this past year. Still, for the love he bears me, Gregory said he wouldn't decide finally at this time, but will speak to the minister general after the council.

"He insisted I sail with him for Provence tomorrow, once again his lucky talisman. I agreed, hoping for a change of heart once the business of the council is concluded. From Marseilles, we continue by barge up the Rhone River to Lyons. The proceedings at Lyons Cathedral will likely have begun by the time you receive this. Christ willing, I hope to return by late June in the company of Fra Salimbene. The man is a chronicler and has an infinite passion for history, especially as it relates to his own Order.

"The days grow hot here, but icy when compared to the conflagration in my breast. To think I once mourned my lost chance to gain treasure in Cathay, and all the while a greater treasure lay hidden in the city of my birth. Each night, I thank God for my good fortune in finding you. I once dreamed of bathing in the clear pools of Cathay, but now wish only to bathe and frolic in the dark pools of your eyes.

"Beneath the window of my chamber, a gaggle of aging crones scavenges like crows through a grassy field. They wheel about in their black skirts, circling as slowly as my restless nights in their searching, but with their aprons full of kindling they turn at last for home. So shall I circle our pope until I finally return to you, my quest fulfilled. Until then, remember your lonely servant and keep me in your prayers, knowing that I remain always,

Innamorato tuo,

Orfeo"

Amata scanned the letter several times over, twisting a stray wisp of hair in her fingers as she read. Disappointed though she was by the news about Conrad, she found herself returning to the passages that proclaimed Orfeo's love. She'd seen a happier man while she watched him recuperate at the Coldimezzo, slowly absorbing the loss of his carter friend—an Orfeo with crinkling eyes and quick laughter. She welcomed his passion, words to melt any woman's heart; the fire burning in him sent urgent, soothing heat pulsing through her own limbs as she read.

Yet other words in his letter troubled her. Maybe it was just the way traders talked, but her mind recoiled when he compared her to "treasure" and "good fortune." She wondered, was he truly spurred by love, or driven foremost by his costly ambition to trade in faraway places? Maybe she'd just become overly leery of fortune-hunting suitors since the incident with Roffredo Gaetani.

The word "Cathay" jumped out at her too. She recalled his stories of his friend Marco, who never met his father until his seventeenth year. *No child of mine shall suffer such separation*, she thought, *and neither shall I*. She didn't want a husband in name only. This was something she and Orfeo had to resolve before she could make a final commitment. Fortunately, thanks to Uncle Guido's willingness to act as her trustee, marriage was now an option, not a necessity.

Footsteps shuffled through the cloister behind her. Her uncle glanced at her as he passed, hands clasped behind his back, lips pursed with curiosity.

"A letter from Orfeo," she said. The count didn't reply, but she understood the question in his eyes.

"I know I should love him," she said, "but some of what he says worries me. I'm sure of this, though: I prefer him to any other man. Is that a strong enough foundation for marriage, Uncle?"

Guido smiled with the sage expression of one who'd already crossed that sea. "You'll know the answer when you see him again, Amatina. In any case, one may wed for love and wake to discover that loving day in and day out can also be a chore."

Amata thrust out her lip and plucked at it as she pondered. "But should I marry for any other reason, wouldn't I eventually have to win my husband to love anyway—to save us both from desperation?"

"You'll do fine, child," her uncle said. "You survived among barbarians. I predict you'll survive marriage to Orfeo, too."

He resumed his stroll, musing to himself. *Peculiar generation, marrying for love. Never would've happened in my day.*

ORFEO PULLED HIS CLEANEST bliaut over his tunic, flattened his hair with his hand, and followed the pope's messenger to the minorite refectory. Gregory had invited Orfeo, as the nephew of San Francesco, to sup that evening with him and the friars scheduled to testify on the second day of the General Council.

The pontiff's entourage occupied the entire head table. A hand waving from the far end of the table caught Orfeo's eye. Fra Salimbene had saved a space on a bench, between himself and Fra Girolamo d'Ascoli, the friar who'd helped Orfeo gain access to the pope. The smallish, nimble Girolamo, with his delicate features, silvery-white tonsure and bright blue eyes, marked a chiseled contrast to the stout and sloppy Salimbene.

Gregory, in terrific humour, beamed all around at the company. He prayed a blessing on the meal and added a thanksgiving for the happy outcome of the General Council's first day, especially for the successful reconciliation with the eastern church.

Arriving late at Lyons cathedral that morning, Orfeo had found himself pressed back against the door by the crowd packing the transept. He'd spoken with Gregory enough beforehand, however, to understand that healing the rift between the churches was the first item on his friend's agenda. Standing on tiptoe, and helped along by the comments of the people in front of him, Orfeo had just been able to glimpse the brightly-garbed eastern delegation as they came forward and knelt before the papal throne. In a loud voice they declared: "We accept the primacy and all the customs of the western church." They agreed further to each of Gregory's sticking points, which included the *filioque* clause in the creed that proclaimed the progression of the Holy Ghost from the Father *and* the Son, and the use of unleavened bread in the liturgy of the Eucharist.

While Gregory repeated his pleasure at the day's events, Orfeo whispered to Fra Girolamo: "What did the eastern church gain in return?" He knew that, as Gregory's envoy to the Byzantine Emperor Michael Palaeologus, Girolamo well understood the subtleties of the negotiations.

"Very little," the friar replied in a low, fluid voice. "We promised to tolerate the Greek liturgy."

"Nothing more?"

"You must understand, young layman, Michael's capitulation has nothing to do with religious issues. The Saracens encroach further on his empire every year. He needs our military support, and is in no position to haggle." He dabbed his bread in a bowl of broth and with just a wisp of smile added: "God achieves His ends through wondrous means, not disdaining even the heathen hordes."

As the level of conversation rose around the table, Fra Salimbene chimed in: "You can be sure the remainder of the council will go harder on our Holy Father. The cardinals took four years to elect him to succeed Clement. In the future, he wants them confined to individual cells after the death of a pope. He'd stop all income for the cardinals while they're isolated in their conclaves—until they've chosen the next pope."

"That's but one issue," Girolamo said. "Tomorrow won't be pleasant either. The indictments against the secular clergy begin." Although both the preaching and minorite friars were by now well represented among the ranks of the prelates—bishops, archbishops, and even cardinals—Gregory believed all the evils of the world stemmed from the *secular* priests and prelates who vowed obedience to no religious community.

Salimbene swiped his sleeve at a rivulet of gravy trickling among the folds of his chins. He winked and grinned. "*Non est fumus absque igne*. There's no smoke without a fire. Even a few cardinals may get singed there."

"Including your own Cardinal Bonaventura?"

Salimbene's bemused glance at the question confirmed his own sense of naivete in these church matters. "No, no," the friar said. "He leads the testimony against the seculars."

Orfeo followed the eyes of the two friars to Fra Bonaventura, seated beside the pope. The cardinal attacked a particularly fatty pork roast.

"Our minister general's become nearly as rotund as you, Fra Salimbene," Girolamo noted with an impish smirk. He spoke with the restrained diction of a well-practiced elocutionist, allowing the word "rotund" to resonate all around and echo off his palate before it rolled from his lips.

"Aye, and about time too. You'll note he hasn't my happy disposition or ruddy health yet, though. A bit on the peaked side for my taste. And those dark hollows around his eyes." Salimbene shook his head in mock sympathy. "Even His Holiness worries for him. Do you see the look of concern in that papal visage?"

Orfeo grinned at their disrespect for Bonaventura, whom all the rest of the world lionized. Since the papal party arrived in Lyons, he'd several times overheard gossip that Gregory was grooming Bonaventura to succeed him—depressing news in terms of his goal to release Amata's friar.

He returned to the subject of the morrow's debate. "Sounds like I should get to the cathedral fasting in the morning and find a spot in the front row."

"There'll be lively entertainment for sure," Salimbene agreed. "You'll want a good view. Stick this half-loaf in your pocket." The friar stabbed a chunk of bread with his eating knife and held it out to Orfeo. "If you've never seen the cathedral windows from inside by first light, you've another treat awaiting you."

ORFEO STEPPED FROM the warm June morning into the chill gloom of the cathedral. As best he could tell from the light cast by the single candle flickering on the main altar, he was the first to slip through the giant transept doors.

Not only had Lyons itself grown since his visit here as a boy, but work on the cathedral had progressed to the point where all Provence boasted of its new stained-glass windows. He'd come to Lyons once with his father, for the annual linen fair that began the week after Easter and lasted all through the spring. The cathedral crawled with activity. Orfeo saw noble men and women willingly bend their necks to the yokes of supply carts and, like beasts of burden, drag the wagons filled with stone and wood, oil and grain to the building site. At night the workers ranged the carts in a semicircle around the construction, with tapers or lamps burning on each wagon. They celebrated the watch with hymns and canticles and laid out their sick atop the wagons. Afterward they carried the relics of saints to each infirm person for his or her relief.

While images from that trip crowded his memory, his eyes adjusted to the darkness; the shape of the cathedral's interior emerged slowly. He noted that the building had none of the blocky, heavy-pillared weight of the Roman-style churches of his own land. Slender columns soared skyward, causing his eyes to turn instinctively toward the ceiling, searching out their highest point, somewhere up there in the domed shadows where one might hope to find the mysteries of God unveiled. All moved upward, directed to the heavens. Uncle Francesco *might* have loved this, he thought, despite its obvious cost. Where the early Orders amassed and stored, his uncle scattered and dispersed, casting off his wealth, discharging his friars to the four winds. His had been a *movement* in every sense of the word, just like this new church design.

While the trader stared up at the clerestory, dim light filtered through the figures in the lancet windows and the delicate tracery of the rose windows above. Angels and saints and Biblical figures crowded every square and curve, while the ordinary craftsmen of Lyons looked on from the corners or bent to their daily tasks of baking or felting or weaving, letting the admiring viewer know who'd paid for these fabulous creations. But the subdued prelude hardly prepared him for the many-voiced motet that followed. As the sun cleared the skyline to the east of the Rhone, light suffused the entire apse. Rays of magical shades splintered in every direction; all the colors of Joseph's robe slanted down onto the high altar and the golden papal throne set up for the council, knifing through the murky nave like streams of rainbow-robed, celestial beings. He imagined the astral choirs raining down their unceasing alleluiahs in praise of the Most High as they rode those beams to earth.

Unhappily, the enchantment couldn't last. The door from the portico outside the transept began to open and close as the citizens who'd come to watch the day's debate filed in. Orfeo stationed himself at the corner where the transept met the nave so he'd have an unobstructed view of the pope and the friars at the front of the church. He reached into the pouch at his belt and took out the dry loaf he'd saved from dinner.

"*Vin, monsieur?* A pour from my jug for a penny."

Here was an agreeable surprise—a surprise because one of Gregory's proposed reforms would cleanse the churches of desecration by peddlers. Orfeo suspected the pope would be doing well if he managed to chase the whores from the darkest corners.

The main portal at the west end of the nave swung wide and Orfeo shoved the last of the bread into his mouth. Walking beneath a white canopy, Pope Gregory X paced the procession into the cathedral. He wore a snow-white chasuble, segmented into quadrants by a pale blue cross. His silk slippers and tiara were also white, the tassels of the tiara backed with gold silk. In his right hand a modest wooden crook served as the crosier measuring his deliberate tread. While he mounted to his throne and the cathedral canons settled the canopy over the papal chair, Orfeo's linen-trader eye noted the chasuble had been fashioned of plain Rheims serge. The cardinals followed next, in red cassocks and copes and broad-brimmed red hats, followed by the bishops and clergy and the witnesses from the minorite and preaching friars. The opposing camps of the Orders and the seculars settled, as if by a prearranged understanding, on opposite sides of the nave. The friars ranged along the south wall, facing Orfeo; the seculars sat with their backs to him.

He tried to catch Salimbene's attention, but the friar neither deviated from his serious aspect, nor in any way acknowledged he'd noticed him. Old Fra Illuminato, the Bishop of Assisi, settled on Bonaventura's right, acting as his secretary in the absence of Bernardo da Bessa. Orfeo also recognized Girolamo d'Ascoli and others of his dinner companions: the French minorite Hugues de Digne, and the friar-Archbishop of Rouen, Odo Rigaldi. On Bonaventura's left sat the white-robed minister general of the preaching friars of San Domenico.

Pope Gregory spoke first without rising, glancing from one camp to the other. "There are those who claim secular priests and prelates are no longer fit to preach or hear confessions or celebrate the Eucharist. Many cities have petitioned me for friars to perform these functions, for they have lost confidence in their own clergy. The clergy replies that the friars behave worse than they do, and deprive them of their rightful income by encroaching on duties that are the prerogatives of the seculars alone. Today, we begin the examination of both charges, and will listen first to the friars' legation."

He motioned to Cardinal Bonaventura. The minister general of the minorites rose slowly, a placid but imposing presence. His manner indicated he too had heard, and believed, the rumors that he would succeed Gregory as pope. The friar spoke almost wearily, Orfeo thought, like a banker listing his till.

"The world seems far worse now than it was of old. The clergy weaken the laity, both in morals and in faith, by their evil example. Many are unchaste, keeping concubines in their houses, or sinning here and there with diverse persons. Simple folk might think these sins acceptable to God, did not we friars preach against them; and deluded women might think it no fault to sin with these priests, as it is well known some have been persuaded to do. An honest woman fears to lose her reputation if she confesses secretly to such clergy.

"The late papal legate to Germany suspended clergy who solicited nuns of any Order to sin—suspended them both from office and from benefice—and excommunicated all who actually sinned with them. Many came under this sentence.

"Yet these same excommunicated clergy went on in their parishes as if nothing had happened, crucifying Christ daily afresh. Their confession and absolution became void, and the laity had no right to attend their masses. Thus were whole parishes swept to hell by communicating with an excommunicate. The devil gains more souls by this means than in any other way.

For the unchaste priests, the illegitimately born, the simoniacal—all have lost the power of binding and loosing from sin.

"Still they hamper the friars in their ministrations. If we were never to abide in any parish but by the will of the local priest, we should scarce ever be allowed to stay. Whether of their own volition or at their bishops' instigations, they would eject us from their parishes sooner than heretics or Jews."

A rumble vibrated along the opposite side of the nave. "Generalities. Libelous generalities," someone muttered loudly enough to carry back to the friars.

The archbishop-friar, Odo Rigaldi, sprang to his feet. "In 1261, Pope Urbano asked me to summon a council in Ravenna to collect money against the invading Tartars. You parish clergy refused to contribute until you'd discussed the encroachments of the friars on your privileges." Odo glared darkly through the rows of seculars, and continued in a shrill voice. "Wretches! To whom shall I commit the confessions of the lay folk under my pastoral care if the Orders aren't to hear them? I cannot in safe conscience commit them to you, for if the people come seeking balm for their souls, you give them poison to drink. You lead women behind the altar under pretense of confession, and there you deal as the sons of Eli dealt at the door of the tabernacle, which is horrible to relate and more horrible to do. Therefore does the Lord complain of you through the mouth of the prophet Hosea, '*I have seen a horrible thing in the house of Israel: these are the fornications of Ephraim.*' And therefore are you grieved that the friars hear confessions, since you fear to have them learn secondhand of your own evil deeds."

"More generalizations," intoned the same flat voice that had complained earlier.

"Does the Bishop of Olmutz grumble about generalizations?" Odo pointed to a priest leaning against the wall of the nave. "Tell me how I can commit women's confessions to the priest Gerard here present, when I know full well he has a whole house full of sons and daughters, and that he might not unfairly be described in the words of the Psalmist, '*Thy children shall be like young olive trees around thy table?*' And would that Gerard were singular in this matter."

He raked the clergy with his eyes and finally settled on a bishop in the front row. "And you, Henri de Liege. Are not two abbesses and a nun among your concubines? Didn't you once boast that you sired fourteen children in twenty-months? Isn't it true that you are illiterate and that you were elevated to the priesthood only eleven years after you became a bishop?"

He sat down heavily, the veins swollen on his thick neck, while the accused Henri sneered and fired back: "We're condemned by a friar cardinal and a friar archbishop. Yet the ranks of friars elevated to the prelacy stink every bit as ripely of the same scandals you'd attach to us."

Orfeo watched Gregory's sad, pensive face as the debate progressed. The pope no doubt expected such acrimony and seemed prepared, for now, to let it take its course.

Henri's taunt had prompted the Dominican minister general to his feet. Framed in his white garments and cowl, he had the aspect of the saints in the cathedral's stained-glass windows. He spoke in a conciliatory monotone.

"When Albertus Magnus of our Order accepted the Bishopric of Ratisbon for the sake of carrying out sorely-needed reforms, our general treated his consent as a terrible fall. 'Who would believe that you, in the very evening of life, would set such a blot on your own glory and on that of the Friars Preachers that you've done so much to augment? Consider what has befallen those prelates who've been drawn into such offices, what their reputation now is, how they end their days!' Thereupon, Albertus resigned his See and died as a simple friar at Cologne.

"Although I've passed many years at the head of my Order, I cannot recall a single instance in which his Holiness the Pope (not referring to the good pope here present) or any legate or cathedral chapter, has ever asked me or any of our superiors, or any of our provincial chapters, to find them a worthy bishop. On the contrary, they picked their own friars at will, either for reasons of nepotism, or from some other unspiritual motive, and so no blame can rest with us for their choices."

He took his seat, but Fra Salimbene rose immediately to continue the theme. "I too, in my travels, have known many Friars Minor and Friars Preachers raised to bishoprics, rather by favor of their families and their fleshly kindred, than by favor of the Order. The canons of the cathedral church of any city care little to have holy men of religious orders set above them as prelates, however clearly the latter may shine in life and doctrine. They fear to be rebuked by them, while they'd rather live in fleshly lusts and wantonness."

"Oooh. Lust and wantonness again!" Mock horror echoed from the clerical side of the church

"Aye, so I said. And may Christ grant you greet the arrow at mid-flight for your mockery."

Salimbene mopped his florid face with a large cloth. The cathedral had warmed considerably, packed solidly with churchmen and onlookers. "I received this story from Fra Umile da Milano, who dwelt at our place in Fano," he continued. "One Lententide the montagnards sent and begged him for God's sake and the salvation of their souls, that he deign to come to them. They would fain confess to him. So he took a companion and went among them, working much good there with his salutary counsel.

"One day a certain woman came to confess to him. She revealed that she'd twice been not only invited, but compelled to sin by the priests to whom she'd come for confession before. Fra Umile therefore said to her: 'I have not invited thee to sin, nor will I so invite thee; but rather I invite thee to the joys of paradise, which the Lord will grant thee if thou love Him and do penance.' And while he gave her absolution, he saw she clutched a dagger, and said, 'What means this knife in thy hand at such a moment as this?' She answered, 'Padre, in truth I was purposed to stab myself and die in my despair if ye had invited me to sin as the other priests have done.'"

The friar warmed to his own oratory, his plump cheeks shining so ruby red Orfeo feared he might burst of apoplexy. "I've found priests lending out money to usury," he said, "forced to enrich themselves to support their numerous bastards. I've found priests keeping taverns under the sign of the hoop and selling wine, and their whole house full of bastard children, spending their nights in sin and celebrating Mass the next day. And after the people have received communion, these priests thrust the leftover consecrated hosts into clefts of the wall, though these are the very body of our Lord. They keep their missals, corporals, and church ornaments in an indecent state—coarse and black and stained. The hosts they consecrate are so little as scarce to be seen betwixt their fingers, not circular, but square, and all filthy with the excrement of flies. They use rude country wine or vinegar for the Mass ..."

"A failing certain to offend a friar notorious for imbibing fine wines across half of Christendom!" a voice boomed from the back of the cathedral. One of the cardinal observers rose from his bench and swooped down the nave toward the center of the controversy, his scarlet cope flying out behind him. With his black, beetling brows, yellow eyes, and sharply-hooked nose, he called to Orfeo's mind nothing so much as the red-tailed hawk closing hard upon its prey.

Orfeo turned to the people around him. "Who's that one?" he asked. Most of the crowd shrugged, but a man clad in the long black gown and square-cut cap of the university whispered: "Benedetto Gaetani. A country-man of yours, judging from your dress. He aspires to the papacy."

Benedetto bowed low toward the pontiff's throne. "Pardon, Holy Father. I know this day has been reserved for the testimony of the friars, but I can no longer keep silent about the outrages I've witnessed in my own district. As Your Holiness knows, I am an Umbrian, a man of Todi. My entire life has passed on the same soil that nurtured these minorite friars."

He gestured toward Bonaventura. "My esteemed brother cardinal knows full well his vagabond sons are every bit as corrupt as clergyman. They abuse their liberty with gluttony and familiarities with women. He knows better than any here why the minorite authorities have been forced to renounce over and over again the friars' spiritual direction of the Poor Ladies.

"As for their vows of poverty, Fra Bonaventura's sons have such success begging all over the country, they must keep servants at their heels to carry their money coffers. How they spend it, the tavern-keepers know. These friars write down the names of the alms givers, promising to pray for their souls, but as soon as they cross over the next hill, they take their pumice stones and scrape the parchment clean so the same sheet can be sold many times over. They court popularity with the people by granting easy penances and avoiding unpleasant duties like excommunication."

The two would-be popes glared at one another across the nave. Then the steely calm in Bonaventura's eyes unexpectedly gave way in a flicker of confusion. He spread his fingers across his chest, laboring for breath. After a moment the minister general rose unsteadily to his feet, his face grey as ash. He tugged at the red cord beneath his chin that held his cardinal's hat in place; his jaw worked as though he were about to speak, but he sat again without rebutting Benedetto's accusations.

Cardinal Gaetani seized upon his silence. He jabbed his finger at Bonaventura and renewed his diatribe. "Those friars who would imitate their founder in holy poverty, you force outside the Order or, worse yet, torture and imprison. Even Giovanni da Parma, revered everywhere for his sainted reputation, has sat in fetters these sixteen years. Is it not true, Fra Bonaventura? Do you deny ought I've said?"

The minorite general struggled to regain control of the argument. "I only wanted accord within the Order." His complexion had gone white as lime. He groaned again, more loudly and painfully this time, and curled forward in his seat like a withered leaf licked by flames. The frail Illuminato tried to catch him, but Bonaventura's weight carried them both to the floor. A collective shout rose from every quarter of the cathedral. Orfeo thought he saw a smile tease the corners of Cardinal Gaetani's thin lips.

The merchant turned his attention back to the center of the pandemonium, in time to see Fra Illuminato make the sign of the cross over his master. The secretary then did a curious thing. He lifted Bonaventura's hand to his lips, as though he meant to kiss it. Instead he lapped at one of the dying man's fingers with his tongue, eased a ring from the finger, and dropped it into his own pocket.

A stunned Gregory stood before his throne, leaning on the crosier. "Holy chrism, someone!" he called out finally. "He needs the last rites!"

Orfeo, too, stared in wonder at the stricken cardinal. Here was Fra Conrad's all-powerful captor stretched out before him, face-to-face with his mortality and as helpless in its grip as the mortally-wounded Neno had been. Like Cardinal Gaetani, Orfeo found himself fighting the urge to exult, for he could finally glimpse a happy ending to his quest.

XXXVII

MPRESSIVE, AMATINA. WHO taught you such skills?"
Count Guido watched his niece prepare a sheet of vellum for copying:
scraping the fine parchment with her pumice stone, softening it with
chalk, and finally smoothing it with a plane. She stretched the vellum on her
high sloping desk, punched tiny holes in the margins with a metal stylus, and
finally used a ruler to draw faint horizontal lines between the holes in the
margins. On a lectern beside her desk lay a single page, cut carefully from
Fra Leo's scroll and covered by a stencil with a window framing the line to
be copied.

"Sior Jacopo showed me how to ready a sheet. It's good 'busy work' and
keeps my mind and hands occupied. Donna Giacoma hired the tutors who
taught me to read and write."

Teresina's singing echoed in the empty room just off the south loggia
where the desks had been set up. Across the courtyard, the hammering of
carpenters rattled along the opposite gallery. The men framed the wind
break where Amata planned to move the copying operation during the cold
months.

She picked up a thin, sharp knife and began whittling anxiously on a quill
point. Count Guido had announced that he'd be returning to the Coldimezzo
at week's end, and Amata had been fretting ever since. How could she tell
her uncle she wanted to keep Teresina with her? The child had stolen her
heart. But Amata had another motive too. As a tribute to Donna Giacoma
she wanted to pass on the noblewoman's generosity to the female of the
next generation. But could Teresina's grandfather stand to part with her?
He'd poured all his love into the girl since his daughter Vanna's death; she'd

become his entire universe. And even though Teresina could live with her natural father in Assisi, Amata had to admit Jacopone remained ill-prepared for parenthood—even though his health improved daily now that his life once again held purpose and routine.

Guido frowned at the page on the lectern. "This might as well be hen scratching to me," he said. "I could never sit long enough to learn to read. I always hired a notary to keep my accounts."

"An honest one, I hope." Amata smiled, listening to Teresina skipping across the room behind her. *God, how she yearned for children.* If anything, her need had grown stronger since she'd visited the celibate Fabiano. She and Teresina now carried full responsibility for continuing the family line.

Amata had dreamed of her brother the night before, all crooked and crippled, though his face shone with happiness. The eunuch for the sake of the kingdom of heaven! Then the dream changed and she found herself alone with Orfeo in the glade at the Coldimezzo. She prolonged that fantasy as long as she could, thrilling as his strong hands explored her moist body ever so slowly (although the hands might have been her own), pressing her eyes shut, trying to trick the dream into believing she continued to sleep long after the first light of morning intruded through her eyelids.

She might have sunk again into the pleasurable daydream even now had not Teresina poked her head out onto the loggia. "I just saw my papa through the arrow hole. He's running through the alley." The child giggled. "Papa looks like a long-legged stork when he runs."

The slap of Jacopone's bare feet echoed through the house and up the stairs to the loggia. He lurched to a stop in front of them and leaned against the railing, trying to get his wind.

"The friars' delegation," he managed at last, "back from Lyons."

Amata jumped from her stool. That meant Orfeo must be near Assisi too. Maybe he'd traveled with them. She opened her mouth to speak, but Jacopone held up his hand.

"There's more. Bonaventura's dead and the provincial ministers are gathering to elect a new general. It can only bode well for Fra Conrad."

He clapped Guido on the shoulder. "Come, *suocero*. Let's go to the basilica and see what we can learn."

The men left arm-in-arm, with Teresina trotting down the stairs behind them. Amata quickly gathered the manuscript pages from the lectern and locked them away with the rest of the scroll. Although she told all visiting friars that she reserved the upper story of the house to her household, the business with Fra Federico had taught her caution. She untied her ink-smudged apron and stared aghast at the black spots on her fingers and hands. She needed to wash up.

She rushed down the stairs to the ground level, but hadn't moved quickly enough. Teresina's squeal rang from the doorway. She turned to see the child hanging like an oversized, wriggling pendant from Orfeo's neck while he did his best to support her with one arm around her waist. His other hand held a sealed parchment.

A grin emerged from the stubble and dust covering his face as he spotted Amata. He leaned over until Teresina's feet touched the floor again and released her. "Your knight errant returns," he said, "I bring with me the Grail of freedom for your friend Conrad."

He dropped to one knee as she approached, playing his courtly role to the hilt. He reached out for her hand, but she immediately ducked both fists behind her back.

"Do I offend my lady?" he asked.

Teresina laughed. "Her hands are all messy with ink. She's been writing a book."

"I should've known." Orfeo's grin widened and he shook his head as he rose again to his feet. "Did I describe her right, Padre?" he said over his shoulder.

Amata hadn't noticed the friar waiting just outside the doorway, but she recognized his good-hearted laugh even before he stepped into the foyer. "Welcome, Fra Salimbene," she said. "I see by the grace of Our Lord you're robust as ever."

"Have we met, *madonna?*" he asked.

"Aye. Should you visit your niece at the Poor Ladies' house this trip, you'll find her chaperon fled."

"Is it you? The little, lively one?" He scanned her features with amused curiosity. "Here's a story I'll need to hear."

"Once you're both settled and I have a chance to clean up." She turned to Orfeo. "I want to walk with you as far as the gate of the Sacro Convento when you go to release Conrad. I want to see his face when he comes out to take his first breath of free air."

"It won't happen quite that soon, Amatina. We have to wait until the friars elect a new general and present Gregory's pardon to him. The new man should prove a friend, though. Both Gregory and Caetanio Orsini, the Cardinal Protector of the Order, have stated their preference for Girolamo d'Ascoli—the friar I told you about in my letter."

Orfeo's head dropped and he scuffed at the tiles with his boot. "Besides, it mightn't be the best idea for you to see Fra Conrad right away. You don't know how he's changed in two years. If you react with shock when you see him ..."

Abruptly, he stared into her face and fell speechless, unable to finish his sentence. She thought she recognized the same desire in his eyes that she'd seen in the imagined glade, although his face had been clean and shaven in her dream. She wished Teresina and the friar would disappear, if only for a moment, so she might throw her arms around his neck like the child and hug him against her. Her longing hung thus suspended, awkwardly, in the silence between them, until Orfeo finally broke the tension with another dusty smile.

He reached into his pouch. "I brought you a gift from Provence, this little bronze mirror." He rubbed it on his sleeve and held it up before her. "Are you so short of quills, Amatina, that you're forced to write with the tip of your pretty nose?"

SALIMBENE WAVED A GOBLET over his empty platter, blessing the recently departed meal. He patted his stomach and resumed his story. "This Brother Piero of the preaching friars reached such a pitch of madness by reason of the honors paid him and the grace of preaching he possessed, that he believed himself able in truth to work miracles. And coming one day to the place of the Friars Minor, and letting shave his beard by our barber, he took it exceeding ill that the brethren didn't gather the hairs of his beard to preserve them as relics.

"But Fra Diotisalve, a minorite of Florence and an excellent buffoon, answered the fool according to his folly. For, going one day to the convent of the Preachers, he said he would in no wise abide with them, except they should first give him a piece of Brother Piero's tunic so he might keep it for a relic. They then gave him a great piece of Piero's tunic, which, relieving himself after dinner, he put to the vilest use and cast at last into a cesspool. Then cried he aloud, 'Alas! Help me brothers, for I seek the relic of your saint, which I've lost among the filth.' And when they ran to the latrine at his call, and found themselves mocked, they blushed for shame."

The friar drained his goblet and held it out for a servant to refill as he blotted his lips on the back of his hand. While the boy poured, Salimbene continued: "As this same Fra Diotisalve went one day through the streets of Florence in winter time, it happened that he slipped upon the ice and fell face down, stretched out at full length. At this the Florentines, who are much given to foolery, began to laugh and one of them asked him as he lay on the ground: 'Are you hiding something beneath you?' To which Fra Diotisalve replied, 'Certainly. Your wife.' The Florentines took no offense at his reply, but rather laughed aloud and commended the friar, saying: 'God keep him, for he's truly one of us.'"

Amata chuckled, though not as heartily as Uncle Guido and the servants at the lower table. She thought of San Damiano and Salimbene's visits to his niece. Strangely, his humor amused her less than in her convent days. He would still be talking late into the evening, she knew, until the others either faded away to their beds or passed out.

Although she still recalled Conrad's low opinion of Fra Salimbene, Amata had taken the risk earlier that day, with Orfeo present, of showing the

chronicler a few pages of Leo's manuscript. She told him of her plan to make
as many copies as she and Jacopone could manage. The woman had watched
his face closely, his growing excitement as he read. When she asked whether
he wished to join their effort, he volunteered at once. "I may produce but
a partial copy before the wanderlust strikes again," he said, "but I must see
the rest of this chronicle."

"Are you discreet, brother?" she asked. "The Order might not approve
of Leo's history if they knew it existed." The question arose from a sudden
misgiving that she might have been the indiscrete one in mentioning the
manuscript to Salimbene in the first place, that she might be relying too
much on her good memories of his visits to the Poor Ladies' house.

"For the love I bear you and your betrothed, I swear to be tactful!"

Amata had blushed at the word "betrothed." She'd given Orfeo no formal
consent yet, nor would she before they'd had a chance to talk alone. She
noticed that Orfeo responded to the friar's comment with a complacent
smile, however.

"Discreet even in your cups, Fra Salimbene?" She knew it was a rude thing
to ask, but the friar couldn't fault the honesty of her concern.

"*Madonna*! You dishonor me." Salimbene had pouted with all the injured
expression his jovial, round face could muster.

Now, after dinner, Amata prayed that she hadn't erred as she considered
the man across the table, watched his bulbous nose glow ever rosier, and
listened as his voice became ever more boisterous. Orfeo or Jacopone would
have to stay with him whenever he left the house.

She turned to see Orfeo beaming at her, although the others were reacting
to something Salimbene had said. He, too, had been more subdued than usual
that evening. His brother Piccardo had sought him out that morning with
word that their father had passed away during Orfeo's trip to Lyons. Despite
his father's ill will towards him, Orfeo had accepted Piccardo's news with
difficulty.

Amata, oddly enough, felt no particular joy when Orfeo relayed the
message to her, even though Angelo Bernardone had until recently been the
focus of her last, lingering rage. She saw then how the visit with Fabiano
had brought closure to her need for revenge. If her brother, crippled for life,
could forgive their enemies and even bless them for freeing him to a higher,
spiritual joy, could she not allow her loftier instincts to guide her as well? She
was learning, thanks to the host of teachers who had crowded her last few
years. And but for old Bernardone's treachery, Orfeo would not have rebelled
and set out on the odyssey that led him eventually to her.

Amata rose and held out her hand to him, at the same time motioning
the others to remain seated and enjoy the moment. She guided him to the
chairs beside the empty fireplace, where she'd had so many agreeable talks

with Donna Giacoma. She wondered if this might one day be their favorite corner of the house on chilly winter evenings . . . outside the curtains of their canopied bed.

They *would* marry, of course. She loved him and she'd already promised as much when he left to seek Conrad's freedom. And besides liberating the friar, he had helped save her from the Gaetani and defended the children against Calisto's raiders. Good Lord, what more could she ask of the man? Shouldn't she view her nagging doubt as nothing more than perversity on her part?

Yet that voice persisted in her mind, the doubter who questioned his motives. It demanded that for her own peace of mind she put him to some further test, even though their future might be the farthest thing from his mind this evening. And so, when he pulled his chair close to hers, she asked: "Do you ever dream how it will be when we're married? What kind of life do you see for us?"

He thought for a moment, bemused, resting his elbow on the arm of his chair, his chin in his hand. "In the best of schemes?"

She nodded.

He leaned forward. "There lies a world south of here, Amatina, like none you've ever imagined, a world of year-round warmth and unimaginable hospitality. The very opposite of the cold and hostility we've known most of our lives here in Umbria. There's something of our own land there, but with all the color and music and wisdom of the orient blended in. The Emperor Frederick once said, 'If Jehovah had known about Sicily, he wouldn't have made such a fuss about the Holy Land.'"

"Fra Salimbene calls Frederick the Antichrist."

"Nonsense. Frederick was a genius, though he *did* thumb his nose at more than one pope. When he reclaimed Jerusalem from the Saracens, no bells rang out and the patriarch of the city refused to celebrate a mass in his honor. And why? Because he won it through his friendship with the Sultan Al-Kamel, not by force of arms. He married the Sultan's daughter and fifty other Saracen women besides. He shared the Muslim love of wisdom and even admired the Quran, their holy book. Frederick peopled Sicily with philosophers and astrologers from the entire Levant, and hired translators to put all their words into Latin. His favorite treasure was an astrolabe given to him by the Sultan."

For the first time that evening, Orfeo showed some excitement. "In Palermo, where the Emperor built his great fortress, you can see mosques and square white houses, just as in the East. They say that at midday half his court rose to say the prayers of Mohamet. Turks and Negroes ran his household, and he never traveled without taking along his camels, leopards, monkeys, lions, exotic birds—even a giraffe."

"You've seen these creatures?"

"Yes, Amatina, and in my dream you get to see them too. I thought of you when I stood in Lyons admiring the beautiful colored glass of the cathedral there, wishing I could share all the wonders of the earth with you."

"And what work do you do in this dream?"

Orfeo grinned. "I'm at last a trader on the grand scale. I travel throughout the Levant and maybe beyond to Cathay. That part of the dream's unchanged since my days with Marco."

"And I? What do I do while you travel and barter and buy and sell in the great marketplaces of the world? Are we partners in your enterprises too?"

"You enjoy the sunshine of Palermo, *cara mia*." He laughed. "Sailors would never allow a woman on a galley. It's bad luck. You're my patient, dutiful wife." He laughed and added with a shake of his finger: "And *faithful*. Someone must raise our children. My dream includes many children."

"Then you *will* sail home from time to time to keep me pregnant?"

The edge in her question startled Orfeo. "It's only a dream, Amatina," he said. "I thought you wanted lots of babies."

"And so I do. But your dream sounds expensive. You'll need *money* on the *grand scale* to trade on the grand scale."

"But when we combine..."

She put her finger to his lips. "Remember. Uncle Guido is now trustee of my wealth. I've thought of having him put much of it aside before I marry—for Teresina. And of course, I owe so much to the monks of San Pietro, for saving my brother's life. They'd like to expand their guest house." She watched his eyes, for she knew she'd see the answer to her next question there, before she heard it from his lips. "Would you still want to marry me if I had no more income than we need to run this house?"

Even the reflection of candlelight in Orfeo's pupils couldn't rekindle the spark her question had snuffed. "I think you toy with me, *madonna*." He pushed up from his chair just as Teresina came pattering for good-night kisses.

The child adores him, Amata thought. *Look how she lights up when he hugs her. And I love him too, damn it, and I want him to hug me, but I...*

Tiredness washed over her, frustration at the disappointment she'd just seen on Orfeo's face. His "dream" seemed to confirm her worst fears, even if it was only a fantasy.

She kissed Teresina on the forehead, and glanced up to see her uncle coming for the girl. "I'll help *Nonno* Guido tuck you into bed," she said. "I need to talk to him."

"What about?" Teresina asked.

"About you, little cricket."

Orfeo slumped back into his chair, morose and silent, while she led the girl away. She signaled for him to wait until she returned, but he turned away. At the far end of the hall, Salimbene's surviving audience guffawed.

A FULL JULY MOON lit the room where Amata normally slept alone. She'd always relished the luxury of her own room in this house, the room once used by Donna Giacoma's sons, even though the noblewoman had preferred to share the large dormitory with the women servants. The past weeks had been an exception. Teresina's tiny figure curled up on a pallet in the corner, her pale limbs wraith-like in the humid shadows.

Amata rolled onto her back and stretched her arms above her head. Her wide-open eyes stared up at the canopy, and a single tear slid down her temple. This should have been the happiest evening of her life. Love surrounded her from every quarter, yet in a few short hours the sweet wine of friendship had curdled to a sour gall.

Had she been selfish or overly optimistic, expecting these men to under-stand *her* dream? She had hoped Guido would agree to her plans for Teresina without question. After the child finished her prayers and closed her eyes, Amata led her uncle down the hallway, where he listened for a while in silence. A shadow clouded his eyes, though, when she suggested he leave the girl with her. He did acknowledge that a young couple might better raise Teresina, once Amata and Orfeo were married, but he saw no reason for the girl to stay just to learn to read and write. He would sleep on her idea, he said finally.

What demon, then, prompted her to add: "I'm not sure I *should* marry Orfeo. I want a real family. I worry he'll always be gone."

"Rubbish," Guido snapped. "Men *are* always gone. I didn't see my wife for three years while I fought in the emperor's crusade. When a great cause or great business summon, men of spirit must go. The world's expanding, Amata, and the adventurous ones like Orfeo will always seek to push its bounds. You ought to be overjoyed to be courted by a man of such energy."

"But when he looks at me, I fear he sees naught but my dower."

"Perfectly normal." Guido took her by the shoulders and shook her lightly, as though he hoped to jostle some good sense into her head. "What *is* it with you, child?" He stared into her eyes, his face close to hers. The acrid reek of digested wine singed her nostrils as he spoke. "I promise you this, Amata. I'll not consider ceding Teresina to your care before the day of your marriage. I'll not place her in a household where confusion's the rule. The child and I return to the Coldimezzo in three days as planned." Her uncle stalked back to the great hall, muttering angrily to himself. She waited until the hot blush drained from her cheeks and ears, almost afraid to follow him, but sensed she owed Orfeo some word of apology. She hoped he would want to take up their talk again, and that she could find a way to explain her misgivings more clearly.

The hall had nearly emptied when she returned, except for the menser-vants and friars bedding down at the far end. Orfeo still waited, brooding in his chair, but he gave her no chance to speak. Instead, he jumped up and said brusquely: "I'm thinking I should move my gear to Sior Domenico's in the morning and stay over there." He chewed his lower lip. "I'll leave your *friend's* pardon here with you. Fra Salimbene can see the next general gets it."

His curtness stung her, so much so she forgot she'd returned to the hall to apologize. "Will you call on me?" she asked. "I want us to remain friends, no matter what."

He'd replied noncommittally. He mumbled that Sior Domenico might want him to go on the road again and strode off to join the other men.

Amata went to her bed with a sinking heart. Because she hesitated to promise marriage, she had annoyed Guido and wounded Orfeo's pride, and that pride suddenly stood like an unscalable mountain between them. Hope-fully only for this evening. Even as she wound the comforting sheet around her shoulders, Amata dared to wish Orfeo would want to see her again. But would he ever truly understand her?

"*I'm just so frightened*," she finally whispered into her pillow, the very words she'd wanted to say to Orfeo all along.

XXXVIII

ZEFFERINO SHUFFLED THROUGH the tunnel above Conrad's cell, followed by a second step the friar didn't recognize. His first thought was that the gaoler brought a new prisoner to their dungeon.

He raised his head weakly as torchlight approached the opening overhead. The padlock snapped open. Zefferino lifted the grate and he and another friar slouched sideways down the stairs.

The gaoler called out to Conrad and Giovanni as he descended. "Brothers. Fra Girolamo d'Ascoli, your new minister general, is here to speak with you."

The prisoners stumbled to their feet, clinking their chains. At a motion from Girolamo, Zefferino removed a large key from the ring on his belt and squatted at Conrad's feet. He unlocked the ankle manacles and tossed them aside with a triumphant clatter.

The minister general said to Conrad: "Our Holy Father, Pope Gregory X, pardons your offenses against our Order, brother. You're free to go. You're also welcome to stay on here at the Sacro Convento until you are restored to health. I would recommend that you take your time and entrust your care to our brother infirmarian."

Conrad squinted against the torchlight. A rush of blood prickled his unfettered legs. Despite months of hoping, the undramatic suddenness of his release made it barely believable. He shook the cobwebs from his brain to be sure he'd heard rightly.

Girolamo continued: "Someday soon, when you are strong enough, we'll talk again, Fra Conrad. I have a plan for you and want you to be my emissary to the Spiritual brothers, to help me bring them back into the fold. As you are sympathetic to their practices and a former prisoner of the Conventuals, they'll listen when you explain how change is inevitable for the Order to grow and to survive. I'm sure Fra Giovanni here recognized this when he served as general."

Conrad's mind groped like a sleepwalker's. "I'm flattered by your trust, Fra Girolamo," he said, "but I recently made a vow that I hope you will let me fulfill. I promised Our Lord that, were I ever released from this place, I'd work for a time among the lepers. But Fra Giovanni da Parma here is beloved by all the friars. Might he not serve as your emissary?"

"I intend to release this reverend father also," Girolamo said. He peered through the shadows playing off the decrepit old friar. "I doubt he could handle the travel involved in such an enterprise, however." He addressed Giovanni. "Have you ever imagined where you would go if you left here, Padre?"

Giovanni stammered out his answer. "I've thought about it hundreds of times. I want to go to Greccio . . . only to Greccio." In a trembling voice he added: "I want to end my days before the stable where San Francesco recreated the scene of Our Lord's nativity."

While Zefferino unlocked Giovanni's manacles, Girolamo spread his palms toward Conrad. "You see, Fra Giovanni won't do. Tell me about this promise of yours. How long have you vowed to work among the lepers?"

"Until I learn what I need to know."

"And what do you need to know?"

"I can't really say. I'm not sure myself. I know only that God will tell me in His own time and way. It may take a day; I may end my life there, never knowing."

Girolamo rubbed his cheek as he continued to study the prisoners. "My desire for unity in our Order has made me overly hasty, brothers. Obviously, you will both need a time of grace while you readjust to life above ground. Go fulfill your vow, Fra Conrad. But I still hope to use you one day, once you've completed your mission and regained your strength."

A noisy sniffle from the stone steps drew their attention. In the flare of the torch, Conrad noticed tears rolling down the guard's cheeks.

"Fra Giovanni will need a companion to take him to Greccio," he said. "Perhaps Fra Zefferino . . . if you could devise some sort of mask . . . because he worries about his disfigurement. . . ."

Girolamo cocked his head. "You plead on behalf of your gaoler?"

"He's played the good shepherd to us these two years. I think he's already beginning to miss his little flock."

Girolamo glanced around the trio, musing in silence. "What say you, Zefferino?" he asked finally. "Are you ready to turn over your keys to another brother and leave this place?"

A strangled laugh erupted from the gaoler's throat. "I'm ready, but I should go with Fra Conrad. Fra Giovanni needs a younger, stronger companion. Conrad, you and I are two blind, matched bookends."

Conrad touched the scar above his cheek. "I hadn't thought how *I* might appear to others' eyes. Have I a face to frighten children?"

"You've aged, friend, far beyond your years," Zefferino said. "When you came here, your hair shone black as a sable's, but now you wear the winter coat of the ermine. You hobble about like a broken-down donkey, and you'll be as sightless as a bat in the bright light of day. In short, but for your prophet's beard, we are complete counterparts." Forgetting himself momentarily, the gaoler started to move the torch closer to his own face for Conrad's inspection; as its heat warmed his cheek, however, he quickly straightened his arm to its full length. He would never forget the vengeful angel of the midnight forest.

Conrad limped to the stairs and clasped Zefferino's shoulder. "Lead on, then, brother. If you can join with me in singing hymns of praise and thanksgiving, we two shall be such a pair as will confound all those who place their hope in earthly favor."

ZEFFERINO WAS RIGHT about the daylight. Eager though Conrad was to escape the Sacro Convento, he had barely cleared the friary gate when he had to shield his good eye with the sleeve of his robe. With faltering steps he ducked inside the dark interior of the basilica's lower church, his former gaoler close behind. Like an infant learning to walk, he toddled to the tomb of Fra Leo.

He repressed an urge to berate his mentor. Instead, he remembered the hymn of praise he'd mentioned to Zefferino in the dungeon, and mumbled his thanks, trying to reaffirm his faith in God's design.

"Here's something new," Zefferino said behind him. "This plaque wasn't here the last time I came up. It's a woman's tomb. '*Jacoba ... sancta romana.*'"

"Jacoba?" Conrad crossed himself, then reached up beneath the pulpit and probed with his fingertips across the inscription. "The date, brother?"

"It dates from last winter. I told you, it's new."

Conrad's arm dropped to his side. "*Requiescas in pace*, Fra Jacoba."

Zefferino stared querulously at him. "A friar with a female's name?"

"A beautiful and gentle lady, brother, and a story for the road. I'll tell you all about her while we walk." He wondered whether Donna Giacoma had been able to follow through on her plan to make Amata her heir.

Amata would be a grown woman now. He'd hardly thought of her the past year, but suddenly had to know how she fared. He wondered too whether he'd been as absent from her mind as she from his. He hoped not.

A harsh reprimand echoed from the opposite transept. A bank of torches lit up the north corner of the basilica. Shielding his eye, Conrad made out two figures moving through the brightness, scrambling about a series of scaffolds. Except for the ripe language, they called to mind the angels ascending and descending Jacob's ladder. The voice that had distracted him blared again in the gravelly tone and dialect of an aged Florentine.

"My pigments are ready, Giotto. Hurry boy. Get the plaster up here. I want to finish the Virgin today."

Conrad crossed the apse, drawing near the scaffolding to watch the fresco painter at work. An abrupt rebuke stopped him cold. "I'll thank you brothers to keep your distance. Don't distract my apprentice."

Conrad froze. He opened his eye wide, not caring of a sudden whether he could see or not. At first the glare of the torches overwhelmed his sight, and he wondered if God's saints constantly bathed in such brilliance. After a time he could distinguish the colors on the wall, a host of cherubs surrounding a half-completed, enthroned Madonna. In her arms she held what might have passed for a real, human baby—not the miniature Roman emperor the friar was used to seeing in such frescoes.

At the Virgin's left side stood the lifelike image of San Francesco robed in the simple grey-brown habit of the Order. The dark eyes gazed calmly somewhere beyond Conrad; the thick lips neither smiled nor frowned. A golden halo framed the saint's protruding ears and olive face, his stubbly reddish beard and tonsure, his negligible eyebrows. The artist had posed Francesco's right hand across his chest while his other clasped a Bible, or perhaps the Rule of the Order. The wounds of the stigmata were clearly visible on each hand. Conrad noted too the imprints of the nails in each bare foot. The gash of the spear in Francesco's side showed through a rent in his tunic.

The blank, peaceful eyes held the friar's attention. He recalled that Francesco had been near blindness at the time the seraph marked him with the wounds. A rush of gratitude for his remaining eye flooded Conrad's heart.

"Beautiful, *signore*," he murmured aloud to the old painter.

"Beauty is my trade." A trace of sarcasm in the artist's voice caused Conrad to wonder whether the man contrasted his work to the friars who watched him. Certainly he and Zefferino lacked beauty. The Florentine with his delicate sensitivity might even find them repulsive. The bravado that had buoyed him in the cell suddenly evaporated and he pulled his cowl over his head.

"Come, brother," he said to his companion. "I know a place where we can rest and be welcome."

HIDDEN BENEATH THEIR COWLS, Conrad and Zefferino waited in the great hall of Amata's house. The servant Pio hadn't recognized Conrad, even when the friar asked if she still lived there. He wondered whether his voice had also changed in the icy dampness of his cell, although he'd had ample chance to use it in Giovanni's company the past year.

Because he had long ago forgiven his gaoler, Conrad hadn't considered until this moment that Zefferino might not be welcome here. But Amata had seen the friar only once, in the darkness of the abandoned chapel, and the man had not revealed his name until Conrad heard his confession. Zefferino's appearance too had changed as a result of his wounds healing and his time underground. But his companion's reaction to Amata might be something else, should he ever connect her to the novice on the road. Clearly Conrad would be wise to leave that dog sleeping during the few days they'd be staying in Amata's home.

He ducked his head when he heard Amata enter the room. "Peace be with you, brothers," she said. "Do you seek shelter here?"

"Yes, Amatina," Conrad said. "For my companion and myself."

Her hesitation was almost palpable. "Conrad?" Her voice trembled.

"Yes. I'm free."

"Oh, God! Let me look at you!" Her hands moved toward his cowl, but he raised his own to stop her.

"Please. I'd frighten you."

Her hands clenched as she slowly pulled them back. "What did they do to you?"

"Not 'they,' *madonna*," Zefferino interrupted. "I was his torturer."

"You were no more that God's instrument," Conrad snapped. "Don't be hard on yourself."

"Brothers! Enough. No more, please," Amata said. "You're both torturing me now." She laid her hand on Conrad's shoulder. He didn't pull away. "So, do you intend to hide beneath your hood the rest of your life? Remember, you're in the home of your truest friend now." She stroked his head through the fabric. "Why don't you practice?"

Conrad leaned toward his companion. "You too, Zefferino. We must, or else we might as well return to our dungeon."

Together they drew back their cowls. Amata blinked back her tears. The young woman rubbed a knuckle across her cheek and stepped away, glancing from him to Zefferino. To Conrad's relief, she showed no recognition of Zefferino as the friar who had tried to spear her with his pike.

Her eyes finally settled on her friend and the attention caused him to flush. "Conrad. Conrad," she said. "I've missed you so much. I never needed to talk to you more than now." She spoke evenly, as though she saw nothing amiss. She even managed a tenuous smile. "And I have a surprise for you. Come with me."

Amata and Zefferino helped him totter up the stairs to the loggia. Again, he didn't resist as her hand cupped his elbow. He began to sense just how much he'd been starved for the slightest token of affection these many months—and how much affection he'd taken for granted in this household years before.

Cresting the topmost step, Conrad saw two scribes—a friar and a lay-man—bent over writing desks. They were both vaguely familiar, although he didn't trust his sight entirely yet. At times he still seemed to move within a cloud, and thus did Amata's small scriptorium strike him as more fabulous than real.

"Fra Salimbene. Sior Jacopone," Amata said. "Look who's here. Do you remember our Fra Conrad?"

Sorrow darkened Jacopone's face as he raised his head. He stared away over the loggia railing. The friar seemed only curious. Salimbene didn't know Conrad well enough to remember how he once looked.

"An incredible document Fra Leo entrusted to you," the chronicler said, "even though it lacks in the miraculous."

Amata quickly explained what the copyists had on their lecterns. "I hope you're pleased, Conrad. You asked me once to do this very thing." She shot him a tentative glance.

With Zefferino's help Conrad hobbled to each desk, scrutinizing the vel-lums. "You're both fine scriptors," he said. He stopped beside Fra Salimbene. "As for miracles, Fra Leo intended only to write a true history. He wouldn't allow himself to embellish his chronicle with false events, even though his readers might be edified thereby."

Salimbene bowed apologetically, perhaps out of deference to Conrad's condition. "And he was right to do so, of course. I've known many to feign false visions that they might be honored above others, as holy men to whom God's secrets are revealed. And, God knows, many a phantasm has sprung from an addled brain, clouded with its own fumes, until a man takes for a true vision that which is merely fantastic."

He warmed to his subject. "Oh, and the counterfeit relics I've seen in my wanderings! The monks of Soisson boast a dubious milk tooth of the child Jesus that fell out on His ninth birthday. I've seen Our Lord's umbilical cord in three separate reliquaries, although it's certainly possible each might have owned a section of the cord. But I've also seen his entire foreskin in no less than seven sites. They're all displayed with much ceremony each Feast of the Circumcision."

Jacopone set down his pen with a mortified expression. "I touched the foreskin once and was greatly moved. It inspired my prayers for weeks afterward."

Salimbene grinned sardonically, his back to Jacopone. "So it goes with *simple* faith. That's the best argument for miracles and relics after all. Ab-stractions are lost on the widow clutching her mite. But for a vial containing a few precious drops of the Virgin's milk ... would she not gladly part with all the little she owns?"

Conrad frowned but didn't reply. "I'm weary now," he said to Amata, without adding that it was Salimbene who tired him. "Where might I rest?"

When they reached the bottom of the stairs, out of hearing of the scribes, he voiced his misgivings about her judgment. "Sior Jacopone I trust, and I'm glad to see him at a desk, but I fear you've made a mistake in showing Leo's scroll to Fra Salimbene. He may appear detached and footloose, but his sympathies lie with the Conventuals."

"He's a chronicler, Conrad," Amata reassured him. "His interest in the history of the Order far overshadows any opinions he might hold about its factions."

"But once he's satisfied his curiosity?"

"He made a solemn promise to me. To me and to…" Amata broke off, not sure how to characterize Orfeo. She certainly couldn't call him her betrothed as Salimbene had. She wasn't even sure she could still name him as a friend.

"I need to speak to you, Conrad. Maybe Fra Zefferino can spare you to me after supper?"

Zefferino bowed his head.

"If you two wish to nap until then, or if you need anything from our kitchen, you need but ask. My entire household is at your disposal."

After supper she would lead her friend to a shaded corner of the courtyard. For as long as he was willing or able to listen, she would tell him all she'd gained since their separation, and all that she'd recently lost. And if he cared to pour out his own story, she would be his sympathetic audience. So much had changed in their lives these two years.

XXXIX

ORFEO CHECKED THE SAILCLOTH covering the loaded tumbrels, making sure his crew had tied it down securely. At a nearby table, old Domenico counted fleeces, sacks of wool, and bolts of finished cloth. Several carters led oxen across the courtyard and yoked them to the three remaining carts and wagons.

Travel normally energized Orfeo. Not today, however. He tried to keep his mind on business, but he prepared for his journey without zest.

Several weeks had passed since he'd heard that "Amata's friar" had settled into her household once more. She'd sent Orfeo a note of thanks and invited him to come meet Conrad, but he could not allow himself even a reply. He still smarted from their last meeting.

He crossed the yard to check on the carters. Most of these men had trekked with him the previous winter on his last buying trip to Flanders and France. They were a grimy-faced, burly, foul-mouthed lot, clad in leather tunics like blacksmiths with daggers swinging against their thighs. But Orfeo knew his crew could withstand any obstacle thrown up by nature or man. Only one of the teamsters was untried—the middle-aged carter who'd replaced Neno. The rest of the men had accepted the newcomer so far.

Orfeo ran his fingers beneath a yoke, making sure it was protected where it would rub the ox's shoulder, and sighted down the line of vehicles. Around the corner of the rear wagon, framed by the rising sun, a hooded friar approached with stiff, unsteady steps. A long white beard like an eastern patriarch's straggled down his chest. The man raised his head as he drew nearer, looking first at Sior Domenico, then at Orfeo. Orfeo winced when he spied the scarred eye socket and the squint of the friar's good eye. This one could curse a soul with a look and no word uttered.

"Orfeo di Angelo Bernardone," the friar called aloud. He spoke the name, not with the lilt of a question, but dryly, as if solely to confirm his guess. In that instant, Orfeo could imagine the Grim Reaper had come to harvest his life.

"You've found him, friar. What do you want of me?"

"Nothing for myself. You've done me enough good already. God reward you for fetching my freedom from the pope." Gingerly, the friar slipped back his hood, displaying a hoary shock of hair filled with sunlight.

Startled, Orfeo didn't speak immediately. He'd pictured a much younger, even a handsome man—one Amata might be attracted to physically. Her coolness toward him at his homecoming, after he'd returned with the pardon, made him wonder if she'd another reason for wanting to free this Conrad—particularly when she'd said she wanted to wait for the man by the friary gate. Orfeo felt she'd used him, then mocked him and turned her back once she had what she wanted. Now, seeing the former hermit in person, he realized his error. He waved his hand, shrugging off the thanks.

"Glad to help an innocent man." He returned his attention to the yoke.

"I also want to tell you you're a fool," the friar added.

Orfeo's shoulders stiffened. Sior Domenico and several of the carters looked up from their tasks. He noticed they all focused their curiosity on *him*, though, refusing to look directly into Fra Conrad's face.

"I don't think it's your position to tell me what I am or am not," he said and thrust out his chin defensively.

"I'll risk that position, if you tell me you cannot love a woman for who she is, more than for her wealth. I know one who loves you as she loves her very soul."

Clearly Conrad had ripped the scab from an unhealed wound. Pained and embarrassed, Orfeo glanced at his compatriots. "Pardon, Sior Domenico," he said. "I need a few moments to walk apart with this friar."

Conrad fixed his eye on the aged merchant. Domenico looked down at his bolts of linen and dismissed them with a wave of his hand.

Orfeo pulled the priest through the arched portal of the courtyard. What had Amata told him?

The friar spoke first. "From what I see in your eyes, I know I guessed right. You miss her as much as she misses you. And seeing your employer just now has inspired me with an idea. It could work if you want it to, if you'd marry Amatina for love alone, as she desires."

With a look Orfeo urged the friar to speak on. He knew his voice would quaver if he tried to speak now. He'd hear this Conrad out while he regathered his composure.

The friar led him through the plan, punctuating each step with the conditional: *if you truly love her*. His advice made good sense to Orfeo, amazingly so considering the man knew nothing of commerce. When Conrad finished, Orfeo said, "Sior Domenico must consent, of course—and my brother Piccardo, too." But yes, he did want Conrad's idea to work, with all his soul. His heart burned at the prospect. He grasped the friar's hand in both of his and shook it vigorously. "Now it's you who may have saved me, brother," he said.

"Then God grant you a happy outcome," Conrad said. Orfeo finally released his hand, and the friar added: "Be so kind as to deliver a message for me, *signore*, when you go to see Amatina. I didn't say goodbye when I left her house today for fear she'd try to delay me. Please tell her I've gone on to the Ospidale di San Salvatore delle Pareti and will return when I can."

"The lazaretto?"

Conrad nodded. "I also left my friar companion behind at her house without voicing my intention. Again, I didn't want to sound any alarms. He's welcome to follow me if he wishes—or not, as God inclines him. I can't say when I'll return and my choice of habitation might not agree with him." The friar managed a wry smile. "*Addio, signore.* May God bless both you and your lady."

ZEFFERINO HAD TOSSED on his pallet much of the night, before finally dozing in fitful sleep. Anxiety crept like disease through his veins. He hadn't been outside the friary walls since the day the brothers found him nearly dead in the abandoned chapel and carried him to the Sacro Convento. He'd hardly been above ground except to fetch food for his prisoners. With his arm he covered his head, isolating himself from the dark lumpy bodies and snoring of strangers all around him; he curled his legs into a taut ball. His little solace came from Conrad's even breathing on the pallet beside his.

At one point before daybreak, Conrad stirred. Through his half-open eye, Zefferino saw his confrere move to the doorway, just as he'd left after hearing the confession in the chapel. For a moment, Zefferino feared he'd been abandoned again, but the noises surrounding him were human, not animal. He lapsed again into sleep.

When next he woke, it was to the commotion of menservants stashing their bedding, yawning and stretching, and calling God's blessing on their day's work. Conrad's bed lay empty and unrolled. Maybe he'd gone to the latrine first.

Zefferino got up, pulled his cowl tightly around his head, and followed the general movement in that direction. He saw how the others conspicuously avoided looking at him. Conrad might be unaware of such a thing, but to Zefferino their disgust or fear was only too plain.

He soon realized that his companion was nowhere around, not even at the breakfast table. While the friar nibbled desultorily, the woman Amata came to him and asked for her friend. But Zefferino could only shrug and glance around the room. The babble in the hall beat on his ears like the wings of bats swooping through the dungeon tunnels.

"I'll look for him in the chapel," she said. She went off through the hallways calling Conrad's name. Something about her voice ... "*Conrad! Fra Conrad!*" Like the boy friar's in the woods. He could almost hear that voice screaming, "*These aren't God-fearing men, Fra Conrad.*" And then the trumpet blast of the fiery angel, just before Zefferino entered into his agony. He'd never asked Conrad about the angel. After his prisoner's vision in the cell, Zefferino realized the man lived on a loftier plane than he. The guard was leery of prying too deeply into the sacred mysteries.

The others finished breakfast quickly, leaving Zefferino alone at the table in the huge hall. Around him, servants gathered empty bowls and cups. The porridge gurgled in his stomach. The two copyists would begin their day's work soon. Maybe Conrad had gone up to the loggia to help them now that he'd gotten his legs beneath him again.

With lowered head Zefferino climbed the stairs. He found only the scribe Jacopone. He watched as the copyist used his knife to cut a page from a thick scroll and spread it on his lectern. The friar picked up the scroll and examined the flimsy material. He'd heard tell of this "paper;" cheap and convenient compared to parchment, but unlikely to withstand the mildew of a damp monastic library. Look how easily someone had poked a hole through this *rotolo*. He stuck his little finger into the puncture.

"There's a story in that rip you're prodding, brother," Jacopone said. "The manuscript saved our lady's life one black night. A dark shadow of a murderous friar would've ripped out her guts with his pike, except she had that fat scroll strapped around her. I remind her even now to praise God for Fra Leo being the wordy sort."

Zefferino squeezed the scroll with both his hands. "A friar? Why would a friar want to kill someone who's so generous to the brotherhood?"

"You wouldn't call her generous to the brothers if you'd seen her that night—she fought like a hellion and dispatched one of their band herself, though they killed one of ours, too. The friars wanted to kidnap Conrad for some reason. Surprised us in the woods after dark."

Zefferino's eye closed. He heard the fearful rhythm of that night again, the shouting all around him, followed by the trumpet and the fire screaming toward his face.

"You were there too?" he asked.

"I was, though almost too late to help. I made a torch of their leader and the rest of the gang scattered like weasels back to their holes."

The scroll dropped with a heavy thud and unraveled partway across the loggia. Jacopone leapt from his stool and caught it before it rolled over the edge. "Careful there, brother! Are you all right?"

Zefferino tucked his hands into his sleeves and ducked his head. His throat convulsed, until finally he coughed—a hoarse, bitter chortle. "*Angelus Domini*," he said. "The angel of the Lord. *You!*"

The wooden loggia trembled lightly. The woman trotted up the stairs followed by Salimbene, puffing behind her.

"Fra Conrad's gone, brother," she said to Zefferino. "He's left word you can find him at the leper hospital, if you care to follow." She turned to Jacopone, her face pink with excitement. "The messenger came from Sior Orfeo. He'll be here tomorrow and said he hopes to bring good news with him."

Jacopone and Salimbene cheered. "I knew he couldn't stay away for long, *madonna*," the fat friar said.

Amata turned back to Zefferino, unable to suppress her grin. "Apologies, brother, for our private celebration. My comrades know how important this message is to me." She glanced at the note in her hand. "I'm worried about Fra Conrad living among those filthy lepers, though. Do you know why he went there?"

"To satisfy a vow, *madonna*."

"Do you plan to join him? I can have cook prepare food for you to take along. Conrad must have left without eating."

Join him? Join the man who'd abandoned him among his enemies? Zefferino waved his hand in front of his eye, fanning a vision of flames. "With your leave, *madonna*, I'd like to remain here one more night. In the morning, I'll be returning to the Sacro Convento."

IT WAS CONRAD, and not Orfeo, who engrossed Amata's last thoughts before she fell asleep that night. She still thought of the friar as the one man who loved her unconditionally, asking nothing from her in return. Although she'd done her best to hide her aversion the day he returned, she grieved for her friend. Never again would she see those light-filled grey eyes. And what if he contracted leprosy at the hospital, despite the purity of his heart? She murmured a prayer for his safety and protection, but oddly she invoked Donna Giacoma rather than God. Then she curled onto her side and slept soundly until the shouting woke her in the middle of the night.

The servant Gabriella tugged at her arm, half dragging her out of bed and her deep sleep. "Dress quickly, *madonna*. There's a fire in the courtyard."

Moving through a fog of sleep and smoke, Amata jogged from her room, wrapped in her cape. What could have started a fire in the hottest stretch of the summer, with every fireplace but the kitchen's cleaned and banked? Someone must have forgotten to snuff a candle. As she neared the cloister she recoiled at the orange glow of flames dancing like a devilish sunrise against the stone pillars and walls. Servants and guests alike scooped water from the fountain in the center of the yard, while others ran back and forth between the melee and the nearest public well.

She rubbed her eyes and stared into the yard from under a cloister arch. Her stomach heaved and she bit her thumb to stifle a cry. She saw to her horror that the section of wooden loggia holding the writing desks stood at the center of the conflagration. A huge fireball engulfed the steps leading to the south section and the entire south wall. The men fighting the fire raced up the north steps with their buckets and along the side balconies in an attempt to keep the blaze from spreading, but the desks were already gone. Amata stared dumbly through the flames, trying to locate the cabinet where she'd stored Leo's manuscript and the unfinished copies. As she watched, the south balcony collapsed, dragging part of the east loggia with it and sending large chunks of flaming timbers plummeting into the courtyard. Amata spotted part of a lectern in the crashing debris, and her heart sank.

All lost!

The stone walls and tiled roofs might withstand the flames, carpenters could rebuild the loggia, but Leo's chronicle was gone forever. She could only bury her face in her hands. She had *failed* Conrad!

The battle to save the rest of her home raged until daybreak. The night watch roused Amata's neighbors and every well and pail in the quarter went to work as bucket brigades fanned out in every direction from the front entry. Brawny men carried larger tubs in pairs. Amata, meanwhile, helped the women who pursued and beat out the flying cinders to keep the fire from spreading. She dashed from side-to-side in the courtyard and cloister walkways until she felt her lungs must burst from smoke and heat and exhaustion, while the crowds inside and outside her house grew steadily larger and noisier.

At last, soon after a church bell announced the hour of Prime, Maestro Roberto sought her out to announce they'd finally doused the flames. Dazed, she walked with him to the center of the courtyard and stared around at the scorched, cracked stonework and blackened arches. Within the perimeter of the cloister, nothing made of wood, not even the doorframes, had survived. Jacopone sat among the ashes on the stone bench where she'd talked with Conrad the evening of his return. He cradled his head in his arms, mumbling aloud, although no one stood near him. A soot-grimed Pio joined her.

"Pio saved your house, Amatina," the steward said. "He smelled the smoke first and roused the rest of us."

Amata rested her hand on the young man's chest. "Bless you," she murmured. She looked around at the others of her household, who drowned the remaining embers or shoveled debris into piles away from the walls. Neither Fra Salimbene nor Conrad's companion worked among them.

"Are the friars all right?" she asked.

"I haven't seen them," Roberto said.

"I spotted your scribe at the beginning," Pio said. "He was the first to reach the loggia. He must have smelled the smoke too. After I woke the others, I ran back here and saw him already hurrying down the north steps. I thought he looked for water vessels and yelled to him to go to the kitchen, but I never saw him after."

Jacopone shouted across to them at the top of his voice: "*Angelus Domini.* The blind friar foretold it."

"An angel?" Amata raised her brows and looked at Roberto.

He shrugged. "I deal with the practical, *madonna*. I leave it to Sior Jacopone to uncover deeper causes for such happenings."

Wearily, they turned to go inside the house. A single, melancholy trumpet note sounded from the corner where Jacopone sat. Amata pivoted just as the man rushed past her. He ran down the hallway with his long loping strides and out the front door.

"Cuz!" Amata yelled after him, but the penitent had vanished.

XL

A LEPER SQUATTING IN THE SUNSHINE outside a doorway spotted him first. The creature rattled his warning clapper before Conrad reached the bottom of the path that dropped from the forest and divided the two longest buildings of the ospidale. Alerted by the noise, other specters in brown tunics emerged from their cells—women and infants from the left structure, men from the right—and began yipping an eerie gibberish. Conrad stopped cold on the trail. He couldn't have been more horrified watching a graveyard spew up its dead. Once more, Leo had led him into the heart of his deepest fears. He closed his eyes and prayed for perseverance. *Servite pauperes Christi*, he whispered to himself.

Two smaller cottages flanked the leper quarters. Conrad guessed they housed the monks and nuns of the Order of the Crucigeri who tended the inmates. One of the monks poked his head through an open window. A second figure, a tall, lean man with ruddy-brown skin, clothed in the long red gown and cap of a physician, stepped from the building and climbed the path toward him. Only when the lepers saw the physician did the yipping stop.

"Hail, brother." In a husky voice, the man introduced himself as Matteus Anglicus, Matthew the Englishman.

"God's peace be with you," Conrad replied. "I've come to work."

Matteus scrutinized him from head to toe, but didn't avert his eyes the way Orfeo's men had. No doubt he'd seen more than his share of the grotesque in this place and looked Conrad over the same way he would a new patient. "And what would prompt you to work here?"

"Imitation of my master, San Francesco—and a solemn vow."

"Raise the hem of your robe a finger length," Matteus said. Conrad did so, while the physician pursed his lips. "As I expected. You'll need to wait here while I fetch a pair of sandals. Rule One: none of my staff walks barefoot in the hospital compound."

"I haven't worn sandals since my investiture," Conrad objected. "It would violate my vow of poverty."

"Then you must decide which of your solemn vows you intend to keep," Matteus said. "If you're going to serve here, you must start by thinking of my orders as God's will for this place. I leave the patients' spiritual guidance to the monks; the monks leave their physical care to me. If you need balm for your conscience, I can promise you'll live poorly enough. And I'll make your sandals the rudest I can scare up." Conrad nodded reluctantly and the physician smiled. "Welcome, then, brother," he said. "As you've just come from the friars' dungeon, I'm persuaded you're a good enough man."

Conrad stammered: "H-how..."

Matteus pointed to Conrad's eye. "You've been tortured. Your hair is white, but your skin's pale and fresh as a maid's, unused to sunlight in a while. Your beard's not known a razor for a few years. Your ankles are hairless and bear the chafe marks of manacles. Besides which, you wear the ragged robe of a Spiritual and go barefoot—both cause enough to be imprisoned during Bonaventura's rule."

"You know of the division ..."

"I thought to join your Order once, but chose my red robe over your grey one. Pope Honorius forbade the study of medicine to priests sixty years ago; consequently I chose never to become a priest."

Conrad followed Matteus to the compound's edge. He waited there while the physician left to fetch the sandals. A whiff of breeze cooled his forehead, but also carried the sickly sweet stench of putrefying flesh to his nostrils. He resisted the impulse to cover his nose with his sleeve or to search out the nearby carcass or bone pile. He'd entered the world of the living dead and he knew the nauseating flesh he smelled still clung to the skeletal creatures who continued to stare in his direction from the alcoves of their cells. The face of the man nearest him, the one who'd sounded the warning, showed the thick lips and bluish lumps of one new to the disease. His flattened nose suggested the cartilage that shaped it had already begun to decay, though. Conrad forced himself to look at the others. Many, thankfully, hid their faces behind veils, only seeming to return his gaze from their unseeing eyes. But the worst cases ...Conrad saw craters of pus where eyes had once peered out, rotting cavities in the place of noses and mouths, mushy flesh passing for chins, pendulous ears several times the size found in nature, hands without fingers, arms without hands, torsos bloated or shrunken, pitted skin or sup-purating lesions. The lepers watched listlessly, although some of the women turned away their ravaged faces from shame. The few children who squatted like dwarfish old men beside them were equally apathetic, staring at Conrad with adult gravity.

The display of horrors held him in a grip of macabre fascination. The friar wondered whether he might be seeing a vision of his own ineluctable future, his diseased corpse in the late stages of decay. He longed for Matteus' quick return and relaxed only when the physician brought the sandals. The sight of the lepers had left him disoriented. The unwonted sandals added to the bizarre effect, desensitizing his feet. He couldn't feel the pebbles in the dust any more, nor the dust itself, the individual blades of grass. Only universal leather. The entire surface of the compound seemed to be covered with leather.

"The first close-up view is always the hardest," Matteus said. He led Conrad to a room in the cottage behind the lepers' dorter. "You can wait in my cell until we clear a space for you."

The physician's chamber was a cluttered contrast to the man's analytical mind. The cell held a narrow cot in the corner farthest from the door, a small table and two stools beneath its only window, and a longer rectangular worktable that filled the center of the space. A skull and hourglass sat on the smaller table, and on the wall near them hung a painted crucifix—reminders to Matteus' patients of the transitory nature of life and of the salvation to come. Candle stubs, urine flasks, pillularia, aludels, an alembic, mortar and pestle, and a pile of bound manuscripts covered most of the large table. An open book on the table displayed a colored circle, perhaps a urine ring. Conrad remembered reading something like this in a uroscopic text in Paris: if the sick person's fluid appeared red and thick, he possessed a sanguineous humour; if red and thin, he'd be chronically angry. Each shade—purple, green, blue, black—matched its corresponding malady.

Vials of powder labeled with the symbols of metallic elements, a jar containing the narcotic mandragora, and medicinal spices—cinnamon, cubeb, and mace—spanned a mantelpiece hung from one wall. A bookcase near the physician's cot held more volumes than Conrad had ever seen outside a friary library.

"Don't gawk in the doorway, brother," Matteus said. With a sweep of his arm, he added: "I thank Constantine of Africa for these. After wandering throughout the Levant most of his life, he finally settled as a monk at Monte Casino. He dedicated the rest of his cloistered life to translating medical texts for us students at Salerno—old Greek masters preserved in Arabic, as well as works by the Saracens. Thus Galen became our Bible (if you'll forgive the comparison), and we learned by rote all ten books of Ali Abbas' *Pantechne.*"

Conrad scanned the bookcase with mixed emotions, awed by its size, embarrassed by his scholar's curiosity. San Francesco would not have approved! The ordering of the shelves showed more of the logical mind Conrad had noted earlier than did the room as a whole: the fabled Greeks Galen and Aristotle on the top shelf, the Saracen philosopher-physicians below them. He found four of the forty-two compositions of Hermes Trismegistus, the *Theatrum sanitatis* of Abul Asan, a treatise on canine hydrophobia, Avicenna's canon of medicine and, on the next shelf down, the Rabbi Maimonides and his fellow Spaniards, Avenzoar and Averroes.

The bottom shelf appeared to hold writings by Matteus' own masters at Salerno: one Trotula da Salerno, and a pharmacopoeia, *Antidotorium*, by a Maestro Praepositus of the same school. The last stood braced upright by a stack of works on the medicinal use of herbs, including Platearius' *De virtutibus herbarum*. Why, Conrad wondered, were the Christian authors relegated to the lowest position?

He flipped open Galen's *Methodus medendo* and frowned at the frontis-piece: a drawing of the pagan Aesculapius, holding the winged caduceus, flanked by his daughters Hygeia and Panacea. "A good Christian might find much to fault in this collection," he said. "I'd rather see the saintly twins Cosmos and Damian or San Antonio Abbas on this page. They're equally symbols of belief in Our Lord's healing power."

Matteus shrugged. "Believe me, brother, I'd gladly accumulate physicians of our own creed, but I know of few beyond my teachers at Salerno. Sadly, our Holy Mother Church persists in regarding the body as a curse, and ill-ness as a divine punishment. I heard a penitent in Assisi once beg poetically for some form of sickness: '*O Signor, per cortesia, manname las malsania!*' He'd have welcomed anything—quartan or tertian fevers, dropsy, toothache, bellyache, seizures. I ask you, what can my healing art do to counteract such an attitude?"

Conrad reshelved the Galen and chuckled. "I think I know that penitent. You'll be pleased to learn he currently enjoys the best health he's known for years."

"Pleasant news indeed. I pray it's not too burdensome for him."

Conrad rubbed his hairy cheek with his palm. "Tell me, what do *you* believe is the root of illness, if it's not a punishment for man's evil nature or a desire on God's part to test his fortitude?"

"You refer to the case of Job."

"As one example, yes," Conrad said. "Or, since we find ourselves in this ospidale, one might mention Bartolo, the leper of San Gimignano. He bore his fate with such joyful resignation that people called him the Job of Tuscany."

The physician thought for a moment before replying. "In truth, neither I nor my medical confreres can say with certainty where the source of illness lies. As we like to put it, Galen votes '*nay;*' Hippocrates votes '*yea.*' The doctors disagree and no one can decide who's right." Matteus riffled through the pile of manuscripts on his worktable as he spoke. Finally, he retrieved a thin, bound tract.

"Rest a moment by the window, brother, and look this over," he said. "It's very brief, composed by a countryman of mine, Bartolomeus Anglicus. He also happens to have been a lay brother of your Order. Study it, please, until your cell is ready. It will give you some background for the work you'll be doing."

After Matteus left the room, Conrad brought the writing close to his face. He hadn't tried to read since losing his eye. He held the parchment closer to the window's light, sharpening the blurred letters and words by squinting slightly.

Fra Bartolomeus treated first of the causes of leprosy, starting with foods that overheated the blood or were likely to corrupt soon: pepper, garlic, the meat of diseased dogs, carelessly cured fish and pork, and inferior breads made from contaminated barley or rye. He proceeded, in too much detail for Conrad's sensibilities, to describe the contagious nature of the disease: how the unwary might contract it through carnal knowledge of a woman who'd lain with a leprous man, how a babe feeding at the breast of a leprous nurse sucked death through the woman's teat, how it could even be inherited. The parchment trembled in Conrad's hand as he read the last source of leprosy: "Even the very breath or the glance of a leper can prove disastrous." According to Bartolomeus, Conrad might already carry the disease within himself, albeit most of the eyes turned toward him on the path had been sightless.

He swallowed back his disgust at Bartolomeus' frank catalog. The friar exceeded the limits of modesty. But nevertheless, those who contracted leprosy through their carnality *did* receive due punishment for their sin. Neither Bartolomeus nor Matteus would convince him otherwise on that score. As for heredity, didn't the Scriptures state, "*The fathers have eaten sour grapes, and the children's teeth are set on edge?*" Thus, even in this instance, the leper paid the price of his forebear's iniquity. Bartolomeus acknowledged as much when he moved on to the treatment of lepers. "Leprosy is very hard to cure but by the help of God"—obviously, since God had inflicted the disease in the first place.

Nevertheless, Bartolomeus listed several nonspiritual options for the physician: bloodletting (should the leper's strength allow); purging for worms and ulcers; medicines within, plasters and ointments without. The Anglican friar concluded: "to heal leprosy or hide it, the *very best* remedy is a red adder with a white belly, provided the venom be removed and the tail and head smitten off. The body, sodden with leeks, should be taken and eaten often."

Conrad replaced the treatise just as Matteus reentered the room. He sensed his old contentiousness curdling to the surface. But where three years before he'd have disputed this Bartolomeus, today he held his tongue. God had sent him to this place to learn. He needed to ask and listen, not argue.

"Does your experience bear out your countryman's hypotheses?"

Matteus picked up the tract and scanned it quickly, his head bobbing as he read. "Diet," he said finally, tapping at the tract. "We serve only fresh meats here. And this time of year, when vegetables and fruits are available, we effect some total cures."

His answer surprised Conrad. "I thought a miracle alone could cure leprosy."

"In my country, I've heard of healing miracles, notably at the shrine of Thomas of Canterbury. A well in the saint's crypt contains holy water mixed with a drop of his blood, and many claim cures by drinking therefrom. But here, I can only claim success through diet."

"But in that case, why aren't all your patients cured?"

Matteus smiled. "You've a good, inquisitive mind, brother. Maybe we'll make a physician of you, too. And your question's well taken." He traced with his finger through Bartolomeus' manuscript, until he found a reference to leprosy. "The word *lepra*, or 'scaly,' as used by the Greeks, described any number of scaling skin diseases. Many such cases show up here, people forced from their homes and livelihoods by the pronouncement of some priest who knows nothing of medicine—how the blood of lepers squeaks when rubbed on the palms of the hands or swims atop a bowl of clear water, the loss of sensation in the fingers and toes, the copper hue of the skin.

"Some of these skin diseases *are* curable, and I've restored many such sufferers to their families. But what I call 'true leprosy,' what the Greeks named *elephantiasis* due to the thickening and coarseness of the skin, in my experience has no remedy. I've tried purging and venesection and a dozen other remedies suggested by various writers—even the animal cures."

"Ingesting the adder's meat?"

"The red-and-white adder is a rare creature in this part of the world. But I've coated lepers' sores with bezoar made from deer's eyes, following the recipe of Avenzoar. The traditional treatment of wounds, applying the heat of a dying cat or dog, has failed me also." Matteus removed his cap and slumped onto the stool opposite Conrad, suddenly dispirited.

The friar studied his companion's ruddy face more closely, the thinning eyebrows, a slight, discolored lump on the forehead, a swelling in the earlobe he hadn't noticed before. The physician smiled grimly.

"Yes. My turn comes soon." His tone told Conrad he'd already accepted the inevitable.

"So the disease *is* contagious, as Bartolomeus said."

"Apparently, although I've been here fifteen years without symptom before now. Among the Crucigeri who help me, some work but a few years before they contract leprosy. You might needs worry if you remain with us long. Yet one old nun has been here twenty-two years with no sign yet."

"But how, then, does it spread?"

"I wish I knew. I've tried to follow Bartolomeus' clues. For example, I've conducted very *specific* talks with those married before they came here. Most continued intimate contact with their husbands or wives, even after the first symptoms became visible, and usually with no harm to the spouse. The exceptions were those who continued to kiss their partners, even after blisters appeared around the lips."

Matteus shrugged. "I see my candor disturbs you, brother, but I'm trying to give at least a partial answer to your question. Human physical behavior is the physician's concern; the body's no more than the tablet on which we write. As I said earlier, I leave moral judgment to you priests.

"In any event, I've come to believe the mouth is the most infectious part of the leprous body. That's why my staff wears sandals, to protect the soles of their feet from the spittle of our patients."

Conrad raked his fingers through his beard. He pictured Francesco, Leo and the other early friars working among the lepers of this very ospidale some sixty-odd years before: unshod, fasting and subsisting on the meanest food, even kissing these unfortunate souls on the mouth to prove their humility. Yet, he'd never heard of a single instance where their lack of precaution led to a case of leprosy—albeit they'd surely enjoyed God's special protection in their holy service. Conrad concluded that Matteus' theories amounted to little more than guesswork. Nevertheless, he wriggled his toes gratefully in the worn sandals.

ORFEO SURVEYED THE RUINED LOGGIA and the charred planks and timbers heaped in Amata's courtyard. "Not the best setting for my news," he said sympathetically. "I'm glad everyone's safe at least, Amatina."

The woman took his arm and leaned her cheek against his shoulder. "The loggia's nothing," she said. "I'll have it rebuilt before winter. It's the loss of Leo's scroll that grieves me."

"Nothing you could have done would have prevented it. Fra Conrad will understand. He will see it as God's will. Which it *is*."

She managed a subdued smile. "I'm truly happy you've come back, Orfeo. I'd nearly lost hope of seeing you again."

"I thought you didn't *want* to see me. The next time you talk to your friar, you can thank him for setting me straight. I don't suppose Fra Conrad told you, but I'd just loaded Sior Domenico's carts and set my cap for Flanders when he stopped me."

"I *didn't* know. Conrad hasn't been here since he talked to you. Isn't Domenico furious with you for the delay? You'll barely reach Flanders before snowfall now."

"He's no longer my employer," Orfeo said. He kicked at a chunk of charred wood and sent it flying toward the pile near the fountain.

"Orfeo! No! How are you going to live?"

A grin brightened his face. "That's what I came to tell you. Sior Domenico's an old man, worn out from years of trading. I offered to buy his goods and wagons, oxen and all—even his warehouse and stall in the mercato. And he accepted. I can't meet his price out of my own purse, of course, but my brother Piccardo's agreed to put up an equal share as my partner."

"Piccardo would compete against his brothers?"

"For the chance to become his own man, yes. When our father died, Piccardo got a sum of money, but the family business went to Dante as the eldest. Piccardo's been squirming under Dante's thumb ever since.

"Anyway, the rest of the amount we'll borrow from a moneylender. With good fortune and good trade, we'll pay back the whole sum in a few years. And here's the best part: Piccardo is willing to do most of the travel. I'll run the warehouse and market and keep the books here in Assisi."

He turned so he faced her, gently loosing her grip on his arm. He took both her hands in his and stared into her eyes. For a moment the courtyard, the smoky stone walls, even the contours of his body and face blurred as she met his stare. She saw only the fire smoldering from the charcoal centers of his pupils.

"We can marry now, Amatina, begin our family, if you'll have me. It's you I want and love. The money's not that important to me. We'll have enough with each other; the rest will come with time and hard work."

Amata pulled her hands free. "And you'll be content with homely pleasures?"

"I can only vow that I will try my hardest."

"And no more than that can I ask."

She hesitated but an instant before she leapt and wrapped her arms around his neck. "Orfeo. You must know I want you more than anything. This is what I wanted you to say the night we parted."

Orfeo hugged her tightly to his chest. "You must understand, I can be a dull-witted clod sometimes. I take a lot of spelling out. Promise to bear with me in future."

Amata snuggled her face into the warm folds of his tunic until she felt his arms relax. She realized he watched something or someone over her shoulder. When she pulled free, she saw Pio standing awkwardly at the edge of the courtyard. Behind him, in the shadows of the cloister, a gaggle of maidservants suddenly busied themselves with wiping and dusting.

"Dinner's nearly ready, *madonna*," he said.

Orfeo blurted: "Pio, we're getting married!"

The young man grinned from ear-to-ear as he glanced from Orfeo to Amata. In some inexplicable way, his response disappointed her. Perhaps she'd expected a more crestfallen reaction from one who'd had a crush on her for so long.

"*Con permesso, madonna*," Pio addressed his lady with a low swoop, "I wish to marry too."

"You, Pio? But who?" She glanced at the clustered maidservants and saw all eyes turned to Gabriella. The girl flushed scarlet and the whole group disappeared giggling into the main hall, followed closely by the red-faced Pio. Then Amata remembered that on the night of the fire she'd been roused by Gabriella, while Pio had been the first to waken the men. How had she failed to notice? Donna Giacoma, certainly, would have intuited the romance in some secret vein.

She muttered to Orfeo: "It's a good thing I don't know all that goes on in my household at night. I think my laxity, or ignorance, saved the place."

She took his outstretched hand and her step regained its customary spring as they headed for the great hall. "About the money ... I just needed to be sure, Orfeo. We don't really need to resort to a moneylender. And I'll work at your side as hard as any man if need be. Also, I do hope that you—that *we*—will travel *some* of the time. We both know you have some salt water in your veins yet. And I've still not seen the sunrise and the colored windows in Lyons cathedral ..."

XLI

FTER BREAKFAST the following morning, Matteus came to fetch Conrad. "Join me in my rounds today, brother," he said. "I'll introduce you to your patients and your duties."

Under the physician's direction, Conrad dipped a bucket of water from a cistern and followed him across the hard-packed clearing that separated the refectory from the male lepers' dorter. Matteus rapped softly at the door of the first man, one of many who'd been too sick to attend the communal meal. "This is old Silvano's cell. First we clean him and his room, then we feed him," he explained.

Conrad focused his attention on the crucifix nailed to the outside of the cell door, bracing himself against the misery he knew he'd find on the other side. A nauseating stench wafted from the leper's quarters as Matteus nudged the door open. The taste of half-digested gruel soured in Conrad's gorge.

A shriveled figure hunched on a wooden chair in the corner—a blind, ancient creature, mostly hidden in his oversized sackcloth robe. Matteus motioned Conrad to one side of the chair, while he shouted at the leper: "More sunshine today, Silvano. Let's get you and this room some air." They lifted the old man, chair and all, and carried him outside, positioning him so the sunrays warmed his back.

"Here's Fra Conrad," the physician continued in a loud voice. "He's going to care for you from now on." Matteus wrapped a blanket around the leper while Conrad replaced the linen, caked with dried blood and pus, that covered Silvano's sleeping mat. He sloshed water onto the floor and began scrubbing.

When he'd finished, Matteus shook the old leper gently. "We'll bathe you anon," he said. Silvano, starting to revive in the sunlight, nodded for the first time. The physician sent Conrad to the scullery to fetch hot water while he continued down the row of patients, rousting the more able-bodied into the fresh air.

Conrad refilled his bucket from a large cauldron heating in the kitchen. He carried the clean water back to Silvano's cell, where Matteus had him remove the leper's veil and loosen his robe. To Conrad's relief, he managed to hold down his meal as he cleansed Silvano's decomposing body and face. Instead of causing him to retch, as he'd feared, the man's wounds roused a surge of pity and compassion within him. His eyes brimmed as he wrung out his washcloth over the steaming bucket.

Matteus watched closely as the friar placed and replaced the cloth on Silvano's lesions, drawing out as much of the yellowish fluid as he could. Finally, Conrad patted the old man with a towel and wrapped his hands and feet in cloth bandages. He resisted the urge to kiss the man as San Francesco would have done in years past. Matteus' warning from the previous day had had its intended effect. "God's peace and good to you, Sior Silvano," he said instead. The leper waved his hand in reply.

"He means to thank you," Matteus said.

"He can't speak?"

The man gestured toward his open mouth, and only then did Conrad notice the withered stump where his tongue should have been.

As they moved to the next cell, Matteus put his hand on the friar's shoulder. "How do you feel?"

"Ashamed. Even yesterday I thought of them as deserving sinners. They are truly Christ's poor ones as San Francesco said."

"You begin to understand and that's all that matters for now. You'll do well here."

The next patient, a man much younger than Silvano, surprised Conrad. He showed hardly any sores on his body at all—just one withered patch on his back, puckered and wrinkled like the petals of a carnation. His fingers had contracted into a claw, however; his thumb lay useless against his palm, and a milky haze flecked with chalk-like grains filmed the corneas of his eyes. As Conrad bathed the dried patch, he glanced questioningly at Matteus.

"Even among true lepers, brother, you'll find many variations of the disease. Some display no tubercles at all, or one, or only a few. They range in color from light pink, like this one, to a deep rose red. They might appear anywhere on the body. But even though this patch has dried for the moment, it's completely numb. He couldn't feel your water were it as hot as boiling pitch. This area of his flesh is forever dead."

Matteus discussed the leper casually, as though he sat in another room.

The man, in turn, stared straight ahead, showing no interest in their conversation—the same lassitude that had made Conrad's skin crawl the day before, when he imagined he'd entered the world of the undead. He blessed the leper when he'd finished as he had Silvano, but this patient showed less reaction than the old man. Matteus rubbed the top of the leper's bald skull as they left, his lips tightened in a wry smile.

"I've seen many cases similar to his," he added once they were outside. "These lepers I call *borderline*. Like this man they display a single lesion, albeit less dry than his. And while sensation at the spot has diminished, they continue to feel some pain. Their lesions are oval shaped, often with a punched-out center and a distinctly palpable edge." Matteus shook his head. "The disease is so complex. I doubt I'll ever understand it fully."

Conrad returned to the scullery for fresh water, trying to retain as much of Matteus' explanation in his head as he could. He'd much to digest. On the path he passed several of the Crucigeri, also fetching water. He'd met the five monks and three nuns that morning. They greeted him with curt nods now, intent on the task at hand.

These religious were a somber lot compared to Dom Vittorio's black monks—maybe because they moved in a world less removed from final judgment, perhaps because their work left them little to smile about. Conrad admired their silence, and the fact that they'd committed their lives in service to these outcasts. He'd be comfortable working forever among such men—and even the women, modest and equally dedicated creatures.

Perchance, though he was no physician, God had brought him here at this precise juncture because Matteus could now see the end of his own road. He quickly dismissed that notion as prideful, however, an overreaction to Matteus' earlier praise. *Conceit rides out on horseback and returns on foot*, he reminded himself. He'd none of the good physician's unique knowledge; nor did he share the special bond that linked Matteus and his patients. Moreover, in his heart of hearts he continued to believe that God's will, and not man's efforts, determined who was stricken or cured—a creed the doctor from Salerno clearly did not share.

WITHIN THE MONTH, Conrad had blended entirely with the Crucigeri, carrying out his tasks in peaceful monotony. He spoke almost daily with Matteus and often worked alongside the physician after he had finished caring for those lepers assigned to him. The friar had learned much about his patients and the multifaceted spectrum of their disease, but nothing to help him understand Leo's purpose in directing him to the ospidale.

While the late summer nights grew colder, the afternoons remained warm and sunny enough for the patients to remain outdoors. On one such spectacular day, Conrad located the red gown along the line of cells and honed in with his hot-water bucket. Matteus had just settled one of the lepers outside his alcove. "How goes it with you today, Mentore?" he asked.

Without expression the man held up his arms so his sleeves fell back. He had numerous sores on his skin, but Conrad noted they were, for the most part, scabbed over with a purplish-grey crust. The nodules on his face appeared to be in a healing phase also, the first time Conrad had even seen any signs of improvement in a patient. Perhaps Mentore had one of the curable skin diseases the physician had mentioned. The friar peered hopefully at Matteus, but saw in his eyes only a deep sadness.

"Are you ready?" he asked the man quietly.

The leper nodded.

"I'll send a priest to confess you and administer the sacraments," Matteus said. He motioned to Conrad to draw closer. "Bathe him especially well today," he said. "You prepare him to greet his Savior."

"But his wounds appear sounder than the others," Conrad said. "His skin has never looked this good."

"Some of his wounds will disappear altogether by tomorrow," Matteus said. "It's a sign of impending death that everyone here has come to recognize. They look forward to it, if not with joy, at least with relief."

Mentore's face, his occluded eyes, remained totally dispassionate. If the leper felt any emotion, he gave no indication. Conrad recalled his talk with Jacopone, when they traveled the road to Assisi; the subject had been poetry, and experience, and the fitful breathing of the dying. Yet this doomed man sat waiting on his stool, breathing as regularly as his snuffling allowed, impassive as a money changer at his scales.

Conrad dipped his towel into the hot water and washed one of the man's hands. A phrase from Leo's letter came to mind: *The dead leper's nails are crusted with truth*. With what seemed to him to be almost morbid curiosity, he lifted the leper's other arm by the wrist, but both hands ended in stumps at the finger joints. Leo's meaning would have to await another opportunity. This Mentore had no fingers, let alone finger*nails*. The same proved true of his feet. Nothing remained of them but twisted toeless knobs.

THAT NIGHT CONRAD tossed in his sleep, disturbed by a noise like wolves howling. As he gradually came awake in the darkness, he realized that the wordless wail came from the lepers' quarters. *It must be over for Mentore*, he realized. A tap at his door and Matteus' voice calling him to chapel confirmed his guess.

The physician carried a torch, for a cloud cover had blown in during the night and now hid the moon. They crossed the courtyard through a fine drizzle.

The monks had already carried the corpse into the chapel, where it lay stretched out on a table in the nave surrounded by candles. The men and women Crucigeri recited the penitential psalms in unison from opposite sides of the choir. The lepers who could walk massed at the back of the building.

Conrad folded his hands and followed Matteus to the leper's body. He wanted to add his private blessing to the ritual prayers of the community. The tubercles on Mentore's face had vanished entirely, as Matteus predicted. His once-mottled skin actually glistened, as ivory white as the candle flickering near his head.

The leper's arms, resting across his chest, drew Conrad's attention. The wounds on the backs of Mentore's hands had clotted completely, shimmering solid and ebony as spikes in the firelight. With quivering fingers, Conrad raised the topmost hand and turned it over. The lesion in the palm was crusted equally hard and black. Conrad manipulated it with his fingertip and the entire spike, palm and back of hand, moved as one object. Carefully, he replaced the leper's arm in its original position.

Bracing one hand on the edge of the table, he lowered himself to his knees and stared down the nave at the image of the crucified Christ above the altar. In his heart expanded a peace he hadn't known since the day Amata arrived at his hut. All the tensions and anguish of the past thirty-four months could finally wash from his body, riding the waves of his suddenly calm exhalations.

At last he understood! Like Giancarlo di Margherita, he had touched the nail with his own hand—*the nail of the dead leper!*

"TWO THINGS MORE I must know." Conrad sat in Matteus' room after the funeral service. "Can these leprous symptoms manifest suddenly, say within a forty-day period?" He leaned forward, resting his elbows on the physician's table. He held all the threads in his grasp, and lacked but a few confirming knots to tie them off. The tapestry Leo had woven for him might dispel the universal reverence for San Francesco forever. Yet, to Conrad, the true account of the stigmata was more wondrous and lofty than the myth, just as the truth about Francesco's wastrel youth surpassed Bonaventura's sanitized version.

"Normally, they manifest only gradually, over a lengthy period," Matteus said. "But I've known cases where lesions erupted *overnight*, in a burst of searing spasms. In such instances, inflammation covers the backs of the hands, the tops of the feet. The hands in particular become hot and swollen and acutely painful." The physician ran his finger across the veins protruding along the top of his hand, to show the afflicted area.

"This acute state can last a few days or a few weeks before numbness sets in. As the inflammation subsides, the joints and tendons contract; they freeze in the position they occupied at rest during the acute stage, like the clawed fingers you've seen on some of our patients."

"And the eyes?"

Matteus nodded his approval of Conrad's question. "You're a keen observer, brother. It's true, this acute leprosy attacks first the hands and feet—but also the eyes. Usually, it ends in blindness: first because it emaciates the iris; secondly, because it incites palsy throughout the face, leaving the patient unable to close his eyelids against the violence of the sun's rays. This is why we seat our patients with their backs to the sun."

Conrad lowered his head. He patted his white beard against his chest and nodded. "It's all true, everything Leo wrote." A sense of emptiness infiltrated his inner calm, a sensation akin to depression, like the loss Rosanna told him she experienced after childbirth, or that an artist might feel at the end of a long project.

"Brother?"

The concern in Matteus' voice brought the friar back to the moment. Suddenly, he had to share all his conclusions with the physician, all the events and discoveries of his nearly three-year quest. A knowledgeable layman, being less threatened by his findings than a follower of San Francesco would be, might listen with greater patience and sympathy than his religious brothers.

The words that could alter forever his Order's history began to pour from him in that dusky room in the isolated valley sheltering the lazaretto. Conrad spoke of Francesco's love for lepers, of Monte LaVerna and the praises the saint dictated there, of the blindness that began on the mountain, of Donna Giacoma's description of the saint's appearance at death, the snow-white skin and lance-wound like a rose, how Elias seized and hid Francesco's body and how the ministers altered the accounts of his life. Finally he told the physician of Leo's letter and his own quest to search out its meaning. That meaning now seemed evident: the *pauper Christi,* the leper whom Leo served, was none other than Assisi's *little poor man, Il Poverello di Cristo.*

Matteus listened in fascinated silence while the friar unraveled his entire skein. "And your San Francesco," he asked at last, "did he never claim the stigmata himself, never proclaim in the words of San Paolo, *ego stigmata Domini Jesu Christi in corpore meo porto*, 'I carry the wounds of our Lord Jesus Christ in my own body?'"

"He said only, '*my secret is my own.*' Yet, his joy on Monte LaVerna is totally plausible. In his deep humility, he sought always to abase himself. He'd have thanked the seraph more for the gift of leprosy than for the stigmata, believing himself deserving of the first and unworthy of the latter. After LaVerna, he could truly say with his crucified Lord, '*I am a worm and no man.*' He could share Christ's humiliation, without sharing the glory of His wounds."

"But you do accept that he saw an angel," Matteus asked, "even though he may already have been blind at the time?"

The skepticism in the physician's voice offended Conrad, despite his own interpretation of the LaVerna ordeal. "Even a blind man can see with inner vision," he said. After a moment's hesitation, he added softly: "I experienced something similar, in the total darkness of my prison cell."

Matteus studied him in silence for an instant. Finally he said: "Of course. Pardon me, brother. I consider such phenomena from the viewpoint of a medical man. It wouldn't surprise me from a purely medical stance, for instance, to learn that a man fasting for forty days while he meditated on the archangel Michael and on the Holy Cross, should find floating before him a seraph pierced with Christ's wounds. Personally, San Francesco's spiritual moment on the mountain to me is more significant than its physical manifestations."

"How so?" Conrad asked.

"When an emperor rewards a soldier's valor with some impressive token, people cheer the man. Yet the token is only a sign of the valor that earned it." He tugged at the chest of his robe. "My patients gaze with awe and respect on my scarlet gown, yet 'twould mean nothing without the years of study it symbolizes. Do you follow my drift?"

"You're saying it doesn't matter what happened to Francesco *physically* on Monte LaVerna? That the spirituality that earned the physical tokens mattered more?"

"Yes, to me—as a hopefully sincere Christian. I'm more inspired by his lifetime of spiritual attainment, which even I can try to emulate, than by a stigmata forever beyond my grasp or even my imagination."

Conrad stared again at the small nodule on Matteus' forehead. "Yet you may one day share in his humbler wounds."

"So I may, and I'll use that thought from now on to lighten any symptoms of regret." Matteus tapped on the table, debating whether to say more. Finally, he glanced up at Conrad and added: "For purely physical reasons, I never believed the story of San Francesco's stigmata anyway."

In response to the look of surprise on Conrad's face, he held out his upturned hands. "As a student of anatomy, I realized Our Lord could not have been pierced through the palms when the Romans nailed him to the cross. The flesh there wouldn't have supported his weight for three hours without tearing." With his left thumb Matteus pressed on the tendons of his right wrist. "Here's where the spike must needs have been driven to hold him. Yet San Francesco's wounds, from what I've heard, appeared in his palms. I always wondered, too, if he truly received the wounds of the crucifixion, why he did not also show the scalp lacerations of the crown of thorns? And what of the forty lashes Jesus received on his back? I've heard nothing of such stripes on the saint."

"And did you never voice these doubts?" Conrad asked.

Matteus laughed loudly. "You're a fine one to pose such a question, having just emerged from the pit. Have you heard of the preaching friar, Tomas d'Aversa?"

Conrad shook his head, no.

"He sermonized in Naples at one time, while I was a student at Salerno. According to the story, he once publicly cast aspersions on the stigmata. As a consequence, the pope forbade him to preach for seven years, which to a son of San Domenico is tantamount to forbidding *you* your poverty. This Fra Tomas is presently Inquisitor of Naples. He takes out his frustration—which he blames on San Francesco—on your Spiritual brothers, slowly and cheerfully murdering them through various exquisite tortures.

"Which leads me back to your question: no, brother, I have never voiced my doubts, nor do I ever intend to. I've never been one to piss against the wind." Matteus stretched his lips in his characteristic tight smile. "What do *you* plan to do with *your* new-found knowledge?"

Conrad grunted as he arched his back. "I'll explain it to Fra Girolamo d'Ascoli, our new minister general. I think God deliberately kept the truth from me until now, until after Bonaventura's death. Girolamo is a fair and honest man. He'll do what's right."

Matteus whistled softly as he rose from the table. "You do thirst after martyrdom, don't you?" He stooped through the doorway and stared off in the direction of the rising sun. "I shall be sorry to lose you so soon," he said over his shoulder.

"I'm happy here," Conrad said. "With my general's permission, I'll gladly return."

Matteus turned and pointed through the mist toward the western sky. "Look. The arc of the covenant."

Conrad followed his gesture to the double rainbow arching high above the trees. "What did you call it?"

"A pun, brother. The arching sign of God's pledge, his covenant with Noah."

"But you likened it to the Ark of the Covenant, the Holy of Holies where the Hebrews kept the tablets of the ten commandments."

Matteus chortled. "Don't read any deep interpretation into that, brother."

Conrad waved off his remark. "I understand what you're saying. But my mind is already down a different path, my friend. God bless you, Matteus. You've told me where they buried San Francesco."

XLII

CONRAD WAITED FOR Girolamo d'Ascoli in the dim interior of the lower church of the basilica. He had asked the minister general to meet him outside the friary proper as a precaution. He enjoyed the coolness of the tiles beneath his dusty, once-again-liberated, bare feet. Never again, he prayed, would they have to endure the numbing chill of an underground prison vault.

Because it was the Lord's Day, the muralist and his apprentice were not at work. Their scaffolding hovered skeletal and vacant in the northeast corner of the apse. While he waited for the minister general, Conrad savored the artist's completed fresco of the Madonna and San Francesco. Without the painter nearby to complain of interruption, he could study the saint's likeness more closely. Francesco's lips and ears appeared thicker than when he'd first viewed the fresco, and the pupils staring through him to eternity now called to mind Matteus' blind patients. The saint's expression even mimicked the impassivity he'd seen at the lazaretto.

Surely, Conrad thought, the similarity to the lepers was some trick of his diminished vision or the poor lighting afforded by the single oil lamp on the main altar. The artist Cimabue had never seen Francesco alive, and drew the image from his imagination. But on the other hand, wouldn't the Holy Ghost guide his brush in such sacred work?

The door thudded shut at the rear of the nave. A friar approached with short, lively steps through the shadows and stopped near the main altar.

"Fra Conrad!" Girolamo greeted him cheerily. "I hadn't expected you back so soon." His fair eyes glittered in the lamplight.

"Nor had I expected to be here. But I learned something of great importance in my time at San Salvatore, important enough I felt compelled to tell you at once."

"Here in the church? Why not in my office?"

Conrad temporized, not wanting to admit his lack of trust even in this good general, but mumbled finally, "I didn't wish to suffer the fate of the messenger who bears bad news."

Girolamo's brow contracted beneath his tonsure. "And what news is that, brother?"

Conrad pointed to their founder's likeness in the fresco. Perhaps he could startle an admission from the minister general by going straight to his point.

"*Francesco Lebbroso*. Francesco the Leper. It has a ring, don't you think?" Conrad studied Girolamo's face as he spoke, trying to detect the slightest reaction. The blue eyes darted in the direction he indicated, but gave no sign of comprehension.

Conrad continued, using the words he had assimilated in his month with Matteus: "The physician at the lazar hospital would likely have diagnosed him 'borderline lepromatous'—displaying a single, oval-shaped, rose-colored lesion on his side, with decayed sight and macular crusts on the hands and feet."

Girolamo's eyes narrowed. "Aaah. I read your implication, Fra Conrad," he chirped in his bird-like voice. "The question I ask myself is, '*why?*' Did you, as you lay chained in your cell these three years, begin to concoct a conspiracy of lies, agreed to by all the early comrades of San Francesco, perhaps initiated by our master himself? Did your visit to the lazaretto provide fuel for some ember already smoldering in your imagination? You aren't the first to doubt the stigmata, brother, although I must admit I'm shocked to hear such misgivings from *you*. You might be the first to brand San Francesco a leper."

"Please hear me out, Fra Girolamo."

The general sighed, his eyes reflecting a sadness and sympathy usually reserved for the deranged. *I'd such plans for you*, they said, *but I never imagined your mind had slipped this far*. Nevertheless, he motioned to Conrad to proceed.

Conrad took a deep breath and launched once more into the story of his pilgrimage. As he led Girolamo, step-by-step, along the same route he'd just traced with Matteus Anglicus, the minister general listened with folded arms. At one point, he clasped his delicate hands behind his back and paced with lowered head between the fresco and the main altar, occasionally glancing up at the painting. His face remained noncommittal when the friar finally ended his tale.

"Didn't Fra Illuminato explain all this to you when you took office?" Conrad asked. "Isn't this part of the secret lore passed to the succession of ministers general? I had the impression in prison that Fra Giovanni da Parma knew. He hinted as much without actually admitting it outright."

"The post came with no secrets," Girolamo said. "Whether Elias orchestrated such a myth five decades ago, you and I will never know for sure. Bishop Illuminato might know, but he imparted no such secret knowledge to me. Besides, even if your theory is true, I can still empathize with Fra Elias' decision. I might have acted similarly in the same circumstance."

"But you would be fostering a lie. Why would you do that?" Conrad balled his fists inside his sleeves. "San Francesco never would have condoned such a fabrication."

Girolamo paused and studied the detached figure in the fresco. Then he trained his gaze on Conrad again. "By the time of his retreat on Monte LaVerna, San Francesco had already relinquished leadership of the Order to Elias, his appointed Vicar. He spent his last years in contemplation, abandoning himself to holy folly, leaving Elias to manage the practical government of a burgeoning organization.

"All the same," he continued, "Francesco remained the figurehead, the saint who inspired young men and women to cast off their wealth and join our ranks, convinced princes and prelates to mend their quarrels and the laity to reform their sinful habits. Could Elias allow this symbol to be shut away in a lazaretto, even if he knew for certain the source of his master's physical transformation? Could he let the world suspect our saint and founder of sin so great that God must punish him with leprosy? Believe me, brother, San Francesco would have exerted far less power for good, even as a second Job, than he did as the second Christ.

"Elias, better than any man, understood the practicalities of a situation. That is why, when the pope grew eager for a monument to properly venerate San Francesco, he could find no one so qualified as Elias to build this basilica, the project for which your Spiritual friends so castigate him. Elias collected the money and finished the task with undreamed-of speed. Yet, with his work complete, he put his signature to the building most humbly as *Frater Elias peccator*—Brother Elias, sinner."

Girolamo scooped up Conrad's flowing beard as though it were a bouquet proffered by a child and stared affectionately into his face. "You've arrived fifty years too late with your allegation, brother. If Leo truly wanted the world to know of Francesco's infirmity, he should have announced it at the time. Instead, he relinquished his duty to you. Consider, too, that people will believe what they want. I suspect you'll find the stigmata of Our Lord is far more appealing to the popular fancy than your *Francesco Lebbroso*."

The minister general's voice echoed down the length of the nave with the fading weight of finality. As he gradually loosened his hold on Conrad's beard, the black, silent shadows of the church closed around the altar where they stood. Conrad envisioned the spirits of Francesco's early comrades rising up from their chapel tombs, huddling in the gloom, urging him to keep trying, to drag the truth somehow to light.

"But we can prove it," he said. "We can exhume his remains. The physician at San Salvatore said he could tell from the skeleton whether Francesco ever suffered from the disease."

"And how do you propose we do that? No one's seen any trace of the relics since Elias hid them."

"The ring of office you wear. The map to the coffin is etched into its face."

Girolamo seemed momentarily stunned. His lips parted slightly, then closed again. He brought the back of the ring to his mouth, sighed and turned away. Conrad followed him to the oil lamp, where Girolamo held out the lapis lazuli to the light. The stone shone more smoothly and polished than the tile beneath their feet.

"It appeared to have been badly scratched. Bishop Illuminato offered to have it buffed for me." A wry smile tugged at the minister's lips. "His eagerness to remove the markings would *appear* to confirm your story."

"Of course he'd do such a thing! He wants to take the secret to his grave!" Conrad said. "But the same figure is carved here, in the altar stone. I found it by accident one day."

He led Girolamo around the altar to the corner inscribed with the design. He lifted the altar cloth and once more traced his fingers through the grooves of the double arch, the stick figure with the concentric circles on its shoulders—the circles that he now understood represented the saint's head and the nimbus of a halo. And the larger circle enclosing the figure, what else could that be but his sarcophagus?

Girolamo's eyes widened in the dim light. "The ring did have a pattern similar to this."

"I believe the two arcs represent the tabernacles on the main altars of the upper and lower churches," Conrad said. "They contain the holy of holies, the consecrated body of Our Lord, as the original Ark contained the tablets given to Moses. This figure with the halo, enclosed in the crypt beneath the lower arch is San Francesco. We are standing on his tomb at this very moment."

Girolamo chewed his thumbnail for an instant, but seemed unconvinced. "It's possible, I suppose. But I would need much firmer evidence than your inventive reading of this design before I tore out the altar and started digging."

"But you must do *something*," Conrad said desperately. "You could force Bishop Illuminato to admit the truth. We must restore integrity to the legends." Twin pincers of doubt and self-pity squeezed on his chest. Had the past three years been for naught? Had he sacrificed his serenity, his green years, and half his sight to no purpose?

"I'm not even convinced of that need, brother," Girolamo replied. "Or that Bishop Illuminato would support your story." He tucked his arms behind his back again and paraded slowly around the altar, examining the tiles and altar base as though he were seeing them for the first time.

"Here's what I want you to do, Fra Conrad," he said when he'd returned to his starting point. "I want you to say nothing at all of your findings—to anyone—until after the Feast of the Holy Stigmata two weeks from now. Because it is also the fiftieth anniversary of the date San Francesco received the stigmata, all of Christendom will be here—including Pope Gregory, should his health permit. We've planned the event for months and we don't need complications now. Can you promise me this much? Or must I command you to half a month's silence under holy obedience?"

"Why don't you just command me to perpetual silence, as Elias did Fra Leo?"

Girolamo grasped Conrad's shoulder, and said deliberately: "Because, frankly, I'm inclined to believe you; because I know what you've suffered in pursuit of Leo's truth; and especially because I'd prefer your silence to be of your own volition."

Two weeks. Did the minister general mean it? Was this a temporary stall until Girolamo found a way to silence him permanently?

He shifted his weight, hesitant to speak of private, spiritual matters, but the situation had grown drastic. His voice halted as he finally spoke. "I had a vision of Fra Leo—the night I received his message. He repeated the command contained in the letter, to discover the truth of the legends. But he didn't come to me alone. San Francesco appeared beside him, as though to add his personal authority to Leo's urgings."

"And what did *he* say?"

Conrad's head sank. "Nothing. No speech, although I experienced a rush of infinite love from him."

"And therein, perhaps, you'll find the root of your ordeal. '*Whom God loves, He chastises.*' In any case, you have my word that we'll talk further of this matter after the commemoration."

"Here?"

"Here, if you wish, or in my office. You needn't fear me. I'm not a tyrant. I won't cut out your tongue or pluck your remaining eye if you persist in your belief. But I do want two weeks. What say you? Can you spare me that time?"

Conrad folded his hands and made a low reverence to his superior. "From forced obedience, *no*. But out of respect for your person, *yes*. You may count on two weeks, then." He genuflected toward the altar with its golden tabernacle, bowed his head toward the treasured relics he now knew to be buried beneath, and limped back into the shadows of the nave.

THE PUNGENT SMELL of wood smoke clung to the alley outside Amata's house—the odor of a winter morning, not an early September afternoon, Conrad thought. When Maestro Roberto opened the door to him, the steward's dispirited eyes told him something had gone seriously wrong in his absence. Rather than leave the bad tidings to his mistress, Roberto led the friar directly to the courtyard and showed him the ruins of the loggia. Pio, meanwhile, scurried off to find Amata, who joined the two men near the fountain.

Speechless, Conrad shook his head at the charred pedestal of a writing desk protruding from the rubble. His mind and nostrils recoiled from the scent of destruction. Gradually, he became aware of the woman standing beside him. He feared to ask the obvious question, especially after he'd just been stymied by the minister general in the other task Leo had entrusted to him.

"We found no trace of the scroll," Amata said.

Whom He loves, He chastises, Conrad repeated to himself. "How did this come about?" he said.

She hunched her shoulders. "Jacopone blamed it on an angel."

"Only a minion of the fallen angel, Lucifer, would have wreaked such damage."

"Jacopone said *angelus Domini*. But you know how feverishly his thoughts can work."

"I should speak to him," Conrad said.

"He's gone, brother," Roberto interrupted. "Lost the north wind. He's slipped back into his former mind."

"And what of Fra Salimbene and Fra Zefferino?"

Amata shook her head. "They disappeared during the fire. Pio noticed Salimbene running along the loggia early on, though."

Conrad tugged at his beard, trying to recreate the unlikely scene in his head. The portly chronicler was neither the sort to risk danger to his person, nor for that matter to "run" anywhere. It was a glimmer of hope, perhaps.

"Salimbene would not have run off while any chance remained of recovering Leo's chronicle," the friar said. For such a manuscript, the man *would* hazard his life. He might even steal such a manuscript to fill what he knew to be a hole in the Order's history.

"My guess is, he had it with him when he vanished," Conrad said. He made a fist and slapped it several times into his other hand as he deliberated. "He might even have started the fire to cover a deliberate theft."

"In a way I hope you're right," Amata said. "At least we'd know the scroll exists somewhere."

"Most likely in one of Fra Lodovico's cupboards. The Order's too enamored with its past to destroy every trace of Leo's record." He squinted at the blackened wall that once supported Amata's scriptorium. "It's not time yet," he said at last. "When the time is right, Our Lord will manifest the chronicle."

His own remark gave him pause. He caught himself wondering whether the same applied to Francesco's leprosy? Maybe now wasn't the God-appointed time to announce his discovery. Maybe Girolamo had asked him to delay for this reason, giving him the next two weeks to reconcile himself to this very point. Uncertainty seemed to be the only absolute today, and it fluttered his stomach like an indigestible stew.

"I have other news," Amata said tentatively, and Conrad read in her face that this news was good. He smiled. "Your merchant's been here."

"Better even than that," Amata said. "We published the banns in Church two Sundays ago. We want you to marry us, for it was you brought us back together."

Conrad counted on his fingers. "The banns must be proclaimed twice more. The last time will be the Sunday before..."

"Before the Feast of the Holy Stigmata honoring Orfeo's uncle," Amata finished. "We realized that already. Orfeo thinks it a marvelous omen our marriage coincides with the celebration of his Uncle Francesco's greatest distinction. He said we can pretend all the decoration and ceremony is for us. And San Francesco will surely bless our home with many children."

Conrad smiled no longer, but he kept his misgivings to himself. The first test of his promise to his minister general. He simply nodded. "The day before the Feast of the Holy Stigmata it shall be then."

Caught up in her own excitement, Amata failed to notice the shift in his mood. "Bless you, Conrad," she said. "Then it's all set." She spun at once to her steward, all grin and flurry. "Maestro Roberto, we'll plan the wedding feast for that evening. And I need you to post a rider to Count Guido at the Coldimezzo at once, and I must buy *panni franceschi* for my gown. We've so little time." She grabbed Roberto's elbow and fairly strong-armed him from the courtyard, calling back over her shoulder, "I hope to have a surprise for you at the feast too, Conrad."

The friar spread his hands inquiringly, but she only laughed. "It won't be a surprise if I tell you now," she cried before she and the steward disappeared.

When they'd gone, Conrad shuffled to the pile of debris. He bent and plucked a singed fragment of sheepskin parchment from the heap. He could barely read the sooty, truncated sentence, copied in Jacopone's hand, but all the same he folded it and tucked it into his robe. Like Amata, he hoped the chronicle had survived intact and was safe—even if forever inaccessible to him—at the Sacro Convento. Otherwise, this scrap was the sole testimony to five decades of Leo's indignation.

XLIII

HE FINAL DAYS before the wedding, and even the solemnity of the
ceremony itself, passed in a blur for Amata. The mood of the torchlit
parade that swept the newlyweds back to their wedding banquet
changed immediately once the murky portico and stern bell tower of the
church had been left behind. Fra Conrad excused himself, saying he planned
to spend the night below the city, at the Portiuncola. "I'd be useless as the
third wheel of a tumbrel at your party," he explained to Amata.

Freed of all priestly influence, one of the wedding guests struck up a song
to the old Roman god of marriage,

"Hymen, O Hymenae, Hymen..."

and added invocations of Venus and the boy cherub,

"When Cupid's shaft impa-ales thee..."

Wine flowed freely after they'd settled again in the great hall of Amata's
and Orfeo's home. Uncle Guido apparently had brought his entire cellar
with him from the Coldimezzo. Servants mingled with carters, merchants
and nobler guests, and the well-wishing degenerated quickly from the merely
pagan to the bawdy. Reveling in the scene of celebration—the couples dancing, huddling on benches, whispering, blushing—Amata predicted to Orfeo
that several more marriages would be proposed before the night ended,
hopefully not to be forsworn in the sober light of day.

One such couple tried to slip away, but were not unnoticed. They sought
the privacy of a second-story room even though, because of the fire, they
could reach it only by ladder. The woman clung to the ladder at the top while
several drunken men at the bottom tried to pull the rungs out from under
her companion, leaving the man stranded midway in the eternal tug of war

between paradise and the nether world. He finally clambered his way to the room, and the guests cheered wildly as he yanked the ladder from the men and pulled it up behind him. During the commotion, Orfeo whispered to Amata that this was the perfect moment to make *their* escape.

The day had been unusually sultry for mid-September, and no breeze stirred the curtains of their canopied bed. Amata noted with pleasure that they would need no cover for their nakedness tonight. The orange light of the single candle shone perfectly for lovers, dim enough to hide any blemish, bright enough to outline in shadow a woman's soft roundness or the ripple of muscle in a man's shoulder. The aromatic fragrance of honeysuckle perfumed the room from outside the shuttered window.

She loosened the gold cord that gathered her full-length white gown at the waist and tugged the wreath from her hair. Orfeo watched her hungrily, still holding his wine goblet, while she shook her black curls and slipped the gown over her head. She'd wriggled half free of the garment when she said, in as casual a voice as she could muster, "Do you remember, love, the story of the newly-married couple in the Old Testament who spent their first three nights in prayer? Maybe we should ..."

She regretted not waiting until she'd undressed completely, for she missed the expression on his face. She heard him strangling on his wine, though, and an irregular pattern dotted the wall where he'd sprayed it. Orfeo shook his finger at her, but said nothing for fear of choking himself again. She grinned over her shoulder, raising her bottom invitingly as she crawled between the bed curtains.

He'd removed his boots and belt when he joined her, but still wore his parti-colored wedding tunic. "Orfeo, why aren't you undressed?" she complained. His dark eyes sparkled in the shadows.

"You'll have to earn this tunic, like the wife of the nomad chieftain," he said.

He'd keep her waiting because of her teasing. He trailed his finger beneath her breasts and around one of her nipples. "Have you heard the tale of the jester Kareem?"

"O love, this isn't the time for a story."

"You won't mind, I promise. I'll punctuate each sentence with a kiss ... or other pleasure." Slowly he fanned her flame while he related how a certain Sultan had rewarded Kareem for his clever folly with a robe colored like the rainbow, the robe a chieftain's wife said she must own for herself when she saw him approaching from a distance. "Be careful," her maid warned. "Kareem is not the idiot he seems." But the greedy woman only mocked her servant, and invited the fool into her tent. After he'd feasted and drunk, Kareem said he'd only give up the robe for an act of love, for the woman's beauty kindled a different desire in him.

By now, fire coursed through every particle of Amata's body, unquenched by the love dew fairly gushing from the gate of Astarte. Every muscle quivered even before Orfeo entered her. For a luscious, blessed, immeasurable time, he didn't speak, not until her very being erupted and he'd ever so carefully brought her, gasping and trembling, once again to a standstill.

"Now take off the damned tunic!" she panted.

"Exactly what the nomad's wife said to Kareem," he replied. "But no, said the jester, that time was for you, because I love you more than any woman I have ever known. This time is for the robe."

He stood as firm as when they'd started. As she cried out in short involuntary yips to his rhythm, Orfeo began to thrust faster and faster, until at long last he collapsed with a loud prolonged outcry on her chest. Amata wrapped her arms around him, content that she'd pleased him so.

"The robe?" she said.

Breathing hard, Orfeo whispered, "That time was for me. I promise, this time will be for the robe."

Incredibly, he remained primed for more. In the morning, she must ask how he did that, for her limited experience of men told her he accomplished the physically impossible. She didn't want to interrupt him now, though, in his state of heightened excitement, except to insist, "The robe comes off first!"

"Again, the very words of the nomad's wife." He laughed, finally yanking the tunic over his head with her frantic help and tossing it outside the curtains.

His chest and shoulders and back curved so broadly, Amata could scarcely reach her arms around him. All men should spend five years at the oar, she mused, before the waves of ecstasy chased all thought again, pounding through her over and over as Orfeo prolonged for a veritable eternity. "With me, come with me," she pleaded.

"I'll do that, too," he replied in a low voice, "but for now, my pleasure's to give you pleasure."

She let herself go completely, sinking, floating, soaring, until she thought she could bear the sweet aching no longer. Orfeo's breathing grew steadily deeper as he sucked for air, moaning as if he too must break, and this time they collapsed together.

They lay quietly for a long while, and during that tranquil aftermath Amata pressed her hands gently to her stomach, certain the moment of mutual release had miraculously engendered new life in her womb—her secret for now until she knew for sure. At last Orfeo rose up onto his elbows and began to stroke the matted hair back from her damp forehead while he smiled into her eyes. The caring in his touch thrilled her as much as the physical sensation.

Amata giggled when she'd regained her breath, and her voice carried a note of triumph. "The tunic's mine!"

"You too underestimate Kareem," he said softly. He rolled over and sat up on the edge of the mattress, pushing the curtain aside. "'*It's a hot day. I'm thirsty,*' Kareem said to the woman after she'd exchanged one of her husband's old robes for his." Orfeo rose and retrieved his wine goblet. "He took the bowl of water she offered and sat outside on the ground while he drank. In the distance Kareem recognized her husband riding toward the tent, but before the man arrived..."

The goblet slipped from Orfeo's hand and shattered on the tiled floor. "Oh, Orfeo, be careful!" Amata said, but he only grinned mischievously.

"... Kareem likewise smashed his bowl and began to cry. The chieftain dismounted from his horse and asked what had happened to so sadden the man. Kareem explained how, because he'd broken this plain clay water bowl, the chieftain's wife had taken the beautiful robe given to him by the Sultan. The chieftain flew into the tent, furious at his wife's shabby treatment of the simpleton, for he believed hospitality to be a sacred duty. He swore he would beat the woman severely if she didn't return the robe at once."

"And she...?"

"And she, in her wisdom, returned the robe and kept silence."

"Nevertheless," Amata said. "Kareem may have started something by loving the nomad's wife so well. He likely disturbed her dreams for years to come."

Amata had a nightmarish dream of her own to expunge, a tale of her own she'd yet to complete. While Orfeo rested beside her, she began again the story of hermit Rustico and young Alibech, the tale she'd started with Enrico the night of the forest battle. She recounted once more how the anchorite overestimated his power to resist the girl's comeliness, and how he finally taught her to put the devil in hell. At that point, Orfeo interrupted her narrative by taking an active, eager part in the plot, playing the hermit's role to the hilt. But even as Amata hugged him to her, part of her mourned her memory of the unfortunate Rico, who'd never had the chance to know happiness like hers and Orfeo's. Maybe with Orfeo's help, she'd finally lay his ghost to rest.

When Orfeo finally rolled, exhausted, onto his back, Amata mounted him and straddled his hips, imagining her knees girdled a muscular bull ox. "Rustico," she whined, "why do we waste our time resting when we should be putting the devil in hell?"

Orfeo glanced up at her through heavy eyelids. "I *thought* you might want to finish your story." She detected just a hint of worry in that glimpse, the very mood she needed to continue her tale. "It's never-ending," she warned.

"At first, Alibech thought hell must be a most hateful place, for Rustico's devil cost her much pain; but the more she performed this act of devotion, the more delicious it became. Truly, she thought, had the Lord said, 'My yoke is sweet and My burden light.' She wondered that all women didn't desert the city to please God so in the wilderness.

Amata massaged Orfeo's chest and shoulders, pouting sadly. "But alas, the more eager her hell became to receive and hold Rustico's devil, the more the devil fled her, so that she began to grumble, 'Father, I came here to serve God, not to stand idle.' The hermit, who lived only on roots and water and hadn't the strength to answer her every call, explained how he must also tend his garden, and how the devil deserved to be thrust into hell only when he raised his head in pride. The young man finally realized to his dismay that it would need overmany devils to appease her hell entirely, and although he delighted her betimes, the satisfaction happened so seldom, each instance had the effect of a bean cast into the gaping maw of a starving lioness."

By now, the candle had guttered and gone out. Orfeo chuckled in the darkness. Amata cradled his head as he pushed himself up onto his forearms with her straddling him still, and pressed his lips to her breast. *O God, I'll never finish the story*, she thought, while at the same time relishing the notion of continuing it night after night. She'd said it would be never-ending, after all.

She did her best to get the words out quickly. "While this debate continued between Alibech her hell and Rustico his devil, for overly much desire on one side and lack of power on the other..." but she got no further, for Orfeo's devil stormed *her* hell again, bucking upward from beneath her, and refused to bow his stiff neck this time until the first hint of dawn.

In the pale, languid daybreak, Amata silently blessed the courtesans of Acre and Venice, or whoever had taught Orfeo the innumerable, subtle secrets of love and inspired in him the patience and endurance to practice them. For the first time, in the arms of this man who smelled of the sea and the steamy Levant, of wintry mountain passes and piquant bazaars, she'd realized the full sexual potential of her body, the enjoyment for which she now understood she'd been born.

Tears of contentment gathered in the corners of Amata's eyes. "I'm happy as Easter," she murmured from the bottom of her heart, and she thought: *I'm so glad I didn't kill you.* She snuggled her head onto Orfeo's shoulder, rubbing his stomach with her palm, until a soft, brutal tap reverberated through the bedroom door. "*Scusami signore, signora.* San Francesco's procession is beginning. You said you wanted to know." Shy footsteps padded away down the hall as a trumpet flourish sounded in the distance.

Amata loved that "*signora.*"

RESIN TORCHES POPPED and hissed all night in the woods surrounding the Portiuncola. Conrad stepped outside as the sky lightened, watching as more torches wound down the hillside toward the tiny chapel. The guildsmen had turned out in force and unfurled the banners of their various trades to the fanfare of a trumpet just as the rim of the sun crested Monte Subasio.

Conrad, the lover of solitude, deliberately inconspicuous in his mushroom-grey robe, found himself abruptly swirled into a maelstrom of color. With the other friars who'd gathered at the chapel, he followed the company of knights and civil guards up the hillside, hemmed in at the rear by the guildsmen with their bobbing standards, surrounded by clergy—poor country priests in threadbare, shiny black cassocks and white surplices, bishops and cardinals at the forefront in their scarlets and ermines—and somewhere at the head of the procession Pope Gregory himself.

No sooner had they set out than a hurly-burly of townsfolk in varicolored mantles and tunics charged down from the city gate to meet them. In their frenzy, they stripped the lowest branches from the grove of olive trees bordering the path, the grove where Conrad had pried at the immature compost three years before. The waving leaves rippled a pale green counterpoint to the banners of the guilds, like sea foam crashing against a beach pavilion. The Compagnia di San Stefano, a band of lauds-singing Assisan flagellants, chanted a hymn to the stigmata:

"*Sia laudata San Francesco,*
Quel caparve en crocefisso,
Como redentore ..."
"Praised be Saint Francesco,
Who appeared crucified
Like the redeemer ..."

Knights struggled to control their mounts, made skittish by the flaring torches and the crush of shouting humanity. The rich stink of fresh horse dung rising from the dusty path warned Conrad to mind where he placed his bare soles. The sky, unmarked by any cloud, brightened from grey to purple to indigo to brilliant blue in the hour or more it took the procession to reach the city walls and the Porta San Pietro. Here the crowd divided, with the friars and prelates continuing on to the lower church of the basilica, while the mass of laity swarmed to the upper church and overflowed into the Piazza di San Francesco. Conrad separated himself from both groups, climbing only as far as the southern edge of the piazza, that he might better view the entire spectacle.

A few important citizens had been invited to the main ceremony in the lower church: high-ranking rulers and local benefactors. Conrad spotted a bleary-eyed Orfeo and Amata yawning in this group. He realized Amata had probably paid for Donna Giacoma's tomb. Then too, her husband was a blood relative of the saint as well as a personal friend of the pope.

A slightly taller, more slender version of the young man chatted at Orfeo's side—possibly the brother Piccardo who'd joined him in commerce. Amata, meanwhile, crouched beside a stretcher borne by four menservants. One of the servants had a familiar face, but Conrad trusted neither his vision nor memory enough to guess at the man's identity from the distance of the piazza. A lap robe covered the invalid on the stretcher, although a wimple like a nun's identified her as female. Apparently Amata knew the sick woman, who'd likely come to the basilica this day in hope of a miraculous cure. He bit into his lip as he took in the mass credulity raving all around him, frustrated that only he and Girolamo fully understood the falsehood on which the ailing woman's hopes had been raised.

Amata straightened, scanning the line of friars filing into the church. Conrad followed her gaze. He thought he recognized Zefferino by his halting movements, although the friar hunched with head lowered beneath his cowl. Enticing the gaoler from the dungeon of the Sacro Convento had been a mistake; his erstwhile comrade had tucked in upon himself further than ever. He saw too the boy Ubertino who'd warned him of danger two years before. The youngster appeared to chant earnestly, but Conrad noted his eyes darting every which way through the crowd, curious as ever. Conrad wondered whether any Spiritual friars might risk entering the church, or whether they'd observe the solemnity elsewhere, in the safety of their caves and huts and secret meeting places in the mountains. Certainly none of these sauntering friars appeared to be ill-clothed, ill-fed lovers of poverty.

And then Conrad spotted the man he most sought, Fra Salimbene, his arms folded across his gourmand's belly, paired in the procession in anomalous juxtaposition with the lanky Lodovico. A compelling urgency to talk to them about Leo's scroll, regardless of the ceremony in progress, sent him flying down the steps toward the lower church. Catching them outside the friary might be his only chance to learn for certain whether the chronicle still existed or had perished in the fire. Although he wanted to trust Girolamo, the memory of his two years in hell was still too fresh; he knew it might be years before he could bring himself to reenter the Sacro Convento, if ever.

He'd almost caught the line, when a civil guard blocked his path. The man held his pike crosswise as a barricade and pushed Conrad and those around him back against the wall, clearing a path through the small square. "Give way to the Doge of Venice," the guard barked. The excitement in the crowd quieted to a hush as a richly-dressed nobleman stepped from his litter. The man nodded to either side, acknowledging the homage of the onlookers. He'd floated several paces toward the church entrance, when the chatter resumed behind Conrad.

The procession of friars had moved on also. Conrad found himself growing short of breath in the press of people. Salimbene would have to wait. He'd started up the steps again, seeking any clear spot he could find, when he heard Amata's voice shouting after him. "Fra Conrad! There you are! Come to our house for supper."

"If I can," he called back. "I have to speak with Fra Girolamo first."

"You *must*," she cried, gesturing at the woman on the stretcher, but the current of people swept him up the stairs before he caught the rest of her words. He cupped his hands to his ears and waved helplessly. She pressed her hands together in a final plea and he nodded that, yes, he would try to make it.

He managed at last to retrieve his space near the edge of the piazza where he found the crowding more tolerable. Maestro Roberto, in the company of Count Guido and the count's granddaughter, detached himself from the throng. The steward grinned and swept his hand in a dramatic flourish. "Have you ever seen such a show, brother?"

Conrad followed the man's gesture across the piazza. The multitude mostly faced the basilica, some with tears streaming down their cheeks while they beat their breasts and raised their hands toward heaven. Others laughed and hugged their neighbors; Conrad overheard two men apologizing, asking forgiveness for past injury. A few stood quietly, eyes closed while their lips moved in silent prayer. Vendors worked the crowd as always, offering meat pies and pastries to those whose devotion also required mortal nourishment. One man knelt on the back margent of the crowd, his head bowed low, his body shrouded entirely in a heavy black cloak despite the warmth of the morning. The size of the man, his brooding aspect and broad shoulders reminded Conrad of the penitent Jacopone and of the former notary's mad devotion to the counterfeit foreskin. Yet how did Jacopone differ from this person, worshiping stigmata that never existed?

A jumble of emotions—sorrow at the universal delusion he witnessed, wonder at the mob's excitement, indignation at Elias' ancient lie proliferating all around him—left Conrad weary. *People love a good miracle, the more fantastic the better*, he repeated from someplace in his memory. He recalled his talk with Amata on the hillside outside Gubbio, his description of the teams careening up Mont'Ingino with their bulky pedestals. "It doesn't matter who wins," he'd told the girl. "Simple folk need simple images to fuel their devotion, not sermons or tracts."

Images like a humble saint with the wounds of Christ impressed into his flesh! How his words gnawed at him now! Be the wounds real or no, Conrad had to admit the evidence surrounding him. San Francesco's stigmata fired the imaginations and religious zeal of believers from every class, if only for this one day of its commemoration. Had he the right, or duty, to claw at such faith—even if he had the power to convince any of these fanatical devotees to believe him?

The kneeling man tottered to his feet and stared vacantly over the heads of the crowd, his tearful eyes scarlet from weeping, his clotted sandy hair a disheveled tangle. He prayed, oblivious to the bedlam around him, even when the girl Teresina, who'd spotted him too, ran and jerked at his cape, shouting above the clamor, "*Papa*! It *is* you! We've been looking for you everywhere!"

XLIV

THE PUBLIC CELEBRATION of the stigmata lasted late into the afternoon, and Conrad had to wait until after Vespers for his audience. When he entered the sacristy of the upper church where Girolamo had agreed to meet him, however, the friar found instead of the Order's general a tall man in a white cassock and skull cap. He faced out the window, his hands clasped behind his back. The man's thin fingers sparkled with rings of high office.

The churchman turned methodically. His sallow skin stretched like aged vellum over his prominent cheekbones. Mauve pouches sagged beneath the heavy-lidded eyes that studied Conrad for an uncomfortable moment. "Welcome, brother," he said at last in a stately cadence that counterbalanced the whistling of his lungs. "Your general has granted our wish to meet the friar whose curiosity landed him in prison. Orfeo di Bernardone's high praise on your behalf roused our curiosity."

Conrad dropped to his knees on the stone floor and bent his neck. "I owe Your Holiness my life." He remained in that humble posture until he felt the soft pressure of hands on his head as the pope mumbled a Latin blessing. Gregory grasped his shoulders and bade him rise.

"Fra Girolamo cannot join us. He is preparing to travel with the doge, who returns to Venice tomorrow." The pontiff pointed the friar to an empty chair and sat down opposite him. "You see," Gregory said, "*we* need his leadership even more than your Order does. We've asked him to return to Byzantium, to tie up the myriad remaining details of Church reunification."

Conrad wondered exactly how much Girolamo had told the pope about him. Had the general, in exchange for agreeing to undertake the mission to the East, called on the Church's highest authority to keep him from disclosing San Francesco's leprosy?

"Unity among the members of Christ's mystical body is a blessing from God," Gregory continued, "especially unity among brothers. Fra Girolamo spoke to us of his plan to use you as an intermediary to heal the rift in your own Order—once you are healed from your pains, of course. A lofty and tremendous task. He'll need to rely even more heavily than he supposed on friars like you now that we've snatched him back for our own purposes. Speaking privately, as well as on behalf of the Church, we would consider ourselves well rewarded for freeing you."

The pontiff peered intently at his face, which Conrad purposely kept clear of expression. He hadn't yet recovered from his initial surprise. He also wanted to reserve his reaction until he'd heard Gregory's whole proposal. "Fra Girolamo sympathizes strongly with your Spiritual friends. He grew up in Ascoli, in the Marches, where they hide. Nevertheless, he understands that the moderate, practical brothers are better suited to carry out San Francesco's plan to reform the Church—to break down the barriers between priests and people—than the more zealous members of the Order. To my mind your Order should emphasize poverty less and simplicity more, asceticism less and austerity more. The shading is a fine one, but will provide Godly comfort to many more of the faithful than the narrower shadow cast by your friends' rigid practices." The pope gestured toward Conrad's robe. "As a case in point, we'd rather see a friar wearing a habit of good heavy material that will last him many years and keep him from distraction in a chilly basilica than have him clothed in rags. We hope you'll reach this same understanding after a period of reflection."

Gregory rose and strolled again to the window, turning his back to Conrad. Conrad caressed the patched sleeves of his habit. He'd already had this argument with Donna Giacoma and could feel the blood warming his cheeks.

Gregory said: "Fra Girolamo tells us you'd be content serving at a leprosarium, but we believe God has reserved a larger purpose for you. We've suggested to your general that you spend a time of retreat at the friary on Monte LaVerna, there to meditate on the greater design of San Francesco's life, his mission to the Church as a whole, to *all* the faithful."

Ah, this does have to do with silencing me. "Why Monte LaVerna?" he asked with feigned ignorance, for the reason could only be that Francesco had manifested his lesions there. *Gregory and Girolamo mocked him.* "Doesn't the truth remain the same and unalterable everywhere?" he asked, certain now the pope knew to what truth he referred.

The pontiff's back stiffened. "'*Quid est veritas?*' Pilate asked our Lord. What is truth? Unfortunately for all humanity, he didn't wait for Jesus to reply. All of mankind would have loved to hear *that* answer. We've lived twice your years, Fra Conrad, many of them spent reading chronicles and histories purported to be accurate. We've observed that the quills of scribes can pen flat and flexible truths as easily as armorers' hammers beat out swords."

"But I'm absolutely right about San Francesco's leprosy."

Gregory turned his head, a pained expression on his face, as though to underscore Conrad's indiscretion in speaking so directly. The pope plainly favored talking around this issue. "A wise man once imagined God held out to him in His right hand all the truth of the universe. In His left, the Creator held only the active search for truth, including the condition that man should ever err in that search. He said to the wise man: Choose! The man humbly took God's left hand and said: Divine Father, give me this one, for absolute truth belongs to You alone."

The pope's whistling voice crackled as he added: "You must have seen today in the piazza that the truth you cling to is not so simple, so absolute. Your *truth* would be a spear thrust through the heart of the people's *faith*."

Conrad lowered his head. Spurred by his convictions he'd overstepped his bounds. He owed the supreme pontiff total allegiance as well as his gratitude. "Forgive me, Holy Father, for my pride," he said. He closed his eye, thinking his heart must burst from the turmoil and confusion raging there. He continued in a low voice: "I reached much the same conclusion as Your Holiness as I watched the crowd and would be ever remorseful if I damaged the people's devotion. Surely this isn't the time for revelation, I told myself. Yet, in respect of that same truth, shouldn't we at least make a note in some chronicle for those who come after us?"

"No." The word came softly, but firmly, and the pope's hand touched his shoulder. "No, my son." Conrad lifted his face again, surprised by the pontiff's sudden tenderness. "But we owe you something, for the pain you've endured, and because ... because, quite simply, we agree with Fra Girolamo that you're probably right. Your finding should not die more than a ... a temporary death. When God wills, He can resurrect it, as easily as He did His Son. Our compromise, then, is this: a friar companion will accompany you to LaVerna; through him you may begin the *oral* tradition of your *Francesco Lebbroso*. Oral, not written. No more than this shall you do, leaving the rest in God's hands."

"And the companion, is he of my choosing?"

The pope nodded, "Provided your minister general seconds your choice."

God grant that he does, Conrad thought. Some ember of hope had suddenly flared within him. With it came an unexpected calm, a sense of reassurance that a friar of some future generation would finally bring Elias's fabrication to light. He felt his resolve rekindling, but he need say nothing of that to the pope.

"Were Fra Girolamo here, I would also request this evening free that I might take leave of Orfeo and his new bride. I promised to join them for supper this evening."

"I see no problem, brother. And please add my congratulations to your own, for I love him dearly." Gregory paused, smiling, before he asked, "When will you come for your companion?"

"If he could meet me at the Porta di Murorupto after Terce tomorrow morning ..."

The pontiff nodded and agreed to relay the request, then walked Conrad to the front door of the basilica. And thus easily the dilemma that had tormented Conrad since his meeting with Fra Girolamo resolved itself with the finality and infallibility of papal decree.

While Conrad met with the pope, the Piazza di San Francesco had emptied as the crowd scattered to their evening meals. A lone mongrel scavenging scraps the pilgrims had dropped among the paving stones came to sniff at the friar's ankles. The animal followed him to the edge of the square and Conrad wished one more time that he could be back among his forest creatures and that the past three years had never happened. He scratched the dog's head with a sudden longing to see Chiara, the tame deer that browsed outside his hut. Then he shooed the animal back to the piazza and pushed on alone.

THE LONE ISSUE that remained unresolved was the existence, or whereabouts of Leo's missing chronicle. Conrad had hoped to put the question to Fra Girolamo, but with the minister general leaving for Venice he had missed his chance. And he knew that even if he could somehow confront Fra Salimbene or the librarian about the scroll, he wouldn't get an honest answer. He'd be reduced to prying cabinet boards loose under cover of night again, an experience he hoped never to repeat in his darkest nightmares. But his companion on the road to LaVerna ... even as he inherited the story of Francesco's leprosy ... could perhaps take up the legacy of Leo's history.

As he took the familiar turns toward Amata's house, Conrad realized that the sudden shift of events had actually left him with a sense of calm and relief. For three years the weight of Leo's message had bowed his willowy soul like a dense snowfall, straining his every reserve to keep from breaking. But the heat of Gregory's authority had finally melted that burden, freeing him to rebound to his natural upright posture. The yoke of blind obedience harbored within it the liberation of childlike irresponsibility. Fra Leo's vanished manuscript represented another load, one more weight he now willingly surrendered into God's hands. He began to look forward to the retreat on Monte LaVerna; he'd layers of such burdens to shed.

When he arrived at Amata's home, he found the household gathered in the great hall, halfway through the evening meal. At the servants' table sat the four men who carried the litter outside the lower church that morning. At this closer range, he finally recognized the one who'd seemed familiar: *Rosanna's man, the servant who'd brought food to his mountain hut each week.*

Conrad rushed expectantly to the head table reserved for family and special guests, but Rosanna wasn't there. His shoulders slumped. He recognized this disappointment; he'd known it once before, the morning he left for the friary, when Rosanna could not see him off.

Amata caught his eye and motioned to the empty space she'd been saving between herself and Count Guido. Guido greeted the friar cordially and made more room on the bench while Amata signaled a kitchen helper to bring another plate. His mind still swirling with memories of his hermitage, Conrad recalled in that instant the sharp-tongued adolescent who'd popped grapes into her mouth one-after-another while she berated him in his hut. The mature young woman beside him was a living tribute to the wisdom and patience of Donna Giacoma.

"I promised you a surprise, Conrad!" Amata said. "I invited Monna Rosanna to Assisi for the saint's day, though I didn't know of her illness at the time. We're hoping, through the intercession of San Francesco's wounds, to gain better health for her during her stay."

"How serious is she?" Conrad asked.

Amata's face darkened. "*Serious*. The leech thinks she'll not survive without such a miracle. Too many hard childbearings. The blessing and curse of our gender." She managed a weak, prescient smile, recognizing that within the year her own life could be dangling suspended between the wonder and mortal peril of pregnancy and birth.

Conrad buried his forehead in his hand and gritted his teeth. *The dearest companion of his childhood made to suffer because her husband had the self-discipline of a rutting stag!* There'd not been a year since their marriage that she hadn't been with child. Yet angry, frustrated and helpless as he felt, a part of him was forced to admit that Rosanna and Quinto had only fulfilled the biblical injunction to go forth and multiply. Would her life have been any different had she married a man like himself?

Amata sipped from her goblet. She touched her hand to his arm and added: "She's been asking for you since she arrived."

The friar started to get up at once, even before the servant came with his food, but Amata's grip tightened on his sleeve. "She's resting comfortably, Conrad. Have supper first and tell us your plan. We hope you'll stay on here with us for a while. Jacopone would gain by your company too."

She nodded toward a wooden bench beneath one of the hall's tapestries. Teresina had finished her meal and sat beside her father, leaning her head against his shoulder and holding his huge hand in her two small ones. The penitent rotated his head sluggishly.

The portrait of relapse disheartened Conrad. He covered his face momentarily with his hand, then explained how he must be on the road by the following morning. "I can only offer *advice*, Amatina," he said. "Find

Sior Jacopone some writing—as your notary, recording his poems, copying, anything. He has the high-strung sensibility of the artist. For such tortured souls writing is the best, maybe the only, purgative. He might even try living in our friary in Todi. He's known there and would have been well-respected before the mad sorrow seized his spirit."

Conrad could see that his reply disappointed Amata, but the pope had spoken and, moreover, his own spirit needed tending. He would miss all this loving company, but he knew he must release them. He stood at another crossroads, another irrevocable change of direction. While he sipped his broth, Conrad thought again of Rosanna, whom he'd already released twice—when he'd joined the friars and received the news of her betrothal, and more recently when he'd abandoned his hermitage to return to Assisi. Now, apparently, he must let go of her a third, perhaps a final, time.

The soup held no scent or savor for him this evening and he hardly noticed the babble around him. His senses had gone ahead into some dark night, beckoning to his soul to follow, and to follow swiftly. His mind paraphrased a short line from a popular poem: *Bidding my friends farewell, I entered the autumn of La Verna.* He'd barely touched his meal when the kitchen servants began clearing the hall.

Amata remained at the table while the others went off in search of bedrolls. "Conrad?" she said softly. "If you've no taste for food, we can visit Rosanna now. But before you and I say *goodnight,* promise me you'll not sneak off in the morning like you did when you left for San Lazzaro."

"I promise, Amatina." He paused, then added, "I hope God will direct my steps this way again one day, but for now I can't see beyond La Verna."

He found himself groping for the words he knew he was supposed to say. "I will miss all of you, terribly, but the separation will be easier knowing you finally are living the peace Giacomina wanted for you, that we all want for you." Yet he suspected it would not be as easy as he made it sound. Parting from Amata might prove to be as wrenching as the other leave-taking he now faced.

He didn't resist as she took his hand and led him to the room where he'd studied his manuscripts in the past. When he paused in the doorway, Amata whispered, "Orfeo's waiting for me," and discreetly returned to the hall. The fire smoldering in the corner of the room leaked smoke that threaded up the stone chimney to the ceiling, just as he'd remembered, but the woman lying on a mat at ground level breathed without pain. Her eyelids flickered, then widened as she spotted the apparition at the door.

"It's *me*. Conrad," he said.

The orange glow of the firelight reflected off the moisture filming the woman's eyes. "What did they *do* to my friend? Amata warned me you'd changed much in prison, but I never expected ..."

Conrad knelt beside her pallet and put a finger to her lips. "They say God treats those he loves roughly, the way children treat their favorite toys. We must be very loved, you and I, Rosanna." He took her hand automatically, as though they were ten years old again, surprising himself with the naturalness of the act. "Amata said you've been waiting for me."

She rolled her head so she stared up into the smoke. "I wanted your prayers, for the deliverance of my soul, and for the protection of my husband and children when I'm gone. I know I'm done, Conrad." He could barely feel the weak pressure of her fingers in his palm. "I also have a confession to make," she said.

Conrad released her hand and twisted into an upright seated position. Rosanna laughed softly into the dusk. "No, no. Nothing so formal. I confessed to the priest in Ancona before I left, in case the journey proved too hard for my health. To you I confess only as friend-to-friend. Please, take my hand again."

He did so, but more self-consciously this time. "Through all the years of my marriage to Sior Quinto," Rosanna continued, "I've been in love with another man. Does that shock you?"

Conrad's breathing ceased momentarily. But for her feeble condition, he'd have let her hand drop again. Although she'd called this cleansing of her conscience informal, he reacted like a resolute pastor. "Did you love him in the carnal sense?" he asked, dreading the answer even as he questioned her.

Again Rosanna chuckled, the sound escaping in faint bursts of air. "No. Only in my girlish fantasies—and now in my matronly dreams. I think he's surely the most naive dolt alive to have missed every clue so entirely."

"You knew him even as a girl? Why didn't you declare your feelings, instead of marrying a stranger?"

"You know daughters have no choice in such matters, Conrad. I did declare my love for him, to my parents, the night they told me of the match with Quinto. I threw the worst tantrum imaginable, and swore I'd only marry ... *you*. Why do you think they rushed you to the friars?" The pallet rustled as she rolled with much effort onto her side. "And look how we've ended. Two battered old rag dolls who should have been the happiest couple alive. I know you loved me too, even if it was only the puppy love of a young boy."

The constriction in his throat kept Conrad from replying. Light from the rising moon touched a corner of the room, fighting through the drooping leaves and a chink in the wall. He suddenly recognized the loneliness of his entire life in that single pallid beam.

"Say it Conrad. Let me bid you *addio* in peace."

He clasped her hand in both of his, tracing over the frail fingers with the tips of his own. He finally spoke, huskily. "We know our souls don't die, Rosanna. We mustn't make too much of saying goodbye. We'll talk again one day, in a happier mansion."

"*Say* it Conrad. Please."

He tried to regain his feet but her hand tightened in his. "*Conrad!*"

He released her hand and placed it on her stomach. "God knows I loved you, Rosanna. Until this very instant, God alone has known that I never *stopped* loving you. I'm just realizing it myself." He smiled. "I guess that proves I really *am* a naive dolt, as you said."

He touched his lips to her humid forehead, then put his hands under her shoulders and half lifted her off the pallet. He held her against his chest for a prolonged moment, fighting back the tears he knew wished to flow as he let go of her this final time. He lowered her body again to the mat and this time allowed his lips to brush hers.

"Thank you, Conrad," she whispered.

"*Addio*, Rosanna. Goodbye, my friend."

He clambered to his feet then and shuffled to the door. There he faltered, gripping the doorframe while he stared up through the cloister at the brilliant sky. With a nod toward the stars he said: "I'll see you there."

AN URGENT STRIDE launched Conrad through the doorway. He followed the moonlit path into Amata's courtyard. There the light tangled in his snowy beard, setting it aglow and enticing a shower of pale moths who danced about his face and head and settled in his hair. He wished he might take root there in the midst of the fire's debris, sprouting moss and lichen like a hoary oak, host to a million beetles, shading Amata's gentle household with his leaves, limbs crawling with her lively *bambinos*.

But his pilgrimage could afford him no such luxury. His was a distant destination. Not merely Monte LaVerna, that mere stop along his path, but no place less than the kingdom of God— hid within him, as Jesus preached.

Tomorrow he'd pass Leo's burden to his chosen road companion, the friar of the next generation, Fra Ubertino. He'd not found God in all that quest, nor in the patched grey habit that now covered his shivering frame. He knew the Father dwelt far deeper than all human striving, than the bit of charred parchment in his pocket and the pure soul of the Order that it represented, or even than the huge basilica that had displaced its soul. Far beyond any *thing* Conrad might name or even think, than his most clever *notion* of a God, which was only an invention.

He felt certain that the path to God would vanish into mystery, perhaps into a place of utter nothingness, though surely not a *place*, nor yet a void—nowhere but only love. The Spirit-rapt Apostle had divined it: "*God is Love.*"

And there, in the heart of Original Love, he knew he'd meet Rosanna next.

EPILOGUE

A FTER HIS TIME on Monte LaVerna, Fra Conrad da Offida gained fame as an itinerant preacher and visionary. Permanently devoted to the cause of his Order's Spiritual faction, he died at the friary of Santa Croce in Bastia in 1306 and was later beatified. A contemporary, Fra Angelo Clareno, testified that Conrad wore the same tunic for 50 years, a tribute of sorts to the stubbornness and toughness of both the man and the material. Sixteen years after his death, Perugian raiders stole Blessed Conrad's bones and enshrined them in their own city.

Ubertino da Casale evolved as a leader of the Spirituals in the late 1200s. In his book *Arbor Vitae* (*The Tree of Life*), he mentions Leo's lost manuscript. Ubertino quoted from the manuscript those excerpts passed to him by Fra Conrad, but was branded a liar for not producing the actual script. To this day, it remains missing.

In 1294, Cardinal Benedetto Gaetani was elected Pope Boniface VIII and plunged the papacy into the longest and worst crisis of its history. If one accepts Conrad's reasoning that Abbot Joachim of Flora's prophecies actually pointed to the year 1293, one might plausibly argue that Boniface represented the coming of the Abomination of Desolation foretold by the abbot's vision.

Jacopone da Todi entered the Franciscan Order in 1278. He too became a leading figure among the Spirituals. His poetic Lauds, written in the vernacular, earned him the love of the people and the scorn of a rival poet, Dante Alligheri. Because Jacopone vociferously attacked corruption within the Church, Pope Boniface VIII incarcerated him in the papal dungeon. But that is another story.

The year her father joined the friars, the teen-aged Teresina left with Orfeo, Amata, and their four children for Palermo, Sicily. There, Orfeo established an outpost, trading throughout the Levant a scant few years before the Sicilian Vespers—and that too is another story.

On April 14, 1482, Pope Sixtus IV canonized the former minister general, Fra Bonaventura. In 1588, Pope Sixtus V further declared the saint a Doctor of the Church with the specific title Seraphic Doctor.

In 1818, a team of workers digging in the crypt beneath the Basilica di San Francesco's lower church discovered the remains of the saint—550 years after their disappearance. The relics have never been tested for signs of leprosy.